John Anketell

Poems on Several Subjects

John Anketell

Poems on Several Subjects

ISBN/EAN: 9783744716185

Printed in Europe, USA, Canada, Australia, Japan

Cover: Foto ©Andreas Hilbeck / pixelio.de

More available books at **www.hansebooks.com**

JAMES STEWART, ESQ.

OF KILLYMOON, COUNTY OF TYRONE.

SIR,

As I owe you infinitely greater obligations than to any other individual now alive, gratitude and inclination immediately point out the unrivalled patron to whom I fhould dedicate my book; this duty, therefore, I now endeavour to difcharge with the utmoft alacrity; but cannot avoid lamenting that I am unable to lay before you materials more deferving of your notice, though I truft that, even in their imperfect ftate, they will experience a portion of your kind indulgence: I muft, however, intreat your pardon for the liberty I have taken in addreffing my work to you, without firft confulting you on that occafion; and which I would not by any means have ventured to affume, but that I feared your well known modefty would

a   have

have deprived me of an opportunity of thus publicly gratifying my feelings, had I previoufly applied to you on this head.

THE very friendly and polite letter with which you, Sir, were pleafed to furnifh me when I commenced the taking in of fubfcriptions for my Poems, not only ferved to infure confiderable fuccefs to my undertaking; but effectually fuppreffed every fufpicion of literary fwindling, a fcandalous fpecies of fraud and meannefs which I am inexpreffibly concerned to find fome of my clerical brethren are accufed of having fallen into; as your name is venerated and efteemed in every part of this kingdom which I happened to vifit. I thank GOD I have never been in the habit of fawning adulation; and yet, fuppofing me to be addicted to flattery; who will be daring enough to infinuate that any eulogium expreffed by me, could convey an idea of your real deferts?

To you, Sir, my brother curates of the eftablifhed church of *Ireland* look up with

con-

confidence for reprefenting, in the enfuing feffion of Parliament, the many difficulties under which they have long and pati. ently labored; and for endeavouring to procure a decent relief of their hardfhips from the juftice and humanity of the Legiflature. For my own part, fhould PROVIDENCE gracioufly vouchfafe to pre- ferve my life for a few months longer, my continuing to exercife the office of a cler- gyman, or of refiding in *Europe*, entirely depends upon a fpeedy augmentation of the curates' falaries ; for I neither expect, nor anxioufly wifh for, ecclefiaftical pre- ferment.

I FONDLY hope your conftituents in the county of *Tyrone* are duly fenfible of the honor they conferred upon themfelves, by appointing you to that important ftation in the *Irifh* fenate, which you have filled with confpicuous dignity, and unfullied integrity, during a period of twenty-five years; that they will never act fo bafe and unmanly a part as, by deferting you, to deprive themfelves of the happinefs of returning to the Houfe of Commons, as long as you exprefs a defire to fit in Parliament, a gentleman whofe eminent public and private virtues advance the worth of any Society in which he is a member; and that they unanimoufly join with me in imploring the beneficent Ruler of the Univerfe to beftow upon you the higheft degree of temporal and eternal felicity!

I have the honor to be,

SIR,

with the moft fincere refpect

and regard,

your much obliged, obedient,

and very humble fervant,

JOHN ANKETELL.

STEWARTSTOWN,
July 1, 1793.

I RECEIVED my claſſical education at the Free-ſchool of *Armagh*, under the care of that moſt reſpectable character, the Reverend Doctor *Grueber*. I finiſhed my ſtudies, as a penſioner, in *Trinity College, Dublin ;* and ſince the 1ſt of November, 1773, have ſerved a curacy in the dioceſe of *Armagh*. I have lived to ſee ſeveral gentlemen highly promoted in the church, who, at the time of my ordination, had hardly commenced the *Latin* Grammar; which I am induced to attribute to their own ſuperior worth, or the ſuccefsful interceſſion of powerful connexions, without the ſmalleſt impulſe of ſpleen or envy; and I ſolemnly proteſt that I do not glance the moſt diſtant reflection at his Grace, the Lord Primate, whom I hold in the greateſt and moſt diſintereſted eſteem, for the truly venerable and exemplary diſcharge of the duties pertaining to the important ſtation which he has filled for a long ſeries of years. As I am well aware that any little merit I might, poſſibly, poſ- ſefs, could be eaſily eclipſed by bodies of greater

moral

moral magnitude; fo I can fafely affirm that no influence has ever been exerted, to my knowledge, either directly by myfelf, or through the medium of any other perfon, to procure for me ecclefiaftical preferment. Still, however, it is probable that, as men are apt to rate their own value pretty highly, I might, in fome meafure, have been chagrined at the manner in which I fuppofed myfelf to be overlooked, but that I, happily, am not of a querulous difpofition; and, moreover, I confidered that the function in which I am engaged was, out of a variety of employments offered to my choice by an indulgent parent, that to which I had uniformly given the preference; and, befides, any latent complaints which might, otherwife, have invoked an hear--ing, were effectually ftifled by an obfervation, that many of my fraternity, of infinitely more enlarged deferts, and of much longer ftanding than myfelf, remained equally unnoticed. Indeed, fome years ago, on perceiving the real neceffaries of life confiderably advanced in price, I was prompted to take the lead in endeavouring to fketch out a plan for obtaining an addition to the annual falaries of the curates belonging to the eftablifhed church in *Ireland,* which might render their lives more comfortable, and forward the caufe of religion, by giving them what wealth

in

in other cases is found to confer a greater weight
with their congregations; but by the indolence
or timidity of my reverend brethren, with whom
I had a confultation on that fubject at the vifita-
tion of *Armagh*, and not a few of whom, perhaps, fhould have defired a profperous iffue of it
even more anxioufly than myfelf, I was fuffered
fingly, to wait upon his Grace the Lord Primate,
relative to this bufinefs. His Lordfhip honored
me with a conference of fome length, and feem-
ed by no means averfe to the fcheme; but was
pleafed to fuggeft to me that " the difturbances
" then prevailing, to an alarming extent, among
" the *White-boys*, in the province of *Munfter*,
" were rather inimical to the profecution of the
" plan at that period, as the fituation of the be-
" neficed clergy was precarious and unfettled."
Being myfelf a weak and unfupported advocate,
I was conftrained to fubmit in filence to the argu-
ments adduced by his Grace, and poftpone the
propofed petition to both Houfes of Parliament,
until a more favorable opportunity fhould occur.
The late liberal increafe of the *Regium Donum*
granted to a very deferving body of men, the
Prefbyterian minifters of this kingdom; and the
yearly enlargement of the gaugers' falaries; in-
clined me fondly to conceive, that they were the
harbingers of a fpeedy augmentation to the noto-
rioufly

rioufly inadequate provifion for the maintenance of the inferior order of the clergy, as by law eftablifhed; but my hopes on that head have been hitherto premature. If to expend the principal part, often the whole, of their patrimony, on an education to qualify them for the facred office of the altar, and which precludes them from embarking in any other worldly vocation; if to have long fubmitted, with more than patience, to a pitiful income, and to which, in the country at leaft, no perquifites are annexed; if regularly to inculcate leffons of loyalty and due fubordination, and to ftrengthen their precepts by practical example, can intitle any men to the particular regard of government; I will venture to affert, without hefitation, that my brother curates have an unqueftionable claim to that regard, by having conftantly given the moft undeniable demonftrations of their unfhaken attachment to the king and conftitution. However, fhould their conduct or condition have no weight with the legiflature, fo as to acquire for them a moderate alleviation of the difficulties under which they labor, by a reafonable acceffion to their falaries; I truft an act will pafs in the enfuing feffion of parliament, for entirely abolifhing the inftitution, as an ufelefs burthen on the ftate; or for tolerating the members of it to profecute, without

any

any odium affixed thereto, whatever other *lay* occupations are juft and honeft in themfelves, in conjunction with their *clerical* profeffjon. By this humane indulgence, fome of them may be happy enough to be appointed to the lucrative offices of ftewards or overfeers to noblemen, or gentlemen of fortune in their vicinity, for it is fuperfluous to fpeak of their being agents, private tutors, or domeftic chaplains; others, fhould they happen to write a fair hand, or have a fmattering know-ledge of arithmetic, may be fo lucky as to ferve, occafionally, in the enviable rank of clerks to magiftrates, merchants, or attornies; and not a few of them, like their great predeceffor, Saint *Paul*.may be able to fecure a flender fupport for themfelves and, perhaps, a wife and feveral help-lefs children, by the labor of their hands, and the fweat of their brows; for to them the tanta-lizing delicacies of life muft remain totally inac-ceffible.

FAR be it from me to accede to the popular charge fo confidently urged againft our Reve-rend Bench of Bifhops, of flagrantly, nay, almoft altogether, neglecting the duties of their facred function, becaufe fuch an accufation is evidently and grofsly exaggerated; but I fincerely wifh I could pronounce it to be utterly unfounded, and

b   that

that *Bath*, and the other *Englifh* pools of *Bethefda*, fafhionably celebrated for the removal of actual or apprehended bodily grievances, might, if pof- fible, be lefs frequently reforted to by them ; as I am led to imagine that a more attentive, per, fonal infpection into the clerical eftablifhment of their refpective diocefes ; and a preference, ge- nerally at leaft, confined to acknowledged merit ; might liberate our churches from many modifh divines of quality, who, totally indifferent about the temporal or eternal welfare of their flocks, connect themfelves to the facerdotal miniftry, for the fake of its loaves and fifhes ; and indecently hurry through the folemn, public fervice of God, as a mere matter of courfe, without feeling them- felves the fmalleft fpark of pious warmth animat- ing their fouls ; or the moft faint defire of im- preffing upon their hearers that devout affection of mind which it is a duty peculiarly incumbent upon them to endeavour to infpire ; or by a fhamefully effeminate, and affectedly lifping, de- livery, literally addrefs the congregation in a tongue unknown, as not being uttered in a tone of voice fufficiently audible to be underftood ; though thofe very gentlemen may be the moft vociferous *Nimrodians* at the death of a fox or an hare ; and not the leaft joyous companions at a convivial affembly, zealoufly difpofed to perform

the

the ~~rites~~ of *Bacchus*, jolly god of wine. I have been told that, in *England*, a clergyman of a moral character, of even contracted abilities as an author, is frequently snatched from obscurity, by the fostering hand of a bishop; but here, as in arts and sciences, we unfortunately fall short of our sister kingdom; and, in the inauspicious climate of *Ireland*, those weak plants, the curates, seldom bear the fruits of affluence, produced by the invigorating heat of prelatical patronage; but are left to wither and decay, and bring their grey leaves " with sorrow to the grave." And, indeed, I conceive the appointment of *Englishmen* or *Irishmen* to the bishopricks in this kingdom, could occasion no material, salutary difference in this case; because *British* gentlemen must naturally have a prevailing partiality for a country which contains their dearest ties and connexions; and lamentable experience has shewn, that the inhabitants of *Ireland* seldom feel a powerful predeliction for the vulgar, non-patrician offspring of their despised native soil; for the exceptions to the general rule are so very rare, that it is needless to bring them forward into view.——As to myself, I shall readily own, that a wish to realize something for the advantage of my family, should they survive me, and, in some measure, to improve, or innocently amuse, my readers; were

the

the motives which led me to offer the following
Effays to your perufal; for *fame* is a flippery,
uncertain baggage, in whom I am not willing to
repofe much confidence.

My verfification of Mr. *Hervey*'s Meditations
among the Tombs was finifhed before I had reach-
ed the nineteenth year of my age. It was my
particular ftudy to adhere as clofely as practicable
to the words of the original; and where I have
found myfelf under the neceffity of departing
from that rule, for the fake of the metre, I fear
I fhall forfeit your approbation. I am fenfible
that many of my lines, perhaps all, are rough
and frigid; and it is poffible that I could have
rendered them more harmonious, by frequent
revifals and alterations; but might I not, in that
cafe, deviate fo far from Mr. *Hervey*'s expreffions,
as to be not only a more indifferent imitator, but
a merely fuperficial poetafter? And is it not infinitely more eligible to enjoy a feeble, though
unerring ray, which uniformly guides us to a
great and durable light, than to look for direc-
tion in our path from a glittering, momentary
meteor, which fuddenly attracts our notice, but
in an inftant vanifhes to fhine no more?—I have
feveral times, it may be much too often, made
ufe of the monofyllables *do, did, doth,* &c. but
                                              I muft

I ~~muft~~ beg leave to obferve, that *verbs* are too
~~confequential~~ in the formation of either profaic
or poetical compofitions; and too neceffary for
the prefervation of found fenfe, and grammatical
accuracy, to be rafhly excluded from that place
which propriety of fpeech requires they fhould
retain : And I will take the liberty of hinting,
that the equally often repetition of the conjunction *and,* or any other word in the *Englifh* language, might produce fenfations in us alike harfh
and difgufting.——Probably it may be objected,
that regular poetry prefcribes the total rejection
of *triplets.* I do confefs I think *Alexandrines*
wholly inadmiffible, as being affected and unna-
tural; but, in a poem of confiderable length, I
certainly do look upon *triplets* to be juftifiable,
as, according to my notion of them, they relieve
the reader from a tedious, unpleafant monotony,
when judicioufly introduced; but whether or
no I have confined-myfelf within the bounds of
methodical exactnefs in that refpect, I muft entirely fubmit to your generous and candid decifion.——Four beautiful lines of Mr. *Pope*'s Elegy
on the Death of an unfortunate Lady, I have
preferved, becaufe I could not conveniently omit
them; but as I had not the unpardonable ef-
frontery of making any change in them; fo neither had I the audacity of falfely arrogating them

to

to myself.——But fome perfon may be tempted to exclaim with indignation, Have we not Mr. *Hervey*'s Works in their native elegance of drefs? Why, then, fhould any part of them be impofed upon us, when only clad in rags? To this humiliating expoftulation I reply by another queftion, Have we not alfo the holy fcriptures, the plain, infallible guides to falvation, laid open before us? and•do we not ftand in need of inceffant exhortations to accept of, and turn to our everlafting advantage, thofe treafures of ineftimable felicity? That portion of Mr. *Hervey*'s valuable productions which I have prefumed to exhibit in a new fhape, is confeffedly of the higheft importance, and claims our moft ferious confideration. Daily experience demonftrates that we are all the mortal fons of fallen *Adam*.——Infancy, youth, vigorous manhood, and infirm old age, are alike expofed to the refiftlefs and unrelenting fhafts of death. The grifly tyrant pays no refpect to the bloom of beauty, the parade of wealth, or the haughty difplay of power; but levels in the duft of indifcriminate and impartial equality, the mighty potentate, and the defpicable flave. Here we have no abiding place, but are rapidly approaching to that ftate, either happy or miferable, which muft be our lot to all eternity! How unfpeakably interefting is it, then, to have always

2   in

in our view any warnings which may ftimulate us, in this our fhort and probationary exiftence, to prepare for admiffion into the glorious, incomprehenfible joys of immortality? Perhaps the novelty of the matter may induce my fellow-creatures to caft an eye over my verfification of the Meditations among the Tombs: But let me earneftly befeech them not to ftop here: Let me intreat them, in the warmeft manner, to compare it minutely with the original; which cannot fail of ultimately bringing with it a reward, amply compenfating for a tafk which, at firft, may be irkfome and forbidding. On every examination, let my inferior performance fuffer under the correcting hand of criticifm; yet I fhall be abundantly repaid by the comfortable fuppofition, that the folemn employment will be productive of the moft falutary benefits to all thofe who may permit themfelves deliberately to engage in it.——Cheerfully fhall I defcend to the loweft ftep of literary reputation, fhould I, as it were by furprize, become an humble inftrument in the hands of PROVIDENCE, of perfuading even a fingle individual among the race of mankind, to choofe " the one thing needful;" to wean his affections from a vain, tranfitory world; and endeavour, fincerely and heartily, " to make his calling and election fure," by " fo numbering his days as to apply his heart unto wifdom."

For

FOR our Saviour's Sermon on the Mount, I ſhall offer no other apology, than to exprefs my regret at not being able to do more juſtice to words uttered immediately by the mouth of GOD himſelf. The elegant ſimplicity of the diſcourſe in the original; the benevolence of the doctrines it contains; and the dignity of the Divine Preacher; are circumſtances which have always made the moſt ſenſible impreſſions on my mind; and will, I truſt, prove ſome excuſe for my having ventured to lay before you, though in an infinitely meaner garb, a ſubject of ſuch eminently conſpicuous excellence and perfection. I cannot, however, ſuppreſs my wonder, that Mr. *Pope*, Mr. *Addiſon*, Dr. *Young*, or ſome of our moſt celebrated poets, have neglected to anticipate me, in ſeizing on the truly profitable opportunity of adding unfading honors to their brows, by introducing into their works a verſification or paraphraſe of this incomparably valuable, ſublime, philanthropic, and edifying portion of holy writ.

MY little piece on the Attributes of GOD, is by no means conceived to poſſeſs any other merit than that of a fervent, though weak, deſire of diſplaying a few of the boundleſs, and inexpreſſibly to be reverenced, titles peculiarly applicable to the great Creator and Governor of the Univerſe;

verfe; and of implanting in our fouls becoming and venerable ideas of our almighty and benefi-cent Sovereign and preferver. · For my own part, neither the execution of this, nor of any others among my poetical attempts, when compared with the performances of refpectable authors, could meet with a cordial reception from me; and how can I imagine, that, when my own offspring ex-perienced but little of the fond partiality fo gene-rally prevalent in parents towards their children, they fhould be relifhed much by thofe to whom they are not in any degree allied?

The five following Effays, like the preceding ones, are juvenile productions, well intended, though poorly finifhed, and whofe concifenefs will, very probably, be the beft advocate to in-fure their forgivenefs. In the lines on *Age*, the word *momentary* I underftand as oppofed to *eter-nity*; and the fame term in the lines on *Death*, muft fignify *fudden*. The expreffions, *aged youth*, introduced into the poem on *Death*, may appear, at firft fight, to be fomewhat contradictory in themfelves, but may, I flatter myfelf, be foon reconciled to plain fenfe, by obferving, that they are defigned to reprefent death as *aged*, when we reflect upon the length of time wherein he has exercifed his power in the world; and *youthful*,

c   from

from a confideration of the many ages in which he may yet continue to retain his dominion.— I am not ignorant that the generality of my readers are too intelligent to require any explanations of this fort; but I look upon it as a duty which I abfolutely owe myfelf, to give every information that may ferve to elucidate my meaning, and render it as univerfally plain and evident as poffible.

In the year 1771, a fociety of gentlemen in *London* offered a confiderable præmium for the beft infcription, in metre, blank verfe, or profe, to be engraved on the monument erected in *Weftminfter-abbey*, to the memory of General *Wolfe*. A glowing efteem for the General, and not an impudently ambitious motive of being a candidate for any pecuniary reward, prompted me to write a fort of eulogium on him. Not pleafed with my firft effort, I fcribbled a fecond and a third one on the fame fubject; and, probably, would have perfifted longer in giving birth to fimilar compofitions, had I not concluded that the public, to whom they were anonymoufly conveyed through the channel of the then *Dublin Chronicle*, were heartily tired with thofe already offered to them. The three firft are now printed as they were originally written; and the fourth

is

is an alteration of the lines which were connected with my propofals for taking fubfcriptions; but whether or no any actual improvement has been made on this occafion, I muft not prefume to determine.—It is worthy of remark, that, out of a multiplicity of competitors who entered the lifts, no one proved fuccefsful; from a conceived impoffibility, without doubt, of determining who was fairly intitled to a preference; or a wifh not to offend fo many difappointed, though very refpectable, rivals.

THE Riddle mentioned as fent to me by a young Lady, was a very ingenious performance; and, had I not unfortunately loft it, would have accompanied my folution of it.

THE Reverend Mr. *Noble*, mafter of *Ennifkillen* Free-fchool, in the county of *Fermanagh*, is the gentleman alluded to in my Rebus, and to which I have fubjoined an anfwer.

MY lines on dry, warm Weather in Spring, fucceeded by Rain, are founded upon real obfervation; though I apprehend I fhall, with fome fhow of reafon, be accufed of prolixity in my manner of handling the fubject. Grammatical accuracy requires that, in the concluding paragraph of it,

the

the pronoun *you* fhould be underftood as prefixed to the monofyllable *who*, in three different lines.

THE trifles which go under the appellation of *Songs*, I would have entirely fuppreffed, but that, upon clofe examination, I cannot difcover that they contain any fentiments or expreffions which are inconfiftent with the ftricteft morality and decorum; and perhaps the perufal of them may contribute to the harmlefs entertainment of feveral among my fubfcribers.

FOR my paftoral Sketches on each Month of the Year, I do not recollect any model which I fought to copy after. They were the amufement of a few leifure hours; and if they fhould be fo fortunate as to fecure the approbation of my friends, I feek for no other gratification.

Mr. *Cunningham*'s charming Poems on Morning, Noon, and Evening, fuggefted to me the notion of attempting fomething in the fame way, to which I added my lines on Night. Mr. *Cunningham*'s meafure is feven fyllables; mine confifts of eight.——I pretend not to a rivalfhip—to fuperior excellence I humbly bow—but fhould I be allowed to have been fuccefsful enough to introduce any natural, defcriptive images into my

little

little performances, I fhall be perfectly contented with the decifion.

As I muft rely upon your generofity to forgive the extreme length of my Fable; I fhall not aggravate my offence, by exhaufting your patience with tedious interceffions for pardon.

I WAS myfelf a fpectator of the patron, or rural meeting, held annually on Eafter Monday in *Stramore*, of which I have attempted a defcription.——The barony of *Trugh* contains two parifhes, *viz. Donagh* and *Erigal*, the former of which is diftinguifhed by the name of Upper, and the latter by that of Lower, *Trugh*.——The *Blackwater*, is a river that takes its rife in the fouth-weft part of the county of *Tyrone*, which it afterwards, in a courfe of feveral miles, feparates from the county of *Monaghan*; and laterally, after dividing the county of *Armagh* from that of *Tyrone*; it empties itfelf into the celebrated lake, *Loughneagh*.——*Stramore*, is a word in the *Irifh* language, which fignifies a large plain, or meadow.——Where I have faid

> What tho' no mafter ever taught them how
> To drop a court'fy, walk genteel, or bow;

muft be underftood generally, not univerfally.——
Glafslough, is the name of a market-town, delightfully

fully fituated in Upper *Trugh*.——*Skernageerah,* now called *Emyvale,* is a fmall village alfo in Upper *Trugh.*

THE Occafional Prologue and Epilogue were written during the time of the late *American* war, when the combined fleets of *France* and *Spain* were in the *Englifh* channel; and I think it neceffary to take notice, that I have introduced into them three or four lines which I judged applicable, from my productions on the death of General *Wolfe.* They were defigned for the comedy of the *Weft Indian,* which was intended to be performed for a charitable purpofe, by a number of gentlemen belonging to the *Stuartftown* Volunteer Company. The Prologue was meant to be fpoken in the character of Enfign *Dudley;* and the Epilogue in that of Mifs *Rufport;* but by the death of Mr. *Gabriel Cornwall,* on whom I have written the fucceeding Elegy, and who was to have acted the part of *Belcour* in the play, the reprefentation of the comedy was never carried into effect.

As Acroftics are a very cramped fpecies of compofition, I fhall only obferve on that head, that my pieces of this kind are inferted in my book, merely from an idea that they are the property

perty of my fubfcribers, which, therefore, common honefty requires me not to with-hold from them; and that I have not, as is too often the cafe, proftituted my pen, in lavifhing extravagant encomiums upon giddy females, whofe cenfurable levity of deportment intitled them to very few compliments indeed!

In the room of about two thoufand lines, more imperfect and unfinifhed than even thofe which I have fubmitted to your infpection, I have fubftituted the Epiftle of *Tarico* to *Inkle;* the Song of *Chevy Chafe,* in *Englifh* and *Latin* metre; and a few portions of holy writ verfified.

When I was a fchool-boy, a relation of mine, long deceafed, was fo kind as to lend me the *original* poem of *Tarico* to *Inkle,* which he got from an intimate friend, the author of it, who had been dead many years before it came into my hands. I took a copy of it, which, together with the original happened to be miflaid fhortly afterwards. When nearly feven years had elapfed, at which time I was a ftudent in *Trinity College,* I was lucky enough to recover my copy; but the original is totally loft. On my return from the country to town, I had it publifhed in the then *Dublin Chronicle,* from which it found

its

its way into feveral newfpapers in *Ireland* and *England*. It was alfo printed in the form of a pamphlet in *Dublin*, where it met with a very rapid fale; and I underftand it went through repeated editions in *London*, in a fimilar fhape, and was purchafed with great avidity. Unlefs the fingular elegance of the epiftle fhould ferve to detect the impofition, I could fafely pafs with the public as the author of it—a kind of fraud, however, which I fhall never be guilty of. Into the poem, as now printed, I have incorporated ten or twelve lines of my own, and made three or four alterations in the original, too immaterial to be particularized.

The poetical beauties of the *Englifh* Song of *Chevy Chafe*, have been fo unqueftionably eftablifhed by the prince of *Critics*, Mr. *Addifon*, in the *Spectator*, that it would be fuperlative impudence in me to expatiate upon the merits of it: I fhall, therefore, add no more, than that I have connected with it a *Latin* metre verfion, which I copied out of a *London* edition of a book nearly ninety years old; and as I regard it in the light of a very curious production, and not generally known, I imagine it will prove an acceptable treat to many purchafers of my book.

THE

THE concluding portions of scripture consists of very striking, and highly awful extracts; on which account, infinitely rather than for any value I lay upon my verfification of them, I fervently hope they will be serioufly perufed, and meditated upon, by all thofe into whofe hands they may chance to fall. Old gold is faid to acquire purity from its age.—Long contracted friendships are moft highly efteemed.—The worth of vafes, paintings, &c. is eftimated in proportion to their antiquity.—Yet all thefe are of a perifhable nature!—And fhall we not prize, in an incomparably higher degree, the long delivered oracles of GOD, which have " brought life and immortality to light," and can alone make us wife unto falvation? It is inexpreffibly to be lamented that the Bible is, in thofe days of modern refinement, an antiquated, neglected book; but as fafhions and cuftoms are ever on the change in other inftances, poffibly it may yet become polite to ftudy the written word of GOD; and when that happy period arrives, may its duration be as permanent as the world itfelf!

IT may now be afked, Would it not be more in the line of my profeffion to print fermons, than poetical attempts? To this ftartling queftion I reply, That though I actually am poffeffed

d   of

of materials of that fort, yet they demand an higher polifh than I may be capable of beftowing upon them, to infure for them a favorable recep- tion from the world, or render them likely to produce any defirable effects in the hearts of my readers. Befides, luxury, debauchery, and dif- fipation, fo univerfally engrofs the time and at- tention of the more elevated orders of mankind ; and the lower ranks of life but too generally efteem themfelves juftifiable in adopting the ex- ample of their *betters*, as in a temporal point of view they are denominated; that ferious dif- courfes are of too aufere and gloomy a com- plexion for their perufal. Would it not be un- pardonable confidence in me to obtrude dull, mufty lectures concerning fobriety, temperance, and felf-mortification, upon hours which were devoted to voluptuoufnefs and fenfual gratifica- tions? Would it not argue extreme weaknefs in me to expect they would be cordially treated by avowed libertines, who glory in their fhame, and whofe conduct proves that they reckon it a mighty degradation of their dignity, to affociate with the vulgar mafs of mortals, for even a cou- ple of hours weekly, in the public worfhip of God? And would it not be really to " caft pearls before fwine," to addrefs grave, religious fubjects to perfons continually immerfed in car-

nal

nal enjoyments, or the profecution of worldly
affairs?——Empty romances; filthy treatifes on
loofenefs and obfcenity, or blafphemous, diaboli-
cal fatires againft morality and devotion; feem
to be alone calculated for fuch diffolute, impious
fons of deftructive infidelity and profanenefs.——
How falutary a courfe would it be for fuch pe-
rifhing, bewildered wretches, to think foberly
and often of the poifonous paths in which they
are impetuoufly pofting; and confider, that though
they may call this day their own, to-morrow may
confign them to the icy bofom of the grave,
where, alarming fuggeftion! repentance cannot
enter, nor reverfe the final doom denounced by
offended PROVIDENCE againft obftinate, incorrigible guilt? Let them for a moment ftop their wild
career, and attend to the practical leffons of a
faithful monitor, experience, which teach that
difeafes and death are the neceffary companions
of brutifh furfeits, and grofs indulgence. Let
them liften to the voice of wifdom, which proclaims aloud, that a reftriction of inordinate, de-
praved appetites, is the grand criterion to diftin
guifh between rational beings and the beafts which
have no underftanding.——Let them remember
that, whilft they, peculiarly crowned with the
bleffings of a bountiful GOD, inhabit magnificent
edifices; are fuperfluoufly loaded with coftly ap-

parel;

parel; all lulled in the lap of eafe and indolence; repofe their bodies, unacquainted with laborious toil, on foft and downy couches; and are pampered with fuperabundance of generous wines, and delicious meats; their poor fellow-creatures, defcended from the fame original parents, and called into exiftence by the fame great Creator; may be deftitute of every thing but rags to protect them from the inclemency of the weather; may not have fo much as a bed of ftraw on which they might ftretch their weak and labour-worn limbs; may want " a cup of cold water only," to allay the parching thirft of ficknefs; or a morfel of bread to filence the importunate cravings of hunger; nor own even a clay-built fhed to cover the miferable victims of indigence and woe. Let them recollect, that " riches make to themfelves wings, and fly away;" and whilft the gratifying opportunity is within their reach, let them ftem the ruinous torrent of unbridled fenfuality, and turn its ftreams into the healing channel of charity and moderation; the advancement of religion; and the fupport of induftry. How exquifitely delightful muft their internal feelings be, while they contemplate their having acquitted themfelves as the true fervants of God; the darling children of humanity; and the patriotic friends of their country; by feeding the hungry;

cloathing

cloathing the naked ; adminiſtering to the wants
of the neceſſitous ; and reſtoring to the community many uſeful members of ſociety, who, but
for their timely interference, might have been irrecoverably loſt ! Thus would they act as the happy
inſtruments of heaven, and ſecure for themſelves
crowns of glory which ſhould never fade away.
But alas ! I ſpeak in vain.—Can the votaries of
Mammon—can thoſe who make a god of their
bellies—who baſely and wickedly deny themſelves
the benefits of the MESSIAH's blood, poured out
for their ſalvation—who plunge greedily into unbounded enormity and licentiouſneſs, and reject
with ſullen, perverſe contempt the precepts of the
Prophets and Apoſtles of old ; and the pathetic,
ſublime exhortations of eminent, modern divines
—can they prevail upon themſelves for a moment
to attend to any admonitions offered by ſo obſcure,
ſo inſignificant a perſon as I confeſſedly am ?

HAVING given a feeble, though candid, cri-
tique of the matter contained in my book ; and
inſerted in my Preface a few notes and explanations with which I was unwilling to burthen the
body of the work ; permit me now to dwell for
ſome time on the treatment I experienced in my
application for ſubſcriptions.

HIS

His Excellency, the Earl of *Weſtmorland*, receives *only* twenty thouſand pounds ſterling, as
an appendage annually to the office of lord lieutenant of *Ireland*. Would it not, then, be very
unreaſonable' in me to ſuppoſe, that, out of ſo
paltry a ſalary, he could ſpare the *enormous* ſum
of five or ſix *Britiſh* ſhillings for a volume, the
principal part of which conſiſted of *Iriſh* manu-
factures, very indifferently fabricated, as his vice-
majeſty would naturally conjecture, from the ſpe-
cimen laid before him in my propoſal? Or why
ſhould I audaciouſly expect that his Excellency
would condeſcend to give his name to my book,
becauſe, forſooth, he might have done ſo in ſome
other inſtances; or, becauſe ſome hundreds of
very reſpectable characters had countenanced my
adventurous undertaking?

To give any encouragement to ſuch trifles as
poetical eſſays muſt, doubtleſs, have been thought
unbecoming the venerable function exerciſed by
the Lord Chancellor and Lord *Carleton*. Had
my book, indeed, been gorgeouſly bound and
decorated, and offered for ſale at the auction of
the late Mr. *Denis Daly*'s ſuperb library, it is poſ-
ſible that Lord *Fitzgibbon* might have become at
leaſt a bidder for it. I had, it is true, the *barren*
honor of being indulged in about a minute's con-
verſation

verfation with his lordſhip, and of paying two or
three *fruitleſs* viſits at his houſe afterwards, as at
the introductory one I received no anſwer. However, I ſhall make myſelf quite eaſy on this head,
by determining that, in the trouble I had in endeavouring to procure a ſecond interview with
his lordſhip, I have conferred upon him a compliment equal to his gracious reception of me.—
We have thus diſcharged mutual acquittances in
full; and here let the matter reſt.

So eleemoſynary an appearance had the ſub-
ſcription drawn from the Marquis of *Downſhire,*
that I repaid it with diſdain, together with legal
intereſt for the time I held his money in my
hands; leſt his lordſhip ſhould have any juſt
grounds to tax me with owing an obligation to
him. The Marquis, indeed, has been ſo deeply
engaged in erecting public places of divine wor-
ſh; in making piouſly political preparations for
futurity; and in extenſively patronizing the ſtaple
trade of *Ireland;* that *mental-webs* are quite of too
thin a contexture for his lordſhip's notice.

LORD *Clonmell* aſſured me, without bluſhing,
that he " had taken an oath never to read a line
of poetry." Though the declaration ſurprized
me not a little, yet, coming from ſo high autho-

rity, it ferved to remove from my mind an erroneous notion which it had until then labored under—that an oath was not required from noblemen, except in very extraordinary cafes.——— But why fhould I complain that his lordfhip did not deign to facrifice a little to my ruftic mufe, fince King *David*, *Homer*, *Virgil*, *Horace*, *Shakefpeare*, *Milton*, *Pope*, and all the celebrated bards, ancient and modern, are perpetually excluded, in common with me, from his lordfhip's prefence?

Lord *Northland*, the governor of the county in which I refide, after *barely* fubfcribing for my Poems, threw out fome infinuations that he " probably might not get the book, having been difappointed in that way on fome preceding occafions;" and mentioned that he was not at all acquainted with me. Being piqued at the unpolite tenor of his lordfhip's behaviour towards me in general, and his alledged ignorance of a perfon who had been a curate for many years, at the diftance of only half a dozen of miles from his lordfhip's country feat, though never, I grant, a gueft at his table, by previous invitation, or perfonal intrufion ; I returned his fubfcription, and reminded him that, in the memorable election at *Omagh* in 1768, when his lordfhip was a candidate for the honor of reprefenting the county of

Tyrone

Tyrone in parliament, he might, possibly, be able to recollect that my father and his interest had warmly supported him, without ever soliciting or obtaining a return of any sort from his lordship, or any of his connexions; and I hinted, at the same time, that he need be under no concern about the publication, since I had relieved him from the terrifying apprehensions of losing his cash.

I TAKE it for granted that Lord *Cloncurry* has been a considerable sufferer in some trans-actions relative to books; else he surely would not have been so exceedingly cautious, in a gla-ringly trivial concern, as to offer me only the *half* of a single blue paper copy subscription, and from an avowed suspicion that the work might never be delivered to him. As an acquiescence with his lordships terms would have been a vio-lation of the conditions specified in my proposals, and in some measure a tacit confirmation of his lordship's doubts; he found that the *prodigious* sum of a *British* half-crown, from even so emi-nent a personage as a peer of the realm, could not divert me from the principles upon which I commenced my undertaking.

Mr. Justice *Downes* would not recollect that I had been his cotemporary and acquaintance in *Trinity College, Dublin.* This particular, how-

ever,

ever, is not of fo very furprizing a nature, when we confider that a long lapfe of time, an unretentive memory, or the enjoyment of profperity on one fide, are circumftances which, fingly or conjointly, may effect it. But, befides, none are fo forgetful as thofe who will not remember; nor any as flow of comprehenfion as they who will not underftand; and the difproportion between a judge and a country curate is fo truly immenfe indeed! as not to admit of a permanent and familiar affociation between them.

A COUNSELLOR learned in the law, not far from *Earl-ftreet*, apologized, by telling me that " ftudies of a different nature from poetry claimed his time and attention."——A frothy novel lay open before him on the table, from which, I dare venture to fay, he extracted highly interefting legal intelligence!

A QUONDAM collector in *Armagh*, with much rudenefs, rather inconfiftent with his ufual *French* grin, fignified his refufal; and fuggefted that he " might, perhaps, encourage my publication, had it been in the line of my profeffion." For my own part, I am led to imagine that the gentleman himfelf was not turned out of his employ‑ ment, for any practical or theoretic improvements made by him in the " line of his profeffion;" and I muft alfo add, that whether my poems were moral,

moral, mixed, or comic, was a matter of which he had not the moſt diſtant knowledge, when he uttered his more than doubtfully *may-be* promiſe of ſubſcribing.

A GROCER in *Armagh*, whoſe father, I under-ſtand, was a clergyman, declared that " hurry of buſineſs abſolutely prevented him from an opportunity of reading any thing except his day-book and ledger."—I heartily congratulate him upon the proſperous ſituation of his affairs ; but I hope, for his own ſake, that he has had the precaution to have thoſe books ſufficiently volu-minous to admit into them the inſertion of the Bible and Common Prayer Book ; becauſe I would be ſenſibly concerned to ſuppoſe that he had devoted the whole of his reading to the ſer-vice of *Mammon*.

IN ſome of my wealthy, beneficed brethren I diſcovered a total void of fraternal affection, and a full meaſure of nauſeous acidity. I forbear mentioning names, out of reſpect to the profeſ-ſion ; and leave them to the feelings of cool re-flection. But am I not to conceive that a ſhyneſs of carriage between clergymen, founded upon no better grounds than a fortuitous diſtinction in terreſtrial acquiſitions, bears the ſemblance of ſcornful loftineſs, altogether unbecoming in thoſe who call themſelves the ambaſſadors of the meek

and

and lowly Jesus? Nor is it to be wondered at that the lowest order of the clergy fhould be trampled upon, in fome degree, by thofe in an high ftation among the laity; when their more amply provided for fellow-fervants in Christ's vineyard, not only treat them with negligence or difrefpect on too many occafions; but feem to look upon them as inferior beings, tainted, as it were, with a fort of leprofy for having affumed the prieft's office, and therefore to be cautioufly avoided as infectious animals. Some people protefted they " had made a folemn refolution never to fubfcribe to any book?" Probably the determination was formed at the moment of fpeaking to me.—Others gravely told me they " would think of the bufinefs." None of thofe confidering perfons have yet communicated to me the refult of their ferious deliberations.—Many declared they " made it a rule " not to fubfcribe to any book, but that they would purchafe mine, when publifhed." Their fincerity I truft I fhall very fhortly have an opportunity of putting to the teft. Several affured me they " would call upon me again;" which, however, thofe evafive promifers intentionally omitted doing.—And not a few ftood aloof at the *exorbitant* demand of five fhillings, prompt payment, for a book, who would not hefitate to expend ten times that fum in reducing themfelves below the ftate of a brute, by

a drunken

a drunken debauch; or a ftill larger fum, in en-
tailing infamy, wretchednefs, and profligacy of
conduct on a fondly credulous, but bafely de-
luded, female.—Shame! Shame! Shame!—Yet
fuch things are.

But fome people object to the bufinefs of fubfcription in the bulk; and fuggeft, that a " good
book will fell of itfelf, without fuch a fupport,
and a bad one does not deferve any aid of this
nature." That blafphemous, obfcene, inflamma-
tory, immoral effays fhould be univerfally difcoun-
tenanced, I will readily admit; and yet woful
experience puts it beyond all doubt that they are
too generally patronized and read: But I am
firmly of opinion, that many valuable productions already have been, and probably hereafter
may be, loft to the world, merely becaufe the
authors of them were in too ftraitened circumftances to bring them into public view without
the help of fubfcription, which, however, they
had not, or may not have, the perfeverance or
good-luck of fuccefsfully fecuring.

Let me now obferve, by the way, that gentlemen who are really at *home* fhould, in fuch cafes,
affign fome other excufe for declining an interview with thofe who call upon them, in preference to the ufual one offered by their fervants,

that

that they are *abroad*. The custom may be fashionable; but it is inconsistent with the dictates of Christianity, or of worldly prudence. For how can it be expected that domestics will be faithful or conscientious to their employers; or that they will not, when an opportunity presents itself, have a tendency to outwit and cheat those who so very improperly instruct them to impose upon others? Or how can masters, who pretend to have the smallest veneration for truth, reconcile such conduct to the express language of Scripture, which represents GOD as utterly abominating every species of fraud and deceit? Might not indisposition; an hurry of business; or a prior engagement be urged, and that with veracity, as an infinitely better apology on such occasions?

POSSIBLY some friend may be induced to hint, how imprudently I act, in thus exasperating so many noble and consequential characters, and provoking them to become my enemies. In answer to this I reply, that in the only opportunity they ever had of serving me in a very inconsiderable degree, and when they had a prospect of being partly repaid, they did not manifest a disposition of even faintly promoting my advantage. Of their friendship I had no patronizing proof; for their enmity I feel no excruciating apprehensions; and should they meditate revenge against

myself,

myfelf, or my innocent pofterity, I truft the pro-
tecting juftice of God will confound their wicked
and malicious machinations. But am I to dread
the lafh of perfecution from thofe whom I would
not falfely compliment with abject, unmanly encomiums of liberality?—No. I have not the
flighteft fears of fuch unwarantable attacks. I
exult in the knowledge of being an inhabitant of
a country where genuine freedom erects its glorious countenance, and for whofe felicity I feel
an uniformly glowing zeal; where the fhield of
equitable juftice defends the innocent from the
attacks of ferocious defpotifm, and curbs the daring extravagance of democratic licentioufnefs;
and whofe public inftitutions I am not fenfible of
having, at any period of my life, violated.———
Without the moft diftant view to the biaffing
impulfe of intereft, I love my king with an ardor
of affection, perhaps as immaculate, and, I am
confident, as unabating, as the higheft officer of
ftate.—I heartily approve of the privileges lately
extended to thofe of the *Romifh* perfuafion in *Ireland*, which their long tried good conduct abfolutely intitled them to; for I am not fo illiberal
as to lay to the charge of the aggregate body of
the people, any outrage or violence committed
by fome ill-minded, mifguided individuals among
them; and I hope and believe that gratitude,

and

and perfonal advantage, will cordially attach them
to the fupport of a government, which has ma-
nifefted fo unequivocal a regard for the promo-
tion of their welfare.—Though my mind recoils
with abhorrence at the idea of a frantic, fanguinary revolution in the ftate, and that fpirit of
reftleffnefs and levelling which unhappily agitates
the breafts of the public in too extenfive a degree; yet, in common with all thofe who are
not actuated by profit or prejudice, I am a ftre-
nuous advocate for a *parliamentary reform;* becaufe I conceive it would contribute effentially
towards the quiet of the community at large;
and becaufe I cannot reconcile it even to common fenfe, to affirm that our conftitution, though
long the envy and the admiration of the world,
may not, as being of human inftitution, be capable of improvement: However, I muft can-
didly acknowledge, that I imagine a reformation
in the morals of the people is previoufly indif-
penfable, in order to qualify them for enjoying a
legiflative renovation with a proper and beneficial
relifh.—For the Houfe of Lords, in its collective,
fenatorial capacity, as a venerable branch of the
legiflature, I entertain the utmoft refpect; though
to feveral members of that body I am far from
owing any obligations; nor have I experimental
proof to affert that, without exception, rank and

fortune

fortune confer true nobility of foul upon their poffeffors.—Though I am unalterably wedded to my prefent religious profeffion; yet I truft I can, without partiality or bigotry, embrace all the deferving individuals among my brethren of mankind; and unfeignedly pray for the reformation of thofe who are deplorably funk in vicious, abandoned practices.—But I fhall never forget myfelf fo far as to pay a bafe and whining court to that " purple and fine linen" which may, poffibly, be worn by a niggardly, auftere, and infolently mean fellow-mortal.

AND now let me afk, On whom are there fuch natural claims for the encouragement of dawning genius, as on thofe who wallow in affluence? Or who are equally open to animadverfion, when they penurioufly fail to perform their duty in this particular? They who are in the fruition of rank and power, will always find an abundant ftock of groveling parafites, difpofed to flatter their vanity, and with mendicant fervility folicit their favours; nay, who are meanly contented to wafte their lives in the vifionary enjoyment of benefits, daily promifed, though never meant to be really fulfilled: But as to myfelf, I fpurn at the idea of affociating with the fawning herd of fycophants. Senfible as I am of being conftitu-

f   tionally

fionally averfe to offend, yet I cannot boaft of
ftoical apathy enough to ftifle my refentment for
unmerited haughtinefs, or boorifh incivility.——
Though I truft I fhall always defpife the littlenefs
of pride ; yet I hope I will never tamely fubmit
to unprovoked infult, or faftidious arrogance·
Worldly wifdom may teach leffons of obfequious
adulation ; but the dignity of human nature with
prevailing influence recommends to me a more
praife-worthy independence of fpirit. My fituation in life is far from being enviable; but I
thank God I would not be reduced to the inevitable neceffity of ftarving, by being deprived of
the poor, I had almoft faid, beggarly income,
attached to my prefent laborious, defpicable, and
unproductive clerical employment; for my fer-
vices in which, a confcientious difcharge of my
duty was, comparatively fpeaking, nearly the
whole of my reward. Should ecclefiaftical preferment ever reach me, it fhall arrive unfought
for ; and at its abfence I fhall never repine :——
But I here ferioufly declare, that unlefs fome ad-
ditional relief fhall be made in the enfuing feffion
of parliament, for the pitiful falaries allowed to
the curates at this day, I will bid a final adieu
to my prefent profeffion ; apply myfelf to fome
lay occupation ; and leave an open for an ill-
fated fucceffor in the miniftry to undergo the
drudgery

drudgery of an office, more scandaloufly provided for, though denominated a bud in the flourifh-ing, foliage-clad tree of the eftablifhed church, than that of even a journeyman taylor in *Dublin*. Should, however, this procedure be called a quar-rel imprudently waged againft my bread and but-ter; I fhall allow that, fifty or fixty years ago, an annual falary of 50*l.* to a curate would, appa-rently at leaft, admit of fuch a charge; but this forry pittance, at the prefent day, will hardly purchafe bread alone for him; and therefore the butter, *&c.* muft be wholly omitted in his hum-ble bill of fare.

BUT it may be objected that, as the yearly income of a curate is fo wretched a provifion, none fhould embark in that function, who are not poffeffed of a decent competency befides.— I grant the argument fhould be conclufive, if none but people of independent circumftances are to be advanced to clerical promotions. But I will contend for it, that exemplary characters, and fhining abilities, are not entirely confined to—I was going to aver are rarely difcoverable in—the families of the great and wealthy; and had PROVIDENCE defigned to exclude from the miniftry the lower ranks of mankind; our blef-fed Saviour would not, furely, have chofen for

his

his Apoſtles ſuch vulgar beings as fiſhermen and tentmakers! In the profeſſion of the law or of phyſic, men of enlarged capacities, let their ex- traction be what it may, will certainly riſe into conſequence by diligent exertions; in the army, by conſpicuous acts of courage, and regularity of diſcipline, they ſometimes undoubtedly do; but, in the church, I aſk, does this appear to be the caſe? And are not many men left to languiſh in actual penury, who, by being more comfortably provided for, would have proved eminent orna- ments of ſociety; valuable patterns of piety; and liberal diſpenſers of charity to their poor fel- low-creatures? GOD is my witneſs that I do not, in the fainteſt manner, allude to myſelf, nor buoy myſelf up with the moſt remote pretenſions to eccleſiaſtical preferment; but I wiſh the prieſt- hood to be decently furniſhed with the neceſſaries of life; and, for the ſake of juſtice, religion, and humanity, to have that claſs of men to which I belong, relieved from the contempt which it is expoſed to, from the inadequate means of ſup- port allotted to it.

PERHAPS it may be deemed expedient for me to mention the mode and quantity of wiſhed-for acceſſion to the curates' annual ſalaries. Though I muſt not be ſo impertinent as either to recom-

mend

mend or prefcribe any plan for the adoption of parliament; yet, fhould I be honored by a public call from them, I may, poffibly, be able to throw out fome hints, which may ferve to lighten the weight of their deliberations on that fubject.

HAVING taken a difagreeable view of the dark fide of the picture; let me now tafte the pleafing fenfations arifing from the reverfed obfervation of it; and after returning my unfeigned thanks to my fubfcribers in general, to acknowledge my particular obligations to Lord MOIRA; Lord CHARLEMONT; Lord KINGSTON; Lord ANNESLEY; the Bifhop of ELPHIN; the Bifhop of KILLALA; Lord CASTLESTEWART; Lord LONDONDERRY; the Right Hon. THOMAS CONOLLY; the Right Hon. JOHN O'NEILL; the Right Hon. ARTHUR WOLFE, Attorney General; Mr. JONES AGNEW; Mr. MERCER, *Arno's Vale;* Counfellor THOMAS DICKSON; Mr. VAUGHAN, *Villa;* Rev. Dr. O'CONNOR; Rev. Dr. CHICHESTER; Rev. Dr. BENTON; Rev. Archdeacon DICKSON; Rev. Dr. MERCER; Major MOLESWORTH; Mr. JOHN CORRY MOUTRAY; Mr. ECCLES, *Fintona;* Mr. M'CAUSLAND GAGE; Mr. JAMES HAMILTON, *Strabane;* Rev. Mr. MORTIMER, *Comber;* Mr. CH. LYND; Mr. WILLIAM TIGHE; Mr. MORRIS, *Lifburne;* Mr. WILLIAM LENOX; Mr.

JOSEPH

JOSEPH CURRY; Mr. JAMES SCHOALES; Mr. JAMES MURRAY, and several other gentlemen in the friendly and sociable city of *Derry;* Mr. MARRIOT DALWAY; Mr. RICHARDSON, *Drum;* Mr. CARY, *Bangor;* Mr. WILLIAM HARKNESS, *Dublin;* Dr. M'CANN, *Armagh;* Reverend Mr. HUDSON; Revd. Mr. ROE, *Strangford;* Mr. PHIBBS, *Hollybrook;* Mr. CRAWFORD, *Crawford's Burn;* Rev. Dr. LESLIE, *Tanderagee;* Rev. Mr. MORRIS, *Ballyclog;* Rev. Mr. ARBUTHNOT, *Cavan;* Rev. Mr. CUPPLES; Dr. JACKSON, *Lurgan;* Captain BUCHANAN, *Artillery;* Rev. Mr. CAMPBELL, *Newry;* Rev. JAMES KNOX; Mr. JAMES HAMILTON, *Capel-street;* Dr. LIVINGSTON, *Newry;* Mr. CUNNINGHAM, *Port;* Counsellor FRANCIS KNOX; Mr. WILL. ARMSTRONG, *Mary-street;* Mr. JOHN ASHE, *Capel-street;* Mr. CHARLES CARROTHERS, *Jervis-street;* Rev. Mr. O'NEILL, *Hibernian Chapel;* Mr. DE LA MAZIER, *Dame-street;* Revd. Mr. NELIGAN; Mr. THOMAS NICHOLSON, *Bride-street;* Dr. M'CLELLAN, *Poynts-pass;* Rev. Mr. HUTCHINSON, *Donaghadee;* Mr. CROSBIE MORGELL; Dr. KING, *Armagh;* Mr. ROSS, *Strabane;* Mr. BENJAMIN NEVIN; Mr. WALKER, *York-street;* Dr. PLUNKET, *Dublin;* Mr. MARK WHITE, *Dorset-street;* Counsellor SPEER; Mr. JOSEPH RICHARDSON, *Stramore;* Mr. SIMON, *Mount Pleasant;* Mr. GRIFFITH,

GRIFFITH, Surveyor of *Killybeggs*; Revd. Mr. STEWART, *Grange*; Mr. TURKINGTON, *Rich-hill*; Rev. Mr. HENRY, *Armagh*; Mr. MACAY, *Drogheda*; Mr. THOMAS, *York-ftreet*; Counfellor GEORGE ROBINSON; Revd. Mr. SIMPSON, *Colerain*; Mr. STUART, *Grace-hill*; Mr. SMYTH, *Lifdillon*; Rev. Mr. ADAMS, *Stewartftown*; and many other gentlemen whofe names it is unneceffary to enumerate at prefent.

A multiplicity of unavoidable obftacles which confpired together to retard the publication of my book, will, I truft, fuccefsfully plead my excufe with my fubfcribers previous to the prefent year; and to thofe who patronized it within that period, I do not apprehend there is any apology abfolutely due.——Indeed, I am well convinced that thofe who encouraged it upon the fmalleft fcale, will be moft clamorous againft me, in a groundlefs charge of defigned procraftination.——And I could mention the names of feveral gentlemen, who frequently recommended it to me, not to be too precipitate in putting my work to prefs, but to render it as productive as I conveniently could; though they themfelves had liberally contributed to the advancement of my undertaking.

NOT-

NOTWITHSTANDING that my fatigue of body, and anxiety of mind, during a very extenfive application for fubfcriptions, muft have been feelingly fevere; yet fo confiderable was the expence neceffarily attending the execution of the bufinefs in which I had involved myfelf, that the favings of a play in *Dublin*, for the benefit of a favorite theatrical performer, acquired without much trouble, and fquandered, perhaps, in the courfe of a very few weeks afterwards on vanity, wantonnefs, and intemperance, will, probably, exceed the fum I fhall be able to realize by the entire fale of my books; but fhould I fail to difpofe of the whole edition, I fhall be an actual lofer, without, however, prefuming openly to repine at the iffue of an affair in which I voluntarily embarked. The neatnefs of the type; the goodnefs of the paper; and the quantity of matter contained in the work; free it, as far as relates to thofe particulars, from the imputation of its being a mere *catch-penny job*; but as to the aggregate quality of the mifcellanies themfelves, I fhall only venture to obferve, that I have rendered thofe pieces which belong to myfelf as faultlefs as my contracted abilities enabled me to do, at the time of my compofing them. My expectations of emolument were never very fanguine; and though I account the encouragement

of

of literary efforts an eafy tax upon the public;
yet I always wifhed to acquire my profits by an extenfive circulation of my books, and a very fmall
profit on each of them; rather than have it af-
ferted with any color of juftice that I held them
at an unreafonable price.

Should I be induced to come a fecond time,
before the awful tribunal of the public, which,
however, depends upon a variety of circumftances, it fhall not be through the medium of fubfcription: For, though I met with numberlefs
inftances of friendfhip, hofpitality, and patronage
during my late folicitations in that way; yet I alfo
experienced fo much vulgar, unmannerly treatment, from perfons whofe external appearance
alone gave them any pretenfions to the appellation of gentlemen; that the certain acquifition
of one thoufand guineas, fhould not prompt me
to engage in a fimilar fcheme. It was, I grant,
a perfectly optional matter with thofe to whom
I applied, whether or no they would become
fubfcribers; but furely it would not have been
any diminution of their dignity, to fignify their
refufal in conciliating terms of politenefs. To
the language of acrimonious invective my mind
is ftrongly repugnant; yet, to a perfon endued
with the fmalleft fenfibility of foul, unprovoked
fheers, churlifh fhynefs, or an harfh and haughty

denial,

denial, muſt prove unſpeakably mortifying and irkſome; though I muſt confeſs that my feelings have not, at any time been, ſo tenderly affected by a genteel apology, as by a ſullen, ungracious compliance, which, therefore, I made it a rule uniformly to reject, as I thought it bore the evident appearance of an intended affront. Refined urbanity is not, I own, attainable by all men; but pride, inſolence, and incivility ſhould be for ever baniſhed the company of rank and wealth; becauſe they diſplay ſtrong ſymptoms of ignorance, and a want of real worth; and are productive of hatred and contempt, inſtead of that veneration and eſteem which becoming affability would certainly acquire.

HAD I cultivated that natural bias to rhyme which I have actually checked for ſeveral years paſt, my poetical eſſays would, probably, have been much more numerous, and have appeared to greater advantage, than they do at preſent; but, in truth, I have no anxious wiſh to be called a Son of the Muſes, whoſe maternal advances I have ſo long avoided; and poverty, the generally allowed inheritance which they confer upon their children, has not, I am ready to acknowledge, any inviting charms for me, however cloſely it may be related to my two-fold profeſſion of poet

and

and curate.—I can eafily reprefent to myfelf ran-
corous juries of partial readers fitting in judgment upon me, and pafling fentence againft me
for the harfhnefs, the flatnefs, the barrennefs of
my productions; but as the peevifh, quibbling
remarks of inferior fnarlers cannot reach me; fo
neither fhall I feel any uneafinefs, fhould even
the gigantic cenfors of literature, the *Monthly
Revciwers*, make a cowardly attack upon me
from their impenetrable lurking-places; nor offer them any other fop to avert their vengeance,
than a copious draught of my foporiferous effays,
fhould they feel any thirft for fuch a potion : For,
at the moft, they can only convict me of being
a country curate, and a forry verfifier! And how
can they depreciate my infignificance, by barely
pronouncing me to be what I have already an
experimental fenfe of being, and am willing,
without controverfy, to admit of?—I envy not
the mental or bodily attainments of any one; nor
do I mean to prefs forward as an impudent com-
petitor with any writer of approved excellence,
for epic or lyric wreaths to adorn my temples.
All riders do not manage the winged *Pegaffus*
alike. Some require the conftant ufe of the curb,
to keep him within proper bounds. Others can
lay the flackened reins upon his comely neck,
and journey on with gentle pace, fecure from

danger.

danger. Many, when even mounted on his back, demand unremitting care to retain their feats, and the conftant ufe of whip and fpur to urge him on his way. I have got only my foot in the ftirrup, and may find it nearly, if not altogether, impracticable to beftride the famed charger. However, my humble mufe, which has hitherto ventured to crop only a few tender fprigs at the bottom of *Parnaffus*, may, poffibly, be encouraged, in time, to undertake the bold attempt of climbing a little way up the hill, though at the fummit fhe well knows fhe never can arrive. I implore not a decifion partially deftitute of juftice; but requeft that thofe who examine the " beams" which are difcoverable in " my eyes," may confider that " motes" are, peradventure, lodged in " their own;" and that

> " Whoever thinks a faultlefs piece to fee,
> " Thinks what ne'er was, nor is, nor e'er will be."

I pretend not to that fublimity of diction, or luxuriancy of invention, fo evidently incompatible with my limited fphere of action; but which would, without doubt, evince themfelves with confpicuous elegance in a more elevated ftation; and phrafes which, falling from me, might be condemned as bombaftic and affected; woul , when flowing from the pen of a right reverend or right

honourable

honourable author, be accounted eafy and natural. Among the many fynonimous terms with which the *Englifh* language fully abounds, perhaps I have been always fo unlucky as to prefer the leaft eligible word; but had I ftudied to conform to the capricious choice or humor of every petty, felf-created critic; the endlefs variety of clafhing judgments which, in fuch a cafe, muft have been confulted, would have utterly annihilated the pieces now offered to your infpection. For who could lay in a claim to approbation, or be expofed to reproof, for a tranfaction in which he was totally paffive? How could any production be compleated, which required perfect unanimity from perpetually difcordant opinions? Or who could affume the appellation of an author, whilft, on all occafions, he was excluded from the privilege of delivering his ideas and fentiments in expreffions of his own adoption? All I afpire to is a candid acknowledgment of the few proofs I have given of acquitting myfelf with tolerable decency.—I ftand in great need of fuch indulgence; and I fondly conceive that my demand is not improper or extravagant.

THOUGH I do not amufe myfelf with the groundlefs imagination that a fecond edition of my mifcellanies will be importunately called for,

or

or that honorable mention will be made of them
by the mighty arbiters of tafte and learning; yet,
as a cordial friend, I would advife my fair coun-
trywomen to perufe with attention fomewhat more
than the firft hundred pages of my book; and
fhall I dare to prefcribe the like ftudy to thofe
of my own fex?—When the ball, the rout, the
gaming-table, or the drunken feaft, with perni-
cioufly captivating temptations throw out their
fafcinating baits; and pleafure, with all-bewitching
blandifhments, allures her unguarded, thoughtlefs votaries into the dangerous vicinity of deftructive fenfuality and licentioufnefs; methinks
the timely interpofition of a monitor, reminding
them that they are but animated duft—the creatures of a day—and that the carnal objects of
their defire, if purfued with unreftrained avidity,
will prove fubverfive of their never-ending happinefs, and, by fhortening the flender thread of
life, accelerate the commencement of their everlafting torments—fhould be embraced with a degree of affection proportioned to the magnitude
of the important admonitions which it inculcates.
The confideration, that all is " vanity and vexation of fpirit" here below; that the " things
which are feen are temporal" and tranfitory;
that thofe who paffionately attach themfelves to
riches, or terreftrial gratifications, fhall hardly

" enter

" enter the kingdom of Heaven ;" and that the grave, which has been the receptacle of our fore-fathers, muſt, in a very ſhort time, become alſo the repoſitory of us, their children ; ſhould teach rational beings, who know, from daily warnings of mortality before their eyes, they cannot eſcape the ſhafts of death, and who will be finally tried at the judgment-ſeat of GOD for all the thoughts, words, and actions of their lives ; to ſhun the baneful ſnares of the world, the fleſh, and the devil ; and zealouſly ſtrive to lay up for them-ſelves celeſtial treaſures, which fade not away ; which " ruſt and moth cannot corrupt ;" nor thieves or robbers forcibly poſſeſs themſelves of.

But hark ! do I not hear it whiſpered on all ſides, that to ſolicit ſubſcriptions perſonally, is too mean an employment for a clergyman ? Well, be it ſo. And, pray, is there leſs diſhonor in venting ſuch half-ſuppreſſed, malevolent and ſlan-derous inſinuations ? Is it not more ſhameful in landlords to grind the face of their poor tenants, by mercileſs, oppreſſive exactions of rent ? Is it leſs diſgraceful, in the way of trade, to impoſe upon the ignorance of thoſe with whom we have any dealings, and take advantage of the confi-dence which they place in our integrity ? Or to beſpatter, frequently without foundation, the cha-

racter

racter of thofe with whom we appear difpofed to affociate upon the moft intimate footing? And let me now fubjoin, that it is likely a moderate annual addition to my falary, might have pre-ferved me from that troublefome, difgufting bu-finefs, for enabling me to bring forward my work; and more than likely, that the poffeffion of even a fmall ecclefiaftical benefice, would have rendered me as lazy as the bulk of my *then* cle-rical brethren are found to be.

On the death of my predeceffor, a general application was made by the members of the eftablifhed church to the Reverend *Alexander Staples*, their rector, for appointing me to the vacant curacy of his parifh, and to which requeft he readily acquiefced. This fingular invitation, which I do not mention from any oftentatious motive, I cheerfully accepted of, becaufe the ex-change introduced me to a more numerous con-gregation, and a more pleafing fociety, than I could have participated of in the immediately ad-joining curacy from which I removed; and I feel fenfations of a particularly pleafing nature in ob-ferving, that I have uniformly enjoyed every pub-lic and private teftimony of efteem from the pa-rifhioners at large, during a refidence of fifteen years among them; nor could I forgive myfelf

for

for omitting an honorable notice of their friendly attachment to me; . the grateful remembrance of which can only be obliterated by the extinction of life itfelf.

I SHALL conclude a tedious, infipid preface, with again fincerely thanking my fubfcribers, and fervently wifhing them an exemption from all poffible earthly diftrefs, and the fruition of pure, eternal felicity.

JOHN ANKETELL.

STUARTSTOWN,
July 1, 1793.

h   CON-

h 2　　　　　　　　　　　On

CONTENTS.

SUBSCRIBERS NAMES.

ABBREVIATIONS.

b. p. blue paper.—b. bound.—g. gilt.

HIS Grace the Archbishop of Cashel.

His Grace the Duke of Leinster, 1 g.

Right Hon. the Earl of Shannon.

Right Hon. the Earl of Clanbrassil.

Rt. Hon. the Earl of Moira, 2 b. p.

Rt. Hon. the Countess of Moira, 2 b. p.

Rt. Hon. the Earl of Charlemont, 4 b. p.

Rt. Hon. the Earl of Kingston, 4 b. p.

Rt. Hon. the Earl of Farnham.

Rt. Hon. Earl Annesly, 7. b. p.

Rt. Hon. the Earl of Enniskillen.

Right Hon. and Rev. Viscount Lifford, 2 b. p.

Right Hon. Viscount Gosford.

Right Hon. Viscountess Gosford.

Right Rev. the Bishop of Kildare, 2 b. p.

Right Rev. the Bishop of Elphin, 4 b. p.

Rt. Rev. the Bishop of Raphoe, 1 g.

Rt. Rev. the Bishop of Killaloe, 2 b. p.

Rt. Rev. and Hon. the Bishop of Ossory, 2 b. p.

Right Rev. the Bishop of Killala, 4 b. p.

Right Rev. the Bishop of Kilmore, 2 b. p.

Rt. Rev. the Bishop of Cork and Ross.

Rt. Hon. Lord Castlestewart, 1 g.

Rt. Hon. Lady Castlestewart, 1 g.

Right Hon. Lord Blaney, 1 b.

Rt. Hon. Lord Mountjoy, 2 b. p.

Right Hon. Lord Londonderry, 4 b. p.

Rt. Hon. Lord Caledon, 2 b. p.

Rt. Hon. Lord Oxmantown.

Rev. Doctor Beaufort.

George Birch, Esq. Roscrea, Co. Tipperary.

Lieut. Mat. Brown, Royal Navy.

Captain William Buchanan, Artillery, 10 b. p.

Rev. Dean Carleton.

Annesley Cary, Esq; Portarlington, Queen's County, 1 b.

Miss Charlotte Cary, do. do. 1 b.

Richard Chaloner, Esq. King'sfort, County Meath.

Miss D'Arcy, Hyde Park, County Westmeath.

Thomas Going, Esq. Traverstown, County of Tipperary, 1 b.

Rev. James Gordon, Vicar of Barragh, Author of a new System of Geography, 4 b. p.

Captain William Grattan, late of the 64th Regiment.

Richard Griffith, Esq. Millecent, County Kildare, 1 b.

Denis

Denis Bowes Daly, Efq. M. P. 1. b.

Captain Richard Houghton, 63d. Regiment.

Major Boulter Johnston, 70th. Regiment

Captain Richard Kitfon, 8th. Dragoons, 1 b.

Mrs. Lennen, Mullingar, County Weftmeath.

Sir Hercules Langrifhe, Baronet, M. P. 2 b. p.

Rev. Mr. Ledwich, Rector, of Aghaboe, Queen's County,

Captain Nettles, 17th Dragoons.

Captain Nicholl, 70th Regiment.

Charles O'Neil, Efq. M. P.

Crofbie Morgell, Efq. M. P. 1 b.

Right Hon. Hercules Langford Rowley, M. P.

Thomas Sims, Efq. Springfield, County Weftmeath, 1 g.

Rt. Hon. Sir Skeffington Smith, Bart. M. P. 1 b.

Hon. and Rev. Dean Stopford.

William Tighe, Efq. M. P. 4 b. p.

George Maxwell, Efq. London, 1 g.

Thomas Anketell, Efq. Dominica, 12 b. p.

County of Antrim.

Edward Jones Agnew, Efq. M. P. 4 b. p.

Thomas Andrews, Efq. Belfaft.

Rev. Richard Babington, Gilgorm Caftle

Rev. Thomas Babington, Mallindober.

Rev. John Bankhead, Broad Ifland, 1 b.

Joh Barclay, Efq. Lambeg.

Mr. Daniel Barry, Glen-oak. 1 b.

Mr. John Begg, Watchmaker, Belfaft.

Mr. Duke Berwick, Belfaft.

Mr. Daniel Blow, Printer, Belfaft.

Edward Brice, Efq. Killroot.

Rev. Mr. Briftow, Sovereign of Belfaft.

Rev. Mr. Briftow, Prebend of Rafharkir.

Rev. James Brown, Kilraghts.

John Brown, Efq. Linen Hall Street, Belfaft.

Rev. Doctor Bruce, Principal of Belfaft Academy.

Mr. John Bruce, Surgeon, Antrim,

Mr. John Cranfton, Belfaft.

Mr. Alexander Cranfton, Belfaft.

Alex. Crawford, M. D. Lifburn.

Rev. Mr. Cupples, Carrickfergus.

Marriot Dalway, Efq. Bella Hill, 4 b.

William Darby, Efq. Lifburn.

Samuel Detacherois, Efq. Lifburn.

Rev. Rich. Dobbs, Dean of Connor.

Rev. Saumarez Dubourdieu, Lifburn.

George Dunbar, Efq. Belfaft, 1 g.

James A. Parrel, Efq. Larne.

John S. Ferguffon, Efq. Belfaft.

Rev. Mr. Fletcher, Vicar of Aghalee.

Mr. James Fulton, Attorney, Lifburn.

Mr. Richard Fulton, Lifburn.

Wm. Watts Gayer, Efq. Lifburn.

Robert Gordon, Efq. Belfaft.

Mr. Nichols Grimfhaw, White Houfe.

Mr. James Grimfhaw, White Houfe.

Charles Hamilton, Efq. Portglenone.

James Hamilton, Efq. Bufh-bank.

Mr. Jacob Hancock, Senior, Lifburn. 1 b.

Mr.

Mr. Jacob Hancock, Junior, Lisburn.

Mr. John Hancock, Lambeg House, 1 b.

Rev. Mr. Henry, Randalstown.

Mrs. Heyland, Glen-oak.

Mr. Robert Hodgson, Bookseller, Belfast.

Mr. Alex. Holmes, Larne, 1 b.

John H. Houston, Esq. Belfast.

Samuel Hyde, Esq. Belfast.

Miss Jones, Moneyglass.

Messrs. Henry Joy, and Co. Belfast. 2 b. p.

Rev. Mr. Jonhston, Derriaghy.

Rev. Sinclair Kelburn, Belfast, 1 b.

Richard Gervas Ker, Esq. Red Hall, 2 b. p.

Sir William Kirk, Carrickfergus.

Mr. John Knox, Watchmaker, Belfast.

Thomas Lea, Esq. Collector of Larne.

William Legg, Esq. Malone.

Mr. James M'Clean, Watchmaker, Belfast.

James M'Donnel, M. D. Belfast.

Alexander M'Manus, Esq. Mount Davis.

Mr. Wm. Magee, Printer, Belfast.

Rev. Mr. Marshal, Ballymoney.

M. Campbell Millar, Surgeon, Antrim.

James Moore, Esq. Clover Hill.

Roger Moore, Esq. Clover Hill.

Thomas Morris, Esq. Lisburn, 1 b.

Mr. Jacob Nixon, Surgeon, Belfast.

Mrs. O'Hara, Crebilly.

John Hamilton O'Hara, Esq. ditto.

Right Hon. John O'Neill, M. P. 4 b. p.

Rev. Mr. Patterson, Carmoney.

Mr. Robert Patterson, Carrickfergus, 1 b.

Mrs. Perry, Carrickfergus.

Charles Ranken, Esq. Belfast, 1 b.

Mr. William Robinson, Ballycraggy. 1 b.

William Rogers, Esq. Lisburn.

John Shepard, Esq. Lisburn.

William Stewart, Esq. Willmount.

James Stuart, Esq. Grace Hill, 1 b.

Mr. Hamilton Thompson, Belfast.

Mrs. Trail, Lisburn.

Rev. Doctor Trail, Rector of Lisburn.

Mr. Matthew Tuton, Belfast, 1 g.

Rev. Mr. Vance, Belfast.

James Wallace, Esq. Lisburn, 1 b.

Mr. George Warnick, Belfast.

Ezekiel Davys Wilson, Esq. M. P. 2 b. p.

Mrs. Elizabeth Wilson, Belfast.

Mr. Andrew Young, Antrim.

Mr. Robert Young, Senior, ditto.

Mr. Robert Young, Junior, ditto.

County of Armagh.

Rev. Mr. Ash, Kilmore.

James Ashmur, Esq. Newry, 1. b.

Joseph Atkinson, Esq. Crow Hill.

Robert Atkinson, Esq. Hayes Hall, 1 g.

Rev. Mr. Barker, Market Hill.

Rev. Mr. Biffet, Rector of Louggall.

Rev. Dean Blacker, 1 g.

Mr. James Boyd, Lurgan.

Robert Boyd, Esq. Acton.

William Brownlow, Junior, Esq. Lurgan.

Rev. Mr. Buckby, Rector of Sligo.

John Henry Burgess, Esq. Armagh, 1. b.

Rev. Mr. Carpendale, Armagh.

Mr. Samuel Carson, Surgeon, Armagh.

William Clark, Esq. Summer Hill. 1 g.

Samuel Close, Esq. Elm Park.

Rev. Mr. Creery, Tanderagee, 1 b.

William Cross Esq. Dartan.

Adam Cuppage, Esq. Lurgan.

Joshua Desvoeux, Esq. Lurgan.

Richard Eustace, Esq. Lurgan, 1 b.

Rev.

Rev. Mr. Gamble, Lurgan, 1 b.

John Godiy, Efq. Tanderagee.

George Gray, Efq. Graymount.

John Greer, Efq. Silver Wood Houfe

Thomas Greer, Efq. ditto, 1 g.

Jofeph Hall, Efq. Lurgan, 1 b.

Rev. Dean Hamilton, Armagh, 1 b.

Mr. Thomas Haughton, Lurgan, 1 b.

Rev. Mr. Henry, Armagh.

Rev. Mr. Hudfon, Rector of Fork Hill, 1 g.

Mrs. Huggins, Englifhtown, 2 b. p.

Wm. Huggins, Efq. ditto 2 b. p.

Alexander Jackfon, M. D. Lurgan, 1 g.

Robert Jackfon, Efq. Armagh, 1 b.

James Johnfton, Efq. Nappagh.

Alexander King, M. D. Armagh.

Rev. Doctor Leflie, Tanderagee, 4 b. p.

Rev. Doctor Lodge, Rector of Kilmore.

William Loftie, Efq. Tanderagee.

John M'Can, Efq. Armagh, 1 b.

Luke M'Can, M. D. Armagh, 1 b.

Andrew Macartney, Efq. Rofebrook, 2 b. p.

Edward M'Clellan, M. D. Poynts pafs, 1 b.

Mr. Charles M'Garry Poynts-pafs, 1 b.

Mr. James M'Gowan, Lurgan.

Rev. Mr. M'Illree, Portadown.

Henry M'Veagh, Efq. Lurgan.

Mr. William M'Williams, Armagh, 1 b.

Mr. Charles M'Reynolds, Innkeeper, Armagh.

Rev. Mr. Magee, Lurgan.

Mr. James Malcomfon, Lurgan.

John Marfhall, Efq. Armagh, 1 b.

Rev. Mr. Martin, Ballymoire.

Rev. Mr. Maunfell, Rector of Drumcree.

Major Molefworth, Fairlong, 4 b. p.

Sir Capel Molyneux, Bart. 1 g.

George Murray, Efq. Armagh.

Mr. Wm. Nicholfon, Tallbridge, 1. b.

John Park, Efq. Attorney, Armagh 1 b.

Doctor Patton, Tanderagee, 1 b.

Mrs. Peebles, Hamilton's-bawn. 1 g.

George Perry, Efq. Armagh 1 b.

Mr. Samuel Pilkington, Tynan, 1 b.

Mr. Alexander Prentice, Armagh.

Mr. Thomas Prentice, Armagh.

Rev. Mr. Quin, Rector of Tynan, 2 b. p.

Rev. Mr. Radcliff, Lifnadil, 1 g.

John Read, Efq. Ballymoire.

Jonathan Richardfon, Efq. Ballynick.

George Robinfon, Efq. Barrifter.

Mrs. Roe, Brookhoufe.

Jonathan, Seaver, Efq. Heath-hall.

Rev. Alexander Staples, Rector of Madden.

Alexander Thomas Stewart, Efq. Acton, 1 g.

Rev. Mr. Stewart, Grange, 1 b.

Rev. Mr. Stinton, Lurgan, 2 b. p.

Counfellor Stringer, Armagh.

Rev. Mr. Strong, Fairview.

Mr. William Turkington, Richhill, 1 g.

Mr. William Thompfon, Lurgan.

James Verner, Efq. Church-hill. 1 g.

Mr. George Walker, Ballileeny, 1 g.

Rev. Dean Warburton.

John Waring, Efq. Dartry-lodge.

Mr. John Watfon, Portadown.

Mr. Charles Whittington, Armagh.

Rev. John Young, Eglis.

County of Cavan.

Rev. Jofeph Arfkine, Cavan.

Rev. Archdeacon Caulfeild, 1 g.

Mr.

Mr. John Caulfield, 1 g.

Rev. Doctor Cottingham, Cavan.

James Fleming, Esq. Bellville.

Rev. Doctor Hales. Killishandra.

John Moutray Jones, Esq. Belturbet, 1 b.

Neal Kenny, Esq. Ballyhays.

Wm. Mayne, Esq. Frame Mount.

Rev. Albert Nesbitt, Vicar of Denn.

Edward O'Reilly, M. D. Cavan.

John Lloyd Saunderson, Esq. Belturbet.

County of Derry.

James Acheson, Esq. Derry. 1 b.

Henry Alexander, Esq. M. P.

William Alexander, Esq. Derry.

William Armstrong, Esq. Derry.

Rev. Isaac Ash, Rector of Tamlaght, 1 b.

Rev. Doctor Barnard, Maghera, 2 b. p.

Rev Mr. Barnard, Maghera.

Mr. William Beatty, Derry.

Rev. Mr. Black, Derry.

Miss Mary Brown, Magherafelt, 1 b.

Mr. George Brown, Surgeon, Derry.

Rev. Mr. Bruce, Rector of Aghadowey, 1 g.

Rev. Mr. Bryan, Rector of Kilcronaghan.

John Buchanan, Esq. Derry.

Rev. Mr. Burroughs, Rector of Ballyscallon, 1 b.

Rt. Hon. Thomas Conolly, M. P. 4 b. p.

John Caldwell, M. D. Magherafelt.

John Church, Esq. Churchland, 1 b.

Rev. Mr. Clarke, Ballinderry. 1 b.

Rev. Mr. Colthrust, Garvagh.

Mr. Andrew Crawford, Castledawson, 1 b.

Mr. John Crawford, Castledawson, 1 b.

Mr. John Cunningham, Derry.

George Curry, Esq. Derry.

Joseph Curry, Esq. ditto. 1 b.

Samuel Curry, Esq. ditto, 1 b.

Mr. Samuel Davison, Derry.

Mr. Henry Delap, Derry.

Miss Douglas, Derry, 1 g.

Dawson Downing, Esq. Rosegift, 1 b.

Rev. Mr. Downing, Maghera.

Marcus M'Causland Gage, Esq. 7 b. p.

Mr. John Galt, Colerain.

Mr. John Given, Farloe, 1 b.

Mr. Samuel Given, Colerain.

Mr. Glenhome, Lengfield.

Rev. Mr. Graham, Rector of Kilrea, 2 b.

Samuel Graves, Esq. Castledawson.

William Graves, Esq. Ballronan, 1 g.

Rev. Mr. Hamilton, Rector of Ballikelly.

Rev. Mr. Hamilton, Newtownlimavady, 2 b. p.

John Harvey, Esq. Derry, 1 b.

John Hart, Esq. Ballimagard, 1 b.

Kennedy Henderson, Esq. Cottage.

Langford Heyland, Esq. Bovagh, 1 g.

Miss Jane Hill, Bellaghy, 1 b.

Captain Holland, Coolafinny.

Mr. John Hopes, Maghera, 1 b.

Rev. Dean Hume, 2 b. p.

Mr. James Hutcheson, Colerain.

Rev. James Jones, Tamlaght O'Brilly, 2 b. p.

Rev. J. Pitt Kennedy, Derry, 1 b.

Mr. Alexander Kennedy, Ballymoy.

Mr. William Kerr, Derry.

Mr. Samuel King, Derry.

Alexander Knox, Esq. Derry.

Mr. Thomas Kyle, Derry.

Mr.

Mr. William Lawrance, Colerain.
Miss Mary Leckey, Agivey.
Averell Leckey, Esq. Magilligan.
William Leckey, Esq. ditto.
William Leckey, Esq. M. P.
Miss Ledlie, Balligonny, 1 b.
Rev. Mr. Lendrum, Artrea, 1 b.
William Lenox, Esq. Derry, 4 b. p.
Mr. Francis Loudon, Maghera, 1 b.
Hugh Lyle Esq. Colerain.
William Christopher Lynam, Esq. Magilligan.
Miss Lynd, Colerain.
Conolly M'Causland, Esq. Fruit Hill, 1 b.
Conolly M'Causland, Esq. Wallworth, 1 b.
Conolly M'Causland, Esq. Daisie Hill.
Rev. Marcus M'Causland, Rush Hall.
Mr. John M'Clintock, Derry.
David M'Cool, Esq. Derry.
Rev. Mr. M'Ghee, Rector, of Desart Martin.
Mr. James Macklin, Schoolmaster, Derry.
Henry Edward Macneill, Esq. Belsbrook.
Rev. Mr. Mansfield, Rector of Erigal.
John Millar, Esq. Moneymore, 1 b.
Samuel Montgomery, Esq. Derry.
Robert Moore, Esq. Derry, 1 b.
Mr. Samuel Moore, Derry, 1 b.
James Murray, Esq. Derry, 1 b.
Mrs. Jane Simpson Ogleby, 1 g.
Henry Patterson, Esq. Millbrook, 2 b. p.
Rev. Mr. Patterson, Tubbermore.
Robert Patterson, Esq. Grillogh, 1 b.
William Patterson, M. D. Derry.
Mr. James Preston, Derry.
Alexander Purviance, Esq. Garvagh.
Mr. Hugh Rankin, Heathfield.
John Richardson, Esq. M. P. 1 g.

Rev. John Ruxton, Tamlaght.
Rev. George Vaughan Sampson, Derry.
Adam Schoales, Senior, Esq. Derry.
James Schoales, Esq. Derry.
Mr. Richard N. Scot, Derry.
William Scott, Esq. Derry.
Mr. Robert Sharp, Colerain.
John Sheil, M. D. Castledawson.
Rev. Mr. Simpson, Colerain.
Mr. Robert Sinclair, Maghera, 1 b.
Thomas Skipton, Esq. Beechhill, 1 b.
George Smyth, M. D. Derry.
William Smyth, Esq. Lisdillon.
James Sterling, Esq. Derry.
John Stevenson, Esq. Fort William.
Mrs. Stirling, Walworth.
Samuel Strain, Esq. Magherafelt.
Mr. Alexander Templeton, Derry.
James Thompson, Esq. Derry.
Mr. Andrew Torrins, Moneymore, 1 b.
Rev. John Torrens, Glenone, 1 b.
Rev. Doctor Torrens, Ballinaskreen, 1 g.
Right Hon. Lord Tyrone, M. P. 2 b. p.
Rev. John Waddy, Lower Alla.
Rev. Richard Waddy, Cumber.
William Walker, M. D. Derry. 1 b.
Miss Wallace, Magherafelt, 1 b.
Rev. Rich. Watson, Retreat, 1 b.
Mr. George Wood, Derry.
Rev. Mr. Young, Rector of Macofquin.
Miss Hatton Elizabeth Young, Macofquin.
Rev. Mr. Young, Derry.

County of Donegal.

George Cary, Esq. Red Castle.
Daniel Chambers, Esq. Rock-hill, 1 b.

2
Rev.

Rev. Doctor Chichester, Cloneah, 1 b.

Charles Colhoun, Esq. Letter-kenny.

Matthew Davis, Esq. Ballyshan-non, 1 b.

Rev. Mr. Delap, Ray.

Rev. Francis Gouldsbury, Upper Moville.

Rev. Francis Gouldsbury, Junior, Insh.

John Hamilton, Esq. Brown-hall, 1 b.

Rev. Thomas Hamilton, Lower Moville.

Miss Mary Ann Hatton Harvey, Malin-hall, 1 g.

Rev. Mr. Hawkin's, Rector of Killinard, 2 b.

Rev. George Homan, Culdaff, 1 g.

Lieutenant Huey, Castle Forward.

Rev. Doctor Kearney, Fort Ste-wart.

Rev. Doctor Knox, Rector of Lif-ford, 2 b.

Rev. James Knox, Rector of Aghanloo, 2 b.

William Knox, Esq. Killcaddon.

Doctor Lamy, Raphoe.

Rev. Joseph Love, Stranolane.

Rev. Josiah Marshall, Fahan.

Richard Maxwell, Esq. Birdstown.

John Montgomery, Esq. Fairview, 1 b.

Rev. Mr. Pemberton, Taugh-boyn Parsonage.

Rev. Mr. Sandys, Donagh.

Mrs. Smyth, Ture, 1 g.

Rev. Mr. Spence, Donaghmore,

Rev. Mr. Thomas, Aghanunshan, 1 b.

Rev. Doctor Waller, Rector of Rayes.

Mr. James Watt, Ramelton.

Robert Young, Esq. Culdaff, 2 b.

Thomas Young, Esq. Lougeask, 1 g.

William Young, Esq. Mount Hall, 1 b.

County of Down.

Miss Addington, Mount Pleasant.

George Anderson, Esq. Newry.

James Andrews, Esq. Comber.

Hon. and Rev. Dean Annesley.

James Atkinson, Esq. Newry, 2 b. p.

John Aughenleck, Esq. Strang-ford, 1 b.

Miss Aynsworth, Strangford, 1 b.

Rev. Mr. Barber, Rathfriland.

William Beath, Esq. Newry.

Samuel Black, M. D. Newry.

William Black, M. D. Newry.

Rev. Mr. Blacker, Portaferry.

Richard Blood, Esq. Barnvale.

Mr. Thomas Bradshaw, Milicross-lodge.

Rev. Henry Bunbury, Rostrevor, 1 g.

Thomas Bunbury, Esq. Bloom-field, 1 b.

Rev. Mr. Burroughs, Dromore.

Rev. Mr. Campbell, Newry, 8 b. p.

Arthur Cary, Esq. Bangor.

Mr. James Christy, Stramore.

Rev. James Hamilton Clewlow, Bangor.

Mr. James Clibborn, Waringstown.

Mr. John Conran, Maze.

Mr. Robert Cosgrave, Newry, 1 b.

Miss Crawford, Crawford's Burn, 1 b.

John Crawford, Esq. ditto, 1 b.

Arthur Crawford, Esq ditto, 1 b.

George Crazier, Esq. Banbridge.

Mr. Robert Delap, Bannville 1 b.

Rev. Archdeacon Dickson, 7 b. p.

Rev. Doctor Dickson, Portaferry.

Andrew Durham, Esq. Belvedere, 1 b.

Charles Echlin, Esq. Echlinville.

Mr. Alexander Falls, Newry, 1 g.

John Fivey, Esq. Loughbrickland.

William

William Fivey, Efq. Union-lodge, 1 b.
Rev. Mr. Ford, Ballynahinch.
Matthew Forde, Efq. Seaford, 1 b.
William Galway, Efq. Portaferry, 1 b.
Hugh Gillefpie, Efq. Comber.
William Glenny, Efq. Newry, 1 b.
Meffrs. William Glenny and Sons, Newry.
Mrs. Gordon, Newry, 1 b.
Thomas Knox Gordon, Efq. Loy-alty-lodge, 1 b.
Rev. Andrew Greer, Mellille.
Rev. Arthur Grueber, Union-lodge.
Roger Hall, Efq. Narrow Water, 1 b.
Savage Hall, Efq. ditto, 1 b.
George Hamilton, Efq. Tyrella.
Hugh Hamilton, Efq. Ballina-hinch.
Mr. Samuel Hana, Newry, 1 b.
Mr. George Hawthorn, Greenan, 1 b.
Steele Hawthorn, Efq. Down-patrick, 1 b.
Rev. Mr. Hazlett, Dundonald.
Rev. Mr. Huey, Flufh-hill.
Rev. Francis Hutchinfon, Do-naghadee.
Mifs Jackfon, Banbridge.
Mr. Thomas James, Newry.
Henry Jenny, Efq. Harrymount.
John Moore Johnfton, Efq. Rock-vale.
Rev. Doctor Kennedy, Rector of Kilmore.
Thomas Dawfon Lawrence, Efq.
Rev. Doctor Lennon, Newry.
William Livingfton, M. D. Newry.
Rev. Mr. M'Cruce, Comber.
Mr. Hugh M'Celland, Banbridge.
James M'Cully, Efq. Ballyhart.
Thomas Mercer, Efq. Arno's-vale, 9 b. p.
Rev. Hugh Montgomery, Rofe Mount, 1 g.
Rev. Boyle Moody, Newry, 1 b.

Rev. Mr. Moor, Rector of Moira.
Rev. Mr. Mortimer, Comber,
Benjamin Nevin, Efq. Donagha-dee, 1 b.
Mr. Thomas Nevin, Downpatrick, 1 b.
Robert Jaffray Nicholfon, Efq. Stramore.
William Nicholfon, Efq. Ballow, 1 b.
Samuel Norris, Efq. Strangford, 1 b.
Mr. Patrick O'Hanlon, Newry.
Mifs Orr, Newtownards, 1 b.
Mr. Thomas Phelps, Moyallan, 1. b.
Eldred Pottinger, Efq. Craiga-vade, 1 b.
Mrs. Pollock, Newry.
Mr. John Quin, Newry.
Chriftopher Reed, Efq. Newry.
John Reed, Efq. Portaferry.
Mr. Jofeph Richardfon, Stramore, 4 b. p.
John Riddle, Efq. Comber.
Rev. George Rogers, Chancellor of Dromore.
Rev. Edward Roe, Strangford, 1 b.
John Ruffel, Efq. Edenderry.
Hen. Savage, Efq. Green Park, 1 b.
James Savage, Efq. Rock Savage, 1 b.
Patrick Savage, Efq. Portaferry.
William Sharman, Efq. Moira, 1 g.
Rev. Mr. Shaw, Banbridge.
John Simon, Efq. Mount Pleafant.
Mrs. Simon, Mount Pleafant.
Rev. Mr. Sinclair, Newtownard.
Thomas Smyth, Efq. Fadam.
Rev. James Skelton.
Hon. Robert Stewart, M. P.
Mrs. Stewart, Newtownards, 1 b.
Mrs. Frances Stewart, ditto, 1 b.
Mr. John Sugden, Gilfort. 1 b.
Mr. Francis Taggart, Newtown-ards.
Mr. John Maxwell Templeton, Newry.

John

John Thompfon, Efq. Newry.
Victor William Thompfon, Efq. Newtownards.
Rev. Thomas Tigh, Drumgooland, 1 b.
J. B. Trotter, Efq. Downpatrick.
Mr. Jofeph Turbott, Longubrickland, 1 b.
George Vaughan, Efq. Villa, 11 b. p.
Robert Waddle, Efq. Ifland Derry, 1 b.
Mr. Thomas Wakefield, Stramore.
Mrs. Elizabeth Walker, Newry, 1 b.
John Walker, Efq. Newry.
Mr. James Wallace, Banbridge.
Hon. Robert Ward, M. P. 1 g.
Vere Ward, Efq. Strangford, 1 b.
Rev. Holt Waring, Kirkcubbin.
Holt Waring, Efq. Waringftown.
Samuel Caulfield Waring, Efq. Waringfield.
Mr. Launcelot Watfon, Newry, 1 b.
Rev. Ralph Wilde, Downpatrick.
Mr. Richard Wolfenden, Lambeg.

County and City of Dublin.

Samuel Adams, Efq. Dawfonftreet.
Townly Ahmuty, Efq. Brideftreet.
W. J. Alloway, Efq. Dublin.
Mrs. Eliz. Archbold, Ufher's-quay.
Clement Archer, Efq. M. R. I. A.
John Ardill, Efq. Great Longford-ftreet, 1 b.
Mr. Edward Armftrong, Boltonftreet, 1 b.
Mr. William Armftrong, Maryftreet, 2 b.
Mr. John Afhe, Capel-ftreet, 1 b.
Rev. Gilbert Auftin, Dublin.
Benjamin Ball, Efq. Kildare-ftreet.
John Ball, Ffq. Barrifter.
Rev. Mr. Ball, Merrion-ftreet.
Thomas Bell, M. D. York-ftreet, 1 g.

Mr. Charles Berry, Dame-ftreet.
Anthony Blackburne, Efq. Barrifter, 1 b.
Rev. Mr. Blacker, Dorfet-ftreet.
Mr. J. Theophilus Boileau, Brideftreet, 1 b.
Solomon Boileau, Efq. Queenftreet, 1 b.
Theophilus Bolton, Efq. Molefworth-ftreet.
Mrs. Bolton, Mary's-abbey, 1 b.
Mr. Boyle, Abbey-ftreet.
William Power, Efq. Summerhill.
Doctor Boyton, Jervis-ftreet.
Mr. William Boyd, Merchant, Dublin, 1 b.
Walter Bourne, Efq. Aungierftreet, 1 b.
Thomas Boys, Efq. Dorfet-ftreet, 1 b.
John Bradfhaw, Efq. York-ftreet.
Rev. Mr. Brickell, Caftleknock.
Rev. Mr. Brinkley, Profeffor of Aftronomy.
Arthur Browne, L L. D. S. F. T. C. D. 1 g.
Rev. Archdeacon Brown, Dublin.
Guftavus Brook, Efq. Marlborough-ftreet.
Rev. Dr. Burrowes, J. F. T. C. D.
Beresford Burfton, Efq. Barrifter, 1 g.
Mrs. Bury, Granby-row, 2 b. p.
Charles Bury, Efq. Mary's-abbey.
Ponfonby Caldwell, Efq. Dublin.
Major Cane, Dawfon-ftreet.
Richard Cooban Carr, Efq. Dublin.
Coote Carroll, Efq. Dublin.
Mr. Charles Carrothers, Jervisftreet, 1 b.
Mrs. Clark, Bride-ftreet, 2 b. p.
Mr. Clark, T. C. D.
Doctor Cleghorn, Dublin.
Mr. Michael Clarke, Chancerylane.
Richard Colles, Efq. Barrifter.
Mr. Robert Collins, Bride-ftreet, 7 b. p.

Rev.

Rev. Dean Coote, Stephen's-green.

Henry Coulfon, Efq. Peter-ftreet.

Mr. John Coulter, Capel-ftreet.

Mr. John Cox, Skinner-row.

Right Hon. Lord Creighton, Dublin.

James Crawford, Efq. Streamf-town.

Mr. Abraham Creighton, Capel-ftreet.

Mr. Crofton, Summer-hill.

Wm. Cufack, Efq. Summer-hill.

Captain D'Arcy, French-ftreet.

William Davis, Efq. Bifhop-ftreet, 1 b.

John Johnfton Danah, Efq. York-ftreet.

Arthur Dawfon, Efq. M. P.

Mr. James Dawfon, Caftle-ftreet.

Mr. John Dawfon, Bride-ftreet, 1 b.

Robert Day, Efq. M. P.

John Deering, Efq. T. C. D.

Mifs Jane Delap, Dublin, 1 b.

Rev. Doctor Dobbin, Finglafs.

Francis Dobbs, Efq. Barrifter.

Mifs Dodd, Camden-ftreet.

Richard Dawfon, Efq. Dublin, 1 g.

Langrifhe Doyle, Mufic Doctor, Dublin.

Timothy Drifcoll, Efq. Barrifter, 1 g.

Arthur Dunn, Efq. Dominick-ftreet.

Mrs. Dunn, Sackville-ftreet.

Henry Duquery, Efq. M. P. 1 g.

Mrs. B. D. Dublin, 2 b. p.

Rev. Doctor Elrington, J. F. T. C. D.

Robert Euftace, Efq. York-ftreet, 1 g.

Jofeph Farran, Efq. Golden-lane.

Mrs. Elizabeth Farran, Eccles-ftreet.

Mrs. Farran, Golden-lane.

Alexander Filgate, Efq. T. C D.

Thomas Filgate, Efq. T. C. D.

Mr. John Finlay, Euftace-ftreet.

Mr. James Finlay, Notary Public, Dublin.

Jonathan Fifher, Efq. Dublin.

Surgeon Fitzfimons, Crow-ftreet.

John Burk Fitzfimons, Efq. Dublin.

John Forde, Efq. Dominick-ftreet, 1 b.

John Forfter, Efq. Dorfet-ftreet, 2 b. p.

Luke Fox, Efq. Barrifter.

Rev. Mr. Gamble, Paradife-row.

Mrs. George, York-ftreet, 1 g.

Rev. Doctor Gibfon, Dublin.

William Perceval Gilborne, Efq. Dublin.

Fortefcue Gorman, Efq. Stafford-ftreet.

Mrs. Graham, Dominick-ftreet.

Rev. Mr. Graves, J. F. T. C. D. 1 b.

William Gray, M. D. Dublin.

Waterhoufe Sheppey Green, Efq. Dublin, 1 b.

Rev. Doctor Grueber, Summer-hill.

Mr. Frederic Gueft, Dame-ftreet.

James Haire, Efq. Capel-ftreet, 1 b.

Rev. Doctor Hall, S. F. T. C. D.

Mrs. Frances Hamilton, Summer-hill, 2 b. p.

Mifs Hamilton, Dorfet-ftreet.

Mifs Hamilton, 111, Capel-ftreet.

Mr. James Hamilton, 111, Capel-ftreet.

William Harknefs, Efq. Dublin, 4 b. p.

Captain Richard Harman, Sum-mer-hill.

Michael Harris, Efq. Golden-lane.

Mifs Ann Harrold, Dublin, 1 b.

Mr. Haftings, Dawfon-ftreet, 1. g.

Arch. C. Hawkeley, Efq. Dublin.

Amory Hawkefworth, Efq. Bar-rifter.

Mifs Hendrick, Dublin, 1 g.

Captain Henry Hewitt, Summer-hill.

Andrew

Andrew Higanbotham, Efq. Dublin.

William Hogan, Efq. Ufher's-quay.

Mrs. Anna Hudfon, Skinner-row.

Edward Hudfon, M. D. Dublin.

Right Hon. Lord Headford, M. P.

Henry Jackfon, Efq. Pill-lane.

Richard Jebb, Efq. Barrifter.

James Johnfton, Efq. Arran-quay.

Robert Johnfton, Efq. Barrifter.

William Johnfton, Efq. Exchequer-ftreet.

Alexander Jaffray, Efq. Ely-place, 1 b.

Rev. Doctor Kearney, S. F. T. C. D.

R. S. Keating, Efq. Granby-row. 1 g.

Thomas Kelly, M. D. Dublin.

Rev. Nicholas Ward Kennedy, Dublin.

Rev. Walter Blake Kirwan.

Mrs. Knox, Dominick.ftreet.

Francis Knox, Efq. Barrifter, 1 b.

James Lambert, Efq. Aungier-ftreet.

Right Hon. David Latouche, M. P.

John Latouche, Efq. M. P. 2 b. p.

Peter Latouche, Efq. 2 b.

Mrs. Ladaveze, Stephen's-green.

Rev. John Leahy, A. M. Dublin.

Jofeph Leathley, Efq. Marlborough-ftreet, 1 b.

Thomas Leland, Efq. French-ftreet.

Rev. Mr. Ledwich, St. Michan's.

Rev. Alexander Leney, Crumlin.

Mrs. Lill, Merrion-ftreet.

Alexander Lindfay, M.D. Dublin.

John Lloyd, Efq. Lower Abbey-ftreet, 1 b.

John Lynam, Efq. Rutland-fquare, 1 b.

John Lyfter, Efq. Barrifter.

James M'Clatchy, Efq. William-ftreet.

James M'Clelland, Efq. Barrifter.

Mr. Wm M'Clelland, Linen-hall.

Robert M'Clintock, Efq. Capel-ftreet, 1 b.

Richard M'Cormick, Efq. Dublin.

Rev. Doctor M'Dowel, Mary's-abbey.

Thomas M'Mullan, Efq. T. C. D.

George Maconchy, Efq. Barrifter.

Mr. Richard M'Owen, Capel-ftreet.

Mr. John Maffit, Great Strand-ftreet, 1 b.

John Maxwell, Efq. Dublin, 1 b.

Robert Maxwell, Efq. Barrifter.

Edward Mayne, Efq. Barrifter.

Andrew De La Maziere, Efq. Dame-ftreet, 2 b. p.

Mark Maziere, Efq. Eccles-ftreet.

Mr. James Medlicott, Grafton-ftreet.

Rev. Doctor Mercer, Crumlin, 7 b. p.

Robert Mercer, Efq. Capel-ftreet, 2 b. p.

William Mitchell, Efq. Dublin, 1 b.

Rev. George Millar, J. F. T.C.D. 1 b.

Alex. Montgomery, Efq. Dorfet-ftreet.

Rev. Doctor Moody, Dublin, 1 g.

John Moore, Efq. Summer-hill.

Mr. Ralph Mulhern, High-ftreet.

Rev. Doctor Murray, V. P. T. C. D. 1 g.

Mifs Ifabella Nicholfon, Bride-ftreet, 1 b.

John Nicholfon, Efq. Bride-ftreet, 1 g.

Mr. Thomas Nicholfon, Bride-ftreet, 1 b.

Mr. William Nicholfon, Bride-ftreet.

Mr. Daniel Norris, North Great Georges-ftreet, 1 b.

Surgeon Ralph Smyth O'Bre, Dublin.

Rev.

Rev. Dr. O'Connor, Caſtleknock.

John O'Donnell, Eſq. Dorſet-ſtreet, 1 g.

Thomas O'Kelly, Eſq. Great Longford-ſtreet, 1 b.

James Ormſby, Eſq. Dawſon-ſtreet.

John Orr, Eſq. Merchant's-quay.

Mr. Thomas Orr, Henry-ſtreet.

Mr. Thomas Orr, Dublin.

Wakefield Orr, Eſq. Queen-ſtreet. 1 b.

Charles Palmer, Eſq. T. C. D.

John Parſons, Eſq. Barriſter.

Mr. James Peebles, Dublin.

Robert Perceval, M. D. Dublin.

Counſellor Plunket, Dublin.

Patrick Plunket, M. D. Dublin, 2 b. p.

Mr. William Porter, Printer and Bookſeller, Skinner-row.

William Preſton, Eſq. Glouceſter-ſtreet.

Major General Pringle, Dublin.

Andrew Ram, Eſq. Dublin.

Stephen Edw. Rice, Eſq. Dublin.

Benjamin Richardſon, Eſq. Grafton-ſtreet, 1 g.

Joſeph Ridgeway, Eſq. Cuff-ſtreet.

William Ridgeway, Eſq. Barriſter.

Rev. Doctor Robinſon, Dublin, 2 b. p.

John Robinſon, Eſq. Aſton's-quay.

Mrs. Rudd, Merrion-row.

Joſeph Roleſton, Eſq. Barriſter, 2 b p.

John Rutherford, Eſq. Abbey-ſtreet.

Thomas Ryan, M. D. Dublin.

Rev. Dudley Charles Ryder, Dublin.

John Semple, Eſq. Marlborough-ſtreet.

Surgeon Short, Peter's-row.

Rev. Mr. Sleater, Bride-ſtreet.

Dr. Stevenſon, Muſic Doctor, Dublin.

Thomas Stevenſon, Eſq. Peter-ſtreet.

Bowen Southwell, Eſq. Dublin, 1 b.

George Stewart, Eſq. Surgeon General, Dublin.

Henry Stewart, Eſq. M. P.

John Stewart, Eſq. Abbey-ſtreet, 1 g.

John Stewart, Eſq. Barriſter.

Mrs. John Stewart, Dawſon-ſtreet.

Hon. Miſs Stewart, Cuff-ſtreet, 1 b.

Stephen Stock, Eſq. Dame-ſtreet, 1 g.

Rev. Mr. Stokes, J. F. T. C. D.

Rev. Mr. Stopford, J. F. T. C. D. 1 b.

Mrs. Tate, Eſſex-ſtreet.

Edward Taylor, Eſq. Ely-place.

Mr. Thomas, York-ſtreet, 1 b.

Miſs Thomas, York-ſtreet, 1 b.

Rev. Mr. Thomas, York-ſtreet, 1 b.

John Norris Thompſon, Eſq. William-ſtreet.

Henry Tiſdall, Eſq. Mechlinburgh-ſtreet.

Thomas Truelock, Eſq. Suffolk-ſtreet.

Mrs. Tuthill, Dublin.

Samuel Tyndall, Eſq. Jervis-ſtreet.

John Verſchoyle, Eſq. N. Great George's-ſtreet.

Mrs. Veſey, Lucan.

Mrs. Vincent, Granby-row.

Rev. Mr. Uſher, J. F. T. C. D.

Thomas Walker, Eſq. York-ſtreet, 4 b. p.

Rev. Mr. Ward, J. F. T. C. D.

Mr. William Watſon, Senior, Printer, Dublin.

Commiſſary Chriſtmas Weekes, 1 g.

Mrs. Maria Weekes, Dublin, 1 g.

Miſs Marian Weſt, Skinner-row.

Mark White, Eſq. Dorſet-ſtreet.

Mr. Sam. Whyte, Grafton-ſtreet.

Richardſon Williams, Eſq. Dublin, 1 b.

Geo. Wilſon, Eſq. Stephen's-green.

Thomas

Thomas Winder, Efq. Cuftom-houfe 2 b. p.

Right Hon. Arthur Wolfe, Attorney General, 4 b. p.

John Wolfe, Efq. M. P. 2 b. p.

Alex. Worthington, Efq. Dublin.

Mifs Martha Wright, Summer-hill.

Peter Wybrants, Efq. Dublin.

Owen Wynne, Efq. M. P.

Right Hon. Barry Yelverton, Lord Chief Baron.

Rev. Doctor Young, S. F. T. C. D.

John Young, Efq. T. C. D. 1 b.

County of Fermanagh.

Colonel Mervin Archdall, M. P.

Mrs. Armftrong, Springtown.

Mr. John Armftrong.

Major Brooke, Colebrook.

Captain Cole.

William Corchoran, Efq. Liffinele.

Mrs. Corchoran, Liffingle.

George Griffith, Efq. Ennifkillen, 3 b. p.

Mrs. Griffith, Enifkillen, 1 g.

Mr. Robert Gunnis, Drumard, 1 b.

Rev. Mr. Fleetwood Lowtherf-town.

Rev. Arthur Forfter, Drumard, 1 b.

Mr. James Hall, Ennifkillen, 1 b.

Captain James Hall, 9th Dragoons.

Mr. George Henderfon, Lowtherf-town.

Mrs. Martha Humphrys, Drum-ard.

Mrs. Humphrys, Ennifkillen, 1 b.

Gorges D'Arcy Irvine, Efq.

Charles Irvine, Efq. Park-hill.

Rev. Thomas Hudfon, Drum-keeran.

Rev. Mr. Keenan, Templecarn.

Rev. William Leflie, 1 b.

Rev. Mr. Macufker, Maghericul-money.

Rev. Traver's Madden, Glebe-hill, 1 b.

Mr. Conftantine Maguire, Ennif-killen.

Rev. Mr. Moffit, Templecarn.

Rev. Mark Noble, Ennifkillen, 2 b. p.

Rev. Mr. Nixon, 1 b.

Mr. Hugh Ovens, St. Catharine's, 1 b.

Rev. William Ovens, Cofbyftown, 1 b.

Rev. Doctor Smyth, Ennifkillen.

Rev. Mr. Stack, Rector of Derry-volan.

John Watkins, Efq. Derrybrufk, 1 b.

Mr. William Whitaker, Ennif-killen, 1 b.

County of Leitrim.

Rev. Mr. Bennet, Carrick-on-Shannon.

Mrs. Cullen, Skreeny, 1 b.

Richard Cuningham, Efq. Port, 1 b.

Thomas Dickfon, Efq. M. P. 3 b, p.

Rev. Mr. Henderfon, Carrick-on-Shannon.

William Parfon Percy, Efq. Gara-dice,

County of Louth,

Simon Baily, Efq. Dundalk.

Sir Patrick Bellew, Bart. Bar-meath, 1 g.

Rev. Mr. Bryfon, Ballymafcanlon,

Rev. Charles Crawford, Drogheda.

Mr. William Davidfon, Lurgan-green.

Rev. Thomas Englifh, Charles-town, 1 b.

John Forbes, Efq. M. P. 2 b p.

Right Hon. John Forfter, Speaker of the Houfe of Commons.

Mr. Patrick Gernon, Drogheda, 1 b.

Rev. Mr. Gerrard, Dunleer, 2 b. p.

k   Rev.

Rev. Mr. Gibfon, Clonmore.
Chriftopher Jenney, Efq. Park.
Thomas Lloyd, Efq. Ravenfdale, 1 b.
Mr. Patrick Macay, Drogheda, 1 g.
Mr. Anthony M'Dermott, Thomaftown, 1. b.
Zachariah Maxwell, Efq. Dundalk.
Henry Maxwell, Efq. Dundalk.
James Metcalf, Efq. Drogheda, 1 b.
Edward Morris, Efq. Caftlebellingham, 1 b.
Mr. George Murphy, Dundalk.
Mr. John O'Donnell, Ardee, 1 b.
William Meade Ogle, Efq. M. P.
John Ogle, Efq. Ravenfdale, 1 b.
Alexander Rogers, Efq. Ballymafcanlon.
George Schoales, Efq. Drogheda.
Henry Smyth, Efq. Corcreigh, 1 b.
Rev. Moore Smyth, Kilcurly, 1 b.
Mr. Robert Speers, Ardee, 1 g.
Mr. John Stanley, Surgeon, Drogheda.
M. Taylor, Efq. Ravenfdale, 1 g.
Robert Thompfon, Efq. Ravenfdale.
Edward Tipping, Efq. Ravenfdale.
Mr. Archibald Wright, Dundalk.

County of Mayo.

Rev. Doctor Benton, Caftlebar, 2 b. p.
Right Hon. James Cuffe, M. P.
Frederic Dennis, Efq. Caftlebar, 1. g
Rev. James Hazlett, Foxford.
George Jackfon, Efq. Profpect.
Rev. Charles Kent, Deel Caftle.
Right Hon. Henry King, M. P. 2 b. p.
John Ormfby, Efq. Gortnar-abbey, 1 b.
Rev. George Paley, Killala.
William Ruttledge, Efq. Profpect.
Rev. Jofeph Wilfon, Caftlebar.

County of Monaghan.

Mrs. Anketell, , Trugh Lodge, 4 b. p.
Charles Anketell, Efq. ditto, 3 b.p.
Matthew Anketell Efq. do. 3 b.p.
Mr. William Anketell, Dungillick, 3 b. p.
Oliver Anketell, Efq. Ivy Hill, 4 b p.
Mr. Roger Anketell, Mount Anketell, 3 b. p.
Mr Roger Anketell, Dungillich.
Mr. Thomas Armftrong, Bloomfiel', 1 b.
Mr. William Armftrong, do. 1 b.
John Bartley, M. D. Monaghan, 1 b.
Mr. James Brown, Printer, Monaghan,
Mr. James Burgefs, Monaghan, 1 b.
Rev. Thomas Campbell, D. D. Killevin.
Mr. Nathaniel Craven, Surgeon, Monaghan, 1 b.
Rev. Robert Chriftie, Erigal, 1 b.
Mr. William Crookfhanks, Glafslough.
Rev. Mr. Davis, Caftleblaney.
William Forfter, Efq. Monaghan.
Robert Graham, Efq. Gortgranagh.
M. George Johnfton, Stramore, 1 b.
Mr. James Johnfton.
Mr. Leflie Kirk, Monaghan, 1 b.
Rev. Mr. Lendrum, Monaghan.
Mr. John M'Clea, Monaghan, 1 b.
John M'Murren, M. D. Monaghan, 1 b.
Mr. Edward Mitchell, Tonanumry.
Mr. Henry Mitchell, Monaghan.
Mr. William Mitchell, Monaghan.
Mr. William Owen Mitchell, Monaghan, 1 b.
John Montgomery, Efq. M. P. 2 b. p.

Mrs.

Mrs. Montgomery, Rosefield, 1 b.
Mrs. Montgomery, Brindrim, 1 b.
Robert Montgomery, Esq. do. 1 b.
Rev. Charles Murray, Erigal.
John Mungan, M. D. Monaghan.
Edward Richardson, Esq. 1 b.
William Richardson, Esq. Tullaghan, 1 b.
Mrs. Rogers, Monaghan.
Mr. William Shaw, Balinode, 1 b.
Thomas Singleton, Senior, Fort Singleton, 1 g.
Thomas Singleton, Junior, Esq. ditto, 1 g.
Surgeon Speer, Glaslough.
John Steele, Esq. Carrickmacross.
Mr. George Sweeny, Monaghan.
Mr. Nicholas Thetford, Monaghan.
Mr. Joseph Whiteside.
Mr. Richard Williams, Glaslough, 1 b.
Mr. Andrew Young, Monaghan, 1 g.
M. Walter Young, Monaghan.

County of Roscommon.

Rev. Mr. Crawford, Elphin.
Arthur French, Esq. French Park.
Henry Fry, Esq. Fry-brook, 1 b.
Rev. J. K. Gouldsbury, 1 g.
Rev. Mr. Kenny, Elphin.
Richard Lockhart, Esq. Boyle.

County of Sligo.

Philip Birne, Esq. Creggs, 1 b.
Rev. R. Chambers, Clover-hill.
Joshua Edward Cooper, Esq. M.P. 2 b. p.
Rev. Alexander Duke, Dromard.
John Everard, Esq. Sligo.
William Gillmor, Esq. Ballyglass, 1 b.
William Griffith, Esq. Ballytrena, 1 b.
Rev. William Grove, Charlesfort.
John Jones, Esq. Johns-port, 1 b.
Robert Jones, Esq. Ardnaree.

John Johnston, Esq. Auburn.
Rev. John King, Ardnaree.
Rev. Joseph King, Sligo,
Rev. Arthur Knox, Ardnaree.
John Martin, Esq. Sligo, 2 b. p.
Rev. James Neligan, Ardnaree, 1 b.
Charles Nesbitt, Esq. Scurmore.
Charles O'Hara, Esq. M. P. 2 b.p.
John Ormsby, Esq. Cummin, 1 b.
Thomas Ormsby, Esq. Castledargin.
Roger Parke, Esq. Dunally.
Rev. Mr. Perceval, Temple-house, 1 g.
William Phibbs, Esq. Hollybrook, 1 b.
Rev. Stephen Radcliff, Drumcliff.
Mr. Andrew Todd, Surgeon, Sligo.
Rev. Charles West, Ahamplish, 1 b.

County of Tyrone.

Rev. James Adams, Stuartstown, 1 g.
Rev. Mr. Alexander, Kildress.
Mr. John O'Connor Arbuthnot, Arboe, 1 g.
Robert Bailie, Esq. Donaghendry, 1 g.
William Bailie, Esq. Ternaskea.
Counsellor Bailie.
Humphry Bell, Esq. Belmont, 1 g.
Surgeon Best, Moy.
Mr. Thomas Boardman, Dungannon, 1 b.
Mr. Thomas Bolton, Coal Island, 1 b.
Rev. Mr. Boylan, Caledon.
Mr. Francis Bryans, Moy.
Rev. Doctor Buck, Desertcrete, 1 g.
John Cairns, Esq. Dungannon, 1 b.
John Caldwell, Esq. Augher, 1 b.
Mr. John Campbell, Aughnacloy.
Mr. William Campbell, Drumkern.
Mr. George Caruth, Coal Island.

James

James Caulfield, Efq. Drumreigh, 3 b. p.
Mrs. Caulfield, ditto, 4 b. p.
Rev. Charles Caulfield, Killiman, 2 b. p.
Thomas Caulfield, Efq. Moy, 1 b.
Mr. Robert Cole, Aughnacloy.
Mr. James Collins, Cookſtown.
Mr. William Collins, Stuartſtown.
Mr. James Cooke, Cookſtown.
Robert Cowan, Efq. Trelick, 1 b.
Charles Crawford, Efq. Newtown-ſtewart, 1 b.
Rev. Doctor Crawford, Strabane.
Rev. Mr. Crawford, Belville.
John Crozier, Efq. Mullaghmore.
Rev. James Devlin, Donaghendry.
Rev. Doctor Dillon, Dungannon.
Daniel Eccles, Efq. Fintona, 1 g.
Mrs. Eccles, Fintona, 1 g.
Nathaniel Edie, Efq. Strabane, 2 b. p.
Rev. Mr. Evans, Donaghmore.
Rev. Mr. Evans, Dungannon, 1 b.
Mr. James Falls, Aughnacloy.
Mr. Richard Falls, Balligawly, 1 b.
Mr. James Fleming, Stuartſtown.
Mr. Thomas Findeliter, Aughnacloy.
Rev. Archdeacon Friend, 2 b. p.
Mifs Mary George, Coagh.
Mrs. Girvan, Tamnaghlane, 1 b.
Rev. Mr. Graham, Caledon.
Mifs Graves, Dungannon, 1 g.
Mr. Benjamin Greer, Moy, 1 b.
Mr. John Greer, Drungould, 2 b.
Mr. Thomas Greer, Milton.
Mr. Thomas Greer, Junior, Rhone hill, 1 b.
Mr. William Greer, Dungannon, 1 g.
Major Hamilton, Cookſtown, 7 g.
Mifs Hamilton, Strabane, 4 b. p.
James Hamilton, Efq. Grange.
John Hamilton, Efq. Crofscavanagh, 1 b.
Thomas Hamilton, Efq. Strabane.
Wm. Hamilton, Efq. Defertercte, 1 b.

Thomas Hannington, Efq. Dungannon, 1 b.
Tho. Harvey, Efq. Green-hill, 1 b.
Rev. John Hervey, Strabane, 1. g.
Mr. John Holbert, Cookſtown.
John Huggins, Efq. Glenarb, 1 g.
Rev. Francis Houſton, Caſtle-caulfield, 1 b.
Mrs. Hunter, Lower Beck, 1 b.
Mr. Thomas Jackson, Tullidowy.
Rev. Mr. Ingram, Leck Patrick, 1 b.
Mifs Johnſton, Coal Ifland, 1 b.
Mr. John Johnſton, Coal Ifland, 1 b.
Mrs. Irwin, Drumglafs, 1 g.
Mr. Thomas Irwin, Caledon, 1 g.
Mr. James Irwin, Aughnacloy, 1 b.
Rev. Mr. Kenedy, Gortinglufs.
Mr. John Kennedy, Coal Ifland.
Mrs. Laird, Stuartſtown, 1 b.
Mr. Francis Lang, Cookſtown.
Mr. Thomas Lawfon, Coagh, 1 b.
Robert Lindfay, Efq. Loughrey 1 b.
W. Crymble Lindfay, Efq. Fort Edward.
Mr. James Little, Stuartſtown.
Mr. John Little, ditto, 1 b.
Mr. Samuel Little, ditto.
Mrs. Lowry, Rockdale, 1 g.
Rev. John Lowry, Clogherney, 1 g.
Robert Lowry, Efq. Pomeroy, 2 b. p.
Charles Lynd, Efq. Mullintain, 4 b. p.
Mifs M'Clelland, Coagh.
Mr. John M'Crea, Aughnacloy. 1 g.
Mr. Wildridge M'Dowall, Aughnacloy.
Rev. Mr. M'Kay, Bray.
Mr. George M'Williams, Aughnacloy.
John Maxwell, Efq. Ahenis.
Mr. William Maxwell, Surgeon, Omagh.
Mr. Ben. Mansfield, Cloghfin, 1 b.
Mr.

2

Mr. Anthony M'Reynolds, Stuartftown, 1 b.

Mr. Samuel M'Reynolds, Dungannon, 1 g.

Mr. Andrew Mecord, Stuarftown, 1 b.

Mr. Robert Moffit, Bells-grove.

Mr. Edward Moore, Aughnacloy.

Mr. John More, Dunaghy.

Rev. Anketell Moutray, Favorroyal, 3 b. p.

John Corry Moutray, Efq. ditto, 3 b. p

Mr. Jofeph Mulhollon, Ardpatrick.

Mr. Stewart Mulligan, Attorney,

Rev. Mr. Morris, Ballyclog.

Rev. Doƈtor Murray, Dungannon, 1 g.

Mr. Andrew Newton, Coagh, 1 b.

Mr. Jofeph Nicholfon, Berna.

Mifs O'Neill, Stuartftown.

Mr. James Orr, Strabane, 1 b.

Mr. David Park, Stuartftown.

Mr. James Park, ditto.

Mr. John Park, ditto, 1 g.

Mr. William Park, Donarifk.

Mr. Robert Peebles, Tullyhog.

Mr Frederic Porter, Strabane.

Mifs Pringle, Glebe-lodge, 1 b.

John Pringle, Efq. Lime Park.

Mr. Robert Read, Eary, 1 g.

James Reynolds, M. D. Cookstown.

Alexander Richardfon, Efq. Woodmount, 1 g.

Charles Richardfon, Efq. Ballymena, 2 b. p.

David Richardfon, Efq. Drum, 1 g.

James Richardfon, Efq. Bloomhill, 1 b.

Rev. Doƈtor Richardfon, Clonfeckle.

Mr. William Richardfon, Moy.

Mr. James Robinfon, Stuartftown.

Mr. Robert Robinfon, Senior, Stuartftown, 1 b.

Mr. Robert Robinfon, Junior, Stuartftown, 1 g.

Mr. William Rofs, Strabane, 4 b. p.

Thomas Ruffell, Efq. Dungannon.

James Seaton, Efq. Perrymount, 1 b.

Rev. David Shuter, Thorn-hill.

Mr John Simpfon.

Mr. Andrew Sloan, Coal Ifland.

Mr. John Sloan, Surgeon, Caledon.

Mr. Hugh Smith, Suartftown, 1 b.

Mr. Alexander Speer, Attorney, 1 b.

Solomon Speer, Efq. Barrifter.

Mr. Thomas Speer, Dungannon, 1 g.

Rev. Doƈtor Stack, Reƈtor of Omagh.

Ephraim Stamus, Efq. Strabane.

John Staples, Efq. M. P. 3 b. p.

Hon. Mrs. Staples, 4 b. p.

Alex. Stewart, Efq. Dungannon.

Benjamin Stewart, Efq. do. 1 b.

Rev. Mr. Stewart, Rakelly.

James Stewart, Efq. M. P. 3 b. p.

Hon. Mrs. James Stewart, 4 b. p.

William Stewart, Efq. Killymoon, 1 b.

Mifs Sarah Sturgeon, Ballyhullan.

Rev. James Taylor, Gortin.

Rev. Robert Thompfon, Irelick, 1 b.

Mrs. John Twigg, Rohan, 2 b. p.

Mr. John Twigg, Coal Ifland, 1 b.

Rev. Mr. Vefey, Drumglafs, 1 b.

Mr. William Warnick, Augher.

Mrs. Watfon, Stuartftown, 1 b.

Mr. Alexander Watfon, do. 1 b.

Mr. John Watfon, Farlough.

Mr. William Weir, Stuartftown, 1 b.

Mr. Matthew Whitefide, Stuartstown.

Mifs Wilfon, Stuartftown.

Mr. Wm. Wilfon, Stuartftown.

SUBSCRIBERS NAMES.

Subscribers Names that came too late for Alphabetical Insertion.

Richard Anderson, Esq. Barrister, Digge's-street.

James W. Bell, Esq. Barrister, Ormond-quay.

Rev. Mr. Harpur, Granby-row.

Charles Farran, Esq. York-street, 2 b. p.

Richard Guinnes, Esq. Barrister, Mercer-street.

Samuel Guinnes, Esq. Barrister, Nassau-street.

Pemberton Rudd, Esq. Barrister, Merrion-row.

ERRATA.

Page	Line	
43,	7,	for *tho'*, read *though*.
48,	5,	for *why*, read when.
53,	13,	for *whife*, read *while*.
62,	3,	for *Jefus*, read Jesus.
63,	11,	before *ere*, infert *more*.
71,	21,	for Providence, read PROVIDENCE.
75,	5,	for *burning*, read *cunning*.
75,	20,	for *themfelves*, read *themfelves*";
90,	9,	for *fecrets*, read *fecret's*
92,	17,	for *Lord*, read LORD.
92,	20,	for *father's*, read *Father's*.
94,	9,	for *meafures*, read *meafure*.
97,	13,	for the fecond *their*, read *the*,
104,	8,	for *with*, read *will*.
104,	9,	for *will*, read *with*.
116,	13,	for *fhalt*, read *fhall*,
126,	1,	for *confiders*, read *confiderft*,
127,	22,	for the firft *their*, read *the*.
130,	14,	for *gave*, read *give*.
131,	1,	for *Lord*, read LORD.
153,	8,	for *banifh*, read *vanifh*.
256,	7,	for *you*, read *do*.
264,	10,	for *vovid*, read *wovit*.
296,	25,	for Lord, read LORD,
299,	1,	for *Lord*, read LORD,
327,	21,	for *Jefus*, read JESUS.

HERVEY'S MEDITATIONS

AMONG THE

T O M B S.

IN A LETTER TO A LADY,

V E R S I F I E D.

MEMENTO MORI!

As I to *Cornwall* lately went abroad,
I ſtopp'd at a large village on the road ;
And being forc'd a ſhort time there to ſtay,
Unto the neighb'ring church I bent my way.
The ſacred doors, like heav'n, to which they guide,
Were for a worthleſs ſtranger open'd wide.
Glad, ſuch an opportunity to find,
To ſpend ſome minutes there I was inclin'd.

The ſolemn place, ſo awfully retir'd,
With pleaſing, mournful thoughts my ſoul in-
  ſpir'd ;

B

Which

Which ufeful were, I truft, in fome degree,
While they poffeffed and enliven'd me;
From which if any good you can receive,
The narrative frefh happinefs will give.

The ancient pile was rais'd and beautify'd,
By hands of men who ages fince had dy'd;
And fituated in a large grave-yard,
Whence tumult, noife, and hurry were debarr'd:
The body fpacious, the ftructure great,
The whole in grand fimplicity compleat.
A row of pillars in the midft appear'd,
Whereon the nobly-modeft roof was rear'd.
Each object grave and venerable feem'd,
From the dim light which through the windows
      gleam'd.
The filent, gloomy afpect of the place,
Did with folemnity the fcene increafe.
My mind with pious terror was poffefs'd,
As penfive thro' the inmoft aile I prefs'd;
Which ev'ry ruder paffion wholly quell'd,
And all th' allurements of the world repell'd.

Having due praife to GOD Almighty paid,
Who in eternal Majefty array'd,
Has heav'n his throne, the earth his footftool
      made;

On

On a fine altar-piece I fix'd my eye,
Which once *Stow*'s mafter-builders did employ;
And which with fervent gratitude was giv'n,
An humble prefent to the LORD of Heav'n ;
Who gracioufly a helping-hand did lend,
Enabling them with joy their work to end.

How lovely, Gratitude! doft thou appear,
When great JEHOVAH is the object dear!
Gratitude's the beft principle that can
With real virtue fill the foul of man :
Something difinterefted it fhews forth,
And, grant the term, of noble, gen'rous worth.
Pray'r chiefly doth regard our future ftate,
Repentance our fall'n Nature indicate ;
But Gratitude in *Eden* held its reign,
When for no crime our parents could complain ;
And will in Heav'n perpetuated be,
Where GOD's inthron'd to all eternity.

This temper fweet, in accents fuch as thefe,
Its fenfe of benefits receiv'd difplays ;
" I am oblig'd ; nor know I how to prove
" My ardent thanks for your furpaffing love."
Surely we thus moft properly declare,
Our praifes for GOD's goodnefs are fincere ;

B 2   Our

Our great Creator's courts to decorate,
And with due honors beautify his feat.
His dwelling-place was glorious heretofore,
Let it not now be fordid, mean, or poor.
A mind ingenuous will feel great woe,
And ev'ry people deep reproach muft know;
Who on their houfes fuch expence employ,
In cedar wainfcot and vermillion dye;
While GOD's own building, fhameful to relate,
Stands quite neglected, in a filthy ftate.

With *Solomon*'s addrefs my foul was pleas'd,
When for GOD's ufe a temple he had rais'd.
He had erected, with vaft fkill and charge,
A noble ftructure, exquifitely large;
But he his work review'd, and, ftruck with awe,
The pow'r tranfcendent of the GODHEAD faw.
The building was too elegant and blefs'd,
By the moft mighty king to be poffefs'd;
For entrance to unhallow'd feet, too clean,
Yet for GOD's dwelling infinitely mean.
The wife King own'd it was furprizing grace,
That GOD Almighty " there his name fhould
    place."
The paffage, with true delicacy fraught,
Difplays a grand fublimity of thought:
Therefore I fhall not hefitate to fhew
The pious fentiments which thro' it flow.

                        " Will

" Will God, indeed, vouchfafe to dwell on earth,

" The place which gives to wretched mortals
　　" birth?

" Behold! the Heav'n of Heav'ns can't thee con-
　　" tain,

" Sure in this houfe much lefs thou can'ft re-
　　main !"

Unequall'd words! and worthy of his pen,

Whofe wifdom fhone o'er all the fons of men!

Who would not choofe, then, rather to pof-
　　fefs

Such elevated piety and grace,

Than all the coftly furniture to own,

With which his facred dome fuperbly fhone?

　With admiration we are apt to praife

The coftly edifice at which we gaze;

And while with joy its grandeur we behold,

The merit of the architect is told.

Perhaps the ancient temple having feen,

The difciples' remark our own had been,

Which they have fuperficially made,

" What ftones and workmanfhip are here dif-
　　" played !"

But much more noble feelings we fhall fhew,

To pay, with *Solomon*, the thanks we owe;

With joy our celebrating voices raife,

Jehovah's great benignity to praife.

　　　　　　　　　　　　That

That God, the High and Mighty, whom we trace,
In boundlefs glory thro' the rounds of fpace ;
Should will in fpecial manner there to live,
A mortal building for his houfe receive ;
Should manifeft a wonderful degree
Of benedictive grace and majefty ;
His prefence fhew to finners, and declare
He'd " make them joyful in his houfe of pray'r !"
This fhould our hearts more fenfibly delight,
Than coftly ftructures gratify the fight.

Nay, the eternal God does not refufe
Our fouls his fpirit's dwelling-place to choofe ;
And of ourfelves a fanctuary make,
And ev'n our bodies for his temple take.
Ye who rely on critics' catching wings,
And nicely weigh the difference of things ;
Quickly approach, and by your judgments fhew
" Whether of joy or wonder more we owe."
Himfelf he humbleth, as the fcriptures tell,
To view the beings that in Heaven dwell,
'Tis a moft condefcending proof of love,
Of angels and archangels to approve ;
When lowly from their heav'nly thrones they all
In homage to their great Creator fall.
And will He poor, polluted duft regard,
And with a gracious union us reward ?

Unrivall'd

Unrivall'd honor! Privilege divine!
Be this ineftimable portion mine!
Then will I not for regal titles ftrive,
Or keep the haughty claim for pow'r alive.

But let me think what fanctity of mind,
And upright converfation is enjoin'd,
Of fuch relations to raife my weak voice;
Remember this, " and tremblingly rejoice."
Durft I, whilft thro' thefe hallow'd courts I walk,
Contract iniquity in deed or talk?
Or could *Jerufalem's* High-prieft permit
Himfelf a known tranfgreffion to commit;
While he into th' holy of holies made
His yearly folemn entrance; and array'd
In facred robes, with reverence beftow'd
Becoming worfhip to Almighty GOD?
No, truly. In fuch circumftances, fure
No thinking man could poffibly endure
Temptations, the remoteft, to affail,
And o'er his probity of heart prevail.
I all indecency of carriage dread,
Left I by it to evil fhould be led.
Why is not, then, this jealous, holy ftrife,
Carry'd thro' all our ordinary life?
Why to ourfelves is not juft honor fhewn,
As beings fanctify'd to GOD alone?
Whom living temples of himfelf he makes,
As the unerring word of fcripture fpeaks?

If

If we our conduct as true Chriſtians guide,
GOD ſays he " dwells in us," and will abide.
That this one doctrine of religion would
With ſtrength abiding on our ſouls intrude!
Inſtead of countleſs laws 'twould regulate
Our lives, and holineſs in us create.
From ſuch convictive pow'r we would deſire
A purity of purpoſe to acquire;
To walk and live deſerving of his care,
Who makes us his paternal kindneſs ſhare;
And who, with majeſty tranſcendent crown'd,
Our union with himſelf and ſon has own'd.

I caſt my eyes next on the letter'd floor,
Which, like *Ezekiel*'s roll, was written o'er.
I ſoon perceiv'd that the ſimilitude
Held alſo in another manner good;
And the inſcriptions uſher'd in a train
Of vary'd " lamentations, woe, and pain."
My obſervation they did much excite,
And to peruſe them ſilently invite.
And what would theſe dumb monitors relate,
If I ſhould on them ſome time contemplate?
" That under their circumferences lay
" Such and ſuch pieces of deceaſed clay,
" Which once had liv'd, could play, converſe, and
         " move,
" And thro' life's various ſcenes of action rove;
                          " That

" That to preferve their names they had the care,
" And of their memories the truftees were."

Now being rouz'd from deep contemplation,
Ah! cry'd I, is fuch my fituation!
The everlafting GOD doth me furround,
And bones of fellow-creatures laid in ground!
With the revering Patriarch, fure I,
" How terrifying is this place!" fhould cry.
Devotion, and a fober frame become,
To all eternity, this holy dome.
O! may I never enter lightly here,
But with an awe profound, and godly fear!
From all irreverence may I be free,
And banifh ev'ry fign of levity!

" That they were wife!" th' infpired Pen-
    " man faid,
When for his people his laft wifh he made;
He breath'd it out, and Nature's will obey'd.
But what is wifdom? It we cannot find
To fpeculations critical confin'd;
Refearches into Nature cannot fhew,
Nor hiftory entire this gift beftow.
In his next afpiration the divine
Lawgiver fays, " that this they would define!"
That they had apprehenfions to difcern
Their fpiritual welfare, and their foul's concern!

That they had eyes, and wifh'd things to purfue,
From which their peace eternal would enfue!
How can the race of mortals, poor and mean,
Knowledge fo infinitely rich attain?
I fend them not, the rev'rend Teacher faid,
To read the works of all alive or dead;
By thinking of their latter end they can
This awful fcience with lefs trouble fcan.
This fpark of Heav'n is very often loft,
By glitt'ring pomp of erudition croft;
But fhines moft evidently in the gloom,
And dreary habitations of the tomb.
Drown'd is this gentle whifper in life's cares,
Amidft the noife of fecular affairs;
But in retirement moft diftinctly fpeaks,
And for its dwelling contemplation takes.
Behold how providentially I'm brought
To wifdom's fchool, fo worthy to be fought!
A very faithful mafter is the grave,
And thefe tombftone's inftructive leffons leave.
Come, calm attention! and my thoughts compofe!
And, heav'nly Spirit! blefs what you difclofe!
That fo thefe awful pages I may read,
As " to falvation to grow wife" indeed!

Searching mortality's records, I found
That with memorials they did abound

Of

Of numbers who, promiscuously here,
Had bid adieu to earthly joy and fear.
Huddled they were, and did together lie,
Of rank regardless, or seniority.
Within this house of mourning, for chief seats,
Or for the highest rooms, were no debates.
On eager expectations none here dwell,
Of being honor'd in their darksome cell.
Men of experience and years who, when
They liv'd, were oracles to other men;
At feet of babes contented were to sleep,
And here uninterrupted silence keep.
Masters and servants, with like ornaments
Were clad, who lodg'd in these cold tenements.
The poor as soundly slept, as softly lay,
As the possessor opulent and gay.
All the distinction that in them I found,
A grassy hillock was, with osiers bound,
Or sepulchres with imagery crown'd.

Why, said my working thoughts, should we
    complain
For rank or precedence, as things so vain;
Since equal meanness is each person's fate,
When this is changed to another state?
Why should we, then, exalt ourselves so high,
Or debase others for their poverty;
Since we must all, on our allotted day,
In common mix, in undistinguish'd clay?

Oh!

Oh ! that this cogitation might pull down
The pride of other people, and my own ;
And our imaginations fink as low,
As our frail dwellings muft in fhort time bow !

Among thefe relics, doubtlefs, we will find
A jarring int'reft, and difcordant mind ;
But like fome able dayfman, Death has laid
On the contending parties hands, and made
Their former variances all obey,
And to an amicable end give way.
Here thofe who, living, were at enmity,
By Death are brought to dwell in unity.
Here all embitter'd thoughts they drop, nor know
The fmalleft difference 'twixt friend and foe.
Perhaps their crumbling bones together all
Unite in common, as they mouldring fall.
Thofe who were filled with invet'rate hate,
And for each other ills did meditate ;
Here to their quarrels put a peaceful end,
And friendly in the grave together blend.
O ! that thefe afhes would fuch counfel give,
That we together might in friendfhip live ;
Refentment's fever from our minds erafe,
Nor fuffer paffion's fiercenefs to increafe ;
Mindlefs of injuries, and free from ftrife,
To pafs the thorny road of human life ;

That

That no more variance the quick might dread,
Than's in the congregation of the dead!
But I fuch general remarks fufpend,
. And to particular my thoughts now bend.

Yonder white ftone doth evidently fhew
An emblem of the innocence below;
And tells each paffenger, that underneath
A tender infant lies, confign'd to Death,
When it had fcarce receiv'd the gift of breath.
There lies the peaceful infant, without pain,
Nor knows what labor and vexation mean;
There it " lies quiet," with no care opprefs'd,
It fleeps profoundly ftill, " and is at reft."
When in the right'ous laver of the LORD,
It was to fecond, fpotlefs birth reftor'd;
Regenerated, 'twould no longer ftay,
When its impurities were wafh'd away;
But, bound for Heav'n, ftretch'd out its callow
        wings,
And took a fpeedy leave of earthly things.
What did the little fojourner, then, find,
So hateful and difgufting 'mongft mankind;
That it fo foon to leave them was difpos'd,
And on the world its eyes for ever clos'd?
Its Saviour would not drink, before he dy'd,
When he the vinegar and gall had try'd.

                                    And

And had our new-come ſtranger to its lip
The cup of life rais'd, and begun to ſip ;
But, when the bitter potion it had prov'd,
Refus'd the draught, and ſtraight its head re-
      mov'd ?
Was this the reaſon that the babe ſo ſhy,
Look'd on the light with a ſcarce open'd eye ;
Then did to more inviting regions haſte,
The ſweets of undiſturb'd repoſe to taſte ?

O happy Voyager ! who, launch'd abroad,
Directly to the wiſh'd-for haven rode !
More happy they, who, by the billows toſt,
The dang'rous tempeſts of the world have croſs'd,
And to ſafe harbours have at laſt attain'd,
By many ſtorms and grievous troubles gain'd !
Who " thro' various tribulations driv'n,
Have enter'd finally the port of Heav'n ;"
To their convoy divine have bliſs ſecur'd,
And to their fellow-toilers joy procur'd ;
Have giv'n examples with good counſel fraught,
By which ſucceeding pilgrims might be taught !

O fortunate probationer ! who were
Choſen without exerciſe of pain or care !
'Twas thy peculiar privilege to be
From all the woes of thy ſurvivors free ;

                 Which

Which oft the braveſt fortitude oppreſs,
And on the firmeſt faith inflict diſtreſs.
Affliction's arrows, with fore anguiſh barb'd,
Are for our choiceſt comforts oft reſerv'd.
Temptation's fiery darts for ever fly,
By *Satan* aim'd at our integrity.
But you, ſweet babe, by Providence belov'd,
From ſuch diſtreſs and danger were remov'd.

Think, then, ye mourning parents, nor com-
    plain
For breathleſs children, as ye weep in vain.
Why ſhould you be in lamentations drown'd,
While your young babes with victory are crown'd,
Before the ſword was drawn, or cruel ſtrife
Had ſhed its venom on the ills of life?
Perhaps Almighty GOD foreſaw ſome wile,
Some tempting evil that ſhould them beguile,
Of ſore adverſity, a dreadful ſtorm,
Or of dire wickedneſs, a monſtrous form.
How then in words which nothing can avail,
Againſt that kind precaution dare you rail?
That, which your dear and pleaſant plant con-
    vey'd,
Free from temptation, to a fragrant ſhade;
Before the lightnings flew, the thunders roar'd,
And its deſtructive rage the tempeſt pour'd?

Remember

Remember that of them you're not bereav'd,
But from " the coming evil they are fav'd."

And let furvivors, doom'd to bear the heat
And burden of the day, with joy relate,
That this for their encouragement they've got,
More honor's won by having bravely fought,
Than fhould the victory with eafe be gain'd,
Or a rich prize be with fmall toil obtain'd.
They who with refignation could obey
Afflictive Providence's angry fway;
And who glad homage to the crofs have paid,
On which their blefs'd Redeemer once was laid;
Who did their minds with perfeverance fill,
And faithfully perform their mafter's will:
Thefe, after they on earth God's praife have fung,
While fervent gratitude infpir'd each tongue;
Perhaps in Heav'n like brighteft ftars will blaze,
And fpread around them their refulgent rays;
Shall in God's everlafting kingdom fee
Stronger joy beam forth in an high degree.

Here a fond mother's grief is funk to reft,
The blafted hope of a kind father's breaft.
Like a well-water'd plant the youth up grew,
Shot deep, rofe high, and manhood had in view.
But as the cedar juft began to tow'r
Its branching head within the verdant bow'r;

And

And promis'd in a little time to lay,
O'er all the trees, an arbitrary fway;
Behold unto the root the axe is laid,
The blow is ftruck, by which its honors fade.
And did he fall alone? O! no; the joy
And comfort of his father, brought fo nigh;
And all the hopes which fill'd a mother's heart,
At once were blafted by Death's fatal dart.

Doubtlefs, it would have pierc'd one's heart,
    to view
The tender parents their dead fon purfue.
Perhaps, o'erwhelm'd with tears, void of relief,
On this fame fpot they ftood, choak'd up with
    grief.
This thought difturbs me; and methinks I fee
The griev'd pair at this fad folemnity.
Their hands they wring, in agonizing pain,
And weep their lov'd, loft fon; but weep in vain.
Is it but fancy all? or do I hear
The mother's anguifh for her breathlefs dear;
Of her foul's darling taking her laft leave;
While for her pangs no comfort fhe'll receive?
Dumb fhe remained, while with pain fhe fees,
The end put to the awful obfequies:
She leans upon the partner of her woes,
'Till irreprefible her torture grows.
Her forrows of all comfort her bereave;
She haftily advances to the grave;

     .   And

And faſtens one more look on her lov'd boy,
The laſt, alas! ſhe ever muſt enjoy;
And as ſhe looks, with mournful words ſhe cries,
With broken accents, and heart-rending ſighs;
" Farewell, my ſon! my deareſt ſon, farewell!
" Would to GOD I had died ere you fell!
" Farewell, my child, to happineſs and you!
" To both I now for ever bid adieu!
" Think not that pleaſure can for me be found;
" My head ſhall ſink with ſorrow to the ground."

From this afflicting ſight let parents know,
What to their childrens' intereſt they owe;
If they thro' moral paths would have them run,
And the deſtructive wiles of *Satan* ſhun.
If your own bodies' offspring can you move,
If you regard thoſe pledges of your love;
O! ſpare no pains; be diligent to teach
Counſel, by which they may to Heaven reach;
By which they ſaving wiſdom may receive,
And in the " nurture of the Lord may live."
Then may their life yield comfort to your mind,
Or in their death you'll conſolation find.
If their ſpan is prolong'd, their blameleſs ways
Will be a ſtaff for your declining days.
If in the midſt their years be lopp'd away,
With greater hopes, and with leſs fears, you may
Commit their lifeleſs bodies to the clay;

Than

2

Than the furvivors you can fend to know
What benefits from education flow.
The future hopes of having them reftor'd,
Will folace for your prefent lofs afford;
When you receive them to your longing arms,
Highly improv'd in noble, godly charms.

A trial hard it is, I muft confefs,
And more afflictive than I can exprefs,
A blooming child, fprung from your loins, to
    leave
In the receffes of the gloomy grave:
Upon your knees whom you have dandled long,
And caught delightful accents from its tongue;
Join'd to your love by many a fond tie,
Become now both the comfort of your eye,
And the fupporter of your family!
Doubtlefs you would in keeneft anguifh mourn,
To have the dear one from your bofom torn.
But O! you and the child would more be croft,
To have his foul from GOD for ever loft;
For early fin, or fhameful want of grace,
Debarr'd from ev'ry hope of faving peace;
And doom'd to regions of corroding pain,
With fiends in endlefs torments to remain!
How would it your diftreffes aggravate,
Confcious of your neglect, when now too late,

If

If thefe reflections fhould your mind employ,
While weeping you attend your breathlefs boy !
" This child, tho' capable to know long fince,
"{ Between what's good and ill the difference;
" Is from the world remov'd, before it knew
" The mighty end for which life's breath it
      " drew.
" A momentary life it had from me,
" But no inftructions fraught with piety ;
" Nothing from me its happinefs t' infure,
" In that ftate which it now muft ftill endure.
" The breathlefs corpfe is in the coffin plac'd,
" And left in the cold, filent grave to wafte :
" And what good reafon have I to fuppofe,
" Its prec'ous foul enjoys more fweet repofe ?
" Why may I not more juftly apprehend,
" Eternal punifhment muft be its end ;
" That by a judge impartially fevere,
" 'Tis fentenc'd endlefs mifery to bear ?
" Ev'n while I weep at its untimely fate,
" In utter darknefs it may deprecate
" Its hated birth-day, and for ever mourn,
" That 'twas of fuch a wicked parent born."

  Nought but the worm that fhall for ever live,
Can anguifh like felf-condemnation give.
. Racks, pains, and tortures muft be eafy things,
Contrafted with remorfe's gnawing ftings.

                    How

How very earneftly I wifh, that they
Who have the management of children, may
Take againft confcience, fcourges timely care,
Which at the laft intolerable are,
By ftriving early in their minds to move
Knowledge of CHRIST, of truth a cordial love!

On this hand one is lodg'd whofe tomb does
    fhew
A tale indeed of pitiable woe!
Well may the little images recline,
O'er the dumb afhes hang their heads, and pine!
None can the melancholy ftory hear,
But fure muft drop, the fympathizing tear.
Juft twenty-eight his age; fudden his death;
Himfelf in prime of life depriv'd of breath:
-" His bones with manly marrow were replete,
" Full were his breafts of milk," when cruel fate
Did from the body call his foul away,
And give the carcafe to its parent clay.
Perhaps his mind, with many pleafures fraught,
Of th' evil hour had entertain'd no thought.
And who could any apprehenfions have,
So bright a fun the world at noon fhould leave?
Men thought his hill ftood in a firm-fix'd place;
Long life feem'd written in his fanguine face:
Large trains of earthly fatisfactions were
    The fure folacers of his greateft care.

                  When,

When, lo! an unexpected ftroke defcends,
From that ftrong arm " which lofty mountains
      rends ;"
Which, like the " moth the felf-thought hero's
      might
Crufhes" refiftlefs into gloomy night;
And that as quickly, and with much more eafe
Than men to death that feeble infect fqueeze.
Perhaps the profpect of his nuptial joy,
Was all that did his warmed thoughts employ.
Perhaps the breathings of his love-fick breaft,
Were in a language like to this exprefs'd :
" Yet but a little while, and I'll poffefs
" The utmoft of all human happinefs :
" I'll call my charmer mine, and in her have
" The greateft comfort that my heart can crave."
In fuch inchanting views did fome kind friend,
Bid on the op'ning grave his eyes to bend.
And foftly hint the momentary fpan,
On earth allotted to that creature, man;
How vaftly out of time would he have thought
The admonitions which he then was taught !
Tho' rich in feeming blifs, and warm his blood,
He on the brink of diffolution ftood.
Dreadful viciffitude ! that bridal joys
Should be exchang'd for Death's folemnities !
Deplorable misfortune ! to be loft
On a fondly-imagin'd friendly coaft !

                   Ev'n

Ev'n in the haven fhipwreck to endure,
And fink when happinefs was deem'd fecure!
O! what a memorable proof is here,
In beft eftate how frail and vain men are!
Ye gay and carelefs look, behold this tomb!
Regard this day; to-morrow ne'er may come!

Who can tell but the joyful bride-maid's fpread,
And carefully prepar'd the marriage-bed?
With richeft covers had it deck'd and grac'd,
And fofteft downy pillows on it plac'd?
When—O! do not on youth or ftrength rely,
Since mortal beings have no certainty;
But truft in GOD, unchangeable on high—
Death, unrelenting death prepares to find,
In the cold earth, beds of another kind.
Unto his grave he muft be carried out,
Not with a fplendid or a joyful rout;
But ftretched in the gloomy herfe he lies,
While mourning friends attend the obfequies.
He muft on this take up his refting-place,
Nor ever change it " 'till the heavens ceafe."
In vain the yielding fair her drefs puts on,
And lacks for nothing but her fpoufe alone.
Did fhe not like *Sifera*'s mother peep
Out of the lattice, wond'ring what could keep
Her much-defired, long-expected love,
Or " make his chariot wheels fo flowly move?"

Little

Little fufpecting her intended mate
Had done with all his tranfitory ftate!
That everlafting cares his mind employ,
None of *Lucinda*, once his chiefeft joy!
Go, difappointed virgin! weep, and know
All is uncertainty of blifs below!
Go, teach thy foul afpiring to purfue
Felicity, immutable and true!
Fidelio once gay and gallant refts,
And Death, his miftrefs, clafps him to her breafts;
She holds him in her icy arms, while he
Forgets, for e'er forgets the world—and thee.

Thus far 'gainft death one's tempted to exclaim,
And him capricioufly cruel name.
By thus beginning with the regifter,
We think all nature's laws inverted are.
He paffing o'er decrepit age's bed,
The bud of infancy has oft ftruck dead;
Youth he has blafted ere to manhood come,
And torn up manhood in its fulleft bloom.
Dreadful thefe providences muft appear;
Yet not unfearchable the counfels are.

Such ftrokes the relatives not only grieve,
From them the neighbourhood furprize receive.
A powerful alarm they loudly found,
To roufe frail mortals from their fleep profound;

And

And are intended as a remedy,
Against our carnal, rash security.
Such paffing-bells in ftrongeft terms proclaim,
The admonition which from JESUS came;
" Take-ye heed, therefore, always watch and pray,
" For ye neither the hour know, nor the day."
We, like intoxicated creatures, flide
On a tremendous precipice's fide.
Thefe difpenfations, with amazing love,
The meffengers of Heav'n themfelves approve;
From our fupinenefs urging us to wake,
And timely circumfpection wifely take.
In words I furely need not them exprefs,
Or their interpreter myfelf profefs.
Let each one's confcience be awake, and then
They will appear thus awfully to mean—
" For your laft end, ye fons of men, prepare,
" Since in the midft of life in death ye are.
" No ftate, no circumftance can afcertain
" Your fafety, nor a fingle moment gain.
" So ftrong and mighty is the tyrant's hand,
" That nothing human can its force withftand;
" His aim's fo certain when his fhafts are fent,
" That of the number not one is mifpent.
" His arrows oft as quick as lightning fly,
" And wound and kill in twinkling of an eye.
" By conftant preparation you can be,
" In all expedients, from danger free.

E   " The

" The fatal ſhafts ſo much in common fall,
" That none can gueſs who'll next obey the call.
" Then be ye ſtill in readineſs to go,
" The final ſummons comes when leaſt ye know."

Important counſel! forth, methinks, it breaks
From ſepulchre to ſepulchre, and makes
In lines addreſſes, and in precepts ſpeaks.
The oft-repeated warning, I confeſs,
Is but too needful for my happineſs;
And may it by co-operating grace,
Effectually work a ſaving peace!
This truth which we with tranſport ſhould re-
  ceive;
And deeply on our memories engrave;
Is only ſketched lightly on the mind,
And leaves nought but a ſlender mark behind.
We view our neighbour's ſick; we ſee them dead;
We then turn pale, and feel a trembling dread;
No ſooner are they to our proſpect loſt,
But either in the whirl of buſineſs toſs'd,
Or in lethargic pleaſures lulled, we
Forget the errand of the Deity.
Our minds unſtable an impreſſion feel,
Like the thin air pierc'd by the barbed ſteel,
Or billows furrow'd by the cutting keel.
To cure this wonderful ſtupidity,
A neighb'ring monument addreſſes me.

It

It a poor mortal's ſtory comprehends,
Call'd to the dread tribunal from his friends;
Without time of the one farewell to take,
Or for the other a ſhort pray'r to make;
Kill'd, as the uſual expreſſions flow,
By a ſudden and accidental blow.

Was it a chance wound? Doubtleſs the ſtroke
   came
From an hand which inviſibly took aim.
The heav'nly angels the great LORD obey,
Who ruleth all things in the earth and ſea;
Except GOD pleaſeth nothing can advance,
'Tis he directeth that which men call *chance.*
Nothing, 'tis plain, can ever come to light,
But what he plans and regulates aright.
If accidents fall out, they ever muſt
Proceed from GOD, and what he wills is juſt.
The LORD, with whom the iſſues of life are,
The warrant and commiſſion did prepare.
The diſaſter, thought caſual, is only
The tool to execute the great decree.
When wicked *Ahab* fell, it was believ'd
He accidentally his death receiv'd.
" A certain man at venture drew a bow—"
To him at venture, for he thought it ſo.
But GOD omnipotent, who dwells on high,
His arm had ſtrengthened, and could deſcry
The ſhaft was aim'd by an unerring eye.

So

So that which men call *chance* is juſt the ſame -
As Providence, chang'd only in its name;
Which can deliberate deſigns reveal,
And its interpoſition ſtill conceal.
How cheering this reflection is, to cure
The throbbing anguiſh which mourners endure!
How admirably fitted to compoſe
Their ſpirits, yielding to a weight of woes!
How excellently ſuited to eraſe
The tears of good ſurvivors, making place, }
Ev'n in the midſt of countleſs griefs, for peace! }

The wall 'twixt this world and the next how
    thin !
We're out of this almoſt as ſoon as in.
Our noſtrils' breath does only ſeparate
Our preſent being from another ſtate :
We may the journey make ſo haſtily,
We live this moment, but the next may die.
From a card-table *Chremylus* aroſe,
And Death in darkneſs did his eyes incloſe.
One night, *Corinna*, gay and ſprightly all,
Was richly dreſſed at a ſplendid ball :
The next, a corpſe, pale, ſtiff, and wan ſhe lay,
And ready to be mingled with the clay.
Young *Atticus* liv'd only to compleat
His ample, coſtly, and commodious ſeat ;
But Death, the dreadful tyrant Death, debarr'd
Him from all pleaſure in the houſe he rear'd.

Hung

Hung were the fafhes to admit the light,
But their Lord's eyes were clos'd in endlefs night.
Chambers were furnifh'd to invíte repofe,
Or pleafure which fociety beftows;
But in the lone, filent manfions of the tomb,
Their owner refts, in his low, earthly room.
Gardens were plann'd according to his mind,
A thoufand noble ornaments defign'd;
But to " the place of fkulls," depriv'd of breath,
Their mafter's gone down to the vale of death.

Many, I doubt not, while I recollect,
This tragical viciffitude expect.
The eyes of that great GOD who fits upon
The circle of the earth, and views with one
All-feeing look the poor fojourners there,
See many tents which now afflicted are:
Afflicted, as when in one night the pride
And ftrength of the *Ægyptians* were deftroy'd:
When the refiftlefs arrows flew abroad,
Shot by the heav'nly meffenger of GOD.
Some from their eafy chairs fink on the floor,
Nor can their fhrieking friends relief procure:
Some in an arbour as reclin'd they lie,
Tafting the fweets which from the bloffoms fly.
Some, as in pleafure-boats they fail along,
O'er dancing ftreams, or laughing meads among;

Nor

Nor is the grim intruder mollified,
Tho' wine and mufic flow on either fide.
Some, intercepted on their journey home;
And as they enter on great matters, fome.
Some are affail'd, as in their hands they hold
The gains for which their juftice has been fold:
And even fome are·taken by furprife,
Juft as they luft or malice exercife.
No care can ftop, no prudence can forefee,
The vary'd ills which wait us conftantly.

Numberlefs dangers compafs men around;
A ftarting horfe may fling one on the ground;
And while his body on the ftones is thrown,
His foul is launch'd into the world unknown.
A ftack of chimnies tumbling from on high,
May crufh the man who thinks no danger nigh:
Or ev'n the dropping of a fingle tile,
May prove as fatal as the total pile.
The thread of life's fo very thin and weak,
It ftorms not only tear, but breezes break.
Occurrences moft common, whence we fear
No harm, may weapons of deftruction bear.
A grape-ftone or an infect, for our doom
Fatal as arm'd *Goliath* may become.
Nay, if Almighty GOD command fhould give,
We from our comforts would our death re-
　　ceive.

The air we breathe's our bane, the food we eat,
Contributes much our life t' attenuate.
The enemy does on us oft encroach,
By many roads that further an approach:
Yea, lies intrenched in our very veins,
And in the feat of life his fort retains.
The crimfon blood with which our health is
        fed,
Is with the feeds of death impregnated.
Inflam'd with heat, or by great toil annoy'd,
The parts defign'd to cherifh are deftroy'd.
Some caufe unfeen its paffage may revert,
Or violence unknown its courfe divert;
By either of which cafes if it moves,
A pois'nous draught, or deadly ftab it proves.

Since the poffeffion of our earthly houfe,
Is fo uncertain and precarious;
Let us be always ready, and prepare
To flit, fince but at will we tenants are.
Except we thus prove good habitually,
We are like wretches that on top-mafts lie,
And foundly fleep, tho' tempefts raging blow,
Or gulphs yawn horrid, or waves foam below.
What fatisfactions can our hearts elate?
Can peace or comfort be in fuch a ftate?
Whereas, a conftant preparation will,
Into our bofoms cheerfulnefs inftill;

                        Which

Which for our peace will efficacious prove,
And which no low vexation can remove;
And a firm conſtancy of mind create,
Not to be quell'd by any dangerous threat.
When the town with ſtrong walls is fortify'd,
And with great quantities of food ſupply'd;
Well guarded by ſtout troops, reſolv'd to fight, ⎫
What then can the inhabitants affright, ⎬
Who may rejoice, ev'n when the foe's in ſight? ⎭
The taſte of life, of death the conſtant mind,
By ſuch, or by much firmer bands are join'd.

I ſaid, ſhould God Almighty orders give,
We from our comforts would our death receive:
And ſee the truth inſcribed by the hand
That ſeal'd Fate's warrant, and gave the com-
      mand.
Yon marble-graced monument contains
My once-lov'd friend's depoſited remains;
There does the body of *Sophronia* lie,
Lamented much, who did in child-bed die.
Alas! how oft the tender branches ſhoot,
When the ſtem withers to the very root!
The infant often is preſerv'd from death,
While ſhe that bare him yields her lateſt breath.
She gives him life; but pitiable thought!
The life ſhe gives, by her own death is bought.

                       And

And tho' her infant's eyes are brought to light,
Yet her's are clos'd in everlafting night.
Or fhe expires, perhaps, in pangs fevere,
And for her offspring does a tomb prepare;
While the complaint of a fad monarch doth
Afford a mournful epitaph for both :
" Alas! the children to the birth are come,
" And there's not ftrength to yield them from the
        " womb !"
In my opinion, we ought not to grieve
So much the lofs we in this cafe receive.
Better, the ftranger in the womb fhould reft,
Than living, by afflictions be opprefs'd.
Better, its eyes fhould in the womb be clos'd,
Than to a world fo dang'rous be expos'd ;
Without the guide of its infantile days,
Wanting a mother, to direct its ways.

Diftinction's eafily in this tomb found,
By the grand ornaments with which 'tis crown'd.
Affluent hands, it feems, the model drew,
Directed by a noble heart, that knew
No niggard boundaries of love, and thought
For the deceas'd enough could ne'er be wrought
Methinks an emblem'd picture it holds forth
Of lov'd *Sophronia*'s elegance and worth.
Does the fair color with her beauty vie,
Or faintly tell her white-rob'd purity?

F   Her

Her good and amiable manners were
Smooth as thefe ftones, polifh'd with fo much
    care:
The whole adorned gracefully, not plain,
Not proudly pompous, or fordidly mean ;
Like her unfeigned goodnefs it appears,
Not oftentatious, but which endears.
But ah! too foon thofe lovely charms have fail'd!
What has the fparkling of thy eyes avail'd!
The beauty of thy bridal youth, how vain!
Or from thy noble birth what didft thou gain!
Alas! too weak the poffeffor to fave
From favage death, or from the yawning grave.
How ineffectual alas! does now
The love of numerous acquaintance grow!
Not thy tranfported hufband's fondeft love,
Nor thy fair fame, as fpotlefs as a dove,
Thy life could lengthen, or death's ftroke re-
    move.
Thefe circumftances on my mind imprefs
The beauty which thofe tender lines exprefs ;
" How lov'd, how valu'd once avails thee not ;
" To whom related, or by whom begot.
" A heap of duft alone remains of thee ;
" 'Tis all *thou* art, and all the *proud* fhall be!"

    Yet tho' unable to divert the blow,
True faith the fting of death can overthrow.

Do not thofe lamps fuch filent truths proclaim?
And the bright heart that blazes like a flame?
The palms that flourifh, and the glitt'ring crown,
In gilt, well imitated marble fhewn?
Do they not to difcerning eyes declare
Her conftant faith, her fervency of pray'r?
The victory which o'er the world fhe found,
The heav'nly wreath with which fhe fhall be
  crown'd;
Wherewith the LORD her goodnefs will repay,
In right'ous judgment at the final day?

 Happy the hufband was in fuch a mate,
The fharer of his bed and his eftate!
Their inclinations nicely were in tune;
Their converfation was all unifon.
How filken was the yoke to fuch a pair?
And in their bands what bleffings twifted were?
With them each joy in mutual increafe grew,
And ev'ry care alleviation knew.
Nothing, they thought, their blifs could fo im-
  prove,
As hopeful children, pledges of their love.
That they might have the happinefs to fee
Themfelves increas'd in their pofterity;
Their mingled graces in their offspring find,
And feel affection of the warmeft kind.

   " Grant

" Grant us this gift," their common pray'rs ex-
    prefs,
" We afk but this to crown our happinefs."

To future things alas! how blind are men!
Unable to difcern what's good, and when!
With an impatient, unbecoming cry,
Said *Rachel*, " Give me children, or I die!"
From this a difappointment fhe receiv'd,
Great as the bleffing which fhe thought fhe crav'd.
Not to a wifh deny'd fhe dates her doom,
But its completion marks her for the tomb.
If children like to flow'ry chaplets are,
Which for their parents balmy odors bear,
Whofe beauties bloom with ornamental pride,
And fhed refrefhing fweets on ev'ry fide ;
Some fell misfortune, or relentlefs death,
May twine itfelf amidft the lovely wreath.
Whene'er our fouls are pour'd out with defire,
Something of fmall importance to acquire ;
The words of our blefs'd LORD we truly may,
" Ye know not what ye afk," to ourfelves fay.
Doth GOD rejeft our wifhes? He denies
In mercy that from which our woes arife ;
And from a principle of kindeft love,
Refufes that which would our ruin prove.
With a fick appetite we oft refrain
From what is good, and languifh for our bane,
                        Where

Where Fancy dreams of fome unmingled fweet,
The bitternefs of woe we often meet :

May, therefore, no defires immoderate,
Bend us to this or that terreftrial ftate ;
But our condition wholly to refer
To God omnipotent, who cannot err !
May we learn wifdom, and be ready ftill
To facrifice our wifhes to God's will ;
And with fubmiffive thankfulnefs fubmit
To be difpofed of as he fhall think fit !
For if, indeed, his precepts to obey,
Be what will certain happinefs convey ;
So, refignation to his will, fecures
That blifs, which to eternity endures.

Here, on the ground a fmall, plain ftone is
    plac'd,
Which with no beautifying fculpture's grac'd ;
But from a frugal fund, one would fuppofe,
Purchas'd it was, and under it arofe.
No coftly ornament is on it found,
Nor is it with one decoration crown'd ;
A very fhort infcription's on it made,
So much effac'd, that it can fcarce be read.
Did the depofitary, void of faith,
Omit its duty to the corpfe beneath ?

Or

Or were the letters thus effaced by
Th' approach of the furviving family,
Which at the tomb met mourning, to revive
The mem'ry of a good, lov'd relative?
For on more clofe infpection I perceive
The body of a father's in the grave.
A worthy and relig'ous father, who
His children left, ere they to manhood grew;
Ere they had worldly fettlements procur'd,
Or with found principles their fouls fecur'd.

Of all confiderations hitherto,
This, fure, is the moft pitiable woe.
The fadnefs of fuch dying chambers leaves
Scenes the moft melting that the mind receives.
There a fond fpoufe and tender parent end,
A gen'rous mafter, and a faithful friend.
He yields there to the laft extremities,
And on the point of diffolution lies.
All art can do, already has been try'd,
But the difeafe has medicine defy'd:
It haftes impetuous in the purfuit,
Its horrible commands to execute;
The filver cord of life to tear amain,
And rend the tie of mutual love in twain,

One or two fervants at a diftance ftay,
Cafting a train of wifhful looks this way;

And,

And, as with grief their fwelling bofoms rife,
Condole their mafter in a flow of fighs.
The grac'ous way wherein he us'd to give
His orders, which with joy they did receive;
Does to their minds his former worth recall,
While down their honeft cheeks the tears faft fall.
His friends, whofe pleafing converfe once could
     ' cheer,
But miferable helpers now appear.
A fympathifing pity's all they now
Can to relieve or fuccour him beftow;
Unlefs it be rais'd and augmented more
By filent pray'rs, in which they GOD implore;
Or pious words of confolation yield,
From proper texts, with which the Scripture's fill'd.
His poor and helplefs children flock around,
Frantic with grief, and in tears almoft drown'd,
Their little fouls they fob out, and complain,
And paffionately cry, but cry in vain;
" Will he then leave us, our weak' ftate to moan?
" And muft we on a wicked world be thrown?"
Thefe parted torrents all together join,
And 'gainft the wretched fpoufe their force com-
     bine;
With complicated woes fhe is opprefs'd,
While tides of forrow overwhelm her breaft.
Sunk in extreme diftrefs, in her by turns
The wife, the mother, and the lover mourns.

                             By

By her his death is much feverer found,
Who had in long-endearing bands been bound.
Alas! where can she find such excellence?
Where place such unreserved confidence?
Can she a counsellor gain so discreet?
Where an example so improving meet?
Where find a guardian, who such pains would
  take,
Merely for her, and for her children's sake?
Behold! how o'er the languid bed she hangs,
Rack'd with a sad variety of pangs;
Most tenderly solicitous to ease
The pains which on her dearest help-mate seize,
And, if 'twere possible, from death to shield
A life, for which her own she'd gladly yield.
A life, for which she solely wish'd to live,
Which only to her offspring bliss could give.
See her hands shake with apprehensive pain,
And from the livid cheek the cold dews clean;
On her kind arms sometimes compose to rest
The sinking head, with racking ills opprefs'd,
Or lay it on her pity-feeling breast.
Behold her heart with speechless ardor rent,
While on the meagre form her eyes are bent;
While her soft passions with vast fondness beat,
And her soul's pierc'd with griefs extremely great.

    The

The fick man, patient and adoring ftill,
Yields and refigns him to the heav'nly will;
And by fubmiffive piety obtains
An healing balm for his afflictive pains.
He's fenfibly affected with the ftate
Of his attendants fo difconfolate;
And pierc'd with anx'ous trouble for his wife,
Who foon muft lead a lonely, widow'd life;
And for the children who, when fatherlefs,
Will be expos'd to multiply'd diftrefs.
Yet, " tho' caft down, not in defpair," for faft
His truft remains, GOD's word fhall ever laft.
His comforters he comforts, when at eafe,
And death with majefty of woe obeys.

The foul, juft going to forfake the corfe,
Makes her laft effort, and collects her force.
Himfelf he raifes on the pillow, and
To his fad fervants ftretches a kind hand;
He to his friends his mournful farewell fpeaks,
And in his feeble arms his dear wife takes;
Kiffes the pledges of their love with grief,
Then thus pours out the fmall remains of life:
" I die, my children dear, you I muft leave,
" But you the everlafting GOD will fave.
" Altho' in me an earthly parent fall,
" In heav'n you have one who is All in All.

" An

" An unbelieving and a wicked heart,
" Can only make you from his joys depart,
" Or you from his endearing love divert."

His heart was full, he could no farther go ;
His utt'rance fail'd him, quite opprefs'd with woe.
After a breathing fhort, but with great pain,
Prompted by zealous love, he thus began :
" On you, dear partner of my foul, on you
" Falls the fole care of our poor orphans now.
" 'Tis true, I leave you under grief weigh'd down,
" But God ftill makes the widow's caufe his own ;
" God, who in faithfulnefs and truth doth fpeak,
" Hath faid, I ne'er will leave you, nor forfake.
" From this my drooping fpirits ftrength receive ;
" Let alfo this my bofom's wife relieve.
" O Father of Compaffion, now I yield
" Into thy hands my foul, with comfort fill'd ;
" Encourag'd by thy promis'd tendernefs,
" Under thy care I leave my fatherlefs."

He fainting fell, when he thefe words had faid,
And lay fome minutes fenfelefs on the bed.
A taper thus, ere 'tis extinguifh'd quite,
Oft blazes quick, and gives a quiv'ring light :
So life, ere 'twas for ever finifh'd, gave
A parting ftruggle, willing to receive
Once more the joy his eyes were wont to leave.

He

He fain would speak, desirous to reveal
The tender thoughts which in his mind prevail.
He more than once essayed, but alas!
Th' organ of speech like a crack'd vessel was;
When he attempted any words to frame,
They all were stopp'd by the obstructing phlegm;
His aspect, tho' in ev'ry air and look,
Affection inexpressible bespoke.
The father all, and husband in his eye,
With stedfast view once more he does espy,
And gaze with ardor on his children dear,
Whom he oft saw with a paternal care:
On that lov'd wife then turns his dying sight,
Whom he ne'er view'd but with supreme delight:
Fix'd in this posture, amidst smiles which pleas'd,
And gleams of heav'n, his last, fond look he gaz'd.

On this, their silent grief no stoppage knows,
But gushes in a rapid tide of woes.
They wept, nor any comfort would receive,
Till time a vent to their afflictions gave;
And 'till religion's consolations stay'd
The wounds which their excess of sorrow made.
Then the sad family search for, and dwell
On the unfinish'd sentences, which fell
From the good lips of him they lov'd so well.
In *Jeremiah*'s prophecy they find
This healing balsam for a wounded mind;

They

They guides to boundlefs wifdom take from thence,
And promifes of vaft beneficence :
" Thy children fatherlefs leave to my care ;
" Them I'll preferve ; nor let your widows fear."
Thofe grac'ous promifes do now impart
Joy to their lives, and comfort to each heart,
They treafure it up in the memory,
As a moft rich and ufeful legacy.
Upon it they rely, and on it build
Their hopes of having ev'ry wifh fulfill'd ;
That all their honeft works, crown'd with fuccefs,
Shall ftill infure unfading happinefs.
The facred pledges of God's favour leave
The greateft wealth felicity can give.
They lack no good, nor evil apprehend,
Since God's their guide, their guardian, and their
friend.

Soon as my own memento is away,
And the memorial of fome one's decay ;
Sad monitors, fucceffive, come to light,
In gloomy order, crowding on my fight,
That which my obfervation fixes now,
Bears than the former a more fable brow.
As I conclude, it underneath contains,
Of fome more aged perfon, the remains.
One would fuppofe that he his ftation grac'd,
As his among the grandeft tombs is plac'd.

Let

Let me approach, and on the ftone perceive
" Who, or what object, flumbers in the grave."
Th' infcriptions on his monument relate,
He once was owner of a large eftate,
Which by attention, care, and induftry,
He faw augmented in a great degree;
And that he in life's bufy period dy'd,
Somewhat advanc'd beyond his noon-day pride.
Then, probably, reply'd my mufing mind,
One of thofe ceafelefs drudges, that we find
At day-break rife, at midnight go to reft,
And eat their bread, with carefulnefs opprefs'd;
Not to fecure the kindnefs of the LORD,
Nor for their wants provifion to afford;
But only heaps of riches to enjoy,
Ten thoufand times more than they can de-
    ftroy.
Did he not fchemes for getting money frame;
And ftrive to raife his family's proud name?
Houfes to houfes join, and field to field,
Until his wifhes to his wealth fhould yield?
That then he'd fit in quiet, and partake
Of things which kept his fenfes ftill awake;
Take fome fhort refpite from terreftrial toil,
And think, perhaps, on ehdlefs things awhile?

But here behold the grofs abfurdity
Of worldly wifdom and fagacity!

How

How fhallow, childifh, filly the pretence
To that which we call mafterly prudence!
When it on *time* beftows more anx'ous cares,
Than when it for *eternity* prepares!
How much infatuated, then, are they
Who fubtly fcheme out meafures for a day;
Who to chimeras carefully attend,
On fleeting fhadows wafte their time, nor fpend
A thought on certainties that ne'er will end!
When ev'ry wheel moves fmoothly on, and all
The fit defigns for execution call;
When long-expected happinefs appears
At hand, and all our fondeft wifhes chears;
Behold! the LORD Almighty laughs on high
At the weak *Babel-builders* vanity;
The labor'd bubbles, touch'd by death, decay,
And into empty air diffolve away.
The cobweb, fpun moft fine and gay, indeed,
Is broke, and fwept away with rapid fpeed;
All the defigns abortive are fupprefs'd,
And in the grave with their projector reft.
So true the verdicts of the LORD become,
Which feal thefe lucky wretches' lafting doom:
" Behold how they on flitting fhadows lean,
" And trouble and perplex themfelves in vain!"

Ye that attended fuch a one at death,
And heard the fentiments of his laft breath;

Speak,

Speak, I befeech you, fay, did he not cry
In the words of crofs'd fenfuality;
" O death! how dreadful thy approach appears,
" To one immers'd in fecular affairs!
" Who with purfuits of prefent pleafures fraught,
" Of hereafter unceafing never thought!
" How am I comforted, what have I gain'd,
" Or what great depth of knowledge is con-
  tain'd
" In being dext'rous in concerns below,
" When I eternal happinefs forego?
" Miftake moft wretched! oh deftructive choice!
" I too much pains employ'd on worldly joys;
" To fleeting toys I was too much confin'd,
" But oh! I then caft heaven from my mind!
" I forgot endlefs ages! that my days—"
Here he was going fome vain hope to feize;
To breathe fome wifh; of fome void comfort
  dream,
Or ineffectual refolution frame;
But fudden tremblings fhook his nerves; ftraight-
  way
His frame diffolved into lifelefs clay.

May an unhappy brother's dying word
To this world's children due advice afford!
May they from their deep lethargy awake,
And benefit from his misfortune take!

       Why

Why ſhould they with impatient warmth com-
    plain,
When they ſome white and yellow earth can't
    gain,
As if the world did not enough contain? .
Why with thick clay ſhould they themſelves preſs
    down,
Why " they're to run for an immortal crown?"
Why ſhould this world ſeem pleaſant to their eyes,
When they ſhould " preſs to their high calling's
    prize?"
Why ſhould they, then, that veſſel overload,
In which their everlaſting all is ſtow'd?
Or ſuperfluities why ſhould they crave,
When they muſt ſwim, their lives alone to ſave?
Yet ſo prepoſt'rous is the life of thoſe,
Who their chief bliſs on affluence repoſe;
Who full of induſtry, time's trifles hoard,
Yet ſcarce wiſh for the riches of the LORD.

    O! may we walk through thoſe toys' glitt'ring
    train,
With wiſe indiff'rence, if not with diſdain!
May we ſuperior to ſuch baubles riſe,
And caſt them henceforth from our wond'ring
    eyes!
Having conveniencies enough for life,
For worldly treaſure let us wage no ſtrife.

                       Let

Let us accommodate ourfelves below,
And let from heav'n our greateft bleffings flow,
Whereas, if we indulge an anx'ous care,
Or lavifh hopes on tranfitory ware,
So firm an union they'll in us create,
That keeneft pangs the parting ftroke await.
By fuch a warm attachment to the joy,
Which will be ravifh'd from us certainly:
Woe 'gainft the agonizing hour we'll gain,
And plant, aforehand, our death's couch with
    pain.

Some got to feventy years, as I perceive,
Before they took their lodgings in the grave;
Some few refigned not their breath before
They of revolving harvefts faw fourfcore.
Thefe, I would hope, by rev'rend duty fway'd,
" In youth due homage to their GOD have paid;"
Ere their ftrength did to toil and forrow turn;
Ere nature languifhing began to mourn;
When keepers of the houfe tremble thro' fear,
And lookers at the window darken'd are:
When ev'n the little grafshoppers fmall weight,
To bending fhoulders feems a burthen great;
And in lethargic, liftlefs fouls, defire
Raifes a faint, and quickly fleeting fire;
Before thofe tirefome hours approach us nigh;
Before thofe heavy moments clofer fly;

H   In

In which there's too much reafon to complain,
" No pleafure nor improvement they contain."

If, then, their lamps were deftitute of oil,
And they expos'd to Satan's fnares meanwhile;
In fuch decrepit circumftances, fure,
At market they're unfit fome to procure.
For, befides great varieties of woe,
Which from enfeebled conftitutions flow;
All their corruptions muft have gain'd great
    force,
By irreligion's uncheck'd, lengthen'd courfe.
Ill habits muft the deepeft roots ftill find,
And twift them with each fibre of the mind;
They muft be all as thoroughly ingrain'd
In their affections, as the foot which ftain'd
Th' *Ethiop*'s vifage of a dufky hue;
Or fpots which in the leopard's fkin we view.
If one who under fuch misfortunes lies,
Should above each oppofing hardfhip rife;
And, fpight of all, to glory onwards flee,
It muft indeed a great falvation be.
If fuch a one, thro' all temptations pafs'd,-
Free from deftruction fhould efcape at laft,
It muft be as if he thro' fire was caft.

This is the feafon that does comfort afk,
And is improper to begin the tafk.

The

The hufbandman fhould now his hook prepare,
Or of the fruit of his hard labor fhare;
Not now begin to furrow up the earth,
Or fcatter feed to bring forth a new birth.
'Tis true, GOD brings all that he wills to pafs;
" Let there be light, he faid, and light there
        was :"
Light inftantaneous, as quick as thought,
A paffage thro' primeval darknefs wrought,
At his command a leprofy moft foul,
Of longeft ftay, is inftantly made whole.
He, in the greatnefs of his ftrength, can raife
Not only finners that are dead four days;
But at his word, reftor'd to life, appears
The wretch deceas'd for even fourfcore years.
Yet do not points of fuch vaft moment try,
Nor truft fo dreadful an uncertainty.
GOD may his help withdraw, his pow'r fufpend :
May in his wrath fwear that thofe who offend,
And to abufe his tender mercy dare,
Shall " never his eternal comforts fhare."

   Ye that are ftrong in health, in bloom of days,
The prec'ous opportunity now feize.
Improve your golden hours, be wife in time,
And to the nobleft purpofe ftrive to climb ;
Tread in thofe paths which may fecure your right
To the inheritance of faints in light;

           By

By which you endlefs youth may call your own,
And gain of glory an immortal crown.
O! ftand not idle all the prime of day,
Nor trifle immenfe, offer'd blifs away;
But hafte, oh! hafte, nor ftill inactive fleep;
Be always ready GOD's commands to keep.
Ev'n while in gay infenfibility,
Loit'ring in fenfelefs eafe, repos'd you lie;
Juft in that moment death his bow may bend,
And, quick as thought, his killing arrow fend.
Not long ago a thoughtlefs jay I fpy'd,
Its pretty feathers drefs with bufy pride;
Or hopping carelefsly from fpray to fpray,
Infenfible that danger near it lay.
Juft then a fportfman paffing by beholds
The bird, as it its gaudy plumes unfolds;
The hollow tube he raifes inftantly,
And takes his aim with an unerring eye.
Swifter than whirlwinds flies the leaden death,
And ftraight deprives the filly bird of breath.
Such may the fate of thofe be who delay
The fair occafion to get grace to-day;
Who wantonly poftpone their happy ftate,
And for improvement 'till to-morrow wait.
Death in their foolifhnefs may them furprife,
While they dream of hereafter being wife.

Some

Some came, no doubt, to this their laſt retreat,
With length of days and piety replete;
" As ſhocks of corn in blooming vigor blow,
" And, fill'd with plenty, ripe in harveſt grow."
Theſe were the children of true light, and who
God's wiſdom in their generation knew;
Who were wiſe in what ſhould them moſt employ,
Wiſe for that happineſs they now enjoy.
They richer and more honorable were,
Than all the votaries of *Mammon* are.
Swift wings were furniſh'd for the wealth of one,
Which is now irrecoverably gone;
Whiſe the poor gatherers are ſent away,
Thro' fields of want and penury to ſtray;
Where not one drop of water they can gain,
To cool their tongue, or eaſe their ſcorching pain.
Whereas, the others always are ſupply'd
With riches, which ſhall with them ſtill abide;
Which leave them not, but conſtantly afford
Them comfort in the city of the Lord.
No pow'r created could their wealth o'erthrow;
Wealth which God only could on man' beſtow:
And ſuch, O pleaſing thought! may I attain!
May each poor, longing ſinner ſuch obtain!
Riches, which ever-ſaving faith inſure,
Treaſures of knowledge, heavenly and pure;
Riches, which bleſs us by atoning blood,
And with imputed right'ouſneſs endu'd.

Their

Their bodies here a " certain quiet fhare,
And lie in " habitations free from care."
Here they have from them ev'ry burden caft,
And have from ev'ry fnare efcap'd at laft.
With racking pain the head no longer aches;
Complaints in tears the eye no longer makes;
The flefh no more with pangs acute is torn;
Nor longer with diftempers ling'ring worn.
Here from their hardfhips they get a releafe,
And here for ever their afflictions ceafe.
Here low'ring danger never does them harm,
Nor threatens them with any harfh alarm;
But fweet tranquillity makes foft their beds,
And fafely watches their repofing heads.
Reft then, ye prec'ous relics, in the tomb,
Reft quiet in this hofpitable gloom;
'Till the laft trumpet gives the welcome found,
And wakes you fudden from your fleep profound;
" Arife, fhine forth, in heav'nly light array'd,
" On you the glory of the Lord's difplay'd."

To thefe, how calmly did life's ev'ning run!
How kindly pleafant was their fetting fun!
Then, when their flefh and heart fail'd them thro'
    fear,
How did the mem'ry of the Lord them cheer!
Who, to preferve them from the fting of guilt,
His fpotlefs blood in fpeechlefs mercy fpilt!

2

How

How did their Saviour their fouls revive,
For their juftification now alive!
How cheering the well-grounded hope of grace,
And for their fins, with GOD Almighty peace
Thro' JESUS CHRIST our LORD! this will affuage
Their griefs, and fweeten death's tormenting rage.
Has wealth pull'd all her golden mountains down?
Where's honor with its trophies of renown?
Where are the pomps of a vain world now fled?
At death's approach can they their comforts fhed?
Can they compofe th' affrighted thoughts, or
        buoy
The foul departing in its agony?
The followers of CHRIST feem pleas'd, and death
Is conquer'd even with their lateft breath.
" They on GOD's everlafting arms repofe,"
While he their fainting heads preferves from woes.
His fpirit to their fouls does peace inftill,
And bends the confcience to his holy will.
With the ftrength of thefe heav'nly fuccours fill'd,
They conquerors, not captives, quit the field;
On GOD's moft faithful promife they rely,
Fraught with full hopes of immortality."

    Now they are gone, and reft in quiet peace,
The ftruggles of reluctant nature ceafe.
In gloomy death the body lies afleep;
The foul is launch'd into the fightlefs deep.
                                        But

But fay, who can imagine the furprize,
Which will then feize on their delighted eyes;
When on them an angelic crowd attends,
Inftead of companies of weeping friends?
O how fecurely in their courfe they ride!
Thro' unknown worlds how fafely do they glide!
While thefe celeftial guides direct their flight,
The vale of tears is loft in endlefs night.
Farewel, farewel for ever, realms of woe!
Farewel, malignant beings' rage below!
They're come to ftates with boundlefs comforts
    ftor'd;
" Come to the city of the living LORD;"
While a voice fweeter than the fofteft lyre,
Sweet as the Seraphim's harmonic choir,
Hails their arrival, and rejoicing fings,
And fpeaks their entrance to the KING OF KINGS:
" Ye everlafting gates, your heads now rear,
" And give admiffion to each godly heir."

While good men's bodies flumber in the grave,
Here let us, now, " their fouls and fpirits leave;"
From an entangling wildernefs preferv'd,
For a moft pleafant paradife referv'd;
Settled in realms of unmolefted peace,
Where their difquietudes and forrows ceafe.
They fit with *Ifaac, Jacob, Abraham*,
In the LORD's kingdom, with the holy LAMB.

                                  Here

Here with innumerable faints they fhine,
And round God's throne exalt their voice divine;
Glad in fruition of their prefent joy,
On certain expectations they rely,
That they'll be blefs'd yet inconceivably ;
" When God the heav'ns and earth calls, from
    above,
" That he in judgment may his people prove."

" Their life fools reckon'd madnefs, fince they
    " found
" Their end approaching with no honors crown'd:
" But they are rank'd among the Sons of God,
" And endlefs blifs fhare in the faints abode."
However, then, a vain world may defpife,
Howe'er the truly good it villifies ;
Be this my greateft and fupreme defire,
The utmoft happinefs I can acquire!
" Let me, oh ! let me meet the juft man's fate ;
" Let me enjoy his death, and future ftate."

What figure's that which ftrikes my gazing
    eye,
And from the wall fhines fo confpic'oufly ?
It does not only eminently grace
A grander, and more elevated place ;
But feems, majeftically proud, to bear
A more than ordinary fplendid air.

I   The

The ftone the inftruments of flaughter wears,
Swords, mufkets, cannons, bay'nets, darts, and
    fpears ;
Thefe with each other on its face entwine,
And thence with formidable grandeur fhine.
Let me fee what the monument contains—
It holds a noble warrior's remains.

Wherefore, thought I, is fuch refpect now paid
To this heroic foldier's fleeting fhade ;
'Caufe he the public good fo highly priz'd,
That for it he was gladly facrific'd ?
What endlefs fame is, then, by him procur'd,
Who for our fakes fuch agonies endur'd !
Who, tho' commander of th' angelic bands,
Altho' he all the heav'nly hofts commands ;
Became a willing, bleeding facrifice,
That we to endlefs happinefs might rife !

His life from one, as being mortal, flew,
And which was long to divine juftice due ;
Which to the debt of nature foon would yield,
Ev'n had it fall'n not in the bloody field ;
But Christ gave up the ghoft, and flefh be-
    came,
Tho' he Jehovah was, the great I AM ;
The fountain of exiftence, who alone
Calls blifs and immortality his own.

3

He

He who fuppofed it no fraud to call
Himfelf an equal to GOD All in All;
Whofe outgoings from everlafting ran,
Ev'n he was made in likenefs of a man;
From the land of the living was cut off,
And to vile wretches was a fneering fcoff.
Wonder, O heav'ns! O earth, aftonifh'd be!
That CHRIST fhould feel fuch dreadful agony!
He dy'd the death, of whom we witnefs have,
He's " the true GOD, and endlefs life can give."

The one to willing perils was expos'd,
When he his king's and country's foes oppos'd;
Which, tho' it beaming glories might difplay,
Yet would an ignomin'ous mind betray,
In fuch good circumftances to gainfay.
But CHRIST the bleffed grafp'd the bloody fword,
Tho' he was KING of Kings, of Lords the LORD.
CHRIST JESUS, the fole monarch, took the field,
Tho' in the conflict he was fure to yield;
And put on harnefs, tho' he knew before,
It muft be ftained with his finlefs gore.
The Prince of heav'n his royal felf refign'd,
Not to mere hazard, but fure death to find;
To death, now certain in its quicken'd pace,
With horrors burfting from its grifly face.
And for whom did he thefe dire torments bear?
Not for thofe who at all deferving were;

I 2

But

But difobedient creatures to befriend,
And pardon gain for criminals condemn'd,
A band of evil rebels, void of grace,
An inexcufable and wicked race;
Sinners obnoxious, whom he might leave
The due reward of their crimes to receive,
Without impeachment of his goodnefs; nay,
His vengeful juftice better to difplay.

The one, 'tis likely, dy'd without much pain,
Was wounded fuddenly, and quickly flain:
A bullet lodg'd within his heart, a fword
Sheath'd in his breaft, might inftant death afford;
Or a ftrong battle-ax his brain might cleave,
And in a moment give him to the grave :—
Whereas our Saviour, divine and dear,
Did tedious, protracted torments bear,
Which were as ling'ring as they were fevere.
Ev'n in the prelude to his laft diftrefs,
What loads of grief his facred frame opprefs!
The mighty preffure, exquifitely fore,
Inftead of fweat, drew blood from ev'ry pore,
The crimfon gore fo from his body rain'd,
It ting'd the pavement, and his raiment ftain'd.
But at the laft fcene of the tragedy,
Oh! what a mournful fight might one efpy!
When to the crofs the minifter of woes,
Had nail'd his body with his piercing blows;

Oh!

Oh! for how many difmal hours of pain,
Did that illuftr'ous fufferer remain,
In fight of GOD, of angels, and of men!
His temples with the thorny crown in fcars;
His hands and feet cleft by the iron bars;
His flefh all cover'd with fevereft fmart,
Trembling and agonizing in each part;
And torments of unfpeakable diftrefs,
On his blefs'd foul, his very foul did prefs!
So long he hung, in fympathizing tone,
Nature for him thro' all her realms made moan.
The earth, fuch barbarous indignities
Beheld amaz'd, and trembled with furprize;
The fun, when thefe black actions came in view,
Shudder'd with horror, and its beams withdrew.
Nay, fo long did this fufferer fuftain
The laft extremity of bitter pain;
That, quick as thought, the alarm of it fled
To the dark regions of the diftant dead.
Still, O my foul, with this vaft truth be fill'd,
The Lamb of GOD was feiz'd, was bound, was
    kill'd;
Slaughter'd with greateft inhumanity,
And fuffer'd agonizing death for thee!
His executioners fo ftudious were,
Their cruel means of torture to prepare;
That ere its fatal dregs he had drank up,
Each drop of gall he tafted in the cup.

                    Once

Once more; the one did like a hero die,
And fell in battle, fighting gallantly.
But went not *Jefus* as a fool to reft?
Not mark'd with fcars of glory on his breaft;
But as fome wicked villain on the rack,
With lafhes of the vile fcourge on his back.
Yes, CHRIST the bleffed, bow'd, ere he was dead,
On the accurfed tree, his fainting head;
And the beneficent Redeemer dy'd,
Between two wicked felons crucify'd;
CHRIST was 'twixt heav'n and earth fufpended.
     high,
Outcaft from both, and whom each did deny.

What fuitable returns of ardent love
Can we make to the holy ONE above?
What worthy thanks can he from us receive,
Who dy'd for us, that we thro' him might live?
He did in ignomin'ous anguifh die,
That we might flourifh in the heights of joy;
And, plac'd on thrones of endlefs glory, raife
To our Redeemer fervent fongs of praife.
Alas! we impotent and fenfelefs clay,
Cannot to CHRIST fufficient duty pay.
He only who does fuch rich gifts beftow,
With grateful warmth can make our bofoms glow,
Then let, moft gracious IMMANUEL,
Thy tomb of gratitude in our fouls dwell.

Infcribe

Infcribe the mem'ry of thy matchlefs grace,
Not in thofe characters we can erafe;
But in that precious and heav'nly blood,
Which from your veins in gufhing torrents flow'd.
With neither ax nor chiffel it prepare,
But with that fpear which your blefs'd fide did
    tear.
Let it in characters confpic'ous ftand,
Indelible, not made by mortal hand;
On marble tables do not it imprefs,
But fix it on our inmoft hearts' recefs.

   Let me obferve one thing ere I leave
This entomb'd hero, and his garnifh'd grave.
Thefe methods oftentatious, how mean,
Which ftrive to bribe the votes of fame, and gain
Some little ftock of pofthumous renown,
To future times thus proudly handed down!
How poorly polifh'd alabafter fhews
The great advantage that from virtue flows!
Or how does mimicry of fculptur'd ftone
Exprefs the memorable deeds we've done!
His countrymen think with affecting grief,
On the great merit of this bleeding chief:
His patriotic zeal, in honor's caufe,
Would be remember'd with the beft applaufe,
Long as the nation is with fafety crown'd,
Without fuch artful means to fpread the found.
                 Such

Such are the methods by which I would ſtrive
To keep my certain memory alive.
Let ſuch memorials be, then, imprefs'd
Deep on each of my fellow-creature's breaſt.
Let my ſurviving friends a witnefs bear,
That for myſelf alone I did not care;
Nor wholly in my generation live,
Without attempts ſome benefits to give.
O! let a long, uninterrupted line
Of tender deeds, on my inſcription ſhine;
And let my wiſhes for the happy ſtate
Of all my friends, be ſhewn upon the plate.

Let all the poor, as by my grave they preſs,
Point at the ſpot, and thankfully confeſs,
" There lies the man, who to each varied grief,
" With ceaſeleſs tendernefs ſtill gave relief;
" Who kindly viſited my painful bed,
" And me in poverty with plenty fed.
" How oft did his inſtructions guide me right,
" And to my caſt-down ſpirits yield delight?
" 'Tis owing to the ſeaſonable ſtore
" With which God blefs'd him, to relieve the
        " poor,
" And the wiſe counſels which he us'd to give,
" That I exiſt, and now in comfort live."
Let a man who once trod ungodly ways,
Once ignorant, his eyes to heaven raiſe;

Let

Let such a one within his bosom talk,
As o'er my grave he takes his pensive walk,
" Here lie the relics of that friend sincere,
" Who for my soul had such paternal care.
" I'll ne'er forget how heedless and how gay
" I posted onward in perdition's way;
" I tremble when I think what endless woe
" Would very soon my wretched soul o'erflow;
" Had not his admonitions, always right,
" Mark'd out the way, and stay'd my thoughtless
     " flight.
" I of the holy gospel nothing knew,
" Nor had I its abundant wealth in view;
" But since his prudent converse guided me,
" The all-sufficiency of CHRIST I see;
" And, animated by his constant pray'r,
" I'd all things lose, that I might JESUS share.
" Methinks, his speeches, with religion fill'd,
" In my ears tingle, and sound comfort yield;
" Methinks, his godly precepts yet impart
" Joy to my soul, and transport to my heart;
" And will, I trust, yet more and more encrease,
" In shedding on me operative grace;
" Until we meet in mansions not prepar'd
" By men; eternal, in the heavens rear'd."

  But the infallible and surest way,
Foundations for our endless bliss to lay;
       K   Which

Which is as open to the rich as poor,
" To make our calling and election fure ;"
Is to gain godly evidence that we
Have our names blefs'd to all eternity.
However they may be forgotten, then,
Or difregarded by the fons of men;
They will not fail, for ever to afford,
Remembrance in the prefence of the LORD.
This is of all diftinctions far the beft;
This will with never-dying fame be blefs'd.
Ambition, do thou then this object claim,
And holy writ will fanctify thy aim,
Ev'n grace itfelf will fan the noble flame.
Memorials on earth muft fhortly ceafe,
And in oblivion fink, in quiet peace.
Thofe for whom we the greateft zeal exprefs'd,
Soon muft in filence in the coffin reft.
Ev'n letters cut into the folid ftone
With iron pens, muft foon become unknown.
But thofe who in the book of life inroll'd,
Have rank'd their names in the MESSIAH's fold ;
The bleffed LAMB has openly declar'd,
That blifs unfading fhall by them be fhar'd.
When a flight of revolving years fhall lay
Majeftic columns level with the clay ;
When brazen ftatues can no longer ftand,
Under deftructive Time's corroding hand ;

Still

Still incorruptible thefe honors rife,
And bloom triumphant in the fplendid fkies.

Lo! yonder entrance leads, as I fuppofe,
To the vault where the filent dead repofe.
Let me now turn afide, and take one peep
At thofe who in this habitation fleep.
The door on rufty hinges flow turns round,
And grates the ear with harfh, difcordant found :
As it not many vifitants enjoys,
It gives me entrance with reluctant noife.
What can this fudden trembling mean, while I
Pafs thro' the place where lifelefs bodies lie?
In thefe ftill rooms, my fpirits, nothing fear,
For " ev'n the wicked ceafe from troubling here."

Good Heav'ns! how difmal is this folemn fcene!
Here, ev'n at noon-day, night and darknefs reign.
What doleful, gloomy folitude it wears !
Not one fmall trace of cheerful joy appears ;
Sorrows and terror feem here to have made
An habitation for their hateful head.
Hark! how at ev'ry ftep the awful found
Does murm'ring from the hollow dome rebound.
Echoes, that long have flept, are now awake,
And round the walls in fighing whifpers fpeak.

A beam or two finds thro' the grates its way,
And from the coffins' nails cafts a weak ray.

So many half-hid fpectacles of woes,
Half which the baleful twilight dimly fhews;
My former apprehenfions much increafe,
And add frefh horrors to this gloomy place.
I read th' infcriptions, and by them I find
The relics of the great are here reclin'd.
No poor or vulgar dead could, fure, receive
So pompous a retirement for their grave.
The moft illuftr'ous, and right nobly great
To this have laid claim as their laft retreat;
And in this place, indeed, they all appear
A fhadowy pre-eminence to fhare.
In filent pomp, and mournful rank they lie,
In fepulchres which fhine confpicuoufly.
While with fmall ceremony meaner dead
" In the pit's ftones prepare their filent bed."

My apprehenfions wake from their furprife;
Here are no fprites but which from fear arife,
But it amazes me when I behold
The wonders that thefe nether fcenes unfold,
Thofe who on vaft revenues lately liv'd,
And from whole lordfhips confequence deriv'd;
In half a dozen feet of earth repofe,
While a few fheets of lead the whole inclofe.
Splendid apartments, and rich furniture
No longer can their haughty minds allure,

The

The fhroud's the only, ornament they have,
Inftead of rooms they get the darkfome grave,
No longer gawdy retinues of ftate
Around this folitary dome await;
No more the lordly equipages ply
For their dead mafter, who can't them enjoy;
Nothing but fable banners, which appear
The figns of triumph o'er their flaves to wear;
Or ftatues hid by duft, which, while the gay
Regardlefs world in pleafure rolls away,
The fculptor's hand the workman's fkill has
       fhewn,
And taught foft tears to flow from folid ftone.
Where is the ftar which on the breaft was plac'd?
Or coronet which once the temple's grac'd?
The tattered efcutcheon now we find,
And the atchievement, beaten with the wind,
Are the fole marks of dignity refign'd.
Thofe who drew from grand anceftors their name
And pedigree, here drop their lofty claim.
With creeping things they kindred now retain,
And quarter arms with reptiles the moft mean,
" They to corruption fay, My father be;
" To worms, My mother and my fifter fee!"
O mortifying truth! enough to wean
Defire moft fanguine from a world fo vain;
One would imagine it enough to make
The foul from its deep lethargy to wake;

                  Above

Above its fickly fatisfactions rife,
Its fliting treasures, and its fading joys.
Or should they still with arrogance assume
The style of grandeur in the lonely tomb;
Alas! how weak would the pretence appear!
The oftentatious vanity how clear!

What's the world to thefe heaps of breathlefs
    clay?
What happinefs did their purfuits convey?
What are their pleafures? Bubbles ftor'd with
    nought.
Their honors what? A dream that is forgot.
What the fum total of their blifs below?
Or what gains did from their enjoyments flow?
Perhaps to inexperienc'd men it fhew'd
A form of fomething wonderful and good;
But lo! now Death has weigh'd it in his fcale,
And lin'd it out, what does the whole avail?

Indulge, my foul, a thoughtful paufe, and fee
With mindful look each trifling gaiety,
From which fuch mighty joys were wont to rife,
As your affections feiz'd and charm'd your eyes.
Examine nicely each alluring bait,
Here, of their value form an eftimate.
Suppofe thyfelf firft eminently plac'd,
And with the favorites of fortune grac'd;

Who

Who in the lap of pleafure roll away,
Shining in robes of honor, always gay,
And fwim in tides of boundlefs riches; yet
The paffing-bell will foon thy end repeat.
When once that iron call has fummon'd thee
To future teft, where would thefe pleafures be?
At that fix'd point, how all the vain parade
By the luxurious and great difplay'd;
Their pompous pageantry, and lofty pride,
Will into thin and empty air fubfide!
And is this ftate fill'd with fuch happinefs,
That we fo eagerly fhould to it prefs?

Ye mighty relics of loud founding ranks,
Your names magnificent claim my beft thanks;
Of this world's littlenefs you've taught me more
Than all the volumes which I have in ftore.
A winding-fheet, nobility's array,
And all your grandeur mould'ring into clay;
To us the ftrongeft teftimonies bring,
Of the fmall worth of each terreftrial thing.
Never, in truth, did Providence record
In fo ftrong chara¢ters this awful word,
As in the lifelefs afhes of his Grace,
Or my Lord's corpfe, whofe vital functions ceafe.
Let others cringing, if they pleafe, refort;
And humbly to your wealthy fons pay court;
Ignobly fawning their requefts renew,
And for preferments anxioufly fue;

In

In penfive contemplations oft my mind
Is to their fathers' fepulchres confin'd;
And from their fleeping duft learns to reftrain
My expeclations from all mortal men;
From each undue attachment free to climb
O'er all the little interefts of time;
O'er the delufive joys of pomp to rife,
And all wealth's gawdy tinfel to defpife;
Still above all the empty fhades to live
Which a vain, tranfitory world can give.

Hark! what a found is that? In fuch a place
Each noife my former fears ferves to increafe.
It breaks again upon the filent air,
Solemn and flow—the ftriking clock I hear.
One would imagine that it was defign'd
To fix the meditations of my mind.
Methinks it fays Amen, and fets a feal
To each improving hint it may reveal.
Of my appointed time it feems to fay,
Another portion has now fled away.
It chimes to me juft like the paffing-bell,
And is of " my departed hours the knell."
'Tis the watch-word to vigilance and care,
And crys, " redeem the time," in reafon's ear.
" Catch opportunity's refrefhing gale,
" Catch it frefh breathing, left away it fteal;

" Ere

" Ere it fhall irrecoverably ftray,
" Since life's fhort fpan does by degrees decay.
" Lo all thy minutes are upon the ftretch,
" And ftrive with fpeed eternity to reach.
" Now to eternity thou draweft near,
" And art to endlefs time a borderer ;
" You make advances always to the ftate
" On which you thoughtfully now contemplate."
O ! may the admonition be imprefs'd
Deep on a willing and attentive breaft !
O ! may it heav'ns arithmetic fupply,
" My days to count, my heart to fenfe apply !"

Often, yea, often have I walk'd below
Th' impending promontory's craggy brow ;
I fometimes did thro' lonely places ftray,
And o'er the gloomy defert bend my way ;
Thro' dreary caverns frequently did prefs,
And penetrate their innermoft recefs ;
But Nature never, fure, beheld before
With form fo dreadful and tremendous lour ;
Nor ever was with like impreffions fill'd,
Which with cold awe my breaft and vitals chill'd;
Which each black arch, thefe mouldy walls af-
        ford,
Surrounded, and with rueful objects ftor'd;
Where melancholy, melancholy dread,
Her raven wings inceffantly has fpread.

L

Let me no more in thefe damp places dwell ;
And now, difmal obfcurity, farewell !
And ye, moft doleful feats, and fhades of night !
Gladly I vifit the returning light.

A fuperficial profpeft having caft
On thefe fad domes, where mortals reft at laft ;
My prying mind prompts me without delay,
To a more clofe and intimate furvey.
And could we open lay the tomb again,
And fee what thofe are now, who once were men ;
How would the view, to our aftonifh'd eyes,
Raife in our bofoms forrow and furprize !
How would we ftart the wond'rous change to trace,
The mighty change, of all the human race !
How grieve to fee what foul difhonor's paid,
What fmall account is of our nature made,
When in their fubterraneous lodgments laid !

Lo ! here the gay and fweetly winning face,
Which wore inceffantly attraftive grace ;
And once of fmiles and lovelinefs was full,
Grins horribly a naked, ghaftly fkull.
Eyes, which more bright than diamonds were con-
    fefs'd,
And glanc'd fweet lightning on the coldeft breaft :
Alas ! where are they ? Or where fhall we find
The links which once thefe rolling fparklers join'd?

                          Thefe

These orbs eclips'd, in total darkness loft,
No more bewitching, radiant glories boaft.
The tongue, that could harmonic charms com-
    mand,
And pow'rful eloquence, in this ftrange land
Has " forgot all its burning;" and now where
Are thofe lov'd ftrains that ravifh'd ev'ry ear?
Where is perfuafion's flow, with charms replete,
That could our judgments wholly captivate?
The mafter fkill'd in language, and fweet founds,
Is filent as the night which him furrounds.
The pamper'd flefh, fo lately cloathed gay,
In purple, linen, and in rich array,
Is rudely cover'd here with clods of clay!
Once the nice, gentle creature could not dare
" To lay its foot upon the ground," through
    fear,
So delicate and weak it was;" but lo!
It fleeps in clammy earth enwrapped now;
Inftead of downy pillows refts its head
On a cold, rocky, gravel-formed bed.
Here " ftrong men bow themfelves; and here
The arm's unftrung, ftout finews loofen'd are,
Limbs, of activity and ftrength poffefs'd,
And brawny joints, repofe in fullen reft;
The bones, as bars of iron ftrong, become
An heap of duft in the lone, darkfome tomb.

The

The man of bufinefs here forgets his aims,
And lays afide his pleafing, fav'rite fchemes;
He ceafes to perplex himfelf in vain,
And difcontinues the purfuit of gain.
A total ftand does in this place arife
To commerce, and the fale of merchandize.
Here, as when *Solomon* his temple rear'd,
No ftroke of hammer or of ax is heard.
The winding-fheet, the coffin, and the tomb,
To our devices give the utmoft doom;
" Hitherto they may, but no farther come."
The fons of pleafure here in endlefs night
Take a laft farewell of each dear delight.
No longer does the fenfualift here
Anoint with oil, or fragrant rofe-buds wear:
No more his time on lively mufic wafte,
Nor revel longer at the drunken feaft.
Inftead of tables fumptuoufly fill'd,
With all the plenty elegance can yield;
Himfelf the poor voluptuary gives,
A treat whereon the fatten'd infect lives;
" The reptile on his flefh feeds eagerly,
" And the worm feafts on him delicioufly."
Here all the winning graces difappear,
And blooming beauty drops her luftre here.
Oh! how her rofes wither and decay!
Her lillies languifh in this chilling clay!

How

How the grand leveller contempt does throw
On what with pleafure made our bofoms glow!
With what deformity has he defil'd
What had before the world in bondage held!

   Now could the captivated lover gaze
On the dear nymph which once could fo much
      pleafe,
What great aftonifhment would on him feize!
" Is this the charmer, whom not long ago
" I fondly doated on, and loved fo.
" I faid fhe was incomparably fair,
" That fhe did fomething more than mortal
     " fhare.
" Her form in fymmetry itfelf was drefs'd,
" And elegance fhone in her air confefs'd;
" The graces all attended in her train,
" And peerlefs beauties forg'd the filken chain.
" Mufic was in her words; but when fhe fpoke
" Encouragement, my raptures fhe awoke.
" How my heart danc'd to the delightful found,
" While in her converfe I all comfort found!
" Can fhe, fome weeks ago the queen of love,
" Now fo infufferably loathfome prove
" Where are thofe blufhing cheeks, alas! now
     " fled!
" And where thofe fweet lips, as the coral red!

                  " Where

" Where that white neck, on which the curling
    " load
" In glossy ringlets elegantly flow'd!
" With numberless perfections of the face,
" Accompany'd with each becoming grace!
" The dreadful alteration me amaz'd!
" On the bright meteor I fondly gaz'd:
" While like a splendid star it shone, methought
" It was with lasting and firm transport fraught.
" But how, alas! has it so soon decay'd!
" Fall'n from an orb in which it only stray'd!
" Shall the sole trace that it on earth must leave
" Be a vile body, putrid in the grave!"

Lie, poor *Florella!* lie deep as you must,
In obscure darkness, mixing with the dust.
Let night, with her impenetrable shade,
For ever o'er thy beauties be display'd.
Thy dome and thy condition now agree;
To thy disgrace let no eye witness be:
But let thy living sisters view thy state,
When in the glass their form they contemplate.
When the sweet image pleasingly shall rise,
And vast perfections open to their eyes;
When boundless charms, with animating grace,
And consc'ous elegance, glow in each face;
When tempting minutes dangers great conceal,
And vain ideas in their breasts prevail;

4   Then

Then let them think what horrid gloom is drawn
Over a face which once like their's did dawn;
A face, in which the brighteft features fhone
With brilliant beauty, blooming as their own.
They by fuch feafonable thoughts may find
Bounds to the toils they have to drefs affign'd ;
And may acquire more earneft care to clean,
Not outfide cafkets, but the pearls within.
It then might prove their higheft wifh to live
In ev'ry virtue grace divine can give;
To have their minds with real goodnefs ftor'd,
After the pattern of their bleffed LORD.

And would this any of their charms conceal?
Or from their perfons any honors fteal ?
Quite the reverfe : It would fpread matchlefs
　　grace,
And heav'nly glory, o'er the faireft face;
It would accomplifhments more winning give ;
From it more lovelinefs they would receive.
And what is yet a more inviting thing,
Thefe flow'rs would flourifh in eternal fpring;
Nor fade with nature, nor with time decay,
But bloom for ever in moft rich array;
With ornaments untarnifh'd always fhine,
And ev'n in wint'ry age fhed fweets divine.
But that which fhall their greateft praifes fwell,
And beft thefe noble qualities can tell ;

　　　　　　　　　　　　That

That which muft, fure, the trueft pleafure give,
Is; as the afhes of the phœnix live,
From their hallow'd remains ere long will rife
A form illuftrious to gild the fkies;
As wings of bleffed angels ever bright,
And lafting as new *Zion*'s beaming light.

For me; the thought of this fad change fhall
    ftill
My mind with fhame and endlefs forrow fill,
For paying court to flefh; and make me fear
From joys fo brittle happinefs to fhare.
It fhall inftruct me henceforth not to prize
The comforts which from well-join'd clay arife;
Tho' in one perfon elegantly meet,
A form quite perfect, and a foul moft fweet.
'Tis heav'ns laft, beft, and crowning gift; to
    be
Receiv'd with gratitude, and hail'd with joy;
As the prime bleffing it can to us lend;
Not ftrains of fulfome worfhip to expend;
Nor in th' incenfe of flattery convey'd,
As adoration to a goddefs paid.
I truft that it my doating eyes will cure,
And make me walk in wifdom's path fecure;
Incline me always preference to fhew
To " charms that from meek and good fpirits
    " flow;"

Before

Before each fleeting, ornamental grace,
Which decorates with white and red the face.

   My roving meditations I reprefs
From long excurfions thro' fcenes of diftrefs.
Fancy awhile attention ftrictly paid,
To the foliloquy a lover made;
But judgment now again refumes the fway,
And while her lips inftructive truths convey,
My mind fhe happily directs and bends,
To felf-concerning thoughts which wifdom lends.
Howe'er, when on the whole fcene I look'd round,
With mortal objects, and death's trophies crown'd;
I could not fail to fmite my breaft and figh,
The nobleft of things vifible to fpy
" Under the pale horfe and his rider lie:"
While I in thefe pathetic terms exclaim,
" What ills, thou *Adam*, from thy failings came!"
What direful defolation haft thou brought
On the world, by thy difobedience wrought!
The pow'rful mifchiefs fee that from fin flow!
Sin, the moft ftately bodies has laid low;
Sin has on earth been fo harfh and fevere,
Among the beft of God's creation there;
That deadly bane of nature would have caft
In deepeft hell, where torments ever laft,
My better part, but that our grac'ous Lord
Himfelf a ranfom for us did afford.

       M   What

What due acknowledgments can finners fhew,
For the great gratitude to God they owe!
What can a heav'n of blefs'd believers give!
Or what warm love fhould he from them receive!
Can they with ample thanks before him bend!
Such a deliv'rer, benefactor, friend!

While my mind on thefe doleful objects refts,
A faithful monitor within fuggefts—
" Muft in me likewife this fad change fucceed?
" And am I, in like manner, doom'd to bleed?
" Am I to breathe my laft, and in my turn
" Become a corpfe, and be what I now mourn?
" Is there a time approaching, then, fo near,
" In which this body, carry'd on a bier,
" Shall all this wretched world's temptations leave,
" And be configned to its clay-cold grave?
" While fome kind friend, perhaps, at parting
        " may
" Let fall a tear, and, Oh! my brother! fay?"
Nothing more certain; and which fhall endure
Than laws of *Medes* and *Perfians*, more fure;
A firm decree has ratify'd the doom,
To which at laft all mortal men muft come.

Should now one of thofe ghaftly figures rife
From its confinement, prefent to my eyes;
In dread deformity before me ftand,
With haggard vifage lift a clatt'ring hand,

                                            And

And point it fully to my wond'ring fight ;
Or open its thin jaws, form'd to affright ;
Then with a hoarfe, tremendous murmur fpeak,
And horribly this profound filence break :
Should it addrefs me juft as *Samuel's* ghoft
Did once the fearful, trembling king accoft—
" The LORD fhall give you to the hand of death,
" And thou muft, alfo, foon refign thy breath ;
" Yet but a little while and thou fhalt be
" In the fame ftate wherein you now find me."
The folemn warning, in a way fo grave,
Muft on my mind, fure, ftrong impreffions leave :
Commands in thunder would fcarce deeper fink—
Yet I ought vaftly more to fear, I think,
That which the LORD exprefsly has declar'd,
" Thou fure fhalt die ;" and be for death pre-
   par'd.
Well then, fince fentence is againft me pafs'd,
Since by a right'ous judge I have been caft ;
And know not when the warrant may arrive;
Let me to fin die, to JEHOVAH live,.
Before I death from his juft ftroke receive.
Let me the fhort, uncertain time employ,
Which before execution I enjoy,
In making preparations for that ftate
Where does a blefs'd and better life await ;
That when the fatal time comes, when my eyes
Muft on all objects clofe below the fkies ;

    I may

I may again my Saviour efpy,
Seated majeftic in the realms on high.

Since then this frame, fo wonderfully made,
Muft to the grave be very foon convey'd;
Since all my pow'rs of flefh muft foon give way
To inactivity, gloom, and decay:
Oh! let it always be my earneft care
To ufe them right, while in my pow'r they are!
Let me the poor ftrive always to relieve,
And be " lefs ready to receive than give."
In humbleft pofture let my knees ftill bow,
Before the throne of grace, devoutly low;
While on the earth my eyes are firmly held,
With penitence and dread confufion fill'd;
Or reverently look to heav'n above,
For grac'ous mercy, and forgiving love!
In ev'ry friendly interview let ftill
The " law of kindnefs all my converfe fill;"
Or if my friends choofe rather godly fpeech,
Let ftill my tongue the gofpel of peace teach.
Oh! that in ev'ry public concourfe I
Might, like a trumpet, raife my voice on high;
And in melod'ous accents fpread around
A much more joyful and harmonic found;
While I in elevated language fing
Glad tidings which from free falvation fpring!

B e

Be ſhut ſtill reſolutely cloſe, my ears,
Againſt the wicked whiſpers ſlander bears;
And ſtrictly careful always to refrain
From filthy talking of a breath profane;
Attend to knowledge which from wiſdom breaks,
And ſtedfaſt hear when your Redeemer ſpeaks;
Imbibe the prec'ous truths deep in the mind,
And be they ſtrongly to the heart inclin'd.
Bear me, my feet, to the houſe of the LORD;
To beds with ſick, and domes with paupers ſtor'd.
As all my members ſtill on GOD depend,
May they with rev'rence always to him bend;
And may I be the willing inſtrument,
By which his praiſe may o'er the world be ſent!

Then, ye embalmers, you may ſpare your pains,
Since I by faith procure my greateſt gains;
Theſe works of faith, and labours of my love,
Are the perfumes for which my ſoul ſtill ſtrove.
Enwrapp'd in theſe I'd fear no deadly peſt,
But ſweetly in the bleſſed JESUS reſt;
Hoping that GOD will his " commandment give,"
By which again " my bones" may life receive;
Reanimate them from the ſenſeleſs clay,
At his moſt awful and appointed day;
And as gold from the fire them purify,
" I ſay not ſev'n, but ſev'n times ſeventy."

Here,

Here, then, my contemplation took its flight,
And quickly in the garden did alight,
Adjoining to the mount of *Calvary*,
On which our blefs'd Redeemer deign'd to die.
Having view'd tombs of fellow-creatures dead,
Methought I long'd to fee where CHRIST was laid.
And what a fpectacle, oh! once was here,
In this fo memorable fepulchre!
He " who for cloaths with light himfelf arrays,
" And walks upon the winged winds" with eafe;
Was pleafed frail habiliments to wear,
And with the proftrate dead a dwelling fhare.
Who can for this think any praife too great?
Or can too oft the wond'rous truth repeat?
Who, with the moft tranfporting, grateful fong,
Can think on the glad theme he dwells too long?
He, who inthron'd in glory, fits on high,
'Mongft all the heav'nly hofts diffufing joy;
Was once a body, bloody, pale, and dead,
And on this fpot repos'd his lifelefs head.

How great, Death, was thy triumph in that
    hour!
Ne'er had'ft thou captive in thy gloomy pow'r,
So excellent a prifoner before.
Did I fay prifoner? And was he fuch?
No; he was more than conqueror by much.

Than

Than *Sampson* he far mightier arofe,
When he fhook off his tranfient repofe;
Spoil'd the ftrong gates, and levell'd with the
     ground
The walls that thefe dominions dark furround.
In this, O mortals! in this you muft place
Your only hopes of comfort and of peace.
This dreadful path your Saviour has trod,
And fmooth and eafy made the rugged road.
CHRIST fleeping in the chambers of the tomb,
Has from this manfion driv'n the difmal gloom,
And left fweet odors in each dreary room.
The dying JESUS, (never let that joy
Forfake your bofoms! JESUS who did die)
Your paffport and protection fure will give
Thro' all the territories of the grave.
Truft him; they'll prove " to *Sion* a highway,"
And you fafely to paradife convey.
Believe in him, and you no lofs will find,
But endlefs gains, when to the tomb confign'd.
For hear what to this weighty point GOD faith,
" Whofo believes in me fhall ne'er fee death."
How fublime and emphatical this ftrain !
This much at leaft the mighty truth muft mean :
" The nature of that latter change fhall be
" Made for the better moft furprizingly.
" It fhall no more be for a punifhment,
" But rather as the greateft bleffing fent :

2   " It

" It fhall attended to fuch perfons hafte,
" With fuch a train of folid profits grac'd;
" That they muft not the name of death receive,
" For 'tis then only they begin to live:
" To fay that death could from fuch blifs arife,
" A happy impropriety implies.
" Their exit is the end of their frail ftate,
" As then perfection will on them await;
" Their laft groan is the prelude to their joy,
" To comfort, life, and immortality."

Weak fouls! affrighted at the paffing-bell,
Who at the fight of open'd graves turn pale;
Who fcarce a fkull or coffin can behold,
And not experience a fhudd'ring cold;
Who to the grifly tyrant bondmen are,
And quake when he his iron rod does rear;
To the LORD of your fpirits loudly cry,
And for protection on his Son rely.
By faith you'll from your flavery be freed,
And courage get on this worft fnake to tread.
Old *Simeon*, when JESUS he embrac'd,
Departed with tranquillity, well pleas'd;
When the child CHRIST in arms of flefh he
        grafp'd,
And in faith's arms the Mediator clafp'd.
That bitter perfecutor *Saul*, when crown'd
With his Redeemer, in CHRIST being found;

                                    .Longs

Longs for difmiffion from this cumbrous earth,
And is all rapture at the fight of death.
Sure I fee one more of IMMANUEL's train
Trufting in CHRIST, on his Redeemer lean;
And cheerfully to filent fhades depart,
With a compofed and exulting heart.
Under this pow'rful and blefs'd name, behold!
Numberlefs crowds of finful men grown bold,
Have fix'd their banners, and moft bravely fought,
And " by the Lamb's blood victory have got."
Thou may'ft by the example which the LORD,
The Captain of Salvation, does afford,
Undaunted ev'ry care and danger meet,
And on the king of terrors fet thy feet.
Supply'd with this fure antidote, you may
Round the hole of the afp fecurely play;
And put your hand, unconfcious of dread,
Where the dire cockatrice its den has made.
Thou may'ft feel vipers on thy mortal part,
And yet experience no deadly fmart.
You, by a joyful refurrection, will
Shake them off one day, without any ill.

Refurrection! that cheering word prepares
Joy for my foul, and lightens all my cares;
My mind it eafes of its anx'ous pains,
And an enquiry of vaft weight explains.

N   I would

I would have aſked, " wherefore in this place.
" Lie all theſe corpſes, in ſuch abject caſe?
" And is this, then, their fix'd and final doom?
" Has Death, their conqu'ror, chain'd them to
    " the tomb?
" Will he his captives ne'er from bondage free?
" Wilt thou forget them, LORD, eternally?"
No, ſaith the voice from heav'n, the word divine,
" Hope doth all good and right'ous men con-
    " fine."
There is an hour (that awful ſecrets known
To GOD, the all-foreſeeing LORD, alone)
There is a time, a fixed hour of grace,
In which an act the heav'nly ſeal will paſs,
Whereby they ſhall a full diſcharge receive,
Eternal freedom from the gloomy grave.
Then the LORD JESUS ſhall from heav'n deſcend,
While angels and archangels him attend,
And with the trump of GOD all nature rend.
Deſtruction's ſelf ſhall the dread call adore,
And graves obediently their dead reſtore.
They in the twinkling of an eye awake,
And from ten thouſand years' ſleep quickly break;
They ſpring forth like the bounding roe or deer,
To meet " the LORD eternal in the air."

And, oh! with what congratulating grace,
With how tranſporting, hearty an embrace,

Are

Are the foul and the body once more join'd,
Companions fo affectionate and kind!
But how much greater figns of love are fhewn,
When CHRIST, compaffionate, calls them his own!
The LORD, who in the clouds of heav'n does
   come,
Is their kind friend, their father, and bridegroom.
Yet they are not to fuffer any fears
From all the grandeur in which he appears.
Thofe wonderful folemnities fo dread,
Which awe and ruin thro' all nations fpread;
Serve only to inflame their love the more,
And make their hopes of happinefs flow o'er.
The awful judge, in all his mightinefs
And fplendor, vouchfafes their names to con-
   fefs;
Vouchfafes their great fidelity to tell
Before the beings that in heaven dwell;
And deigns their goodnefs to commemorate
Before the world, who on his will await.

Hark! now the thunders their dread found af-
   fuage;
The lightnings ceafe their terrifying rage;
In filent doubt th' angelic armies fee
Attentive wait the Judge's great decree!
The race of *Adam*, with an anx'ous mind,
Expect a fentence rigorous or kind.

That

That King fupreme, adorable, whofe grace
Is more than life to mortals pureft peace;
And whofe adoption is a crown of joy;
Upon the right'ous cafts a pleafing eye.
O! what a fpeech from his lips fweetly breaks!
What cheering accents, as he grac'ous fpeaks!
And with what ecftacies of joy and praife,
They in the bofoms of the faithful blaze!
" To you, my people, I acceptance give,
" For ye are they who did my name believe.
" Lo! ye are they who have yourfelves deny'd,
" And with firm truft ftill on my pow'r rely'd.
" No fpot or blemifh in your frames I fee,
" Wafh'd in my blood, cloath'd in my purity.
" Renewed by my fpirit, ye on earth
" Have prais'd me, and been conftant unto death.
" Come then, ye fervants of the living *Lord*,
" Enjoy the comforts which he will afford.
" Come, then, ye bleffed of the LORD above,
" Children of light, who fhare my father's love;
" Poffefs a kingdom that fhall ne'er remove;
" Receive the crown that fadeth not away,
" And tafte of pleafures which can ne'er decay!"

The right'ous then, this fmalleft good fhall gain,
That they no more will languifh under pain;
That ficknefs ne'er again fhall fhew her face,
Her doleful vifage, in their dwelling-place.

At

At that great period death itfelf fhall die,
And be quite " fwallow'd up in victory."
That fatal jav'lin, whofe unerring dart
Drank monarch's blood, and pierc'd the mortal
      heart;
Death, which all *Adam*'s children has annoy'd,
Shall at that time be utterly deftroy'd.
That fcythe enormous, which in darkeft fhade
The greateft empires has fo often laid;
Which years and generations can remove,
Shall then perpetually ufelefs prove.
Sin, alfo, which, thou bloody tyrant, fills
Thy hateful quiver with tormenting ills;
Sin, which to thee refiftlefs ftrength could yield,
And crown'd thee victor in each horrid field;
Which drove thy arrows with unbounded might,
Shall then be cover'd in unceafing night.
Whetever's frail, or could our minds deprave,
Shall be thrown off for ever in the grave.
All yet to come is excellence fupreme,
Confummate blifs, and tranfports ftill the fame.

Eternity! O vaft eternity!
Thou doft our boldeft, ftrongeft thoughts defy!
All our refearches thy great depths to gain,
Are ufelefs, ineffectual, and vain!
Who can with landmarks thy dimenfions bound?
Or who find plumbets the abyfs to found?

Arith-

Arithmeticians have rules to fhew
The feafons which progreffive time goes thro':
Aftronomers have inftruments to fpy,
And tell how diftant all the planets lie:
Can numbers ftate, or any lines unfold
The lengths and breadths eternity fhould hold?
" Its height is more than heav'n; what canft thou
    do?
" Its depth is more than hell; what canft thou
    " know?
" Its meafures doth our leffer earth contain,
" And in its breadth it holds the watry main."

Myfterious exiftence! vaft excefs!
Not to be render'd by deductions lefs,
Or by the largeft fums we can exprefs!
Extent impoffible to be confin'd
By any boundaries by us affign'd!
None can fay after wond'rous ages' wafte,
" That fo much of eternity is paft."
For when ten thoufand centuries are gone,
It is but juft commencing to come on;
When millions more have run their ample round,
It will no nearer to its end be found.
When ages, num'rous as the bloom of fpring,
Join'd to the herbage which the fummers bring;
Augmented by the ears of autumn's grain,
All multiply'd by winter's dropping rain;

       And

And when ten thoufand times ten thoufand more,
Added to numbers infinite before;
More than imagination can convey,
Or yet fimilitude have pafs'd away;
Eternity, amazing, vaft, immenfe,
Will only at that period commence;
Or rather (if I in thefe terms may fpeak)
Will its beginning but begin to make.

O ! what a pleafing awful thought is this !
With dread abounding, and yet full of blifs.
May this give the alarm to all our fears,
Quicken our hopes, and animate our cares !
May it inftruct us faithfully to live,
And fortitude to our endeavours give !
An inconceivable and endlefs ftate
Does fhortly, very fhortly us await ;
Let us be diligent *now*, to infure
An entrance into happinefs fecure !
Let us our utmoft induftry apply,
Since no fcene alters in futurity.
The wheel ne'er turns, nor objects change re-
        ceive;
All's fix'd, immoveable, beyond the grave.
Whether we, then, are feated on the throne,
Or ftretch'd on racks, in agony to groan ;
Juftice inflexible, or endlefs grace,
Will a firm feal to our condition place.

The

The faints their happinefs rejoicing prove,
Amidft the fmiles of never ending love ;
Their harps inceffantly to joy they fit ;
No interruption their triumphs admit.
The ruin which the wicked undergo,
Is filled with irremediable woe.
The fatal fentence which the LORD fhall feal,
Is fix'd immoveable, without repeal.
They cannot one faint, glimm'ring hope receive,
Their doleful habitations e'er to leave ;
But all things the fame difmal afpect bear,
And which they everlaftingly muft wear.

The wicked—How my penfive bofom fhrinks,
When on their dreadful mifery it thinks !
It wav'd the horrid theme with careful awe ;
And feems yet willing from it to withdraw.
But it is better for fome minutes, fure,
To cogitate, than endlefs pains endure.
Perhaps, the thought of their fad torments may
Some terrible advantages difplay ;
Perhaps, the thought of their augmented woes
May to my foul fome mighty good difclofe ;
May teach me JESUS with more joy to fee,
" Who from the pit unfathom'd fets me free."
May hurry me, like the avenger's fword,
To this fole city with protection ftor'd,
Which to fad finners refuge can afford.

As

As malefactors in the prison's gloom
Fearfully wait their trial yet to come;
So here the wicked in confusion lie,
And suffer torments to eternity.
They must for ever dwell in this dire place,
For " their departure was devoid of peace."
Their closing eye-lids were with horrors drown'd,
Which dealt inceffantly a direful wound;
And sad forebodings in their minds did raise,
" That the black darknefs would not ever ceafe."
When the laft ficknefs feiz'd their tott'ring
        frame,
And the inevitable fummons came;
When at their life they faw their archer aim;
And to the ftring perceiv'd the fatal reed
Fitted, and pofting with unerring fpeed,
When they experienc'd the deadly dart,
Transfixed deeply in the vital part—
Good GOD! what fearfulnefs muft them annoy!
What horrid dread their ev'ry hope deftroy!
How ftedfaftly their ghaftly eyes they keep,
Shudd'ring at the tremendous, gloomy fteep!
Afraid exceffively this world to leave,
Yet utterly incapable to live!
What pale reviews, what ftartling profpects rife,
Confpiring all their fouls to agonize!
When their paft life they ponder, they behold
Moft melancholy fcenes themfelves unfold;

O   GOD's

God's mercy flighted, unrepented fin,
And grace withdrawing from the foul within.
They forward look, nought opens to their fight,
But that great God who forms his judgment right,
They at the dread tribunal muft appear,
And pay their awful, folemn reck'ning there.
Around them their affrighted eyes they roll,
Viewing the friends who their diftrefs condole,
Who, if partakers in their wicked life,
Muft add frefh anguifh to their former grief;
When they confider, in this dreadful ftate,
That this their guilt muft further aggravate;
When they perceive they have not finn'd alone,
But have made others act as they have done,
If their friends are to holinefs inclin'd,
This heaps new forrow on each troubled mind;
It greatly heightens their diftracting pain,
That they-fhall ne'er enjoy their fight again;
But at a diftance unapproachable,
And parted by a gulph unpaffable.

They at the laft, perhaps, begin to pray,
Striving by that their terrors to allay;
With anx'ous wifh they to the Lord apply,
And for affiftance to Jehovah cry:
With trembling lips their falt'ring words they
  pour,
To that great God, " who kills and can reftore."
        But

But why, oh! why have they fo long delay'd
Pray'rs which to Heav'n they fhould before have
    made?
Could they have hopes of any blefs'd reward,
When to God's counfels they paid no regard?
And why did they incorrigible ftand,
Unmindful ever of his great command?
How oft were they forewarn'd of this fad ftate,
And what dire punifhments would them await?
How oft importunately urg'd by God,
To turn to him, and fhun his vengeful rod?
I wifh the Lord may on them mercy pour,
And fave them at this laft alarming hour!
I wifh they may his kind forgivenefs meet,
Ere deep damnation burfts beneath their feet!
But oh! affronted majefty may then
Regardlefs of all their complaints remain;
Nor deign to work a miracle of grace,
To give fuch obftinate tranfgreffors peace.
He may, for aught that any mortal knows,
" Joy at their griefs, and laugh at all their woes;
" May be unheedful of their agony,
" And mock them when their fear approacheth
    " nigh."

Thus they lie groaning with fevereft pains,
In tortures fpending what of life remains;

       With

With chilling fweat their bodies running o'er,
Which iffues coldly from each open'd pore ;
Convulfive throes now ftruggle with the heart,
Grief infupportable throbs thro' each part ;
Innumerable fhafts of forrow fpend
Their rage upon them, and their confcience rend.

If the ungodly fuffer, then, this death,
And with fad torments thus refign their breath ;
" My foul, do not into their fecret come,
" Left you fhould meet with their eternal doom !
" Do not, mine honor, with fuch men unite,
" But from their meetings take thy daring flight!"
How awfully accomplifh'd are the words,
The truths which infpir'd wifdom ftill affords !
" Sin always bears the moft deftructive load,
" Tho' feemingly in the commiffion good ;
" Like bites of ferpents it inflicteth pains,
" And like the adders, hidden ftings contains."
Then, thefe loft wretches' wicked courfes fhun,
And from their tents with expedition run.

How happy would this diffolution be,
Should it from all their tortures fet them free !
Alas ! thefe tribulations only are
The bitter prelude to their future care ;
Which one drop of the " cup of trembling" give,
Mingled with anguifh they muft yet receive.

No

No fooner fhall the lateft pang expel
The foul, reluctant, from its earthly cell;
But they are hurry'd with moft rapid flight,
To God's much injur'd and offended fight;
Not by the conduct or beneficence
Which bleffed angels cheerfully difpenfe;
But left to infults of the fiends accurs'd,
Who lately tempted them to deeds the worft,
Who now upbraid them for their lives mifpent,
And to eternity will them torment.
Who can conceive their forrow and diftrefs,
Or their confufion properly exprefs;
When inexcufable and guilty, they
In fight of their incens'd Creator ftay?
They are received with an angry brow;
" The God that made them has no mercy now."
The fpring of happinefs, the prince of peace,
Rejects them with abhorrence and difgrace;
He gives them o'er to chains of black defpair,
And to receptacles of gloomy care;
'Till that more public, miferable ftate,
Which at the great day fhall on them await.
The phials then of unrelenting woe,
Will thefe unhappy creatures overflow.
The holy law, of which they made fo light;
The gofpel, which they hitherto did flight;
The pow'r, which they repeatedly abus'd;
The goodnefs, which fo often they refus'd;

Will

Will then, in their exemplary decay,
With richeſt honors their negleɛt repay.
Then GOD the LORD, who ſhall without repeaſ
His juſt diſpleaſure on the wicked deal ;
Will draw the arrow to the head, and bind
Them as the mark of his relentleſs mind.

A reſurreɛtion from the gloomy grave,
Will to their ſouls no privileges give ;
But immortality itſelf ſhall ſhed
Eternal curſes on each wretched head.
Would they not bleſs with warmeſt thanks the
    tomb,
" Where all things lie in everlaſting gloom ?"
Would they not wiſh for ever there to hide,
And in its dark receſſes ſtill reſide ?
Their perſons, though, the grave will not con-
    ceal,
Or o'er their wicked aɛtions draw a veil.
They alſo muſt awake ; they muſt ariſe,
And meet their Judge immortal, in the ſkies :
That great Judge before whom " heav'n's pillars
    quake,
" And earth's foundations to the centre ſhake :"
A Judge, long-ſuff'ring once, with mercy ſtor'd,
A once compaſſionate and friendly LORD ;
But now unalterably fix'd to ſhew
Stubborn offenders, what great evils flow
From

3

From their provoking of Almighty God;
What 'tis to trample on their Saviour's blood;
And what it is with defpite to receive
The grac'ous overtures his fpirit gave,

Oh! what perplexity will then abound!
And what diftraction muft the fouls confound
Of wicked rebels! when the final call
Before God's judgment-feat fhall bring them all!
" What can they do in this day of diftrefs,"
Which feals their punifhment without redrefs!
Where? How? Or from whence can they feek
    relief?
Which of the faints will mitigate their grief?
Where can they find eafe from their wretched
    ftate?
Alas! 'tis all in vain; 'tis all too late.
Friends and acquaintance here no longer own
That they before were ever to them known;
Now heav'n and earth forfake them to the woe
Which they eternally muft undergo;
And ev'n the Mediator's felf denies,
In thefe black moments, any hopes to rife.
To fly, will now impracticable be,
To clear themfelves, impoffibility;
And to implore in fupplicating ftrain,
Would now be unavailable and vain.

                    Behold!

Behold! the book of judgment's open laid,
The ſtricteſt ſcrutiny will now be made;
The ſecrets of all hearts ſhall be diſcloſ'd,
And ev'ry wickedneſs to ſight expos'd;
The things which hitherto were hid in night,
Shall be diſplayed in the cleareſt light.
How empty, ineffectual, and bare
With each refined artifice appear;
Will which the hypocrites have men deceiv'd,
And worthy characters from them receiv'd!
The jealous GOD, the mighty LORD, who hath
Been round their bed; has been about their path;
And hath ſeen all the ways which they have run;
" Before them ſets the things that they have done."
They can't to one in thouſands anſwer make,
But in the awful judgment trembling quake.
Speechleſs with guilt, and branded with diſgrace,
They dare not view the bleſſed angels' face.
Oh! what a favour would the foaming ſea,
By hiding their aſhamed heads, convey!
How very willingly would they be hurl'd
Beneath the ruins of the tott'ring world!

If the contempt that's thrown upon them, then,
Can cauſe ſo inſupportable a pain;
" How will their hearts ſtand," when with woes
     prepar'd,
The ſword of endleſs indignation's rear'd,

And

And fiercely wav'd round each defenceleſs head,
There its abundant agonies to ſhed ;
Or aim'd directly at the naked breaſt,
That they eternally may be diſtreſs'd !
How muſt the wretches ſcream with wild ſur-
    priſe,
Rending the heav'ns with ſad, bewailing cries ;
When " the right-aiming thunderbolts" of GOD,
To execute his orders, " go abroad !"
Go, at the dreadfully commanding word,
To drive them from the kingdom of the LORD ;
Not to involve them in a moment's pain,
Or tortures which but one ſhort hour remain ;
But into all the reſtleſſneſs and care,
The pangs which fires unquenchable prepare,
And griefs of everlaſting, black deſpair !

   O ! miſery of miſeries ! ſad fate !
Too ſhocking for reflection to repeat.
But if it is ſo diſmal to foreſee,
And that when view'd ſo very diſtantly ;
And with ſome comfortable hopes combin'd,
Some expectations an eſcape to find ;
How hard, how inconceivably ſevere,
How vaſtly bitter theſe dire pangs to bear ;
Without a reſpite from ſuch agony,
Thro' hopeleſs ages of eternity !

       Who

Who can the bowels of compaffion fhew?
In whom do fentiments of pity glow?
Who for his fellow-creatures can conceive
Tender concern, their hardfhips to relieve?
Who is he? For CHRIST's fake, and in GOD's
     name,
Let active zeal his fympathy proclaim.
Let him befeech mankind to feek the LORD,
While in their reach he may himfelf afford;

To throw their arms rebellious away,
Ere the acts of indemnity decay;
Submiffively the holy LAMB adore,
Who for his own has perfect blifs in ftore.
Let us to men here act the friendly part,
Let our benevolence itfelf exert,
To prove the feelings of a tender heart:
By warning whomfoever may be gain'd,
Quickly to take the wings of faith unfeign'd;
With undelay'd repentance ftraight comply,
And " from yet abfent indignation fly."

Upon the whole; what great difcoveries,
Immenfe, ftupendous, open to my eyes!
Do thou, my foul, to ferious thoughts re-
     fign'd,
In faithful memory keep them confin'd.

Still

Still recollect them with a prudent breast,
When you lie down, or when you rise from
    rest.
Do thou, when walking, always them receive
As the companions who best counsel give;
To them, when talking, strict attention pay,
As prompters who the soundest truths convey;
And to whatever business you attend,
Heed them as those who will thee best be-
    friend.
If you by these considerations move,
Your ev'ry view will more extensive prove;
All your affections will exalted be,
And rise in value more conspic'ously;
And you will soar on more majestic wings,
O'er tantalizing reach of earthly things.
Thy bosom with these influences fill'd,
That on which your supreme desires you build,
The scope of your endeavours, will be then
The approbation of the Lord to gain;
Who will with glory fill the judgment-seat,
And the decisive sentence there repeat.
His pleasure for thy rule will to thee leave
The greatest happiness you can receive;
His glory be thy aim; his holy grace
With strength unceasing will thy faith in-
    crease.

Wonder,

Wonder, O man, with admiration fee
The great events now near approaching thee;
View the ftrange prodigies which foon will fall
With dread awe on the univerfal ball;
Events fo vaft, that nothing here below,
No finite being can their meafure know.
Events, by which whatever yet was thought
Great in this world, will be reduc'd to nought;
And will to littlenefs and nothing tear
The annals of which mankind took fuch care:
Which (JESUS, for their coming give us grace!
Be our defence, O LORD, when they take
    place!)
Are with the fixed, everlafting fate
Of all the living and the dead replete.
I muft behold the graves then cleaving wide,
And ocean teeming from its mighty tide;
Muft unfufpected multitudes efpy,
And countlefs crowds together fwarming fly;
Muft fee from both the thronging nations fpring,
To hear the fentence of their Judge and King:
Muft fee the world blaze with deftructive flame,
To non-exiftence turn'd, from which it came;
Stand at the downfall of mortality,
And an attendant on dead nature be.
I muft the great, expanfive fkies behold,
Themfelves like fcrolls of paper clofely fold;

                And

And the incarnate GOD, of boundlefs worth,
From brightnefs inacceffible come forth;
On whom ten thoufand thoufand angels wait,
While he confirms both men's and devil's fate.
I muft fee time conceal'd in endlefs night
And vaft eternity difclos'd to fight;
Muft enter on a new exiftence now,
Which never nearer to an end fhall grow,

   Let the moft vain imagination fay,
Ought I not heedfully to watch my way;
The purity of my belief to try,
And not too much on human ftrength rely?
Are there inquiries worthy greater care,
Or for importance can with them compare?
Does not this give an infinite command,
With girded loins before the LORD to ftand;
To trim my lamp, and my beft garments wear,
When I before the " bridegroom fhall ap-
     pear?"
That I, wafh'd in the bleffed, bloody tide,
The fountain open'd in my Sav'our's fide;
Clad with the marriage - garment which was
     wove
By his obedience and tranfcendent love;
May, " unreprovable, be found in peace,
Unblameable," by his abundant grace.

                        Elfe,

Elfe, how fhall I with boldnefs ftand, when all
The ftars of heav'n from their bright orbits
      fall ?
How fhall I come with courage in my face,
Erect and daring, fearlefs of difgrace ;
When ev'n the earth, from its foundations low,
Is like a drunkard, reeling to-and-fro ?
How fhall I then look up with pleafing joy,
And behold my falvation drawing nigh ;
When hearts of multitudes thro' terror fail,
And dreadful agonies their fouls affail ?

  Now, Madam, left my meditations may
Set in a cloud, and any gloom difplay
Unpleafing to your mind, let me once more
The brightning profpects of the juft explore.
Their joyful expectations held in fight,
May ferve our doleful mufings to delight ;
May our fad thoughts exhilarate, which were
Long fix'd on fepulchres and objects drear ;
And have been hovering fo much around
Infernal darknefs, and the depths profound :
As a large plain, with cheerful verdure fill'd,
Can to the eye relief and vigor yield ;
Which fome minute or glaring thing had tir'd,
By being too attentively admir'd.

                  The

The good and righteous repofing lie,
And in earth's bofom quietnefs enjoy;
As wary pilots cautioufly feek,
In ftormy feafons, fome well-fhelter'd creek;
There to partake of harmony and reft,
While dreadful tempefts this low world infeft.
Here they are in fafe anchorage; and here
No hidden fhoals, or foundering fands are near;
Freed from iniquity's prevailing feas,
They live in calm ferenity and eafe;
No powerful temptations now can block
Their paffage, or impel them on fin's rock,
But we fhall very fhortly fee them hoife
Their flag of hope, which with glad breezes
        flys;
Riding before a kindly blowing wind,
Of worth atoning, and a loving mind;
'Till with the fails of faith affur'd they prefs
Into the port of endlefs happinefs.

Then, may the honor'd, much efteemed friend,
The lady for whom thefe lines have been penn'd;
Rich in good works, in heav'nly tempers great,
But with CHRIST's merit vaftly more replete;
O may fhe with a favorable gale,
Enter the harbour, like a ftately fail,
Juft from a noble expedition come,
Return'd fuccefsful, and in triumph home;

                            While

While acclamations, joy, and honour wait
With fhouts inceffant, on her lucky ftate!
While my fmall bark, attendant on the joy,
Cheerfully joining the folemnity,
And a partaker of the victory;
Shall flowly, with a peaceful, gentle wind,
Humbly obfequious, glide on behind;
And both in the lov'd, wifh'd for haven reft,
With perfect blifs, and endlefs fafety blefs'd!

THE

THE

5TH, 6TH, AND 7TH CHAPTERS

OF THE

GOSPEL ACCORDING TO ST. MATTHEW,

BEING

CHRIST'S SERMON ON THE MOUNT,

VERSIFIED.

─────────

LUKE, 21ft Chap. 33d Ver.

" HEAVEN AND EARTH SHALL PASS AWAY, BUT " MY WORDS SHALL NOT PASS AWAY."

─────────

CHAPTER V.

AND when the LORD great multitudes efpy'd,
He ftraightway gain'd a lofty mountain's fide;
Where being feated, his difciples came,
Whom he inftructed in this godly theme:
The poor in fpirit are fupremely blefs'd,
For their's is heav'n, and everlafting reft.
Blefs'd are the mourners, who at laft fhall find
That GOD will comfort the afflicted mind.

Q Blefs'd

Blefs'd are the meek and gentle, who fhall gain
A feat on earth, and endlefs blifs obtain.
Who thirft and hunger for religion's fake
Shall plenty ftill of boundlefs joys partake.
Blefs'd are the merciful, for they fhall know
The fweets of mercy which themfelves beftow.
Blefs'd are the pure, of juft and upright ways,
Who God fhall view, and tafte celeftial eafe.
Blefs'd are the peace-makers, for they fhall be
The fons of God, and his falvation fee.
Thofe who for righteoufnefs' fake feel woe,
And perfecution in this world below,
Are blefs'd, fince heav'n and happinefs await
Their glad removal from a human ftate.
Your cafe is blefs'd when men fhall you revile
And to your charge lay actions grofsly vile;
When varied wickednefs of you they fpeak,
And falfely witnefs 'gainft you for my fake;
Exult exceedingly, with joy elate,
As your reward in heav'n is vaftly great;
For thus with rancour keen did they purfue,
And hate, the prophets who preceded you.
Ye are the falt of earth, which, fhould it lofe
Its favour once, is of nó farther ufe;
But worthlefs grows, and may be caft away,
And trodden down among the beaten clay.
Ye are the light by which mankind fhould move,
Who wifh to merit great JEHOVAH's love.

A city,

A city, fure, that's built on rifing ground,
Muft be confpicuous to all around.
Men light not candles, that a bufhel may
Conceal the luftre which they would convey ;
But, plac'd in candlefticks, they banifh night,
And deal to all the family their light :
Then let your light before mankind fo fhine,
That they may imitate your acts divine ;
And proper glory to your father give,
Who to eternity in heav'n does live.
Let no fuch thought e'er harbour in your breaft,
That I the law or prophets will moleft ;
I came, fubmiffive to my Father's will,
That I the law and prophets might fulfil.
For unto you I verily declare,
'Till heaven and earth fhall vanifh into air ;
No jot or tittle of the law fhall fail,
'Till all's accomplifh'd which it doth reveal.
Who, therefore, fhall the leaft commandment
      break,
And others teach the fame ill courfe to take ;
The heav'nly angels will give him the name
Of leaft, and juftly his tranfgreffions blame ;
But whofo doth and teacheth them fhall gain
The name of great, and heav'nly blifs attain.
Thus I admonifh you, beware, take heed,
Your faith the Scribes' and Pharifees' exceed ;

Or

Or elſe you ſhall in no caſe heav'n enjoy,
And taſte its tranſports, which can never cloy.
You've heard it ſaid, of old men gave command,
Thou ſhouldſt commit no murder in the land,
And whoſo ſhall of murder guilty be,   •
Cannot the judgment without danger flee :
But I ſay unto you, that whoſoe'er
Does enmity againſt his brother bear,
And cauſelefs wrath, and unbecoming hate,
Shall be in danger of the judgment-ſeat :
And he that, *Raca*, ſhall his brother call,
Will in great hazard of the judgment fall ;
But whoſoe'er, thou fool, ſhalt to him ſay,
Should fear hell-fire, and for forgiveneſs pray.
If, when thy gift is to the altar brought,
Thou there remembreſt that thou art in fault ;
And haſt done any thing by which you might
Your brother's anger or offence excite ;
Thy off'ring there before the altar leave ;
And go, and pardon from thy brother crave ;
When thou haſt made him merciful and kind,
Then give thy off'ring with a cheerful mind.
Strive ſoon thy adverſary to appeaſe,
And as you walk, endeavour him to pleaſe ;
Leſt he thy body to the judge ſhould give,
From whom the officer would thee receive,
And ſtraightway hurry thee to priſon, where
You'll ſuffer ſorrow, and corroſive care :

Thus

Thus I assure thee, thence thou shalt not get,
'Till thou hast paid each farthing of the debt.
You've heard 'twas said by men of ancient time,
Avoid adultery, that heinous crime.
But I say unto you, that whosoe'er
With lustful eyes shall on a woman stare;
That man in heart is guilty of this sin,
And needs repentance for his thoughts within.
And if thy right eye chance to give offence,
Then pluck it out, and straightway cast it thence:
For it is better one eye should be gone,
Than all thy body in hell-fire be thrown.
If thy right-hand act any wicked deed,
Then cut it off, and cast it thence with speed;
For it is better one hand should be lost,
Than thy whole body into hell be toss'd.
It hath been said, that whoso is inclin'd
To part from her whom marriage rites have join'd;
Let him a writing of divorcement give,
That so apart they may unsinning live.
But I say, whosoe'er shall from her part,
Whom wedlock made the sharer of his heart;
Save for the cause of fornication, he
Then makes her guilty of adultery;
And he that marries her divorced will,
In sight of God, adultery fulfill.
You've heard that men of old this law did make,
Whene'er you swear, your vows you shall not
     break;

                                           But

But ſhall unto the LORD exactly pay
Whatever thou haſt vow'd to do or ſay.
But I ſay unto you, from oaths forbear,
And ne'er preſume by any thing to ſwear:
Neither by heaven, for it is the place
Where GOD enthron'd ſhews his Almighty face;
Nor by the earth, GOD's footſtool, where around
He deals his mercy, and his love profound;
Nor by *Jeruſalem*, which GOD has made
His choſen city, and its bulwarks laid;
Nor by thy head ſhalt thou thy promiſe plight,
Since not one hair thou canſt make black or white;
But ſtill let Yea and Nay your ſayings guide,
That evil ſwearing you may thus avoid;
For whatſoever farther ſhall extend,
Is wickedneſs, and doth to evil tend.
You've heard that men of old this precept gave,
Eye for an eye, and tooth for tooth receive.
But this commandment unto you I ſpeak,
That you 'gainſt evil no reſiſtance make;
Whoe'er by blows ſhall give thy right cheek pain,
Then turn to him the other, nor complain:
And whoſoe'er at law thy coat demands,
Let him thy cloak get alſo from thy hands:
He that compelleth you to go a mile,
Go with him two, nor him for that revile.
Thoſe who would borrow from you kindly hear;
Give thoſe who aſk, nor turn away thine ear.

You've

You've heard what men of ancient time have faid,
Who this command and admonition made ;
Your neighbour love, and hold him in your breaft,
But all your enemies you fhall deteft.
But I fay unto you approve of thofe
Who fhew themfelves your enemies and foes;
Blefs them which curfe you, and endeavour ftill
To cherifh thofe who wifh to treat you ill,
Thofe who defpitefully fhall you offend,
Let pray'rs and bleffings on their crimes attend ;
That you by gentlenefs yourfelves may prove
The children of the heav'nly LORD above ;
Who makes the fun to rife on good and bad,
Whofe fhow'rs alike the juft and wicked glad.
If you love only thofe who love again,
What profit have you ? What do you obtain ?
Do not the Publicans act even fo,
And to their friends and neighbours fondnefs
       fhew ?
And if your brethren you falute alone,
What do ye more than other men have done ?
Do not the Publicans thus alfo greet
Their friends and,brethren wherefoe'er they meet?
Be ye then perfect, as the LORD on high
Is good and perfect to eternity.

CHAPTER

CHAPTER VI.

TAKE heed you do not charity beſtow,
That men may ſee you, or your actions know ;
Your heav'nly Father will not, elſe, regard
Your alms, or for them give you a reward.
When thou doſt, therefore, deal thine alms a-
    round,
Let not before thee any trumpets ſound ;
You may in ſynagogues and ſtreets perceive
That always thus the hypocrites behave ;
Who hope by oſtentatious deeds to find
Themſelves admir'd and honor'd by mankind.
This I ſay unto you, they ſhall obtain
The earthly glory which they ſeek to gain.
But when thou haſt thy charity convey'd
Let not thy left know what thy right hand paid ;
That ſo thine alms, conceal'd from mortal eyes,
May be diſtributed in ſecret wiſe ;
Your Father, who in ſecret ſees and heeds,
Will then bleſs openly your pious deeds.
And when thou prayeſt, always ſtrive to ſhun
The falſe appearance hypocrites put on ;
For in the ſynagogues they ſtanding love
To ſhew their worſhip, and their faith approve;
And in each corner of the ſtreets they pray,
That they to men their goodneſs may diſplay.

This

This I fay unto you, they fhall procure
The earthly honours that they would fecure.
But when you worfhip, to your room repair,
Shut clofe the door, and enter into pray'r;
Addrefs your Father, who in fecret reigns,
And he fhall openly reward your pains.
But when you pray, be careful to refufe
Vain repetitions which the Heathen ufe;
For by much talk they foolifhly expect
They will be heard, nor treated with neglect;
Be ye not like them, for your Father knows
What things you need, ere ye your wants dif-
    clofe.
In this wife make your fupplications known,
In humble manner, to the LORD alone:
" Father of all, who fill'ft the boundlefs fkies,
" Let to thy name eternal bleffings rife.
" May thy dominion no confinement fee,
" But all exiftence to thy will agree.
" As heav'nly angels thy commands obey,
" Let earth's inhabitants their homage pay.
" Since by thy goodnefs we alone can live,
" May we to-day our daily bread receive.
" As we forgive our debtors what they owe,
" May we, O LORD! thy great forgivenefs
    " know.
" Into temptation let us never ftray,
" But fave us always from each evil way.

R   " The

" The kingdom, glory, and the pow'r thou
    " haſt,

" Which to eternity ſhall firmly laſt.

" Then let the univerſe reſound again ·

" With joyful acclamations of *Amen.*"

If you forgive when mortals you offend,

Your heav'nly Father will like grace extend;

But if to men no pardon you afford,

Neither will you find mercy with the LORD.

Moreover, when you faſt, avoid with care,

The ſad appearance hypocrites then wear;

For they aſſume a melancholy mien,

That ſo of men their faſting may be ſeen.

This I ſay unto you, they ſhall poſſeſs

Rewards for which ſo eagerly they preſs.

But when you faſt, let joy your frame o'erſpread,

Waſh clean your hands, with oil anoint your
    head;

That ſo your faſting, to mankind unknown,

May of JEHOVAH be perceiv'd alone;

Your Father who in ſecret does regard,

And ſee your actions, will your faith reward.

On earthly treaſures do not time employ,

Since ruſt and moth your labor can deſtroy;

And thieves and robbers may themſelves avail

Of your poſſeſſions, and your riches ſteal.

But your chief treaſures let the heav'ns contain,

Where ruſt or moth no entrance can obtain;

                        Nor

Nor thieves nor robbers thence can bear away
The riches which you there fecurely lay,
For wherefoe'er your treafures can be trac'd,
Your hearts will there undoubtedly be plac'd.
The eye's appointed to difpenfe the light,
The body gains by its beholding fight;
If thine eye, therefore, fhall be fingle found,
Thy body will with total light be crown'd:
But if thine eye to wickednefs fhould bend,
Then total darknefs fhall your frame attend.
If then thy light fhould turn to fullen gloom,
How difmally obfcure muft it become!
No man can poffibly with credit ferve
Two lords at once, and truth to both preferve,
For elfe for one his hatred will be known,
While all his love is to the other fhewn;
Or one by him will ardently be priz'd,
While in his heart the other is defpis'd.
Ye cannot *Mammon* faithfully obey,
And likewife own the great JEHOVAH's fway,
I therefore fay, avoid each thought and care
Of what you fhould to cherifh life prepare;
What fort of food you might fecurely ufe,
Or yet what drink with fafety you fhould choofe;
Nor for your body anx'oufly enquire,
What kind of cloaths is proper for attire;
Is not the life of greater worth than meat?
The body more than raiment yielding heat?

The

The winged fongfters of the fky behold,
Who to the fun their varied plumes unfold;
They neither fow nor reap the fertile plain,
Nor into barns collect the hoary grain;
And yet your heav'nly Father feeds them fo,
That they no want or griping hunger know.
Are ye not better than the fowls of air,
Whom he regards with fo much tender care?
Who can by thought a proper plan defign,
Which to his ftature may a cubit join?
Why do ye afk with fuch a thoughtful breaft,
What fort of raiment will preferve you beft?
See how the lillies of the valley rife,
Nor toil, nor fpin, but open to the fkies;
Yet even *Solomon*, in glory gay,
Could never boaft fuch elegant array.
If God the herbage of the fields thus crown,
Which blooms to-day, to-morrow is cut down;
Ye faithlefs people, can ye ftill be blind,
And not perceive to you he'll prove more kind?
Take then no thought about your drink or meat,
Nor fay when hungry, What have we to eat?
Nor when you're dry, What liquid fhould we
     prove,
Which might moft fpeedily our thirft remove?
Or, what apparel is the beft to wear,
To guard our bodies from the chilling air?

                 (For

(For ſtill the *Gentiles* keep theſe things in view,
And think true happineſs they thus purſue.)
Your heav'nly Father knoweth what you need,
And will ſupply you with paternal ſpeed.
But ſeek ye firſt with unremitting pain
The realms of GOD, and right'ouſneſs to gain;
And all theſe things into your pow'r ſhall fall,
If on the LORD with fervent zeal ye call.
No thought of this, then, harbour in your mind,
What good or ill to-morrow has deſign'd;
To-morrow ſhall to-morrow's things convey,
The evil's ſtill ſufficient for the day.

CHAPTER VII.

BE cautious from judgment to refrain,
Leſt you like judgment ſhould partake again.
Whatever judgment you to mortals give,
Such judgment ſhall you from the LORD re-
    ceive:
And as you mete your meaſure to mankind,
Like meaſure ſhall you with JEHOVAH find.
And why doſt thou ſo eaſily eſpy
The mote that lodges in thy brother's eye;

And

And yet confiders not the mighty beam
Which thine eye holds, to thy eternal fhame?
Or how wilt thou thus to thy brother fay,
Let me the mote pull from your eye, I pray;
When lo thine own eye doth a beam contain,
Which chiefly fhould excite a godly pain?
Thy own beam firft, thou hypocrite, remove,
Ere others' feelings you attempt to prove;
Then fhalt thou comfort to thy brother raife,
And from his eye extract the mote with eafe.
Give not to dogs the things that are divine,
Nor caft your pearls before unruly fwine;
Left with their feet they break them and deftroy,
Then turn again, and your repofe annoy.
Still on the LORD with ftedfaft hope believe,
Implore his mercy, and you fhall receive:
JEHOVAH's kingdom feek with zealous mind,
And you eternal happinefs will find:
Knock with firm virtue at the throne of grace,
And you fhall enter GOD's all happy place:
For he that afketh, fhall his wifh fecure;
And he that feeketh, fhall true blifs procure,
And he that knocketh at GOD's bleffed throne,
Shall make felicity fupreme his own.
What man of you whofe fon fhould bread require,
Would with a ftone fulfil his ftrong defire?
Or if a fifh he happen'd to demand,
Would give a ferpent from a parent's hand?

If

If ye then evil, know how beſt to grant
The goodly gifts your children chance to want;
Shall not the LORD much better things beſtow,
On all who to his will obedience ſhew?
Whate'er to you from men you think is due,
Ev'n ſo to mankind you ſhould always do;
For thus the law and prophets you fulfil,
And pay compliance to GOD's holy will.
At the ſtrait gate an entrance ſtrive to gain,
Which leads to pleaſures ever free from pain;
For wide's the gate, and open is the way,
Which guides poor mortals from the LORD aſtray:
Deſtruction's paths extenſive are, and broad,
And many wretches enter its ſad road;
For ſtrait's the way, and narrow is the gate,
Which leads to life, and few go in thereat.
Avoid falſe prophets, who mild carriage bear,
And do externally ſheep's clothing wear;
But you in them will hidden miſchief find,
And breaſts like wolves, as rav'nous and unkind,
The fruits they bear their vileneſs ſhall diſcloſe,
And ſhew their wickedneſs their hearts incloſe.
Do grapes on·thorns for mankind ever grow?
Or do the thiſtles any figs beſtow?
Thus ev'ry good tree uſeful fruit will yield,
But trees corrupt with evil fruit are fill'd.
A good tree cannot evil fruit conceive,
  Nor from bad trees can you good fruit receive.

Each

Each tree which doth not goodly fruit produce,
Is fell'd and burn'd, as of no other ufe.
Wherefore their fruits fhall evidently tell,
Whether from you they merit ill or well.
Not ev'ry one that faith LORD, LORD, fhall gain
The realms of blifs, and endlefs joys obtain;
But he that doth my heav'nly Father pleafe,
Shall join with angels in eternal praife.
In that day many fhall to me exclaim,
LORD, have we not been prophets in thy name?
And in thy name have dæmons overthrown?
And in thy name much wond'rous actions done?
Then will I fay, I never gain'd your heart,
Ye workers of iniquity depart.
Therefore who doth my admonitions hear,
And to my fayings lend a willing ear;
Is like a man who, with true wifdom crown'd,
Rear'd his ftrong edifice on rocky ground,
The rain defcended, floods with rapid rage,
And roaring winds, againft his houfe engage;
But yet it fell not; founded on a rock,
Their force united it could fafely mock.
And ev'ry one that hears thofe words of mine,
Yet doth to wickednefs his foul incline;
Shall to a foolifh perfon be compar'd,
Who on the fand a tott'ring fabric rear'd;
Strong floods rufh on, the heavy rains defcend,
And dreadful ftorms their fury on it fpend;

Awhile

Awhile it weakly ſtrives their forte to ſtay,
And with a craſh then tumbles to decay.

It came to paſs, when Jesus made an end,
All did with wonder to his words attend;
And were aſtoniſh'd at the laws he ſpake,
Which were deliver'd for poor mortals' ſake.
Unlike the Scribes, with boldneſs he diſplay'd
The doctrines which to endleſs comforts lead.

S

ON THE

ATTRIBUTES OF GOD.

IMMORTAL Lord! Jehovah moſt ſupreme!
At whoſe dread word all things from nothing came;
And muſt again, when your commands await,
Return to their primæval, empty ſtate.
By your controul, the kindly-ſhining ſun
Inceſſant moves, his daily courſe to run;
And the pale moon does with her ſilver light,
Diffuſe her ceaſeleſs ſplendor on the night:
As you direct, the planets ever roll,
And tell your mightineſs from pole to pole.
Thou ſov'reign God, omnipotent, moſt juſt,
Who formed *Adam* out of brittle duſt;
And in thy likeneſs did his perſon frame,
And gave him faculties to praiſe thy name!
But he, tranſgreſſing thy moſt ſacred law,
Did on the world thy ſore diſpleaſure draw;
'Till thy bleſs'd Son forſook his throne on high,
To ſave fall'n mankind from their miſery;
And for their ſake endur'd moſt racking pain,
That they thereby might ſure ſalvation gain.
I AM, inviſible, pure, good, and kind,
In whom the juſt do endleſs comforts find.
Incomprehenſible, Almighty God,
Who govern mankind by thy awful nod.

Deathleſs,

I

Deathlefs, all-ruling, uncreated *Lord*,
Who order all things by thy pow'rful word.
Thou God inthron'd, unerring, and unfeen,
Eternal Governor of mortal men.
Infallible, omnifcient, ador'd,
Unpaffive, loving, ever-watchful Lord.
Propit'ous, all-beholding, unconfin'd,
Rev'renc'd and eminent Judge of mankind.
God, incorporeal, unchang'd, moft high,
At whofe great word the dreadful thunders fly.
Moft grac'ous, immaterial, unreftrain'd,
In whofe light bonds the right'ous are detain'd.
Lord undeceiv'd, refiftlefs, and uney'd,
On whofe great mercy we fhould ftill confide.
How can poor mortals gratefully repay
The countlefs bleffings of thy gentle fway!
Tho' we fhould pafs fourfcore revolving years,
And fpend that time in never-ceafing pray'rs;
Nay, fhould we live innumerable days,
And chaunt inceffantly our fongs of praife;
Yet, ftill unprofitable fervants, we
Could never tell thy love fufficiently;
And yet thou doft with tendernefs receive
The poor returns which we fincerely give.
Lord everlafting, to our fouls inftill
A warm defire thy dictates to fulfill!
Make us ftill eager for thy faving grace,
And crown us joyful in the realms of peace!

DESCRIP-

DESCRIPTION OF SUNDAY EVENING,

SPENT IN A

COFFEE-HOUSE,

IN THE

CITY OF DUBLIN.

'TIS Sunday ev'ning, and when pray'rs are
done,
Straight to the coffee-houſe crowds thronging run,
Where from their minds they utterly diſcard
Texts which in church they heard without regard.
Calls for the news, and " Is the packet come?"
With waiters' " Here, Sir!" echo thro' the room.

The tawdry fops, with ſneering, vain grimace,
Adorn'd with ignorance—and flimſy lace,
Strut in mock majeſty, and view with ſcorn
The *lower* creatures who this ſcene adorn.

Here the old dotards ſip their capilaire,
And talk of politics with lofty air;
On ſtate affairs importantly proceed,
And pore on papers which they cannot read.

The

The fpruce apprentice, from his mafter free,
In his beft cloaths haftes here with merry glee;
With powder'd hair refolv'd to cut a dafh,
And treat of money—tho' he has no cafh:
But as the coxcomb will not want his tea,
He muft be trufted—as he cannot pay.

Thus when fome hours in idlenefs they fpend,
Their fteps in fullen mood all homewards bend;
Or to fome tavern, or curs'd ftew repair,
To banifh languor—by increafing care.

If men the Sabbath treat with fuch negle&t,
What can we from them on week-days expe&t?
Will thofe who little heed to Sunday fhew,
And on that day no praife to GOD beftow;
When gilded pleafures, or a thirft of gain,
Provoke their paffions, and their thoughts detain;
Forfake fuch obje&ts, and with fouls fincere,
Addrefs to GOD their fervent, humble pray'r?
Can fuch men hope the LORD will gentle prove,
To thofe who wickedly defpife his love?
Or make them fharers of that heav'nly throne,
Which he has promis'd to the good alone?

ADVICE

ADVICE

TO THE

NON-OBSERVERS OF THE SABBATH.

ALL ye who drowfily on Sunday creep
To hear a fermon—tho' ye foundly fleep;
Awhile with patience to my words attend,
And mark the counfel of a chiding friend.

Ye who muft fleep, fhould always ftay at home,
Nor ever yawning to GOD's temple come;
For his commands thus wickedly ye break,
And of his worfhip open mock'ry make.
Can you indulge a foolifh, empty thought,
That ye are blamelefs, when ye are not caught
In flumb'ring pofture, and may fnugly lie,
If you can fhun each fellow-mortal's eye?
But know, rafh creatures! that JEHOVAH's fight
Beholds your actions in the darkeft night;
Nor are your inmoft, fecret thoughts unknown
To GOD, who governs ev'ry thing alone.

To you, fair nymphs! I next addrefs my theme,
As your great levity rebuke muft claim.

Pray,

Pray, is the church a proper place to court?
Is that a scene for gigglers to make sport?
Should you form parties there, or shameless leer,
Remark your dress, and at each other sneer?
Fly such impieties, nor bring disgrace
By empty carriage, on a charming face;
But wisely strive, by modest, decent ways,
To gain affection, and the Lord to please.

With you, ye fops, rakes, fribbles I conclude,
Who early learn the method to be rude;
And hope each fair one's easy faith to win,
By launching deeply into modish sin.
Beware of prating in the house of God,
Nor vilely use the ogle, wink, or nod.
Endeavour God's consuming wrath to shun,
Nor rashly into endless tortures run:
So shall your days with happiness be crown'd,
And even death will scatter bliss around.

ON AGE.

Lo! hoary age now flowly ftalks abroad,
And bends beneath its momentary load;
Striving with nervelefs limbs, and half-clos'd eyes
To tafte the fweets which want of ftrength denies:
For feeble feventy will not admit
Of joys for vig'rous manhood only fit.
And with what rapid motions do alas!
From youth till age our fleeting moments pafs!
We fhine this minute, and are rais'd on high,
Tho' we, perhaps, muft the next inftant die.
We glide like fhadows vain before the wind,
Which leave not the leaft veftiges behind.

   Think, then, ye fons of men, ere 'tis too late,
What dreadful punifhments muft you await;
If you in vain purfuits have fpent your days,
Nor paid attention to God's holy ways:
For if you fhould his dread commands neglect,
In your laft hours, what peace can you expect?
But if thro' life his will you have obey'd,
Nor have by wicked counfels e'er been fway'd;
Your dying couch fhall yield you calmeft eafe,
And from your minds each fearful thought erafe.
O may we, then, with zeal unceafing ftrive
To keep a fervent love of God alive!
May we the firmeft virtue ftill retain,
That we eternal happinefs may gain!

ON LIFE.

LIFE, potent fovereign of all mankind,
In whofe light bonds with pleafure they're con-
    fin'd!
Thou balmy potion, fweet which ne'er can cloy,
And which we're anxious always to enjoy!
Thou deareft friend to rich men and to poor,
For which all hardfhips gladly they endure!
When tempefts rage, for thee the failors pray,
And for thee caft their dear-bought wealth away.
The pris'ner for thy fake would undergo
The moft fevere and complicated woe.
Each fex and age with equal pow'r you bend,
With like defires they at your fhrine attend,
Do thou, indulgent, my fond wifhes hear,
And to my cravings turn a placid ear!
Grant that my life I on fuch terms may choofe,
That it I ne'er may be afraid to lofe!
O make me always in GOD's nurture live,
And to his precepts due attention give!
Into my breaft a love of him inftill,
And lead me always in his holy will!
From dire commotions let me ever ceafe,
And lull me into everlafting peace!

T

ON DEATH.

DEATH, thou beſt comforter of the diſtreſs'd,
By whom their agonies are huſh'd to reſt!
The good man's bliſs, the wicked's greateſt curſe,
Since their bad ſtate by thee is chang'd to worſe!
Thou aged youth! ſure meſſenger of fate!
Impartial judge of poverty and ſtate!
Whence is it that you always terrors bring,
Tho' you're oft' but a momentary ſting?
And that, tho' veſted with unbounded ſway,
So very few are willing to obey?
How do you cauſe ſuch univerſal dread?
It muſt from conſc'ouſneſs of guilt proceed.
What elſe could make mankind ſo ſtrangely err,
As worldly toys to heav'nly bliſs prefer?
O be thou ever preſent to our ſight,
And guide our footſteps in the paths of light!
Deſtroy each evil thought that may ariſe,
And drive the miſt of error from our eyes!
That we, when our appointed hour is come,
With Chriſtian fortitude may meet our doom!
If virtue was our guide, we may rely
On GOD's firm promiſe " We ſhall never die."

AN

ADDRESS TO THE PUBLIC

BY THE

PUBLISHERS OF THE DUBLIN CHRONICLE,

WHICH WAS INSERTED IN THEIR PAPER
ON THE SECOND OF JANUARY, 1772.

THE infant year in blithſome mood appears,
And with glad ſtrains each jocund boſom cheers;
While ev'ry hour in lively pleaſure flows,
Each merry heart with ſweet contentment glows;
Thus may our friends, for ever free from ſtrife,
In health and happineſs enjoy their life!
May with proſperity each wiſh be crown'd,
And bliſs unſullied ſcatter peace around!

To all our friends who hitherto were kind
We pay the tribute of a grateful mind;
And hope by our endeavours ſtill to pleaſe,
Among the public freſh ſupplies to raiſe.
Our types are new, our paper good and large,
And yet we've added nothing to its charge;
The price was but an halfpenny before,
Now, much amended, it will coſt no more;

And

And it fhall ftill abundantly be 'ftor'd
With all the news the feafon may afford.

 Our modern bards, we truft, will not refufe
To court the favor of their darling mufe;
And grace our *Poets' Corner* with that fire
Which fam'd *Parnaffus* can fo well infpire.
We take our leave, with fondeft hopes that thofe
On whom we do our confidence repofe,
Will now prove friendly, nor their aid delay,
As we will ftrive their kindnefs to repay.

A N

AN

ADDRESS TO THE PUBLIC

ON DROPPING THE

PUBLICATION OF THE DUBLIN CHRONICLE

IN THE YEAR 1772.

SINCE nothing elfe, good friends, will do,
This paper bids you all adieu.
And now we'll tell the reafon why
The *Dublin Chronicle* muft die.
Of advertifements, few or none,
Which are as marrow to the bone,
We could colleƈt; for what we got
Would hardly ferve to boil the pot;
And we muft always, let us tell ye,
Make fome provifion for the belly:
And when the proclamations ceas'd,
Expence and trouble ftill increas'd;
So that we find it better far
To yield, than wage deftruƈtive war.
But yet we ftill vend writing paper,
Which you can no where purchafe cheaper;
With ink, wax, wafers, pens, and quills,
And *Anderfon*'s and *Hoffman*'s pills;

Likewife

Likewife pure, infpiffated juice
Of liquorice, for colds of ufe ;
With *Britifh* oil, and drugs befide,
Too num'rous to be notify'd ;
And alfo books of ev'ry fort,
For tafte, religion, and for fport ;
And many pretty, printed toys,
For blooming girls, or prattlings boys ;
With *Mahomet*, *Zobeide*, and *Timon*,
The dramatic romance of *Cymon* ;
And publications, new and old,
Which any where in town are fold.
In *College-green*, near *Gibfon*'s fhop we live,
Where we with thanks your cuftom will receive.

EPITAPH

EPITAPH ON GENERAL WOLFE,

WRITTEN IN 1771.

Reader, this monumental pile furvey,
Nor, void of pity, turn thine eyes away.
Lo! here entomb'd *Wolfe*'s mortal frame is laid,
Which Nature's debt too foon alas! has paid.
Here fleeps the hero, who, at honor's call,
Hurl'd his dread veng'ance on the hoftile *Gaul*;
Thro' ranks oppofing rufh'd with boundlefs might,
And ftill undaunted dar'd the coming fight:
When glory beckon'd, join'd the bloody field,
And made his foes to matchlefs courage yield:
Who *Bourbon* taught to drop her haughty pride,
And bravely conquer'd—yet more bravely dy'd.

The tears of millions weep thy fudden fate,
And keeneft forrows on thy fhade await.
Love, friendfhip, laurels crown thy facred urn,
And plaintive *Britons* ceafelefs grieve and mourn;
In doleful meafures grace thy patriot name,
And found thy praifes in the lifts of fame;
Record thy valour in the plains of blood,
And dangers flighted for thy country's good;
Tranfported tell, how with thy lateft breath,
Britannia's welfare chac'd the fears of death;
How worth exalted fill'd thy noble breaft,
And lull'd thee finking into filent reft.

EPITAPH ON GENERAL WOLFE,

WRITTEN IN 1771.

WHEN hoftile *Bourbon*, fwoln with vaunting
    pride,
Britannia's wealth and warlike troops defy'd;
When fam'd *Canada* own'd the *Gallic* fway,
And *Quebec* learn'd its mandates to obey:
Then youthful *Wolfe*, brave, emulous of fame,
With *England*'s fons enroll'd his peerlefs name;
The thirft of glory fir'd his manly breaft,
And quell'd the fears that might his peace moleft;
By honor prompted, ev'ry danger grew
An empty fhade, and vanifh'd from his view:
Thus ftrongly arm'd, he hail'd the bloody plain,
Contemn'd the wounds he might in war fuftain;
With dauntlefs courage blefs'd the fatal blow,
And dy'd content at *Gallia*'s overthrow.

    What could a mother's poignant plaints remove
For that loft fon who held her warmeft love?
What eafe her fharp and agonizing woes,
Or calm her anguifh to ferene repofe?
The glowing joy, how *Britain*'s heroes tell
He nobly fought, and crown'd with conqueft fell.
The tears of millions drown *her* fingle cries;
The parent's grief in millions' forrow dies;
While praifes, honors, trophies join to fave
His valu'd mem'ry from the fullen grave. .

LINES on the DEATH of GEN. WOLFE,

AS ORIGINALLY WRITTEN IN THE YEAR 1771.

THO' fculptur'd marble can but faintly tell
How *Wolfe* fought, conquer'd and triumphant fell;
Tho' mortal honors never can proclaim
The boundlefs value of his deathlefs name;
Tho' virtue's friends, in foft, harmonic lays,
In vain attempt to celebrate his praife:
Yet weeping *Britons* thus their fondnefs fhew,
Thus ftrive to pay the gratitude they owe;
In mourning fadnefs labour to deceive
The fullen darknefs of the gloomy grave;
With heart-felt forrow wifh to teftify
That *Wolfe*, tho' dead, to them can never die.
    When glory pointed to the martial plain,
Where carnage, horror, and confufion reign;
Behold the hero ev'ry danger dare,
Spring to the fight, and hail the bloody war!
With fearlefs valour to the van advance,
And bravely curb the arrogance of *France!*
Behold him wounded! in the jaws of death!
Revere his country with his lateft breath!
With eager tranfports catch the joyful found,
That *Britain*'s fons with victory were crown'd!
" I die content, my foes are overthrown,"
He fmiling crys, and finks without a groan.

U   THE

LINES on the DEATH of GEN. WOLFE,

ALTERED.

THO' fculptur'd marble can but faintly tell
How gallant *Wolfe* triumphant fought and fell;
Tho' mortal honors feebly muſt proclaim
The boundlefs worth of his exalted name;
And Virtue's friends, in foft harmonious lays,
In vain attempt to celebrate his praife:
Yet *Britons* thus their fond attachment fhew,
Thus ſtrive to pay the gratitude they owe;
In mourning fadnefs labor to deceive
The fullen darknefs of the gloomy grave;
With heart-felt forrow wiſh to teſtify
That *Wolfe*, tho' dead, to them can never die.

When glory pointed to the martial plain,
Where carnage, horror, and confufion reign;
Behold the hero ev'ry danger dare,
Spring to the fight, and hail the bloody war!
With fearlefs valour to the van advance,
And bravely curb the arrogance of *France!*
Behold him wounded! in the jaws of death!
Revere his country with his lateſt breath!
With eager tranfports catch the joyful found
That *Britain*'s fons with victory were crown'd!
" I fall content, my foes are overthrown,"
He fmiling crys, and finks without a groan.

ANSWER

ANSWER TO A RIDDLE

SENT TO ME BY

A YOUNG LADY.

IN Spring the trees their budding pride renew,
And gaily glitter in a verdant hue;
They, next, with fweet and gaudy bloffoms glow,
From which refrefhing, balmy odors flow;
Succeeding fruit from ev'ry bough depend,
And blufhing clufters make the branches bend :
The ripen'd apples, for man's ufe ordain'd,
Are from the trees by careful perfons glean'd;
And, prefs'd, a cool and pleafant juice afford,
Or fold, increafe the coffers of their Lord.
When rough north winds the leafy trees affail,
The roaring gufts againft their drefs prevail;
Their fhady honors feel a fwift decay,
And, like poor mortals, quickly fade away.
The fhort enjoyments of their beauty fhew
That all is frail and fleeting here below.
The rain defcending from their boughs appears
Like falling drops of melancholy tears.
If my folution of the riddle's right,
An *apple-tree* is what you had in fight.

A REBUS.

A REBUS.

WHAT's that perfon's name, pray, in which
    may be found,
Without any difcount, the fum of a pound?

ANSWER.

IN a *Mark* thirteen fhillings and four pence we
    find,
Which when to fix and eight pence, a *Noble*,
    conjoin'd,
Will make juft a pound fterling, and give us the
    name
Of a man who to learning and merit lays claim.

LINES BY AN UNKNOWN AUTHOR,

INSINUATING THAT

MISS ASHMORE, NOW MRS. SPARKS,

WAS ONE NIGHT INTOXICATED, WHILE PER-
FORMING THE PART OF *SYLVIA*,

IN THE DRAMATIC ROMANCE OF CYMON.

POOR *Sylvia* I pity'd laſt night in the grove,
When unable to tell the ſad tale of her love.
Quoth I, ſurely *Merlin* to ſilence has twitch'd her,
Or elſe the enchantreſs with brandy bewitch'd her.

REPLY TO THE ABOVE LINES.

MALICE, thou bane of frail mankind, for-
        bear
To wrong a nymph ſo exquiſitely fair :
Aſhmore the chaſte, the witty, and the gay,
Could not on brandy throw her time away.
Hopes built on univerſal praiſe muſt fall ;
ſ" Vain's that attempt which ſtrives to pleaſe us
        all !"

ON

ON THE GREATLY DEPLORED

DEATH OF JOHN AVERELL, *D. D.*

LATE BISHOP OF LIMERICK.

THOU grifly tyrant, in whofe cruel breaft,
Nor pity, kindnefs, or compaffion reft!
Infatiate Death! harfh, unrelenting Lord!
Who to the good, bad, rich, and poor afford
Equal refpect; nor ought on earth can fave
Their fhort-liv'd bodies from the darkfome grave!
Could no lefs victim pleafe thy bloody mind?
Or could you not more worthlefs objects find
To fpend your fhafts on, and employ your rage
On thofe who totter with inactive age?
The great, the noble foul at length is fled,
And *Averell* lies among the pallid dead!
Averell, whofe ev'ry kind and tender thought
Was with benevolence the pureft fraught:
Whofe conftant care was to relieve the poor,
And for their fouls and bodies wealth fecure;
Who may in deepeft forrow now deplore
Their once fure friend, who is alas! no more.
In faith, firm hope, and charity he ftill
Guided his actions by GOD's holy will;
And by adhering to the perfect way,
Has gain'd a crown that never fhall decay;
Has purchas'd heav'n, no more to fuffer pain,
But in eternal happinefs to reign.

O N

DRY, WARM WEATHER IN SPRING,

SUCCEEDED BY RAIN.

W HEN vernal *Phœbus* his long ſtation keeps,
And ne'er on duty like a ſluggard ſleeps;
When keen and fervent his wing'd arrows fly,
And cleareſt luſtre crowns the vaulted ſky;
Then hangs each flow'r its weak and drooping
      head,
And mournful gardens weep their beauties dead;
The budding bloſſoms are obſerv'd to fade,
And ſadly beg ſome wat'ry planet's aid;
Diſtending earth its gaping jaws diſplays,
And with dumb wiſhes for refreſhment prays;
The parched fields defy the farmer's toil,
And hungry cattle crop the ſcorching ſoil;
The birds in cluſters ſeek the cloſe retreat,
And panting ſhun the overpow'ring heat;
While ſick'ning nature is oppreſs'd with care,
And univerſal mourning ſeems to wear.
But when from heav'n the wiſh'd-for rain de-
      ſcends,
Its honors fair creation ſoon extends;

                         The

The nodding trees their leafy pride renew,
And with fresh glory boast their verdant hue;
The op'ning flow'rs, restor'd to richest bloom,
Emit a sweet and delicate perfume;
Each blushing hedge then rears its gladsome head,
While glowing blossoms fragrant odors shed;
The fertile lawns their former pomp regain,
And herds in gambols scud acrofs the plain;
Unnumber'd daisies deck each grassy vale,
And gentle zephyrs waft a spicy gale;
The feather'd songsters echo thro' the grove,
And in fond strains repeat their constant love;
The prospect pleasure to the farmer yields,
Who, cheerful, views his plenty-bringing fields;
The frisking lambs the woolly sheep attend,
Whose joyous bleatings the deep vallies rend;
The frugal bees their honey'd treasures hoard,
Which in abundance fragrant flow'rs afford;
The yawning earth receives the limpid food,
And gladly drinks the all-enliv'ning flood;
While smiling nature is elate with joy,
And tastes of comforts which can never cloy.

Thus some poor mariner, diftrefs'd, forlorn,
By adverse winds from his dear country torn;
When foaming furges round the veffel roar,
Which crafhing break with horror on the fhore;

O'er-

O'erwhelm'd with anguifh, fees with ftreaming
  eyes
Surrounding terrors, and inclement fkies;
Laments his family, now left to weep
For him, thought bury'd in the raging deep:
But fhould the tempeft by degrees fubfide,
And fanning breezes give a tranquil tide;
His woes are banifh'd by the welcome wind,
Preceding hardfhips banifh from his mind;
His fparkling eyes his ardent joys confefs,
And fmiles declare his heart-felt happinefs;
The long'd-for port with fwelling fails he gains,
Where reft awaits him from his late felt pains;
His friends, wife, children, his warm tranfports
  fhare,
And mirthful pleafures diffipate his care.

 All hail, dread LORD! who deal with mighty
  hand
To heav'n, earth, fea, and air thy great command!
Who in their proper time to mortals give
The fruits of earth, on which they are to live!
Who in due feafon fend heat, fnow, and rain,
And hoary froft, which binds the level plain!
Let all the world their fongs of homage pay,
And own, rejoicing, thy benignant fway!
With ceafelefs praifes thy vaft worth proclaim,
And in loud pæans celebrate thy name!

   X   A SONG.

A SONG.

My *Phillis* is blooming and young,
    And moves with an elegant grace;
The accents that fall from her tongue
    Redouble the charms of her face.

I fee her each day with delight,
    Nor ftrive to repel the ftrong flame;
I think of her all the long night,
    And clafp her bright form in my dream.

Each female I view with difdain,
    When *Phillis*, dear *Phillis* is by;
She only can banifh my pain,
    She only can gladden my eye.

Fair nymph, kindly cherifh my love,
    Nor rack me with cruel neglect;
Enraptur'd, fhould you but approve,
    I'm loft if my fuit you reject.

Ye Gods! to make happy my life,
    Fulfill this one ardent defire;
Let *Phillis* blefs me as a wife!—
    On earth nought befides I require.

A SONG.

SAY, *Phillis*, muſt I longer ſtrive
    Your flinty heart to move ;
And keep my torment ſtill alive,
    By plunging more in love.

If perſeverance in my flame
    Be an imputed ſin ;
Sure, *Phillis*, you are much to blame,
    That rais'd the flame within.

In your bright eyes the lightning blaz'd,
    Which ſet me all on fire ;
And in my breaſt ſuch tranſports rais'd,
    As never can expire.

I pine and languiſh all the day,
    With hope and fear oppreſs'd ;
In vain attempt to chace away,
    Blind *Cupid* from my breaſt :

The urchin tells me, when I rage,
    " 'Twas Phillis ſent me here."
How can I, then, moleſt the page
    Of one I hold ſo dear ?

Angelic

Angelic accents grac'd your tongue;
   Refiftlefs founds to me!
I fell your captive as you fung—
  O fhall I e'er get free!

Your fex for mildnefs was defign'd,
   For paffions fond and true;
May thofe fweet virtues fill thy mind,
   And fhew their power on you!

Let gentle pity melt thy heart,
   Not kill me with difdain!
But as much tendernefs impart,
   As you have done of pain.

A SONG.

A SONG.

WHAT charms can *Phillis* boaft,
　　To captivate my mind?
And yet alas! I'm loft,
　　Should *Phillis* prove unkind.

Her nut-brown, flowing hair,
　　Drefs'd elegantly plain,
Sure could not form a fnare,
　　To give me fo much pain.

Her fair, angelic face,
　　Where native fweetnefs ftill
Shines with triumphant grace,
　　Has not the pow'r to kill.

Her eyes, where ev'ry glance,
　　And richeft beauties bloom;
And little *Cupid*'s dance,
　　Could never feal my doom.

Her cheeks, in whom refide
　　The lilly and the rofe
Tho' crown'd with fweeteft pride,
　　Did not my griefs impofe.

Her teeth, like virgin fnow;
   Superlatively white,
Ne'er made my bofom glow
   With rapturous delight.

The accents from her tongue,
   Could yield no thrilling joy;
Nor her voice when fhe fung,
   My happinefs deftroy.

Her lovely, fwelling breaft
   May gently rife or fall;
But cannot hurt my reft,
   Or my fond foul enthrall.

Her pretty, dimpled chin,
   Could never caufe my woe;
Nor yet her charming fkin,
   My peace of mind o'erthrow.

Why from her polifh'd arm,
   Tho' fram'd with niceft art;
Should I fear any harm,
   Or wounds to pierce my heart.

What care I for her frown?
   Or for her winning fmile?
Could *that* my comforts drown?
   Or *this* my hopes beguile?

                     But

But whither do I ſtray?
    Some error dims my eyes:
With falſehoods ſhould I play?
    Or deal in glaring lies?

Since *Phillis* can with eaſe
    Pronounce my life or deaſh:
To her I vow my days,
    And yield my conſtant breath,

Then, *Cupid*, lend an ear,
    And to my wiſh incline!
Fulfill this ardent pray'r,
    Make charming *Phillis* mine!

A SONG.

A SONG.

WHEN *Phillis* trips acrofs the plain,
And views me with fevere difdain;
Ye Gods! how can I tamely fee
Her fmile on all around but me!

When fondly I confefs my love,
And warmly hope fhe'll gentle prove;
She, cruel, hears unheeded all,
And feems to glory in my fall.

When late I met the nymph alone,
And made again my paffion known;
Then thoufand tender vows I paid,
But vain alas! was all I faid.

I wept and languifh'd in her fight,
And own'd fhe was divinely bright;
She coldly liften'd to the theme,
And, fcornful, mock'd my ardent flame.

With foolifh rafhnefs oft I fwear
Her image from my breaft to tear;
But adamantine chains deny
That from her bondage I fhould fly.

From

From fleep when I expeſt relief,
The night augments my bitter grief;
And in my dreams, O fad diftrefs!
I fee my rival's happinefs.

Thus comfortlefs I pafs my days,
And, hopelefs, find my woes increafe;
Nor dare prefume but from the grave
The fmalleft refpite to receive.

A SONG.

A SONG.

I ONCE was unreſtrain'd and free,
Like birds that ſport from tree to tree;
'Till *Phillis* aim'd a pointed dart,
And lodg'd its venom in my heart.
What haplefs wretch can long endure
Anguiſh incapable of cure?
Or fay what med'cine can remove
The torments of defpairing love?

Can fuch a fweet, angelic face,
And perfon form'd with matchlefs grace,
Contain an unrelenting mind,
To ev'ry foft emotion blind?
The rougher fex compaſſion knows,
And mourns its fellow-creature's woes;
Then, fure, the gentle, female breaſt
Muſt fympathize with the diſtrefs'd.

O cruel fair! with pity heed,
And heal the heart you taught to bleed;
Nor longer rack your faithful fwain
With agonizing, cold difdain!
So fhall I blefs the happy hour
In which I yielded to your pow'r;
And with my *Phillis* taſte of joy
That fhall my all of life employ.

A SONG.

A SONG.

THAT *Phillis* is gentle, good-humour'd, and
    free
To all but poor *Damon*, the world muſt agree ;
Alas ! him ſhe cruelly treats with diſdain,
And ſeems to taſte pleaſure in giving him pain.

Whenever my paſſion I venture to own,
My ardor ſhe ſcornfully pays with a frown ;
When mutual returns to my love I expeƈt,
I killing indifference meet, and negleƈt.

At her feet when I mournfully languiſh and pine,
And warmly pronounce her ſupremely divine ;
She haſtily ſhuns me with heart-rending ſneers,
With ſmiles heeds my torments, and laughs at my
    tears.

But dare I her aƈtions preſume to upbraid,
Or call to account ſuch an angelic maid ?
Yet of female ſoftneſs ſure void ſhe muſt prove,
Whom tenderneſs, pity, or kindneſs can't move.

Oh *Cupid!* direƈt your keen, well-pointed dart,
And pierce this fair charmer's ſtill obdurate heart !
Let her feel the tranſports, but not the deſpair
Attending a paſſion ſo fond and ſincere !

A SONG.

A SONG.

ON a bank by a rivulet's fide
 Poor *Damon* fat penfive alone;
While the waters feem'd fadly to glide,
 Refponfive to his doleful moan.
" Oh! what fhepherd was e'er fo diftrefs'd!
 " Why do you fo hard-hearted prove!
" Say, how can you behold me opprefs'd,
 " And heedlefsly view my foft love!

" When, dear *Phillis*, your angelic frame
 " All lovely appear'd in my fight,
" I acknowledg'd blind *Cupid*'s ftrong flame,
 " And own'd his omnipotent might.
" But alas! you with fcorn ftill repay
 " Each proof of affection I give;
" And regardlefs hear all that I fay—
 " What mortal more wretched can live!

" Then, ye earthly, frail comforts adieu,
 " Since *Phillis* her bofom has fteel'd;
" I in vain the bright charmer purfue,
 " And reft the grave only can yield.
" May the youth who her favour fhall gain,
 " And happily reign in her foul;
" Never caufe her a moment of pain,
 " Nor ever her actions controul!"

Then

Then by chance lovely *Phillis* was near,
    And heard all his piteous tale;
And, defirous to banifh his care,
    Did for him her paffion reveal:
" My fond *Damon*, I was but in jeft,
    " When I feign'd your love to defpife;
" I could with you for ever be blefs'd,
    " No object's fo dear to my eyes."

The glad fhepherd in tranfports of joy
    The fair one to his bofom prefs'd;
He forgot that fhe ever was coy,
    And fhe clafp'd the fwain to her breaft.
Then to church the fweet nymph he convey'd,
    Where *Hymen*'s mild knot was faft ty'd;
He a bridegroom moft happy was made,
    And fhe a delectable bride.

ON A YOUNG LADY.

ASK me no more for whom I figh;
  Nor dare my paffion to reprove;
No beauty fparkles in an eye
  More brilliant than the maid's I love.
Coynefs to prudery unknown,
  Shines blended with the glow of youth;
Prudence has mark'd her for her own,
  And blefs'd her with the love of truth.
Religion, child of endlefs peace,
  Reigns in her breaft without controul;
And, deck'd with each external grace,
  No virtue's foreign to her foul.

CUPID'S APOLOGY.

AS *Venus* and *Cupid* were taking a walk,
The mother began to her fon thus to talk:
" Dear *Cupid*, pray tell me how comes it that I
" Am fo oft' deceiv'd by a beardlefs, blind boy?"
Quoth he, " Becaufe women rufh into men's arms,
" Before they difplay half the force of their charms.
" Would they act more fhily, and quit fuch odd
    " pranks,
" I'd get much lefs fcolding, and you much more
    " thanks."

ON A YOUNG LADY

WHOSE GLOVES WERE DECORATED WITH THE
FIGURES OF *HEARTS* AND *DIAMONDS.*

THE *Hearts* that deck each filken glove,
  What mortal can unmov'd withftand?
Which hold forth challenges of love,
  When drawn upon the fair one's hand?

Why from the *Di'mond's* mimic charms,
  Should you borrow weak affiftance;
While your fnow-white, polifh'd arms,
  Captivate without refiftance?

Bright *Venus* can, with winning art,
  Conquefts make by blooming faces;
But enflav'd is ev'ry heart,
  When affail'd by countlefs graces.

Since, then, fubmiffive to your will
  Admiring numbers proftrate fall;
Thofe whom your cruel frowns muft kill,
  Let gentle fmiles to life recall!

ON JANUARY.

THE *New Year* comes, and in its train,
Cold chatt'ring hail, and beating rain;
While furious winds, replete with rage,
In loud, tumultuous strife engage.
The rustics, clad in coarse attire,
Now huddle close around the fire;
Where, free from gnawing care and strife,
They lead a cheerful, frugal life;
And, happy in an humble state,
Unenvy'd view'd the rich and great.
The air inclement tempests cloud,
And storms horrific roar aloud;
While clust'ring herds to shelter run,
The direful hurricanes to shun;
And *Sol*, withdrawn from mortal sight,
But seldom deals his partial light.
The fowler, with the rising day,
Thro' thorny brakes directs his way;
And as the woodcocks flush around,
The shot inflicts a fatal wound;
Or while the snipe darts thro' the skies,
Swift death arrests him as he flies.
The water's frozen top employs
Unnumber'd groupes of girls and boys;

1   Who

Who gladly o'er the cryſtal tide,
In daring, active motions ſlide;
Or form'd in parties, joyful throw
Their harmleſs balls of pureſt ſnow;
And jocund, blythe, their ſports purſue,
'Till *February* comes in view.

ON

ON FEBRUARY.

Now *February* bleak appears,
Which fills our breasts with gloomy fears;
And, cheerlefs, makes us oft retreat
To court the fire's enliv'ning heat.
The fruitlefs earth dejected moans
Its doleful fate in deepeft groans.
Now, weighty show'rs of driving hail,
With raging vehemence prevail;
Succeeding cataracts of rain,
With rapid floods o'erwhelm the plain;
And ravage with refiftlefs force,
Whatever dare oppofe their courfe;
Then, frofts in fetters bind the ground,
And fpread their firm-lock'd chains around;
Next, falling clouds of chilling fnow,
Add ftill frefh implements of woe;
While dreadful hurricanes of wind,
Difturb with fears each timid mind:
And yet the chorifters of air
In throngs affemble now to pair;
And jocund, fill each wood and grove,
With fweeteft notes of conftant love.
The farmer views, with heaving fighs,
The tumults that involve the fkies;

And

And aching forrows fill his foul,
While raging, difmal tempefts howl.
Now *Phœbus* peeps abroad by day,
And glads us with his cheering ray ;
Contracting each returning night,
'Till *March* approaches to our fight.

ON MARCH.

IN *March* destructive tempests roar,
And foaming billows lash the shore;
While ev'ry sailor's daring breast
With anx'ous trouble is oppress'd.
Consumptive people waste away,
And sickly mortals now decay;
And while the earth acquires fresh bloom,
They quickly hasten to the tomb.
Rude blasts convulse the northern skies,
And as loud-sounding storms arise;
The jovial rustics quaff their beer,
And hail this season of the year.
The huntsman with his sweet-ton'd horn,
With joyful shouts salutes the morn;
And free from fear, pursues his dogs,
O'er hills and dales, thro' plains and bogs.
The pretty, little, harmless lambs,
Frisk gladly with their woolly dams;
And while the vallies deep resound,
They bleating leap, and sport around.
Now to the cultivated plain,
The farmer trusts his yellow grain;
Which will in proper time afford
A ten-fold produce to its Lord.

But

But lo! the fun, increas'd in light,
Difplays his glory to our fight.
The cheerful, all-enliv'ning fpring,
Inftructs the feather'd race to fing;
While Nature, tafting pureft mirth,
To pleafant *April* gives its birth.

ON APRIL.

Now *April* comes, whose fertile rain
With verdure decks each graffy plain;
And does to fmiling fields difpenfe
Its glad and welcome influence.
The fky ferenely bright appears,
The fun's kind heat the farmer cheers;
The fportive lambkins fkip around,
While ev'ry lawn's with daifies crown'd.
The budding trees their bloom renew,
And put on robes of verdant hue.
The milkmaids now, untaught by art,
To their dear fwains their love impart;
While ev'ry youth, with equal flame,
Returns the paffion of his dame.
The hardy plowman turns the foil,
And drowns in merriment his toil.
The honeft ruftic tells his tale
Over a pot of nut-brown ale;
While belles and coxcombs are array'd
In coftly cloth, and rich brocade.
The warbling birds their carols fing,
And joyful hail the lovely fpring.
The bufy bees now fly abroad,
To feek their mellow, honey'd load;

And

And frugal ants, with prudent care,
Supplies for winter now prepare.
The feafon daily warmer grows,
The cooling breeze more rarely blows;
Still *Phœbus* darts a ftronger ray,
And tells us of the coming *May*.

ON MAY.

FAIR Nature deck'd in mild array,
Now uſhers in the lovely *May;*
While welcome *Phœbus* glads our ſight,
And fills our boſoms with delight.
The bloſſoms pendant on the bough,
With balmy odors richly glow.
The blooming verdure kindly ſheds
Its fragrance on the graſſy meads.
With ſweeteſt notes the vocal thruſh,
Harmonic pipes from ev'ry buſh ;
And whiſtling blackbirds, from each thorn,
Salute, with melody, the morn.
Fond *Ceres* crowns with riſing grain
The fertile, culture-boaſting plain.
The frugal bees collect with care
The ſweets which op'ning bloſſoms bear ;
And hoard a plentiful repaſt
Againſt the winter's gloomy blaſt.
The feather'd ſongſters watch their neſt,
And lull their clam'rous young to reſt ;
Which ſtriplings oft, in wanton play,
Remorſeleſs ſeize, and bear away.
The nymphs and ſhepherds in each grove,
Alternate chaunt their faithful love ;

And

And not a creature now complains,
While jocund, lovely *Maia* reigns.
But lo! the fun ftill clambers high,
And darts frefh glory from the fky;
His fteeds more flowly drive at noon,
And warn us of approaching *June.*

ON

ON JUNE.

BEHOLD now with an aspect clear,
The kindly smiling *June* appear;
While in its train the sun displays
The force of his delightful rays!
The blooming orchards all around,
Are with the sweetest blossoms crown'd;
And the industr'ous, frugal bees,
Collect the honey from the trees.
The cheerful larks now soar on high,
And sing, rejoicing, to the sky.
The hawthorns clad in smiling bloom,
Emit a fragrant, rich perfume.
Fond *Flora*, in her gaudy dress,
Keeps in the gardens her recess;
And now beholds with glowing eyes,
The sweetly-smelling flow'rs arise;
While ev'ry field, and each gay plain,
Exulting owns her pleasant reign.
With joy the husbandmen behold
The cheerful crops their farms unfold.
The welcome cuckoos fly around,
And glad us with a simple sound.
The bashful nymphs now nightly stray,
Where cooling rivers gently play;

And

And by the ruftic fwains uney'd,
Plunge their fair bodies in the tide.
But fee the all-enliv'ning fun,
His daily courfe unweary'd run;
And give, with much reluctance, place
To *July*, which comes on apace!

ON

ON JULY.

Now *July* comes, on which await
A fcorching fky, and fervent heat;
While rays fierce-darting from the fun,
Inceffant move, their courfe to run.
The apples ripen on the trees,
And flow'rets court the bufy bees.
The woods and groves with mufic ring,
As feather'd choirs in concert fing;
And fragrant meadows, blufhing fweet,
The fmell with balmy odors greet.
Say, can the painter's pencil vie
For colors, with the butterfly?
Or with his niceft tints expofe,
Such graces as the blufhing rofe?
The woodbines, deck'd in native pride,
Tho' mounting near the bramble's fide,
Surpafs in ornament and fmell,
Each perfum'd, gaudy, flutt'ring belle.
The chatt'ring, corn-frequenting quail,
And hoarfe-pip'd, meadow-loving rail;
With notes alternate ftrike the ear,
And hail with joy the jocund year.
Now frifking herds fhun *Sol*'s bright ray,
And in refrefhing waters play.

The

The loaded trees luxuriant glow,
And now their mellow fruits beſtow.
But *Phœbus* quickly haſtes away,
Contracting each ſucceeding day;
'Till pleaſing *Auguſt* comes in ſight,
Which yields us longer reſt at night.

ON AUGUST.

Lo blooming *Auguſt*, ſmiling kind,
Elates the careful farmer's mind!
Hark! how the gently-ſwelling breeze,
In mildneſs whiſpers thro' the trees;
And wafting calmly o'er the plain,
Bends into waves the yellow grain!
The dog-ſtar now, with raging heat,
Makes the reluctant hind retreat;
And reſt his weary limbs awhile,
That he again may work and toil.
The trees with juicy apples bend,
And pears from loaded boughs depend:
The peaches with a bluſhing dye,
Invite the taſte, and glad the eye;
While balmy flow'rets all around,
With richeſt honors cloath the ground.
Their ſickles now the ſwains prepare,
And, joyful, to the fields repair;
Jocund to reap, with buſy hands,
The produce of their fertile lands:
Their work with plenty *Ceres* crowns,
And in rich crops their hardſhips drowns.
With hurry ev'ry village teems,
And all one ſcene of buſ'neſs ſeems;

While

While frugal mortals life employ
In buftle, labor, care, and joy :
The morning fees their toil begun,
Which ends not with the fetting fun;
And all the willing tafk purfue,
'Till mild *September* comes in view.

ON SEPTEMBER.

SEPTEMBER, rich with waving grain,
With plenty crowns each hoary plain;
While careful hufbandmen, with joy,
Diligently their time employ;
And cheerful reap the nodding hoard,
Their fertile fields ten-fold afford.
With mellow fruit the orchards glow,
Which mild and pleafant fruit beftow;
Or prefs'd, afford a cooling juice,
Ordain'd by God for mankind's ufe.
The filver moon, with borrow'd beams,
And waning luftre, nightly gleams;
While gilded ftars, remotely bright,
To earth emit a twinkling light.
The bleating fheep, fecure from cold,
Are clofely tended in their fold;
And lowing herds their ftalls contain,
Well fhelter'd from the chilling rain.
The feather'd warblers ceafe to fing
In ftrains which made the woods once ring;
And fettle penfive in the grove,
Forgetful now of making love.
The fun more dimly rules by day,
And fhines now with a fainter ray;

While

While fading hedges fore lament
The leafy honors from them rent.
But fee, loud-fwelling blafts arife
And darker horrors cloud the fkies!
A difmal profpect all things wear
As fad *October* does appear.

ON

ON OCTOBER.

NOW bleak *October* rushes on,
Which seldom owns the cheering sun;
And weak, consumptive beings fear
This sickly season of the year.
The leafless trees dejected mourn
Their once glad beauties from them torn;
While dreadful *Boreas* blows amain,
And strews their honors o'er the plain.
The drooping warblers of the wood,
Now fearful roam abroad for food;
And every naked, lonely bush
Bewails the absent, sweet-pip'd thrush.
Swift round his head the thresher wheels
His flail, whose weight the barley feels;
And to his blows, quick-falling, yield
The ripen'd harvests of the field.
The horrid tempests direful roar,
And surges dash against the shore;
While sailors view, with fearful eyes,
The lightnings flashing from the skies.
Each jolly swain, o'er nut-brown ale,
Now cracks a jest, or tells a tale;
And hearty shouts proclaim around,
That mirth and harmony abound.

Chill'd

Chill'd mortals round the embers crowd,
And joyous fing, or talk aloud;
Then to their homely couches creep,
To eafe their toil in balmy fleep:
While with *November* fhorter days,
Long nights, and nipping colds increafe.

ON NOVEMBER.

NOVEMBER, of unwelcome hue,
Approaches difmal to our view;
While dreadful hurricanes difplay
Their baneful force by land and fea.
The difmal rain its fury pours,
In weighty, quick-defcending fhow'rs;
While muddy ftreams, in fwelling rills,
Rufh rapid down the floping hills;
And clouds of hail fharp-pointed fly,
Darting their vengeance from the fky.
The thrifty houfewife cards and fpins,
Whofe tafk with rifing *Sol* begins,
Nor till he long has funk from fight,
Does fhe to labor bid good night.
The lowing cattle feem to moan,
And for their verdant paftures groan;
Whofe owners, heedful of their cry,
With ftraw and hay their wants fupply.
Now lively folk at balls and plays,
Or charming cards, their fancies pleafe;
And foolifh children round the fire,
Of fairies, ghofts, and fprites enquire;
Till weary grown, they fhrink to bed,
Fill'd with horrific, idle dread.

Now,

Now, in the cold, benumbing night,
The fparrows bend their eager flight
To fnug-thatch'd roofs, where they remain,
Secure from ftorms, and chilling rain.
But lo! *December* next appears,
Which racks our breafts with painful fears.

ON DECEMBER.

ROUGH, baneful hurricanes arife,
And northern tempefts cloud the fkies;
While chilling blafts make mortals know
December comes, replete with fnow.
The wither'd herbage of the fields
Scant food to hungry cattle yields,
That heartlefs crop the poor remains
Of fertile once, and verdant plains.
With plenty deck'd, the feftive board
Does mirth and jollity afford;
And jocund people *Chriftmas* hail
With fports, fongs, jefts, and honeft ale;
Which ferve to banifh fullen care,
And eafe the hardfhips of the year.
The innocent and ufeful fheep,
To places fet with bufhes creep;
And there in plaintive bleatings moan
The pleafant, funny feafon gone.
Thick crowded ftars adorn the night,
And fhed a clear and glitt'ring light.
In mourning clad, the feeble fun
Dejected moves, its courfe to run;
And faint, obfcure, each gloomy day,
Scarce deals to earth a fingle ray.

The

The froſt with hoary honors crown'd,
In cloſe-lock'd fetters binds the ground;
Whoſe keen and piercing pow'rs diſpenſe
To land and ſea their influence,
Which numb the limbs with nipping pain;
And the year ends with cold and rain.

ON MORNING.

BEHOLD the glitt'ring ſtars retire,
  And in thick clouds themſelves repoſe;
Avoiding *Sol's* reſplendent fire,
  While beaming glory round him flows.

The daring cock, with lofty throat,
  Gives notice of the coming morn;
And nightingales of ſweeteſt note,
  Forſake their reſting-place, the thorn.

The huntſman with loud, early cries,
  Now ſtarts the fearful, nimble hare;
And o'er the plains impatient flies,
  The worthleſs, timid prey to ſhare.

From his ſtraw couch the frugal clown
  Haſtes quick to earn his wages poor;
And ſnarling cur-dogs in each town,
  Stand barking at their maſters' door.

The fowler, with obſervant eye,
  Explores each wood and brake around;
And as the warblers ſleeping lie,
  They ſink beneath a deadly wound.

4

Now fifhermen into the flood,
  With ftedfaft look commit their bait;
While in large fhoals the finny brood
  Catch eager at their certain fate.

The linen from the clean-wafh'd pail,
  Is hung to dry upon the thorn;
And fturdy threfhers with the flail,
  Inceffant beat the yielding corn.

The foaring larks, afcending high,
  Freed from the difmal gloom of night,
Tune their fhrill pipes, and gladly fly,
  Rejoicing at approaching light.

The blooming milkmaid fweetly fings,
  As fhe trips lightly o'er the plain;
And kindly fmiling, new-milk brings,
  To her enamour'd, honeft fwain.

The fchool-boy o'er the verdant fod,
  With tardy pace moves on his way;
Regardlefs of his teacher's rod,
  He fpends his golden hours in play.

ON NOON.

THE fun-his lazy car has driv'n
Up the fteep, meridian height;
Illumining the earth and heav'n,
  With keeneft rays of piercing light.

The face of nature looks ferene,
  Frefh glories beam throughout the fkies;
While from the fields and hedges green,
  The aromatic fragrance flies.

The birds in throngs now panting fly,
  And dip them in the limpid flood;
Or in thick clufters joyful lie,
  Clofe cover'd by the fhady wood.

See from on high the larks defcend,
  Unable to endure the heat;
And where the leafy poplars bend,
  The weary hind feeks a retreat.

Swift from its cell the bufy bee
  Flies anx'ous to collect its fweet;
And oxen from the plow fet free,
  In fhades repofe their tired feet.

The

The fchool-boy now indulges play,
  And quits his heavy book awhile;
The brawny ruftics tofs the hay,
  And with loud laughs their tafks beguile.

The mower from his work retires,
  To cool him in the gentle breeze;
And hides from *Sol*'s refiftlefs fires,
  While fcarce a zephyr fans the trees.

In herds the harmlefs, woolly, fheep,
  Throng ardent to the thicket's fide;
And haft'ning down the rugged fteep,
  In leaf-clad coverts joyful hide.

Now from the field the careful fwain,
  Homewards directs his tardy way;
But when refrefh'd, returns again,
  To make amends for his delay.

In the green bow'r, with cheerful throat,
  Each fhepherd chaunts to his lov'd dame;
While fhe with foft, enchanting note,
  Repays his true and conftant flame.

ON

ON EVENING,

THE fober ev'ning, ting'd with red,
Steals flowly on the wond'ring fight;
While *Phœbus* refts on *Thetis'* bed,
And introduces dufky night.

The empty fhadows longer grow,
As objects pafs along the plain;
The gadding cows move homewards flow,
And in their well-known ftalls remain.

Lo! from his work the frugal clown,
Retires now to his fimple treat;
And tir'd with labor, lays him down
On the green bench before his gate.

Protected fafely from the fox,
To their folds hafte the bleating fheep;
And echo rifing from the rocks,
Expands refponfive o'er the deep.

The milkmaid with her fnow-white pail,
Now to her ev'ning tafk repairs;
While honeft fhepherds quaff their ale,
And toaft their charming, comely fairs.

The

The feather'd warblers ceafe their fong,
  And haften joyful to their neft;
Quick flying to their callow young,
  They lull them into quiet reft.

The lads and laffes on the green,
  In fprightly meafures frifk and play;
With ruftic garlands deck their queen,
  Or tumble thro' the new-mown hay.

The leathern-winged bat now flies,
  From the old abbey's crevic'd wall;
While gently from the gilded fkies
  The genial dew-drops lightly fall.

His daily toil the farmer leaves,
  And bends his flow-pac'd journey home;
While wifely provident he faves
  A ftock for winter's barren gloom.

The twinkling ftars refume their place,
  And fhed around a glimm'ring light;
While *Luna* with a filver'd face,
  Gives warning of approaching night.

ON NIGHT.

SEE Night, bedeck'd in dark array,
  Her fluggifh fteeds now flowly drive;
While not a beam points out the way,
  Save what the glow-worms faintly give.

The ftriplings loudly fing thro' fear,
  As they run quickly o'er the plain;
While tippling drunkards guzzle beer,
  To eafe them of their marriage pain.

From the old, ruin'd, folemn dome
  The owl, impatient of the light,
Now dares to venture from its home,
  And fcreaming takes its airy flight.

The prowling fox, with cunning eye,
  His feather'd fpoil prepares to feize;
And as in quiet fleep they lie,
  On turkeys, ducks, hens, geefe he preys,

In crowds the elves affembled now,
  In circles dance upon the grafs;
The fongfters refting on the bough,
  The night in filent flumbers pafs.

The

The faithful watch-dog in the yard,
  Obfervant in his kennel lies ;
His owner's property to guard,
  And keep his dwelling from furprize.

Now fcarce a whifper ftrikes the ear,
  Acrofs the fragrant, level land ;
Their mafks the bloody ruffians wear,
  And at lone corners take their ftand.

The frugal hufbandmen repofe,
  On couches plain their droufy heads ;
But when their centinel cock crows,
  They roufe them from their ftraw-made beds.

The fairies gliding at the door,
  Now thro' the key-hole nimbly creep ;
And lightly tripping on the floor,
  Pinch dirty houfe-maids in their fleep.

The filver moon flits fwift away,
  The ftars emit a weaker light ;
The fkies their gilded robes difplay,
  And bar the gates of fable night.

A FABLE.

A FABLE.

In days of yore, when ev'ry creature
Could glibly talk, as taught by nature:
When larks and linnets tun'd each mattin,
In *Greek* fublime, or noble *Latin*:
When dogs and cats held pretty prattle,
And could, like modern people, tattle:
A philofophic fox would tell ye
His *fummum bonum* was his belly;
And when keen hunger call'd for food,
A turkey, duck, or hen was good:
When pigs taught arithmetic, and
How many planets move or ftand;
And plainly fhew'd twice two are four,
Great truths, from children hid before!
When learned monkies practis'd phyfic,
Could vomit, bleed, draw teeth, or—make fick;
With fevers, agues, rais'd a rout,
And differtations on the gout:
When rav'nous wolves prais'd felf-denial.
Yet ne'er themfelves would make the trial;
But, when the fpirit mov'd, could eat
A tender lamb—'twas harmlefs meat!
When owls demure kept fober fchools,
And laid down methodiftic rules;

Preach'd

Preach'd worldly pleafures all were vain,
Yet could not from fuch things refrain;
When geefe, deck'd richly in brocade,
Made conquefts at a mafquerade;
And were as ceafelefs of good fame,
As any modern, titled dame:
When peacocks fram'd the neweft fafhion,
And made fops' cloaths in ev'ry nation:
When grim baboon turn'd dancing-mafter,
And made each awkward mifs move fafter;
And prov'd the modifh method how
To court'fy, or to fcrape a bow:
When 'mongft the modeft fheep each prude
Could faintly bleat, " Fie, Sir, you're rude:"
When magpies with coquettifh air,
Would laugh, grin, hop, and fondly ftare:
When all the finny brood could play
Up " Water parted from the Sea:"
Rats could diftinguifh by their tafte,
Whofe wheat or barley was the beft;
And would, like villains unconfin'd,
Their neighbours rob, to juftice blind:
When Crifpin Jack-all taught each beau
His fhoes to buckle at the toe:
When friffeur goats drefs'd ladies' hair,
With puddings, greafe, and *French poudre*;
Inftructing foreign modes to prize,
But heartily their own defpife:

D d   When

When frugal bees, at early dawn,
With care explor'd each flow'ry lawn;
And joyful bore the honey'd load,
On eager wings to their abode;
Where, dire diftrefs! each worthlefs drone
Securely feafts, as on his own:
When lap-dogs in an ev'ning fat
To fip their tea, and have fome chat;
War, mufic, politics, fuch ftuff,
For fome time ferv'd them well enough;
Till back-biting alone could pleafe,
Much like the cuftom now-a-days.

When things were thus upon a time,
(No matter when, or in what clime)
A fage affembly met together,
One morning in fine fummer weather;
All thither fummon'd by the afs,
Whofe office that of herald was;
For, *Stentor-like*, his lungs were ftrong,
And fweetly could he bray a fong;
Or o'er a quart of nappy ale,
Roar out a catch, or tell a tale;
In order to deliberate
On fome things of important weight:
Beafts, infects, birds, fifh, one and all,
Hear and obey the vocal call.

The

The place of meeting 'twas agreed,
Should be upon a verdant mead;
Where an extenfive lake difplays
Its cryftal waves to *Sol*'s bright rays;
For then the fifhes in the deep,
Like folk at church, might hear, or—fleep;
Vermin, fowl, cattle round the lake,
Of fome refrefhment might partake.

Tho' mountains then aloud could roar,
And billows fcold along the fhore;
Tho' voices founded from each hill,
And murm'ring ftrains from ev'ry rill;
Tho' plaintive accents fill'd each rock,
And echo dar'd their notes to mock;
Tho' zephyrs chaunted thro' each grove,
And nodding trees vow'd faithful love;
Yet ev'ry noife was ftraight fupprefs'd;
As thus a cow the crowd addrefs'd,
And claim'd attention from the throng,
While words momentous grac'd her tongue:

" My friends and brethren! (certainly
" I with fuch terms may now make free;
" Since they are us'd by all our preachers,
" Our holy priefts, and rev'rend teachers)
" I had a wondrous dream laft night,
" Which caus'd fome pain, but much delight:

" Yet

" Yet think not that I idly fpeak,
" Or that my intelle&s are weak ;
" No vain chimæra I relate,
" Or what is foreign to repeat ;
" For twice before it fill'd my mind,
" Or may I from this time be blind ;
" And you know what's repeated thrice,
" Will come to pafs—fo fay the wife."

Here all attend with ears ere&,
And anx'oufly the tale expe& ;
While Madam *Bas*, elate with mirth,
Thus gives the ftrange narration birth :

" Methought the genius of the flood,
" Slow rais'd him from the flimy mud :
" His head was crown'd with gilded rays,
" Which caft a ftrong, refulgent blaze ;
" His body was array'd in white,
" Which foon difpell'd the gloom of night ;
" And from his lips mild accents broke,
" As thus in folemn tone he fpoke :

' To what I now reveal attend,
' And know I am your deareft friend.
' Lo ! underneath this lake is plac'd
' An herb of moft furprifing tafte ;

2

' Its

' Its wondrous quality is fuch,

' 'Twill make you happy by its touch;

' No dangers fhall on you await,

' Nor fears difturb your peaceful ftate;

' No more fhall men your eafe moleft,

' No more annoy your tranquil reft;

' For, this preventative procur'd,

' Eternal fafety is fecur'd;

' So general is its excellence,

' Such ufeful good does it difpenfe;

' To ev'ry being 'twill fuffice,

' That creeps, or walks, or fwims, or flies;

' The hook no more the fifh need fear,

' Nor birds avoid the fowler's fnare;

' All things by land, in air, or fea,

' May chace their empty dread away:

' Then ftraight convene each animal,

' (I mean that is *irrational*)

' And feek diligently to find,

' This fure preferver of their kind;

' But ye muft all this water drain,

' Before ye can the plant obtain.'

" This faid, he funk; I rais'd my head,

" And tofs'd and tumbled on my bed.

" I have difclos'd what I was bid,

" Nor is the fmalleft tittle hid.

" Like

" Like ſtocks or ſtones ſhall we ſtand ſtill,
" Nor ſtrive thoſe orders to fulfill?
" And careleſs of our happineſs,
" Neglect what may inſure ſucceſs?
" Shall we, regardleſs of our lives,
" Not wiſh to ſhun the butchers' knives?
" And fooliſhly deſpiſe the means
" Tho' hard, to ward off future pains?
" At leaſt my kindred will not, ſure,
" Such ſhameful ſlothfulneſs endure ;
" When they the bright example give,
" You'll all, perhaps, tho' late, believe ;
" Nor longer with indiff'rence hear
" The admonition I declare."

The kine aſſented with a nod,
And rent amain the graſſy ſod ;
The dogs tore us as well as able,
And emulation fir'd the rabble :
All warmly ſtrove, with tooth and claw,
The water from the lake to draw ;
But when the progreſs was but ſmall,
And all prov'd ineffectual ;
When long they tugg'd and toil'd in vain,
And thus could no advantage gain ;
As Mrs. Cow was deeply read
In ev'ry tongue alive or dead ;

Was

Was vers'd in hiftory, and knowledge,
Tho' never bred in *Oxford* college ;
Profoundly fkill'd in algebra,
In civil, martial, and church law ;
And could with grave deportment tell
A ftory very plaufible ;
She order'd filence, and aloud
Again harangu'd the lift'ning crowd :

    " I've heard (I will not fay how true,
" But that point I muft leave to you)
" That *Xerxes'* troops drank rivers dry ;
" Why may not we this method try ?
" I know there are as many here
" As he had, what fhould we, then, fear ?
" And perfeverance will o'ercome
" The hardeft tafk in *Chriftendom,*"

    Quite fure of victory, they think
They can with eafe the waters drink ;
Whole tons moft cheerfully they fwill,
But find the lake o'erflowing ftill ;
Again they drink, but foon perceive
The liquid plain frefh ftores receive ;
At length a bear, with age grown grey,
Stepp'd forth, and begg'd thofe words to fay :

    " I fear we labor with fome evil,
" Some fell delufion of the Devil ;

                  " We

" We find him oft o'er man preside,
" His chief companion and his guide ;
" And oft perfuading him to try
" And court impoffibility.
" We *reafon* want, 'tis true, to fhew
" The paths in which we ought to go ;
" But let us not perverfely run,
" And aim at what can ne'er be done."

He faid ; they heeded what he taught,
Difpers'd, and own'd they were in fault ;
Convinc'd, they were no longer blind,
Unlike fome millions of mankind ;
Who purfue obftinately ftill
Schemes which they never can fulfill.

ON

STRAMORE PATRON.

IN blefs'd *Hibernia's* thrice-renowned ifle,
Where hofpitality and plenty fmile ;
Thro' whofe rich plains clear, fertile rivers flow,
Whofe happy lands no pois'nous creatures know;
Whofe hardy foldiers roaring cannons dare,
And face, undaunted, all the rage of war ;
Where *Ulfter* ftretches its fair paftures forth,
To the cool climate of the wholefome north ;
The county *Monaghan* is known to fame,
For yarn, flax, linen cloth, and ftore of game ;
Here lies the barony of *Trugh*, of old
Replete with fportfmen, refolute and bold ;
Who fearlefs follow'd their fure-fcented dogs,
O'er hills and dales, thro' valleys, glens, and
     bogs ;
Who at the fummons of the fweet-ton'd horn
Leap'd from their beds, and hail'd the jocund
     morn ;
Whofe fwift, ftrong hunters left the fields behind,
And rival'd in their fpeed the winged wind :
In vain the five-bar gate oppos'd their way,
Nor ditch nor drain could ftop them from the
    prey ;

Whether

Whether the cunning fox they hold in fight,
That wily, fowl-deftroying thief by night;
Whether the hafmlefs, timid hare they trace,
Whofe mazy windings oft perplex the chafe;
Or the ftout buck, with tow'ring pride elate,
Who dares, majeftic, his impending fate;
With gleeful fhouts exulting they purfue,
And echo gladly while the game's in view.
The fons ftill own the ardor of their fires,
Their gen'rous breafts glow with *Nimrodian*
    fires;
And in like fports fome vacant hours employ,
To banifh trouble and afford them joy.

Large fhoals of fifhes gambol in each flood,
Here crooked eels quick wallow thro' the mud;
In cryftal brooks there darts the fpeckled trout,
The wide-mouth'd pike here rears his rav'nous
    fnout;
The finny brood, the roach, the tench, and breme,
Plunge thro' each lake, and play in ev'ry ftream;
And all confpire to pleafe the angler's eye,
To feize the bait, or catch the cheating fly.
Here bafks the partridge in the ftubble field,
Great ftore of grous the heath-clad mountains
    yield;
The woodcock flufhes from the clofe-fet brake;
See from the marfh the fnipe to flight betake!

Ducks,

Ducks, teal, and widgeon wing their airy round,
And rails and plover cop'oufly abound.

In lower *Trugh*, near the *Black-water* fide,
A verdant plain extendeth far and wide,
Known by the appellation of *Stramore*,
A place ne'er fpoken of in verfe before.
On *Eafter Monday* hither thoufands run,
To be fpectators of, or join the fun.
Here limping fidlers hafte as well as able,
To glean fome coppers from the giddy rabble;
And here blind pipers merrily repair,
To charm each ruftic's truly ruftic ear.
The fports begin; the mufic plays; and lo!
The lively lads and laffes in a row
Form the light dance, and trip it on the ground,
To the fad bagpipes' or harfh fiddle's found;
And for their dance the ftated tribute pay,
The fum an halfpenny—then march away;
For here no formal complaifance is fhewn,
Nor female partner paid for by the clown.
What tho' no mafter ever taught them how
To drop a court'fy, walk genteel, or bow;
In fprightly meafures on the green they move,
And cheerful hop, as they themfelves approve.

Here *Oonah* ftands; her pumps, you fee, are new,
Her gown ftripp'd linen, and her ftockings blue;

E e 2   Laft

Laſt week in *Glaſslough* were her buckles bought,
How bright they ſhine, tho' purchas'd for a groat!
With three-cock'd hat, and ſmooth-comb'd, flow-
    ing hair,
Her partner *Paddy* hands along the fair;
His brogues are half-ſoal'd, and at ev'ry bound
Their firm-nail'd heels imprint the beaten ground.
Dolly with care her ſcarlet cloak diſplays,
Lac'd tightly in her miſtreſs' caſt-off ſtays;
While *Laughlin* ſtruts, and ſeemingly looks big,
With coarſe black ſtockings, and his one-row
    wig.
Here *Peggy* ſkips, dreſs'd in a yellow gown,
Which coſt in *Skernageerah* juſt a crown;
New cap and ribands ſet her off with grace,
And add freſh honors to her roſy face;
While *Denis* ſmartly trips along to ſhew
His ſheep-ſkin breeches, bought ſome weeks ago.
With nimble ſteps ſee *Bridget* next advance,
And gladly enter on the pleaſing dance;
A new green petticoat proclaims her fine,
And gloves and ruffles render her divine!
Lawrence beholds her with a lover's eye,
And " cuts his capers," as his ſweetheart's nigh;
Diſplays his bath-rug coat with artful care,
And laughs with joy to ſee her fondly ſtare.
There *Sheelah* moves with awkward, ſheepiſh mien,
Her handkerchief and apron, though, are clean;
                         And

And then who can unmov'd, uncharm'd withſtand
The penny ring that decks her yellow hand!
Terrence the lightning of her eyes receives,
And ſwears for her alone he dies or lives;
While his red waiſtcoat ſhoots a pointed dart,
Which pierces her, kind fair one! thro' the heart.

I could recount an hundred other names
Of ruſtic youths, and freſh-complexion'd dames;
Whoſe native beauties feel no ſinful paint,
Whoſe blooming cheeks no borrow'd colors taint:
But as ſome palates ſqueamiſhly are nice,
Ev'n theſe few characters may now ſuffice.

Lo! there at commons two-form'd parties ſtand,
Each graſps the bended weapon in his hand;
Then near each other in the ground are fix'd
Two ſticks at each end, ſome ſcore yards betwixt;
Thro' one of which the wooden ball muſt run,
Before the game is either loſt or won.
And now the ball flies ſwift acroſs the ground,
Now o'er their heads behold it lightly bound!
Anon it falls; the ready heroes near,
Oft intercept it in its quick career.
See one confiding in his active ſpeed,
Reſiſtleſs drive it o'er the graſſy mead;
'Till running forward with unguarded force,
A rival's foot arreſts him in his courſe,

And

And lays him proftrate; then loud laughters rife,
And fhouts of triumph rend the vaulted fkies.
Not long the conqu'ror fhall exulting boaft
His late gain'd vict'ry, which muft_foon be loft:
A trip projects him headlong on the ground,
While roaring clamors echo all around.
Succeffively they ftumble, run, and fall,
Alternate bear away, or lofe the ball;
Till with the exercife fatigu'd, they make
A willing truce, and fome fhort breathing take.

For foot-ball two felected bodies there,
With eager looks and cheerfulnefs prepare:
And firft afide their coats and hats they lay,
As thefe would prove too cumbrous in the play.
Now o'er the plain the ball is fwift impell'd,
And quickly bounds acrofs the verdant field;
Now thro' the air it lightly fkims along,
And from aloft drops in the gaping throng;
Again it flies, again the youths engage
In ftruggling conflict, but unknown to rage:
The thick-foal'd brogue from the fore, bleeding
    fhin
With erring kicks ftrips off the bleeding fkin;
They juftle, trip, kick, wreftle, fall, and rife,
And fhout and fwear with loud, confufed cries;
Nor ceafe their fports, till weary with their toil,
They fit them down, and gladly reft awhile.

Here

Here crowds divert themselves at pitch-and-tofs,
All wish to win, tho' to their neighbours' lofs.
Here *Philip* fquanders all his cafh away,
The price of his good yarn, at idle play.
Behold how *Miles* his rent and tythe forgets,
And ventures all his money here on betts!
See *Murtoagh* rifk the purchafe of his fhoes,
And very juftly ev'ry farthing lofe;
While *Dermot*'s fleec'd of what fhould buy fome
  meal,
And is compell'd to beg, work hard, or—fteal;
And *Teague* rejoices at his lucky fate,
Five fhillings won, make him with blifs elate.

Together there a group of little boys
In their train'd hands the well-fhap'd cockfticks
  poife.
A circle's fwept upon the beaten land,
And in its centre, lo! a prop does ftand:
On this a piece of lead, or button's laid,
The ftated length is meafur'd on the mead,
O'er which they throw; three cafts for ev'ry pin;
Happy's the lad who can the trifle win!
Well pleas'd is he, compleated is his joy,
Who from the circle drives the worthlefs toy!

Lo! here are troops of brawny ruftics feen,
Who with agility fpring on the green.
       Some

Some with hop-step-and-leap themselves divert,
Others at running-leaps are most expert:
Here sev'ral hold a staff in either hand,
With which they bound far o'er the level land:
Some throw the drawing, some the shoulder
  stone,
And inactivity is felt by none.

Here fortune's wheel is quickly turn'd about,
Round which the gulls raise at themselves a
  shout;
While its proprietor, with merry heart,
Acts, as prime gainer in the farce, chief part.
How prone are we to aid the wily foe,
Who for *Eve*'s offspring plots unceasing woe!

Some fav'rite scheme does ev'ry one employ,
And all is cheerfulness, content, and joy.

The sun now streaks the skies with ruddy
  light,
And yields its empire to the pow'r of night;
In splendid pomp the silver moon is crown'd,
And twinkling stars emit their beams around;
When to the tents the men and women drive,
Like bees in summer clust'ring at the hive.
Around they ply with whiskey, rum, and beer,
While cyder, wine, and brandy join the cheer;
        With

With jokes and tales the meeting they pro-
    long,
And crown their revels with an *Irifh* fong;
Make love by turns, and fometimes hop and
    prance,
And blithfome grown, again renew the dance;
Bagpipes and fiddles, with their grating notes,
Join in full concert with the ruftics' throats;
They curfe, tell lies, difpute, talk loud, and
    laugh,
Till urg'd to madnefs by the drink they quaff,
To blows and furious combat they proceed;
Friends fall by friends, and fons by fathers bleed;
Their angry ftrokes to all alike they deal,
The liquors o'er their fenfes fo prevail.
The knotty floe-tree cudgel bruifes fore,
And from their heads draws floods of crimfon
    gore;
Tough afh and hazle give a defp'rate wound,
And ftout fhilelahs on their fkulls refound:
With jars and tumults thus they end the play,
And fights and bloodfhed clofe the parting day.

Suppofe that now their fteps all homeward
    bend,
And heavy deluges of rain defcend;
The new red cloak and petticoat are fpoil'd,
The bonnet, handkerchief, and gown are foil'd;

F f   'The

The tipſy huſband tugs along his wife,
Drunk as himſelf, the torment of his life;
Their tott'ring limbs can ſcarce their load ſuſ-
    tain,
Stagg'ring they tumble thro' ſome miry drain;
Whence hardly dragg'd, along the road they ſtray,
And blindly reeling, oft miſtake their way;
Till partly dry'd and warmed by the fire,
They to their humble, ruſhy beds retire;
Where I muſt leave them to ſerene repoſe,
And thus my ſimple narrative ſhall cloſe.

ON THE

MUCH LAMENTED DEATH

OF THE

REVEREND FOWKE MOORE, *A. M.*

MASTER OF *DUNGANNON* FREE-SCHOOL, IN THE
COUNTY OF *TYRONE.*

A T length the fure-aim'd fhaft of fate has
 fped,
And *Moore* lies number'd with the mould'ring
 dead :
His mortal frame, thro' many years' decay
Exhaufted, yields him to his parent clay.
Tho' pedantry was banifh'd from his breaft,
The man of learning fhone in him confefs'd ;
Unfeign'd devotion, with peculiar grace,
Liv'd in his life, and fmil'd upon his face.
His gentle bofom, free from envy's fting,
Ne'er made dire difcord among neighbours fpring;
But, with the focial virtues fully fraught,
The placid paths of harmlefs pleafure taught :
With jocund innocence, and wit refin'd,
The gentleman and Chriftian were conjoin'd.

    Farewell,

Farewell, blefs'd fhade! may thy example guide.
Thy fellow-creatures thro' life's rugged tide!
May refignation, fuch as thine, impart
Its healing balm to ev'ry wounded heart!
Teach them with thankfulnefs to kifs the rod
Of bitter grief, inflicted by their GOD!
Make them confefs, that he who deals the woes,
Has equal pow'r their forrows to compofe;
And in due time with lafting joys will blefs
The patient fons and daughters of diftrefs!

A N

OCCASIONAL PROLOGUE.

Y E brave affertors of *Hibernia*'s weal,
Whofe bofoms glow with patriotic zeal!
Self-offer'd patrons of the nobleft caufe,
To fave your country, liberties, and laws!
A brother-foldier fondly would impart ,
The warm emotions of an honeft heart;
And pay to *Ireland*'s volunteers that praife,
Which lafting honor to your names fhould raife:
But, from conviction that his nervelefs verfe,
In feeble numbers would your worth rehearfe;
To future *Miltons* he configns the lyre,
To chaunt a theme which *Homers* might infpire.

Now *Gallic* perfidy, and *Spanifh* pride,
In hoftile triumph on the ocean ride;
Together leagu'd, a formidable band!
Menace deftruction to our native land.
If with fuch foes our fate is to contend,
Not I alone a fifter muft defend.
While devaftation and unbridled rage,
Involve in common ev'ry fex and age;
Then thoufand *Dudleys*, feiz'd by ruthlefs pow'r,
In fruitlefs plaints muft weep their natal hour;

And

And time-worn heroes, fpent by years and pain,
Lift their weak hands, and fupplicate in vain.

In days of yore our gallant grandfires fpread
O'er *France* and *Spain* an univerfal dread ;
Thro' ranks oppofing rufh'd with boundlefs might,
And ftill undaunted dar'd the coming fight.
Have then our fathers, candidates for fame,
With well-earn'd trophies gain'd a deathlefs name?
And fhall their fons, when glory calls aloud,
In timid indolence their heads enfhroud ?
With tamenefs fuffer *Bourbon*'s haughty train,
For free-born fouls to forge a fervile chain ?
No.—Dangers flighted for *Ierne*'s good,
Shall found our valour in the field of blood ;
In future times our prowefs fhall be told,
And our example make our children bold ;
While they, like us, each vaunting foe defy,
Refolv'd to conquer, or unvanquifh'd die.

A N

OCCASIONAL EPILOGUE.

WHERE'ER my animated glances fly,
A martial object ftrikes my roving eye.
Hibernia fummons her bold chiefs around,
Whofe ardent breafts revere the welcome found;
Honor erects her banners in the air,
To which the fons of liberty repair;
While fame and glory light fair freedom's fires,
And emulation each brave foul infpires.

In former times what our forefathers were,
Let *Blenhcim*'s plains, and *Dettingen* declare;
Where *Gallic* armies own'd fuperior might,
And funk in death, or fought ignoble flight.
In foreign climes, then, was their courage fhewn,
And fhall we hefitate to guard our own?
Of noble anceftors how can we boaft,
If foes invade us, or infult our coaft?
And faithlefs *Bourbon*'s abject, flavifh band,
Should with impunity defpoil our land?
Forbid it, virtue! and forbid it, fhame!
Such daftard meannefs fhould infect our fame!
Your country calls, while freedom intercedes,
And honor ftimulates to gen'rous deeds;

The

The lordly impulſe ev'ry boſom warms,
And magnanimity provokes to arms.

    Permit me, Sirs, in unaffected ſtrain,
To plead my ſex's cauſe, nor plead in vain;
Soldiers, by duty, ſhould protect the fair;
An helpleſs female's their peculiar care.
To you we leave guns, cannons, bay'nets, ſwords,
Our weapons are an arſenal of—words.
While you with eager ſteps to battle preſs,
A woman's province is—to talk and dreſs.
Our magazines of arrows, flames, and darts,
Are ſolely ſuited to our lovers' hearts.
But while on your protection we confide,
The vaunting threats of *Bourbon* we deride.
Your well-known fortitude ſhall calm our woes,
And lull our ſorrows to ſerene repoſe:
Shielded by liberty's brave volunteers,
Our breaſts exult, and diſſipate our fears.

O N

ON THE

SINCERELY DEPLORED DEATH

OF

MR. GABRIEL CORNWALL,

OF STUARTSTOWN,

SURGEON AND APOTHECARY.

ESCULAPIUS.

THE racking fever, with refiftlefs force,
Has thro' the heart impell'd its baneful courfe;
The ftruggle of contending nature's o'er,
Life's pulfe is ftopp'd, and *Cornwall* is no more.
My boundlefs ftore of medicines in vain
Has been adminifter'd to eafe his pain;
The king of terrors, with malignant eye,
Frown'd on my aid, and bade his arrow fly.

LUCINA.

No more his fkill obftetric fhall relieve
The pregnant dame, and bid her ceafe to grieve;
No more recall her to the joys of life,
And blefs the hufband in his gentle wife.

G g   And

And is, alas! time's fleeting circle run!
Has death bereft me of my fav'rite fon!
Weep, weep, ye matrons, and your lofs deplore,
Cornwall your guardian, breathes alas! no more.

MOMUS.

My feftive board no more his fong fhall hail,
Or hang attentive on his mirthful tale;
Hufh'd are his notes, for ever mute the voice,
That made his jocund friends fo oft rejoice.
The virtues of his fociable mind,
Were form'd to pleafe and humanize mankind;
But death, on cruelty extreme intent,
Our *Cornwall* from the world and me has rent.

CHARITAS.

No more his lenient hand fhall foothe with
    care
The bed of ficknefs, and avert defpair;
No more around his charitable door,
Difpenfe his lib'ral bounties to the poor.
But hark! Heav'n's awful voice affords relief,
And calls, indulgent, to affuage our grief:
" *Cornwall*, tho' loft to earth, fhall never die,
" Supremely blefs'd to all eternity."

Accept, dear fhade! the tribute of my lays,
Which fondly prefs to celebrate thy praife.

The

4

The heart-felt forrow of thy num'rous friends,
Plaintive around thy breathlefs corfe attends.
Revolving feafons would attempt in vain
To eafe their woe, and mitigate their pain;
Did not religion calm the rending figh,
And teach this leffon, " All are born to die."

AN ACROSTIC.

" JOIN voices, all ye living fouls," to raife
Of him due thanks, who taught you GOD to praife:
Heav'n *loft* to man his deathlefs works record,
Nor ftops his mufe till heav'n's thro' CHRIST re-
    ftor'd.
Millions of angels, from the realms of day,
In joyful tranfports hail the noble lay:
Loud fwells the mufic on their golden ftrings,
To fill the concert as the poet fings.
On *Milton's* brows unfading laurels fhine,
No bard more worthy claims rewards divine.

AN ACROSTIC.

GROANING with anguifh at the mournful
    tale,
England's brave fons their breathlefs chief bewail.
No more their ears, accuftom'd to rejoice,
Exulting hear his animating voice.
Rous'd by refentment, when his country calls,
Ardent he flies, and crown'd with conqueft falls.
Loft to the world in vig'rous manhood's bloom,
Wolfe finks, alas!—but triumphs o'er the tomb.
On fame's ftrong pinions wafted to the fkies,
Lo!- all the hero's fragrant honors rife.
From the oblivion of the fullen grave,
Eternal gratitude his worth fhall fave.

A N

AN ACROSTIC.

LET hoary age no more with infolence
Obtrude its precepts, as fole guide of fenfe:
Rawdon the brave, in youthful manhood wife,
Difputes the maxim, and its truth denies.
Rawdon we find with fterling worth replete,
Alike in fenate and in battle great.
While *Ireland* fuch an ornament can own,
Dauntlefs and prudent, for her native fon;
On her detractors fhe with fcorn may fmile,
Nor heed the gibes with which her foes revile.

AN ACROSTIC.

AS *Gallic Conflans* made his haughty boaft,
Dooming to hoftile ravage *Ireland's* coaft;
Mov'd by a *Britifh*, patriotic flame,
In its defence a brave protector came;
Remov'd its danger, lull'd its fears afleep,
And *England* reign'd bright emprefs of the deep.
Like *Jove's* fierce bird, quick darting on his prey,
Hawke flew refiftlefs o'er the foaming fea;
And fcorning rocks, and winds that raging blow,
With intrepidity affail'd the foe:
Knowing no terror when his country fpoke,
Eager thro' tempefts, fire, and death he broke.

AN

AN ACROSTIC.

SUBLIMELY great, the philofophic mind
In *Newton* fhines, unequall'd, unconfin'd.
Regions and caufes in dark chaos loft,
In his folutions cleareft luftre boaft.
Sunk in obfcurity, of proof bereft,
Aftronomy to errors maze was left;
At *Newton's* call, uncertainty withdrew,
Conviction fpoke, and wifdom rofe to view:
No more the mift of ignorance prevails,
Enlighten'd truth its pleafing form reveals.
With rev'rend wonder, and fupreme delight,
The whole creation opens to our fight.
Orb upon orb, in awful order plac'd,
Newton explor'd, and all their motions trac'd.

AN ACROSTIC.

QUICK flew the hoftile news, and *England*'s
    fons
United rife againft the haughty *Dons.*
Elizabeth collects her gallant bands,
Earneft to execute her great commands.
Now rides the vaft *Armada* o'er the main,
Elate with all the arrogance of *Spain:*
Loud roars the tempeft, and the raging waves
Ingulph the vaunters in their briny graves.
Zealous of fame, unaw'd by wars alarms,
A *virgin queen* her dauntlefs fubjects arms;
By Freedom fummon'd, nobly they obey,
Eager to prefs where glory points the way:
The gallant caufe OMNIPOTENCE befriends—
How can they fail whom PROVIDENCE defends?

AN ACROSTIC.

KINDLED by fervent, patriotic zeal,
Illuſt'rous *Alfred* ſought his country's weal :
No turns of fortune could his purpoſe ſhake,
Greatly he ventur'd for his people's ſake.
Alike in council and in war renown'd,
Laws he compos'd, and was with conqueſt crown'd.
Fraught with each virtue, his majeſtic ſoul
Revolv'd, confirm'd, and plann'd, the mighty
　　　whole.
England from him her conſequence firſt drew,
Deriv'd her knowledge, and in glory grew.
True to his GOD, ſuperior to diſtreſs,
Heav'n ſaw, approv'd, and bleſs'd him with ſuc-
　　　ceſs.
Envy in him could no foul blemiſh find,
Goodneſs and royalty were ſo combin'd :
Religion pure, and ſchemes without deceit,
Engroſs'd his thoughts, and ſtamp'd him juſtly
　　　Great.
Applauding ages ſhall record the theme,
Tun'd to the praiſes of his valu'd name.

AN ACROSTIC.

WITH boundlefs force the fenfes to com-
    mand,
Immortal *Shakefpeare* fhall unrivall'd ftand.
" Life's many color'd fcenes" he boldly drew,
Look'd thro' the foul, and ev'ry paffion knew.
Inventive beauties in his writing fhine,
Acknowledg'd wit, and energy divine.
Mute tho' his tongue, to ruthlefs death a prey,
Still fhall the poet tranfports fweet convey.
Harmonious numbers fwell the melting ftrain,
As tender maidens breathe their love-fick pain :
Kindly affectionate the verfes flow,
Expreffing friends or parents' blifs or woe :
Strong rufh the meafures which in colors bright
Paint anger, jealoufy, or mortal fight.
Enrich'd with elegance of ftyle fublime,
Admiring crowds, in ev'ry peopled clime,
Refound his merit, and with candour own,
England's fweet bard all other bards outfhone.

AN ACROSTIC.

KIND PROVIDENCE, attentive to our good,
In tender mercy deals us cloaths and food;
Nor lefs beneficent in other things,
Gives us for governor the beſt of kings.
Guided by motives of the pureſt kind,
Endu'd with ev'ry excellence of mind;
On virtue's bafe intent to found his name,
Religion unaffected ſtamps his fame:
Grac'd with each principle to prove him great,
England's lov'd monarch holds the reins of ſtate.
Touch'd by the orphan's, or the widow's grief,
His lib'ral hand adminiſters relief.
Ever obſervant of his children's weal,
The parent glows with amiable zeal:
His blifs compleated by a matchlefs ſpoufe,
In ſpotlefs truth he pays his marriage vows.
Refpected, equitable, mild, and juſt,
Deathlefs his worth ſhall foar above the duſt.

AN ACROSTIC.

JOYFUL our breasts the happy day record,
On which brave *Marlborough* drew his flaming
    sword:
Heav'n smil'd beningly on the honest cause,
Nor let his valour sink without applause.
Doom'd to the fury of his matchless force,
United armies seek to stem his course;
Keen bursts his thunder, and the motley foe,
Ensanguin'd meets a total overthrow:
Onwards he drives, JEHOVAH leads the way,
Fortune attends, and vict'ry crowns the day.
Madly impell'd by boundless empire's charms,
Ambition urg'd rash *Lewis* into arms;
Reduc'd by adverse fate, and racking shame,
Late he deplores his vain pursuit of fame.
Bright glory pants her radiant beams to shed,
On mighty *Marlborough*'s triumphant head.
Resounding plaudits, and heroic song,
On eagle's wings shall waft his praise along:
Until old time his stated glass has run,
Greatly shall bloom the honors he has won,
High as the stars, and splendent as the sun.

AN ACROSTIC.

COULD my fond thoughts à proper utt'rance
    find,
How would they praife the firft of womankind!
Adorn'd with ev'ry excellence and grace,
Roy'lty holds in her but a fecond place.
Like a good angel haft'ning from the fkies.
On bleffings' wings *Charlotte* to *England* flies,
The virtues which her heav'nly form compleat,
To rank give worth, and dignity to ftate.
Endu'd with female gentlenefs of breaft,
Quiefcent the tumultuous paffions reft.
Unfeign'd devotion, void of fhowy art,
Elates her foul, and animates her heart.
Exalted feelings, and maternal love,
Nourifh'd by piety, her merits prove.
Opprefs'd by indigence, or funk in grief,
From her each wretch is fure to find relief.
Guided by fenfe each weaknefs to controul,
Reafon invigorates and fills her foul.
Enrich'd by wifdom, and chafte honor's laws,
Admiring millions join in juft applaufe.
The jarring int'refts which at courts are feen,
Befiege in vain *Great Britain*'s darling queen.

                    Rais'd

'Rais'd up by God our manners to amend,
In grateful ſtrains our thanks ſhould heav'nward
  tend :
Taught by her bright example, age and youth,
Attach'd ſincerely to the paths of truth ;
In graceful humbleneſs their lives ſhall lead,
Nor fear the ſhafts which lay them with the dead.

YARICO

YARICO TO INKLE.

AN EPISTLE.

—

☞ The following Epiſtle is ſuppoſed to have been written by YARICO, in the beginning of her ſlavery, juſt as INKLE was embarking for *England;* and contains a little hiſtory of her unprecedented ill-uſage, mixed entreaties, tenderneſs, and upbraidings.

—

FROM this ſad place where anguiſh ever reigns,
And helpleſs wretches groan beneath their chains ;
Where ſtern oppreſſion lifts its iron hand,
And reſtleſs cruelty uſurps command ;
Where ſlav'ry its infernal viſage rears,
And racks its victims with inceſſant cares :
To ſoothe her ſoul, and eaſe her aching heart,
Permit a wretch her ſuff'rings to impart ;
To paint her bitter, life-conſuming grief,
And from the doleful ſtory ſeek relief :
To *Inkle* ſhe complains ; to him who taught
Her hand in language to expreſs her thought.
Yet ere your ſails before the winds are ſpread,
A woman's ſorrows with compaſſion read ;

Her

Her dying farewell from her pen receive,
And to her wrongs a tear in pity give.

    Fain would I learn from whence your hate
        arofe,
The cruel caufe and fource of all my woes.
Oh! tell me why am I fo wretched made?
For what unwilling crimes am I betray'd?
Is it becaufe I lov'd?—Unjuft reward!
That love preferv'd you from the ills you fear'd.
If 'twas a fault, alas! I'm guilty ftill,
For ftill I love, and while I live I will:
Nor change of fortune, nor your cruel hate,
Shall cure my paffion, or its warmth abate.

    Falfe as you are, how dare you truft anew
To winds and waves as treacherous as you?
Think'ft will the gods you ferve, if gods they
        are,
For crimes like your's their punifhments forbear?
If injur'd innocence their care be made,
Tho' I forgive, their certain vengeance dread.

    What if your bark, by adverfe tempefts tofs'd,
Should on fome barb'rous coaft, like mine, be
        loft;
Think that you fee your friends and you purfu'd
By favage people, greedy of your blood:

                    Who

Who then will fnatch you from your fell defpair ?
You'll find no *Yarico* to fhield you there.
How would you wifh you never had betray'd,
Or fold for trifling gain an helplefs maid ?

Oh! yet redeem me while you've pow'r to fave,
And make me your's, if I am doom'd a flave!
Your faithful flave indeed I'll ever prove,
And with continued care attend my love.
Think on the vows you have fo often made ;
How did you promife ? How have you betray'd ?
And think, oh! think of the dear load I bear ;
Muft a poor babe a mother's fuff'rings fhare ?
Shall the dear witnefs of our mutual flame
Be born to want, to mifery, and fhame ?
Whofe tender care fhall hufh your infant cry ?
Or whofe indulgent hand thy wants fupply ?
Behold a gift a father's love prepares !
Unceafing trouble, and continu'd fears !
This is the portion deftin'd to be thine,
Thou'rt heir to all the woes that now are mine.

Oh! could my pen in artful language tell
The fad variety of ills I feel!
Would fome kind pow'r affift my thoughts to flow,
Strong as my love, and piercing as my woe ;
To fpeak the anguifh of my bleeding heart,
My bitter pangs, and agonizing fmart;

I   Hard

Hard as you are, you'd mitigate my pain,
Or pitying take me to your arms again.
Remember, as 'tis sure you often must,
When the seas drove you on our fatal coast;
How did my bloody friends your life purfue,
Nor one of all who landed 'fcap'd but you?
Pale with your fears, and breathlefs with the chafe,
With wearied fteps you fled from place to place.
Forlorn, diftrefs'd you knew not where to go,
To fhun the fury of the defp'rate foe;
'Till chance, or rather fome propit'ous God,
Your feet conducted to a fhady wood:
Screen'd from your hunters' eyes, but not your
  fears,
On the bare ground you lay, o'erwhelmed with
  tears.
By me alone was thy retreat perceiv'd,
And oh! by love my foul was ftraight enflav'd!
My arms encircled round your neck were made
A guard and eafy pillow for your head;
Thus in foft flumbers, ftretch'd at eafe you lay,
'Till op'ning morning fummon'd us away.
In hafte I cry'd, " Awake, awake, my dear!
" The chirping birds approaching day declare;
" See how the fainting ftars foretell the morn!
" Awake, my love, and to our cave return."
Whole months fecure in this recefs we pafs'd,
And each new hour came happier than the laft;

Such was our love, fo mutual was our flame,
Our hopes, our fears, our wifhes were the fame.

The various prefents other lovers gave,
I brought to furnifh, and adorn our cave;
With fofteft, party-color'd fkins I made,
Perfum'd with fweeteft flow'rs, a fragrant bed.
Had you a wifh that ever I deny'd?
Or was not with a willing care fupply'd?
O! what returns for fuch a wafte of love!
But ftill would I entreat, and not reprove.
Yet let me mind you of what once you faid,
While oaths confirm'd the promifes you made:
" My *Yarico*, my life, my love, you cry'd,
" My dear preferver, and my choiceft pride!
" Thou kindeft, fofteft cure of all my woe,
" How fhall I pay the gratitude I owe!
" Thou Pow'r that mad'ft me, hear me while I
          " fwear
" Eternal love, eternal truth to her!
" If thou vouchfaf'ft me to behold once more
" My dear, my long loft friends, and native
          fhore;
" If ever I forget her tender care,
" Do thou regardlefs hear my dying pray'r;
" Drive me in bitternefs of want to rove,
" And fhut me ever from the realms above!"

Is

Is he a God whose curses you implor'd,
And shall his hand not grasp th' avenging sword?
Ne'er can you hope in sweet content to live,
Or know the comforts you refuse to give.
Among the vices men abhor the most,
Ingratitude is sure of all accurst.
Can the just gods with pleasure look upon,
Or love a temper so unlike their own?
Kind offices a kind requital claim,
He pays but half, who but returns the same;
Who gives at first a gen'rous temper shews,
The other only pays the debt he owes:
But you, regardless of my cries and pray'rs,
Smile at my wrongs, and mock my falling tears;
Not one return for all the mighty debt,
But cruel rage, and persecuting hate;
This, this is all your nature can bestow,
And thus you pay the gratitude you owe.

Time and my griefs this body shall decay,
My moving frame shall be but lifeless clay;
Then peaceful in the silent grave I'll rest,
Still this warm blood, and calm this glowing
     breast:
But the remembrance of my wrongs shall live,
Your treachery whole ages shall survive;
Men yet unborn will my hard lot relate,
And curse your cruelty, and weep my fate:

And if in diftant years fome haplefs maid,
Shall be by faithlefs, barb'rous man betray'd;
Condemn'd in fharpeft mifery to rove,
Unblefs'd with hope, yet curs'd with fatal love;
One to· whom life and liberty he owes,
From whofe indulgence ev'ry blefling flows;
Then fhall be drawn the juft comparifon,
" So trufted *Yarico*—and was undone."

Think of that morn when on the beech I ftood,
And faw the bark at anchor on the flood.
Straight to your cave with eager hafte I ran,
" Behold, I cry'd, a veffel on the main!
" Away, my love, nor longer let us live
" Unknown to peace fecurity can give."
No more you needed; pleafure in your eyes
Flafh'd like a fhooting light in ev'ning fkies.
Your eager arms around my neck were flung,
In filent tranfports on my lips you hung;
The mighty joy, too great to be exprefs'd,
Glow'd on your cheeks, and ftruggled in your
       breaft.
" Adieu, you cry'd, ye friendly fhades, adieu!"
" And in embraces to the fhore we flew.
" And thou, my cave, my ever kind retreat,
" Scene of my happinefs, my fafety's feat,
" Farewell! and ye, ye cruel men, adieu!
" Adieu to all, my *Yarico*, but you!

" You, my preferver, fhall be ever near,
" Reign in my foul, and ev'ry bleffing fhare."

But why do I purfue th' ungrateful tale?
Why urge a fuit that never will prevail?
Why tell, when nearer to the fhore we drew,
The waving colors you beheld and knew.
" See, fee, my love, what heav'n relenting fends!
" Behold my friends, my countrymen and friends!"
Then loud you cry'd, and wav'd your hand in
     air,
And ftraight we faw the haft'ning boat appear;
With eager ftrokes we cut the yielding tide,
And joyful climb the lofty veffel's fide.
If from a life of long, continued care,
From threat'ning cruelty, and reftlefs fear;
From death, the greateft of all ills we dread,
To be in one propit'ous moment freed;
Be happinefs that can addition know,
Your friends' embraces made it fo to you.

And now the fhip unfurls its crackling fails,
Whofe bending bofoms catch the rifing gales:
Like diftant clouds appears the lefs'ning fhore,
'Till the faint profpect can be feen no more.
" Adieu, my friends, my countrymen, adieu!
" A lafting farewell here I take of you."

Thus

Thus while I cry'd, as confc'ous of my fate,
Unufual fadnefs on my fpirits fat;
By blood ran cold, my bofom heav'd with fighs,
And gulping forrow trickled from my eyes:
But you with well diffembled forrow came,
(Diffembled 'twas, tho' ftill you look'd the fame)
" Oh! whence, my love, this change, this mourn-
   " ful look!"
You faid, and mingled kiffes as you fpoke.
" What means my dear! oh! tell me why you
   figh!
" Why fteals the pearly moifture from your eye!
" Tell me, and let me cure the ills you feel,
" Or fhare the torments which I cannot heal;
" For heav'n-born fympathy my bofom warms,
" And boundlefs love my melting heart alarms."
Pleas'd with your words, fufpecting no deceit,
Artlefs I fwallow'd the enfnaring bait;
Honeft myfelf, I thought the world fo too,
Nor falfehood fear'd, for no deceit I knew.

No more I wept, my griefs were lull'd afleep,
'Till 'twas decreed I muft for ever weep.
Brifk blew the driving winds, the fleeting fhip
Buffs the white waves, and fkims along the
   deep;
When on the deck a fudden fhout is heard,
Barbadoes' welcome coaft at laft appear'd.

        The

The cheerful failors fkip from place to place,
And fmiling joy appear'd on ev'ry face;
But you fat filent, penfive, and alone,
And meditated mifchief yet undone:
Then was the fcheme of my undoing laid,
Then was the curs'd determination made.
Oh! fay what mov'd you to the cruel deed!
Did it from hate, or thirft of gain proceed?
Urge nothing—for if love's not in our pow'r,
Is there from gratitude requir'd no more?
That's the grand tie that fhould for ever bind,
The fureft charm to fix a noble mind.

What tho' the burning fun's difcol'ring rays
Have fhadow'd with a browner dye my face;
Yet was I thought moft lovely to the fight,
The virgin's envy, and the youth's delight;
Nor was my birth unequal to my fame,
I from a race of fov'reign princes came.
My love, the nobleft of the youthful train
With warm perfuafion pleaded to obtain:
Alas! unheeded all their vows I heard,
Nor knew a tender wifh 'till you appear'd
Subdu'd, I yielded up to you alone,
Decreed the flave of love to be undone.

Ye pow'rs divine, who rule the world below,
Relieve, or teach me how to bear my woe!

Give

Give me, oh! give me eloquence to move
His ftubborn heart, and bring him back to
    love!
Oh! make him feel the horrors I endure,
And kindly fly my miferies to cure!
So fhall my life be fpent in endlefs praife,
And lafting honors to your names I'll raife.

And now I ftood upon the long'd-for fhore,
And warmly hop'd the hours of forrow o'er.
You fmil'd, and as you fondly prefs'd my hand,
" Welcome, you cry'd, my *Tarico*, to land!
" Thou kindeft, deareft, tend'reft, lovely maid,
" Now fhall my promis'd gratitude be paid."
Oh! how unmanly is the flatt'ring lye,
Which cheats but to enhance our mifery!
For that which aggravates our troubles moft,
Is to know happinefs, and know it loft.
Such foothing words conceal'd the black deceit,
And lull'd me unfufpecting of my fate.
But now no longer need the mafk be on,
The means were over, for the end was won;
No more th' endearing look your falfehood wears,
But all the monfter in full light appears:
" Take her, you cry'd, my right I here refign,
" Your flave by purchafe, as fhe once was mine."
You ended; and the wretch to whom you fpoke,
(Pride and ill nature fettle in his look)
               Approach'd,

Approach'd, and fternly feiz'd upon my hand;
And rudely haul'd me under his command.
Such cruelty what favage ever knew,
Or hearing could believe you meant it true?
Too true I found it, when with barb'rous fcoff;
And hate unknown before, you fhook me off;
Then plung'd me o'er in ev'ry human ill,
Not to be fpoke, and what I only feel.

Can you forget, or did you ne'er regard,
The fad diftrefs which in my foul appear'd?
How chill'd with horror I could fcarce furvive,
And mad and blafted ftiffen'd yet alive?
How grov'ling at your feet in wild defpair,
I beat my bleeding breaft, and tore my hair?
Then what did rage, and love, and fear, not
        fay,
As madnefs prompted, and my pangs gave way?
" Oh! fave me, and this fatal doom reverfe,
" Which once endur'd there is no greater curfe!
" Or tell me why with vengeance you purfue
" Her who was life and happinefs to you!
" Relentlefs can you ftand to all I fay,
" Unchang'd, unmov'd—Oh! give compaffion!
" Or kindly, with fome well diffembled vow
" Delude me ftill, it would be pious now!
" But oh! I read my anguifh in your look!
" I can no longer, for my heart is broke!

K k   " Yet

" Yet let my heaving breaſt and ſtreaming eyes
" Speak for me what my fault'ring tongue de-
  " nies!
" Recall the former image to your view
" Of her who loves—who was belov'd by you!
" Who now o'erburthen'd with a mother's cáres,
" The tender pledge of our endearment bears!
" I feel the infant ſtruggling in my womb,
" As conſc'ous of its wretchedneſs to come:
" Oh! ſpare the guiltleſs bade! let nature move
" Your heart to pity, though 'tis deaf to love!"
I could no more; your cruel looks congeal'd
My flowing blood, and ev'ry vital chill'd;
No more my boſom heav'd; my dying eyes
Were clos'd, and ſenſe forſook me with my cries:
Oh! had it been for ever gone indeed,
From what a world of woes had I been freed!
But fate conſpiring to protract my grief,
Unſeal'd my eyes, and gave me back to life.

 I found me, when my ſenſes were reſtor'd,
In the curs'd houſe of him I call my Lord:
My bitter wrongs in vain I did deplore,
For you, the ſource of all, I ſaw no more.
How ſhould I act in ſo ſevere diſtreſs!
Words could not paint my anguiſh, nor redreſs;
Yet ſtill to keep a glimm'ring hope alive,
The laſt ſad comfort wretches can contrive;
       I told

I told my fatal ſtory o'er with pain,
And fu'd for pity, but I ſu'd in vain;
Condemn'd to feel unutterable woes,
And all the wrongs that ſlav'ry can impoſe.

Tho' deaf to juſtice, and love's ſofter claim,
Oh! yet redeem me in regard to fame!
For ſtill the living ſtory of my woe
Shall follow, and acclaim where'er you go;
Mankind will ſhun you, and the blaſting tongue
Shall hoot the monſter as you paſs along:
" Behold the wretch, whoſe breaſt to nature
        " ſteel'd,
" For kindneſs hated, for compaſſion kill'd!"
Then, as you taught me, if there is to come
A day of gen'ral, juſt, and awful doom;
If fit gradation be obſerv'd in pains,
Oh! think and tremble what for you remains!
Unleſs ſweet mercy ſhall your heart incline
To ſhun the anguiſh, by relieving mine;
So endleſs torments will you change for peace,
And men, inſtead of curſing you, ſhall bleſs;
The Gods in mercy will the deed regard,
And pay you with a penitent's reward:
Or if the ſtate you brought me to believe
Be but a ſtory, fabled to deceive;
Yet ſweet contentment never hope to own,
Remorſe ſhall find you on a bed of down;

K k 2

In

In vain for eafe to bus'nefs you'll repair,
My wrongs fhall reach you, and avenge me there.

Forgive, thou ftill lov'd author of my pain!
My griefs are heavy, and I muft complain.
Oh! kill me, or fome milder ill provide,
Ere fate quite fevers, or the feas divide!
That thought diftracts me—my ftrain'd eyes grow
      dim,
And nature fhivers at the dreadful theme.
A thoufand things my loaded heart would fay,
But oh! my trembling hand will not obey!
Then let your fancy image my diftrefs,
And yet, oh! yet, while you have pow'r, redrefs!

CHEVY

CHEVY CHASE,

A SONG.

IN ENGLISH METRE.

GOD profper long our noble king,
  Our lives and fafeties all;
A woful hunting once there did
  In *Chevy Chafe* befall.

To drive the deer with hound and horn,
  Earl *Percy* took his way;
The child may rue that is unborn,
  The hunting of that day.

The ftout Earl of *Northumberland*
  A vow to GOD did make;
His pleafure in the *Scottifh woods*
  Three fummer days to take;

The chiefeft harts in *Chevy Chafe*
  To kill and bear away.
Thefe tidings to Earl *Douglas* came,
  In *Scotland* where he lay:

Who

Who fent Earl *Percy* prefent word,
  He would prevent his fport;
The *Englifh* earl, not fearing this,
  Did to the woods refort;

With fifteen hundred bowmen bold,
  All chofen men of might;
Who knew full well in time of need
  To aim their fhafts aright.

The gallant grey-hound fwiftly ran,
  To chace the fallow deer;
On Monday they began to hunt,
  When day-light did appear;

And long before high-noon they had
  An hundred fat bucks flain;
Then having din'd, the drovers went
  To roufe them up again.

The bowmen mufter'd on the hills,
  Well able to endure;
Their backfides all with fpecial care,
  That day were guarded fure.

The hounds ran fwiftly thro' the woods,
  The nimble deer to take;
And with their cries the hills and dales
  An echo fhrill did make.

2   Lord

Lord *Percy* to the quarry went,
    To view the tender deer;
Quoth he, Earl *Douglas* promifed
    This day to meet me here;

But if I thought he would not come,
    No longer would I ftay.
With that a brave young gentleman
    Thus to the Earl did fay :

Lo ! yonder doth Earl *Douglas* come,
    His men in armor bright;
Full twenty hundred *Scottiſh* fpears,
    All marching in our fight.

All pleafant men of *Tividale*,
    Faft by the river *Tweed*.
Then ceafe your fport, Earl *Percy* faid,
    And take your bows with fpeed.

And now with me, my countrymen,
    Your courage forth advance ;
For never was there champion yet
    In *Scotland* or in *France*,

That ever did on horfeback come,
    But if my hap it were,
I durft encounter man for man,
    With him to break a fpear.

                            Earl

Earl *Douglas* on a milk-white steed,
　　Most like a baron bold,
Rode foremost of the company,
　　Whose armor shone like gold.

Shew me, he said, whose men ye be,
　　That hunt so boldly here;
That without my consent you chace
　　And kill my fallow deer.

The man that first did answer make,
　　Was noble *Percy*, he;
Who said, We list not to declare,
　　Nor shew whose men we be:

Yet we will spend our dearest blood,
　　The chiefest harts to slay.
Then *Douglas* swore a solemn oath,
　　And thus in rage did say:

Ere thus I will outbraved be,
　　One of us two shall die;
I know thee well, an earl thou art,
　　Lord *Percy*, so am I.

But trust me, *Percy*, pity it were,
　　And great offence to kill
Any of these our harmless men,
　　For they have done no ill.

Let thou and I the battle try,
    And set our men aside.
Accurs'd be he, Lord *Percy* said,
    By whom it is deny'd.

Then stept a gallant squire forth,
    Witherington was his name;
Who said he would not have it told
    To *Henry* our king for shame;

That 'e'er my captain fought on foot,
    And I stood looking on;
Ye be two earls, said *Witherington*,
    And I a squire alone.

I'll do the best that do I may,
    While I have pow'r to stand;
While I have pow'r to wield my sword,
    I'll fight with heart and hand.

Our *English* archers bent their bows,
    Their hearts were good and true;
At the first flight of arrows sent,
    Full three score *Scots* they slew.

To drive the deer with hound and horn,
    Earl *Douglas* had the bent;
A captain mov'd with mickle pride,
    The spears to shivers sent.

L l

They

They clos'd full faſt on ev'ry ſide,
No ſlackneſs there was found;
And many a gallant gentleman
Lay gaſping on the ground.

O Christ! it was great grief to ſee,
And likewiſe for to hear
The cries of men lying in their gore,
And ſcatter'd here and there.

At laſt theſe two ſtout earls did meet,
Like captains of great might;
Like lions mov'd, they laid on loads,
And made a cruel fight.

They fought until they both did ſweat,
With ſwords of temper'd ſteel;
Until the blood like drops of rain
They trickling down did feel.

Yield thee, Lord *Percy*, *Douglas* ſaid,
In faith I will thee bring
Where thou ſhalt high advanced be,
By *James* our *Scottiſh* king.

Thy ranſom freely I will give,
And thus report of thee,
Thou art the moſt courageous knight
That ever I did ſee.

No,

No, *Douglas,* quoth Earl *Percy* then
 Thy proffer I do fcorn;
I will not yield to any *Scot*
 That ever yet was born.

With that there came an arrow keen
 Out of an *Englifh* bow,
Which ftruck Earl *Douglas* to the heart,
 A deep and deadly blow.

Who never fpoke more words than thefe,
 Fight on my merry men all!
For why, my life is at an end,
 Lord *Percy* fees me fall.

Then leaving life Earl *Percy* took
 The dead man by the hand,
And faid, Earl *Douglas,* for thy life
 Would I had loft my land!

O CHRIST! my yery heart doth bleed
 With forrow for thy fake;
For fure a more renowned knight
 Mifchance did never take.

A knight among the *Scots* there was,
 Who faw Earl *Douglas* die,
And in his wrath did vow revenge
 Upon the Earl *Percy:*

Sir

Sir *Hugh Montgomery* was he call'd,
   Who with a fpear moft bright,
Well mounted on a gallant fteed
   Ran fiercely thro' the fight :

And paft the *Englifh* archers all,
   Without all dread or fear,
And thro' Earl *Percy*'s body then
   He thruft his hateful fpear.

With fuch a vehement force and might
   He did his body gore;
The fpear went thro' the other fide,
   A large cloth-yard and more.

So thus did both thefe nobles die,
   Whofe courage none could ftain.
An *Englifh* archer then perceiv'd
   The noble earl was flain :

He had a bow bent in his hand,
   Made of a trufty tree;
An arrow of a cloth-yard long
   Up to the head drew he.

Againft Sir *Hugh Montgomery*
   So right his fhaft he fet;
The grey-goofe wing that was thereon,
   In his heart's blood was wet.

This

This fight did laſt from break of day,
　'Till ſetting of the ſun;
For when they rung the ev'ning bell,
　The battle ſcarce was done.

With the Earl *Percy* there was ſlain
　Sir *John* of *Ogerton;*
Sir *Robert Ratcliff,* and Sir *John,*
　Sir *James* that bold baron.

And with Sir *George* and good Sir *James,*
　Both knights of good account;
Good Sir *Ralph Raby* there was ſlain,
　Whoſe prowefs did ſurmount.

For *Witherington* needs muſt I wail,
　As one in doleful dumps;
For when his legs were ſmitten off,
　He fought upon his ſtumps.

And with Earl *Douglas* there was ſlain
　Sir *Hugh Montgomery;*
Sir *Charles Currel,* that from the field
　One foot would never fly.

Sir *Charles Murrel* of *Ratcliff* too,
　His ſiſter's ſon was he;
Sir *David Lamb* ſo well eſteem'd,
　Yet ſaved could not be.

And

And the Lord *Markwell* in likewife,
 Did with Earl *Douglas* die :
Of twenty hundred *Scottifh* fpears,
 Scarce fifty-five did fly.

Of fifteen hundred *Englifhmen*,
 Went home but fifty-three ;
The reft were flain in *Chevy Chafe*,
 Under the green-wood tree.

Next day did many widows come,
 Their hufbands to bewail ;
They wafh'd their wounds in brinifh tears,
 But all would not prevail.

Their bodies bath'd in purple blood,
 They bore with them away ;
They kifs'd them dead a thoufand times,
 When they were clad in clay.

This news was brought to *Edinburg*,
 Where *Scotland*'s king did reign,
That brave Earl *Douglas* fuddenly
 Was with an arrow flain.

O heavy news, King *James* did fay,
 Scotland can witnefs be ;
I have not any captain more,
 Of fuch account as he.

Like

Like tidings to King *Henry* came,
  Within as fhort a fpace,
That *Percy* of *Northumberland*
  Was flain in *Chevy Chafe.*

Now GOD be with him, faid our king,
  Sith't will no better be;
I truft I have within my realm
  Five hundred good as he.

Yet fhall not *Scot* or *Scotland* fay
  But I will vengeance take,
And be revenged of them all,
  For brave Earl *Percy*'s fake.

This vow full well the king perform'd,
  After an *Humble Down;*
In one day fifty knights were flain,
  With lords of great renown.

And of the reft of fmall account,
  Did many hundreds die.,
Thus ended the hunting of *Chevy Chafe*,
  Made by the Earl *Percy.*

GOD fave the king, and blefs the land,
  In plenty, joy, and peace;
And grant henceforth that foul debate
  'Twixt noblemen may ceafe!

CHEVY CHASE.

A SONG.

IN LATIN METRE.

VIVAT rex noster nobilis,
 Omnis in tuto sit :
Venatus olim flebilis
 Chevino Luco sit.

Cane, feras ut abigat,
 Percæus abiit ;
Vel embruo elugeat,
 Quod hodie accidit.

Comes ille *Northumbriæ*,
 Votùm vovid Deo,
Lusus in sylvis *Scotiæ*,
 Habere triduo ;

Eprimis cervis *Cheviæ*,
 Cæsos abripere.
Duglasium hæ notitiæ
 Adibant propere :

Qui

Qui ore tenus delegat,
   Se ludum perdere.
At *Percæus* non hefitat
   Ad fylvas tendere;

Quingenis ter teliferis,
   Virtutis bellicæ;
Qui norunt, rebus arduis,
   Sagittas mittere.

Curritur a venatico,
   Damas propellere;
Die Lunæ diluculo,
   Ad rem accingunt fe;

Centumque cervi funt cæfi
   Ante meridiem,
Tunc redeunt, cibis impleti,
   Ad venationem.

De monti fagittarii,
   Apti militiæ,
Proderunt armarii
   Hodie a tergore.

Per fylvas celarent canes,
   Ut cervos capiant;
Ac fimul montes et valles
   Latrata refonant.

M m   Fædinam

Fædinam comes adiit,
 Berinam vifere;
Duglas minatus eft, inquit,
 Hic mecum affore;

Congreffum autem defperans,
 Mora non dabitur.
Quo dicto, Tyro elegans
 Illum alloquitur:

En! en *Duglafius* eminus!
 Armis cum fplendidis;
Bis mille cum militibus,
 Vifui obviis:

Cunctis de valle *Tiviæ*,
 Ad ripas *Tuæfis*.
Ludos, ait, intermittite,
 Arcubis habitis.

Et vobis nunc, O noftrates,
 Tollatur animus;
Haud præflo fuit athletes,
 Gallus vel *Scoticus*,

Mihi, equeftris obvius,
 Quin poftulante re,
Eocum vellum cominus,
 Vi, hafti ludere.

I   Equifeffor

Equiseffor *Duglafius*,
   Audax ille Baro,
Præfuit aliis omnibus,
   Aurato clipeo.

Cujates, ait oftendite,
   Hic aufi pellere,
Ac me invito, impete
   Feras occidere.

Qui primus verbum edidit,
   Percæus nomine;
Qui fumus, ait, non libuit
   Vobis oftendere:

At fanguinem abfumemus,
   Cervos diftruere.
Juravit tunc *Duglafius*,
   Dixitque temere;

E nobis pereet unus,
   Antequam devincar;
Tu comes es, bene notus,
   Egoque tui par.

At, fi qua fides, eft fcelus
   Miferum! perdere
Ullos de his infontibus,
   Immunes fcelere.

       Nofmet

Nofmet pugnemus cominus,
  Viris abfentibus.
Depereat, inquit *Percæus*,
  Huic adverfarius.

Tunc armiger exiluit,
  Witherington nomine,
Regem, ait, fcire noluit
  Hoc, præ dedecore ;

Quod dux pugnaverat pedes,
  Me ftante obiter ;
Vos duo eftis commites,
  Ego, ait, armiger.

Obnixe omne faciam,
  Dum ftare dabitur,
Ac dum vibrare machæram,
  A me pugnabitur.

Angligeni tendunt arcus,
  Quam cordatiffimi,
Decis fex a miffilibus
  Cæduntur *Scotici.*

Adverfus feras fe&antes,
  Mifit *Duglafius*
Torvum ducem, dimicantes,
  Tra&is haftilibus.

                                        Incin&i

Incincti funt celeriter,
    Parum pigritiæ;
Multufque jacet belliger,
    Inanis, animæ.

Pol! dolor erat vifere,
    Ac etiam audire,
Viros plangentes undique,
    Perfufos fanguine.

Comites tandem coibant,
    Multo magnanime,
Inftar Leonum feribant,
    Truci certamine.

Pugnarunt vel in fudore,
    Diftrictis enfibus;
Ac maduerunt cruore
    Æque ac imbribus.

Ut dedas, ait, *Duglafius*,
    Te ducam fubito,
Ubi eris præpofitus
    A rege *Jacobo*.

Proh gratis redimam captum,
    Et celebrabo te,
Equitem quam magnificum,
    Et fine compare.

                                          Cui

Cui *Percæus* ait, minime!
  Quod offers refpuo;
Nollem unquam me dedere
  Viventi *Scotico*.

Tunc eft emiffus calamus
  Ab arcu *Anglico*;
Quo fixus eft *Duglaſius*
  Heu! tenus cerculo:

Qui verba hæc emurmurat,
  Viri, contendite!
Quid ni, mors mea propinquat,
  Speĉtante comite.

Tum *Percæus* exanimi
  Manum it prendere;
Dicens caufa *Duglaſii*
  Se terras perdere.

Vel cor, ait, fundit fanguinem
  Per tui gratia;
Nam nunquam talem equitem
  Non novit noxia.

Miles decernens *Scoticas*
  Duglaſium emori,
In *Percæum* mortem ejus
  Devovit ulcifci:

                                    Hugo

Hugo de monte gomeri,
    Hafta cum fplendida,
Movit decurfu celeri,
    Ferox per agmina:

Præteriens fagittarios
    Anglos impavide,
Percæios ventriculos
    Foravit cufpide.

Tanta cum violentia
    Fodit corpufcula,
Plus tres pedes per ilia
    Tranfivit haftula:

Sic ceciderunt comites
    Quam invictiffimi.
Quum fagittario fubdit res
    Percæum occidi:

Arcum intenfum dextera
    Factum infigniter,
Tres pedes longa fpicula,
    Implevit fortiter.

Hugonem Gomeri verfus
    Sic telum ftatuit,
Vel anferinus calamus
    In corde maduit.

Ad

Ad vefperam ab aurora
  Duravit prælium;
Octava fcilicet hora
  Vix eft præteritum.

Cùm *Percæio* eft peremptus
  Dominus *Ogerton*,
Johannes Ratcliff, *Robertus*,
  Et *Jacobus* Baron.

Jacobus et *Georgius*,
  Equeftris ordinis,
Radulphus Raby Dominus,
  Periit magnanimis.

Pro *With'rington*, fit gémitus,
  Ac fi in triftibus,
Qui pugnavit de genibus,
  Truncatis cruribus.

Perierunt cum *Duglafio*
  Hugo Gomericus,
Carolus Currel a campo
  Nunquam difceffurus.

De *Ratcliff Murrel Carolus*,
  Nepos a forore;
David Lamb bene habitus,
  Exangui corpore.

Ac

Ac etiam *Markwell* Dominus
   Deditus eft neci:
Vix e duobus millibus
   Fugerunt fexdeni.

E ter quingenis *Anglicis*
   Vix tot abiere;
In *Luco* cæfis cæteris,
   Sub fagi tegmine.

A plurimis cras viduis
   Lugetur mifere;
Vulnera lota lacrymis,
   Nec prævaluere.

Cruentata corpufcula
   Secum abftulere,
Millies dederunt ofcula,
   Defanetis funere.

Fertur apud *Edinburgham*,
   Regnante *Jacobo*,
Duglafium fibito cæfum
   Fuiffe jaculo.

O lamentabile dixit,
   Scotia fit teftis,
Haud alius Dux fuperfuit
   Equalis ordinis.

N n.   *Henrico*

Henrico tradidit fama,
   Pari intervallo,
Percæium de *Northumbria*
   Occifum in *Luco.*

Quum Rex edixit, valeat,
   Rebus fic ftantibus!
Spero quod regnum abundat
   Quingenis talibus.

Aft fentient me ulcifcentem
   Scoti et *Scotia,*
Ac vindiсtam inferentem
   Percæi gratia.

Quod eft a Rege præftitum
   Cæfis in montibus,
Quinquies denis militum,
   Nec non Baronibus.

Ac de plebe perierunt
   Centeni plurimi.
Venatum fic finierunt
   Percæi Domini.

Sit Rex et Grex beatulus
   Pace et copia,
Ac abfit a magnatibus
   Malevolentia.

1ft CORIN-

4

THO' I fhould fpeak with mens' and angels'
    tongues,
And grace with eloquence fublime my fongs ;
Yet, lacking charity, I fhould be found
As brafs, or tinkling cymbals, nought but found.
Tho' with the gift of prophecy infpir'd,
Knowledge of myfteries I have acquir'd ;
Altho' enlighten'd intellects I fhare,
And faith, which mountains from their bafe can
    tear ;
Devoid of charity, I muft become
The worthlefs offspring of my mother's womb.
Tho' I beftow my riches on the poor,
Who miferably crowd around my door ;
Or give my martyr'd body to the flame,
Yet, wanting charity, I lofe my name.
Long-fuff'ring charity is meek and kind,
Nor heeds another's blifs with envy's mind :
Is not puff'd up with hateful vanity,
Nor looks on mankind with a fcornful eye :
Doth not with infolence itfelf behave,
Or its juft rights with haughty conduct crave :
To bitter quarrels eafily incline,
Or againft others evil acts defign :

Doth

Doth not in vile iniquity rejoice,
But in defence of truth exalts its voice,
Benignant charity, with gentle heart,
In fympathizing forrows bears a part;
In God's veracity confiding ftill,
Its hopes are built on his unerring will:
And, deck'd with mild habiliments of peace,
Immortal charity will never ceafe:
Tho' tongues fhall fail; knowledge diffolve away;
And faculties prophetic feel decay.
Our prefent minds contracted wifdom deal,
Events foretelling on a narrow fcale;
But when compleat perfection comes in fight,
Its feeble dawn fhall yield to boundlefs light.
When I in childhood ignorantly walk'd,
As children I thought, underftood, and talk'd:
But when I to maturity had grown,
Each childifh tendency away was thrown.
Now objects darkly through a glafs appear,
Which fhall hereafter fpotlefs luftre wear:
And partial knowledge is on me beftow'd,
Until I reach the happy realms of God.
And now faith, hope, and charity abide,
But ftill the laft fhall o'er the reft prefide.

ISAIAH,

YET ſhall the dimneſs leſs obſcure be found,
Than when vexation's arrows flew around;
When on *Zebulun*, and *Naphthali's* land,
At firſt he lightly laid affliction's hand;
And afterwards, upon the ocean's ſhore,
His cup of indignation bubbled o'er;
Beyond fam'd *Jordan*, who, with healing tides,
By *Galilean* regions proudly glides.
The people who long walk'd in gloomy night,
Have been refreſh'd with comfortable light;
They who the darkſome vale of death poſſeſs,
Have ſeen the ſhining beams of happineſs.
Thou haſt the nation greatly multiply'd,
But its hilarity not magnify'd:
Their's is the joy of farmers freed from toil,
Or that of ſoldiers who divide the ſpoil.
The burden of his ſhoulder thou haſt broke,
And his oppreſſive, *Midianitiſh* yoke.
Horrific noiſe, and blood-ſtain'd garments ſhew,
The fatal conflict of the warlike foe;
But this ſhall be with ſacrifices made,
A grateful tribute to JEHOVAH paid.
For unto us is born a child divine,
A ſon beſtow'd of choſen *Judah's* line,

On

On whom shall rest the government supreme;
And this shall be his everlasting name,
Wonderful, Counsellor, the mighty LORD,
Eternal Father, Prince of Peace ador'd.
Of his peace and dominion shall be shown
A constant increase upon *David's* throne;
With judgment and with justice to direct
His holy servant, and his rights protect.
The LORD of Hosts, whose word shall never fail,
Will this perform with unabating zeal.

ISAIAH,

. ISAIAH, 11th Chap. 10 firſt Verſes.

FROM *Jeſſe*'s ſtem a blooming rod ſhall ſhoot,
And a rich branch ſhall flouriſh from his root.
On him ſhall reſt the ſpirit of the LORD,
With wiſdom and pure underſtanding ſtor'd;
The ſpirit of good counſel and of might,
Teaching how to know and fear GOD aright :
Which ſhall expand his faculties of mind,
And ſhew perfeƈtions of an heav'nly kind;
Nor on his intelleƈts of ſight or ſound,
Shall he his puniſhments or judgments found.
He ſhall the poor with righteouſneſs try,
And for the meek reprove with equity.
His awful voice ſhall fill the earth with pain,
And when he ſpeaks the wicked ſhall be ſlain.
Juſtice the girdle of his loins ſhall prove;
His reins are girt with faithfulneſs and love.
The wolf and lamb in harmony ſhall live,
And leopards into friendſhip kids receive :
The calf, the fatling, and the lion's heir
Shall walk ſubmiſſive to an infant's care.
The cow and bear together ſhall be fed,
Nor ſhall their young feel any jealous dread,
But on a common couch their bodies lay;
And like an ox the lion ſhall eat hay.

The

The fucking child shall play, without controul,
Around the stinglefs afp's unpoifon'd hole;
And without danger the wean'd child may reft
His hand on the fell cockatrice's neft.
From fatal proofs of their malignity
My holy mountain shall be ever free:
For as the waters the vaft ocean fill,
So shall the world pay homage to God's will.
A root of *Jeffe* in that day shall rife,
To which the people shall direct their eyes;
To this the Gentiles shall with ardor prefs,
And gain rewards of lafting happinefs.

ISAIAH,

THE truth of our report who deigns to own?
And to whom hath GOD's mighty pow'r been
    fhown?
For as a tender plant he fhall be found,
And as a root in dry and parched ground:
To form or comlinefs no claim he lays,
Nor has he beauty our defires to raife.
Defpis'd, rejected, and beheld with fcorn,
A man of forrows, and to troubles born:
As if afham'd to keep him in our view,
We turn'd indignant, and our eyes withdrew.
Surely he did our miferies fuftain,
And in his perfon bear our grief and pain:
Yet have we reckon'd him to feel the rod
Of an offended and avenging GOD.
For our tranfgreffions he was wounded fore,
And bruifes for our wickednefs he bore:
On him our peace-conferring ftripes were laid,
And by his chaftifemént our debt was paid.
All we, like filly fheep, have gone aftray,
Attach'd, thro' ignorance, to error's way;
And on him hath the LORD impos'd the weight
Which our fins render'd exquifitely great.
Afflicted and opprefs'd with keeneft woes,
His lips refufe his anguifh to difclofe:

        Speechlefs

Speechlefs as lambs beneath the butcher's knife,
Or filent fheep, he yields his fpotlefs life.
He was from trial and confinement brought,
And by whom fhall his pedigree be fought?
With guilt untainted he refign'd his breath,
And for my people's crimes receiv'd his death.
With wicked men he funk into the tomb,
And with the rich partook a mortal doom :
Yet had he done no violence or wrong,
Or with deceit defil'd his heart or tongue.
But it pleas'd GOD his wounds to multiply,
And rack him with unceafing mifery :
When his foul's made an offering for fin,
His feed fhall bloom, his days of joy begin;
And in his hand the fervice of the LORD
An overflowing increafe fhall afford.
He of the travail of his foul fhall fee,
And fatisfaction reap abundantly :
By knowledge fhall my right'ous fervant fave
Numbers, and on himfelf their fins receive.
Therefore his lot fhall with the great abide,
And with the ftrong fhall he the fpoil divide :
Becaufe to death he had refign'd his foul,
And he was mufter'd in the finners' roll :
He on himfelf the crimes of mankind laid,
And interceffion for tranfgreffors made.

1ſt Kings, 17th Chapter.

To *Ahab* the *Tiſhbite Elijah* came,
Who with the men of *Gilead* rank'd his name,
And ſaid, For years, as liveth *Iſrael*'s Lord,
.Nor dew nor rain ſhall fall without my word.
Then unto him did God's command thus ſpeak,
Quick get thee hence, and thy courſe eaſtward
    take;
By the brook *Cherith*, near to *Jordan*'s ſide,
Thou ſhalt remain, and there thy perſon hide.
The water ſhall thy craving thirſt allay,
And ravens bring thee nouriſhment each day.
So he, obedient to the will of God,
By the brook *Cherith*, near *Jordan*, abode.
And ravens brought each morning fleſh and bread,
And with like food each ev'ning was he fed.
In a ſhort ſpace the brook was render'd dry,
As rain had ceas'd its ſources to ſupply.
Then did again God's orders thus declare,
Unto *Zidonian Zarephath* repair :
Lo ! there a widow woman, weak and poor,
By me directed ſhall thy meat procure.
Then riſing he went to *Zarephath* ſtraight,
And as he came unto the city gate,

Behold

Behold the widow woman there he found,
For fire-wood feeking little fticks around :
Then he addrefs'd her, and faid, Bring with
    hafte
A cup of water, my parch'd lips to feaft.
And as fhe went, he call'd again, and faid,
Bring alfo in thy hand a fcrap of bread.
And fhe reply'd, The LORD who hears me
    fpeak,
Can judge I am not miftrefs of one cake;
Of meal a fcanty handful, and no more,
With a fmall drop of oil, compleats my ftore ;
And lo! two fticks I gather, as you fee, .
To drefs a morfel for my fon and me :
That fo we may on our laft victuals dine,
And to the grave our famifh'd frames confign.
Then faid he unto her, Fear not, but go
And execute what you defign'd to do :
But firft for me a little cake prepare,
And afterwards thy fon and thou fhalt fhare.
For thus doth the LORD GOD of *Ifrael* fay,
The ftock of meal fhall fuffer no decay,
Nor any wafte the crufe of oil fuftain,
Until the LORD fhall on the earth fend rain.
Then did fhe with the prophet's will comply,
And long abundance blefs'd her family.
She found no diminution of her meal,
Nor did her little crufe of oil once fail,

                   According

According to the faying of the LORD,
Which he had utter'd by *Elijah*'s word.
It came to pafs, ere many days were gone,
That ficknefs vifited the widow's fon;
And his complaint fo violent became,
The pulfe of life forfook his breathlefs frame.
Then cry'd the wretched mother, bath'd in tears,
O man of GOD, how haft thou fwell'd my cares!
My fenfe of fin art thou come to revive,
And of her child the widow to deprive!
Then faid *Elijah*, Give thy fon to me.
And from her bofom, rent with mifery,
Unto a loft the child he ftraight convey'd,
And on his bed the clay-cold body laid.
Then did he fervently the LORD addrefs,
Why doft thou, LORD, the widow thus dif,
    trefs;
And fummon to the grave her darling boy,
While in her houfe my lodgings I enjoy!
Then on the child he ftretched himfelf thrice,
And befought GOD with fupplicating voice;
O LORD my GOD, thy mercy I implore,
And to this child his foul again reftore!
Then did GOD grant the prophet's warm de-
    fire,
And with the breath of life the child infpire.
And to the houfe, *Elijah*, from his room,
To diffipate the widow's mournful gloom,

Conveys

Conveys the child, and to the mother cries,
Lo thy fon lives! reftrain thy rending fighs.
Then to *Elijah* thus the woman faid,
By this the pow'r of heav'n I fee difplay'd;
That from the LORD a meffenger thou art,
And doft in truth the word of GOD impart.

1ſt KINGS, 18th Chapter.

AND when three years their fleeting courſe
    had run,
Thus to the Prophet was GOD's will made known;
Go, and before the face of *Ahab* ſtand,
And I will pour forth rain upon the land.
Then did *Elijah* with ſubmiſſion go,
Himſelf to *Ahab*, *Iſrael*'s king to ſhew:
While famine, with deſtructive rage replete,
Held in *Samaria* its baneful ſeat.
Then *Ahab* thus to *Obadiah* ſaid,
Whom maſter of his houſehold he had made,
(Now *Obadiah* greatly fear'd the LORD,
And when *Jezebel* drew the bloody ſword
Againſt GOD's prophets, he, their lives to ſave,
An hundred hid, by fifties, in a cave,
And in their ſolitary, dark abode,
Of bread and water due ſupplies beſtow'd.)
Go thro' the land, and cloſely ſearch around,
Wherever brooks or water-ſprings abound;
We may, perhaps, enough of graſs eſpy,
For mules and horſes, leſt the beaſts all die.
So they, to paſs throughout the land, agreed
In different directions to proceed :

Ahab,

Abab, alone, his road by one courfe bent,
And *Obadiah* in another went.
As *Obadiah* journey'd on the road,
Behold, he chanc'd to meet the man of God;
Whom recognizing, he falls down, and cries,
Say, is *Elijah* prefent to my eyes?
And he reply'd, He is; to *Abab* fay,
Lo! here *Elijah* will himfelf difplay.
Then anfwer'd he, What evil have I done,
That thou to certain death wouldft drive me on?
As thy God liveth, before whom I ftand,
My Lord hath fought thee throughout ev'ry land;
And when they faid, He is not here; he took
An oath that in veracity they fpoke.
And now to *Abab* thou bidft me declare,
Lo! in this place *Elijah* will appear:
And it fhall happen, that when hence I go,
Ready compliance with thy will to fhew,
The fpirit of the Lord fhall thee remove,
Where fruitlefs will my fearch to find thee prove:
And when thy orders I to *Abab* tell,
And he cannot difcover where you dwell,
My life fhall fall a forfeit to my word,
But I thy fervant always fear'd the Lord.
Did not my Lord intelligence receive,
That I an hundred prophets in a cave
By fifties from *Jezebel's* fury fav'd,
And dealt the nourifhment which nature crav'd?

And

And now you bid me thus to *Ahab* fpeak,
Elijah's here;—and he my life fhall take.
Then faid *Elijah*, As God lives, to-day
I will myfelf to *Ahab*'s fight convey.
Then *Obadiah* towards *Ahab* went,
And to *Elijah* the King's fteps were bent.
And *Ahab*, when he faw *Elijah*, faid,
Art thou he that haft ills for *Ifrael* made?
He faid, I have not ftirr'd up *Ifrael*'s woe,
But from thee, and thy houfe, their evils flow;
Becaufe God's laws are banifh'd from your mind,
And your whole thoughts to *Baal* are inclin'd.
Now, therefore, for the men of *Ifrael* fend,
And at Mount *Carmel* let them all attend;
Call the groves' prophets, four hundred, to me,
With *Baal*'s priefts, four hundred and fifty;
Who at *Jezebel*'s royal table wait,
And feaft in all the elegance of ftate.
The men of *Ifrael*, as the king decreed,
And all the prophets, to the mount proceed.
Then faid *Elijah* unto all around,
How long fhall ye be fluctuating found?
If God be Lord to him your voices raife,
Or elfe to *Baal* join in fongs of praife.
Then to the filent, congregated crowd
Elijah thus addrefs'd himfelf aloud;
Of the Lord's prophets I remain only,
But *Baal*'s are four hundred and fifty.

Let

Let them two bullocks for us now procure,
And for themſelves the choſen ox ſecure,
Which they may cut, and lay on logs of wood,
But place no fire below to dreſs their food;
And I the other bullock will receive,
But no coals underneath the timber leave:
Then ſupplicate your Gods, while I proclaim
My ſole dependence on JEHOVAH's name;
And let the GOD who ſpeaks by fire be LORD.
Then cry'd the people, We applaud thy word.
To *Baal*'s prophets thus *Elijah* ſaid,
Chooſe your ox firſt, and have it ready made,
For ye are many; and addreſs with faith
Your deities; but lay no fire beneath.
Then the ox which was given them they took,
And did from morn till noon *Baal* invoke;
Saying, O *Baal*, hear us! But they found,
To hear their pray'rs, no condeſcending found.
Then with diſtracting diſappointment ſtung,
Upon the altar which was made they ſprung.
And about noon *Elijah* mocking ſays,
In elevated ſhouts your voices raiſe:
He is a *God*, ſure! and on buſineſs talks,
Or drives the foe, or on a journey walks,
Or, peradventure, ſunk in ſleep he lies,
And muſt be rous'd with loud, repeated cries!
With madneſs fir'd, they call'd with bolder ſtrains,
And prick'd with knives and lancets their fill'd
  veins,

I   Until

Until the gushing streams of crimson blood,
Ran down their bodies like a swelling flood.
And when they prophefy'd till noon was gone,
And ev'ning facrifice was coming on;
Yet was by them no voice or anfwer heard, ‑
Nor any who would their requests regard.
Then faid *Elijah* to the men, Come here.
And to the Prophet they approached near,
While he his active diligence beftow'd
To mend the torn down altar of his GOD:
And for this end *Elijah* chofe twelve ftones,
The number of the tribes of *Jacob*'s fons,
To whom the word of GOD Almighty came,
And faid, Henceforth fhall *Ifrael* be thy name.
Then with the ftones an altar he prepar'd,
Which was in honor of JEHOVAH rear'd:
And round the altar a deep trench was made,
Wherein two meafures of feed might be laid.
Elijah next the wood in order put,
Whereon he plac'd the ox, in pieces cut;
And faid, With water four large veffels fill,
Which on the wood and off'ring you fhall fpill.
Repeat the fame, he faid; which ftraight they did;
And the third time obey'd, as they were bid.
In rills the water round the altar flows,
And in the trench unto the top arofe.
And when the ev'ning facrifice drew nigh,
The prophet thus to GOD addrefs'd his cry;

LORD

Lord of *Abraham*, *Ifaac*, *Ifrael*, hear,
That thou art God let it to-day appear;
And that I am thy fervant, and have wrought
Whatever I was by thy precepts taught!
Attend, O Lord, and make this people know
That reverence to thee alone they owe!
That thou a merciful Creator art,
And' haft reform'd each difobedient heart!
Then the confuming fire of God quick flies,
And burns the wood, ftones, duft, and facrifice,
And in its rapid motion drinks around
Each drop of water in the trench if found.
Then faid the people, falling proftrate down,
The Lord is God; the Lord is God alone!
And to the people thus *Elijah* fpake:
Let none efcape—all *Baal*'s prophets take.
Straight were they feiz'd, and by *Elijah's* word,
Giv'n, at Brook *Kifhon*, victims to the fword.
To *Abab* then the Prophet faid, Prepare
To eat and drink, for rain immenfe is near.
Abab fat down to take fome nourifhment,
While to Mount *Carmel*'s top *Elijah* went,
Where lowly on the earth himfelf he laid,
Holding between his knees his bended head;
And to his fervant cry'd, Straightway afcend,
Thy looks unto the diftant ocean bend.
And he faid, Nought I fee towards the main.
Then call'd *Elijah*, Go fev'n times again.

And

And at the fev'nth time, From the fea, he cries,
Like a man's hand, I fee a fmall cloud rife.
Then he reply'd, Bid *Abab* hafte away,
Left the rain fhould occafion a delay.
And while to *Jezreel Abab* rode, behold,
Rain, wind, and clouds the heav'ns in black in-
    fold.
And lo! *Elijah*, by the LORD fuftain'd,
Entrance in *Jezreel* before *Abab* gain'd.

2d KINGS,

2d KINGS, 5th Chapter.

NAAMAN, leader of the *Syrian* hoft,
Was by his fovereign efteemed moft,
And held in honor, as by him the LORD
To *Syria* deliv'rance did afford:
The title of great prowefs too he bore,
But leprous fores cóver'd his body o'er.
And parties of the *Syrians* went out,
Who thro' the land of *Ifrael* took their rout,
From whence they carry'd off a little maid,
Who to *Naaman*'s wife attendance paid;
To whom fhe faid, Would GOD my mafter were
To the fam'd Prophet of *Samaria* near;
Who the phyfician of found health would prove,
And foon the loathfome leprofy remove!
Then went one to the King, and faid, Behold,
Thus hath the *Ifraelitifh* maiden told.
The *Syrian* monarch anfwer'd, Go to, go,
I'll to the King of *Ifrael* write, and know.
Then *Naaman* commenc'd his journey ftraight,
And brought, of filver, ten talents in weight,
Six thoufand pieces of gold coin, befide
Ten fuits of raiment, deck'd with fplendid pride:
And thus to *Ifrael*'s king his letter ran;
Behold, herewith I fend thee *Naaman*,

My valuable fervant, to obtain
From thee a cure, his leprofy to clean.
And when the letter *Ifrael*'s king had read,
He rent his cloaths, and thus in anguifh faid,
Am I a GOD, to fave or to deftroy,
That this man bids me heal a leprofy?
Wherefore confider now, I pray, and look,
How he to enmity doth me provoke.
And when it to *Elifha* was made known,
The man of GOD, what *Ifrael*'s king had done,
This meffage unto him the Prophet fent,
Wherefore haft thou thy cloaths, defponding, rent?
Let him come to me, and he fhall perceive
That yet a prophet doth in *Ifrael* live.
So he with fteeds and chariot, in ftate
Came forth, and ftood before *Elifha*'s gate.
And from *Elifha* thefe directions came,
Immerfe thyfelf fev'n times in *Jordan*'s ftream;
Then fhall thy malady receive its doom,
And thy found body in full vigor bloom.
But *Naaman* was wroth, and went away,
And was, indignantly, induc'd to fay,
Lo! I thought he will furely come to me,
And ftand, and fupplicate his Deity;
Then ftrike his hand acrofs the part impure,
And thus perform an efficac'ous cure.
Damafcus, *Abana* and *Pharpar* boafts,
Rivers more fam'd than all in *Ifrael*'s coafts;

May

May I not wafh in them, and be made whole?
So he went off, and rage inflam'd his foul.
Then came his fervants near, and faid, My Sire,
Did he fome grievous tafk from thee require,
Wouldft thou not do it? How much rather, then,
When he faith only, Wafh, and be made clean?
In *Jordan*, then, according to the word
Proceeding from the prophet of the LORD,
He fev'n times dipp'd his vitiated frame,
And like a child's his cleanfed flefh became.
Then to *Elifha* he return'd again,
And ftood before him, he, and all his train,
And faid, I know in all the earth around
No GOD, except in *Ifrael*, can be found;
Now therefore, I befeech thee, for my fake
A bleffing from thy grateful fervant take.
Then faid *Elifha*, As the LORD doth live,
Who hears me fpeak, no prefent I'll receive.
And *Naaman* each mode perfuafive us'd,
But ftill the Prophet utterly refus'd.
Then faid he to *Elifha*, Shall I pray,
Be granted to me two mules' load of clay?
For henceforth facrifice or burnt-off'ring
I unto no Gods but the LORD will bring.
For this thing may the Lord thy fervant fpare,
That when the king, my mafter, fhall appear
In *Rimmon*'s houfe, his worfhip to beftow,
And leans on me, and I to *Rimmon* bow:

When

When I in *Rimmon*'s temple lowly bend,
May God his pardon to me then extend!
Then said *Elisha* to him, Go in peace.
And he departed from him a small space.
But thus the prophet's man, *Gehazi*, spake,
When he perceiv'd *Elisha* nought would take;
Behold, my master hath this *Syrian* spar'd,
And at his hand accepted no reward;
But as God liveth, I will inftantly
Hafte after him, and for fome gift apply.
So ftraightway after him *Gehazi* ran,
And when he was obferv'd by *Naaman*,
He quickly from his carriage did alight
To meet *Gehazi*, and cry'd, Is all right?
Then said *Gehazi*, All, my Lord, is well:
My master thus hath order'd me to tell,
Behold, ev'n now two young men to me came,
Sons of the prophets, from Mount *Ephraim*;
For them a filver talent I befeech,
Together with a change of cloaths for each.
Then *Naaman* reply'd, Pray be content
Two talents with the garments may be fent.
And in two bags, two filver talents ty'd,
He forc'd upon him, and the cloaths befide,
Which, upon two of his domeftics laid,
Were, to the Prophet's houfe, by them convey'd.
And when they reach'd the tow'r, *Gehazi* then
Laid up the prefents, and difmifs'd the men.

Then

Then went *Gehazi* to his mafter's room,
Who thus demanded, Whence now art thou come?
And he reply'd, Thy fervant went no where.
Then faid *Elifha*, Felt my heart no care,
When from his chariot the man retir'd,
And for my welfare eagerly enquir'd?
Is this a time garments or cafh to crave?
Or oliveyards or vineyards to receive?
For men-fervants or maidens to apply?
Or feek for fheep and oxen greedily?
The leprofy of *Naaman*, therefore,
Shall cleave to thee and thy feed evermore.
Then did he from the Prophet's prefence go,
A miferable leper, white as fnow.

Genesis,

AND some time afterwards the *Lord* defign'd
To know by trial *Abraham*'s faith of mind;
And he call'd to him, and faid, *Abraham*.
Then he reply'd, Behold, LORD, here I am.
And he faid, *Ifaac* take, thy fole, lov'd fon,
And to the land of *Moriah* go on,
Where, on a mountain which I'll fhew to thee,
Prefent him a burnt-offering to me.
Then *Abraham* got up at dawn of day,
Saddled his afs, to bear him on his way,
Made *Ifaac*, and two young men-fervants rife,
And clave the timber for the facrifice,
And then together all their journey took,
Towards the place of which JEHOVAH fpoke.
And on the third day afar off, behold,
Appear'd the mountain of which he was told.
Then to his young men *Abraham* reply'd,
Remain you here, and with the afs abide;
While the lad and I yonder go to pay
Our worfhip, and return to you ftraightway.
Then *Abraham* on his fon *Ifaac* put
The wood which for the facrifice was cut;
And he took in his hand a knife, and fire,
Then did he with the lad apart retire.

And

And thus fpake *Ifaac*, O my father, heed!
Then anfwer'd *Abraham*, My fon, proceed.
And he cry'd, Lo! the wood and fire are here,
But is a lamb for the burnt-off'ring near?
And he faid, GOD will find a lamb, my fon,
For à burnt-off'ring.—So they both went on.
And *Abraham*, where he was taught by GOD,
An altar rear'd, and duly rang'd the wood;
Then bound his fon, whom on the wood he laid
For a burnt-off'ring, as the LORD had faid;
And took the knife, and ftretched out his hand
To flay his fon, as GOD had giv'n command,
And out of heav'n the angel of the LORD,
Vouchfaf'd to utter his almighty word,
And to him faid, *Abraham*, *Abraham*,
Then anfwer'd he, Lo! here, O LORD, I am.
And he faid, Lay not thine hand on the boy,
Neither do thou to him an injury;
For now your truft in GOD is fully try'd,
Since thou haft not thy only Son deny'd.
And *Abraham* a ram, on looking round,
In a brake by his horns entangled found;
And he feiz'd on the ram, and of him made
A burnt-off'ring in his fon *Ifaac*'s ftead.
Then he the place *Jehovah-jireh* nam'd,
Which, as the Mount of PROVIDENCE, is fam'd.
And the LORD from the regions of the blefs'd
A fecond time thus *Abraham* addrefs'd;

3

By

By myſelf, ſaith the Lord God, do I ſwear,
Since thy lov'd only Son thou wouldſt not ſpare ;
Thy welfare I will conſtantly increaſe,
And multiply exceedingly thy race,
Like ſtars which glitter in the realms of day,
Or grains of ſand along the foaming ſea ;
And thy poſterity, with conqueſt crown'd,
Shall all their haughty enemies confound ;
And in thy ſeed ſhall all the earth rejoice,
Becauſe thou haſt attended to my voice.
Then *Abraham* return'd to his young men,
And they all dwelt at *Beer-ſheba* again.

Exodus,

Exodus, 20th Chapter, 17 firſt Verſes.

AND thus the LORD expreſs'd himſelf, and
    ſaid,
Behold in me the LORD thy GOD diſplay'd,
Who thy deliverance from *Egypt* wrought,
And from the land of bondage have thee brought,
In me alone with fervent zeal confide,
Nor worſhip pay to any gods beſide.
Thou ſhalt not any graven image make,
Nor a ſimilitude unto thee take
Of things in heav'n, or in the earth below,
Or in the waters which beneath them flow:
Thou ſhalt not to them humbly proſtrate fall,
Nor for relief importunately call.
For I the LORD thy GOD will jealous be,
And ſtrictly puniſh all iniquity
Of ſires and ſons in long deſcent, who hate
My precepts, or my orders violate;
But kind and merciful to thouſands prove,
Who my commandments and my perſon love.
Do not the attributes divine profane,
Or take the name of thy LORD GOD in vain;
For GOD will not of wickedneſs acquit
Thoſe who ſuch groſs impiety commit.
Remember to obſerve the ſabbath-day,
And holy adoration on it pay.

Six days thou fhalt thy induftry purfue,
And do the labor which thou haft to do;
But to the feventh the LORD thy GOD lays claim,
On which thou fhouldft devoutly praife his name.
In it by thee, thy daughter, or thy fon,
Or thy man-fervant, fhall no work be done;
Thy maid-fervant, thy cattle, or whoe'er
Taftes, in thy gates, thy hofpitable fare.
For in fix days GOD made heav'n, earth, and fea,
And all they hold, and ceas'd the feventh day;
Wherefore on it a blefling was beftow'd,
To endlefs ages, by Almighty GOD.
Unto thy parents grateful honor yield,
And GOD will long thy life and welfare fhield.
Avoid with care all fanguinary ftrife,
Nor rob thy fellow-creature of his life.
With fix'd abhorrence fhun adultery,
And ev'ry action of indecency.
Let not to fraud thy erring foul incline,
Nor feize by violence what is not thine.
Againft thy neighbour no falfe witnefs bear,
Nor with detraction wound his character.
Do not indulge a covetous defire,
Thy neighbour's wife or dwelling to acquire;
Nor feek his maid-fervant, man, ox, or afs,
Or any property thy neighbour has.]

1ft CORIN-

1st CORINTHIANS, 15th Chapter.

MOREOVER, brethren, I declare once more,
The gospel which I preach'd to you before;
Which ye did also formerly receive,
And which ye still with confidence believe;
Which, if what I said ye in mind retain,
Will save you, if ye trusted not in vain.
For at the first I openly made known,
The doctrine that had to myself been shewn;
How, as the word of scripture testifies,
CHRIST for our sins became a sacrifice;
That in the bowels of the earth he lay,
And from his prison burst on the third day;
Of *Cephas* first, then of the twelve was view'd,
And next before more than five hundred stood;
Of whom the greater part alive is found,
But in death's icy slumbers some are bound.
Himself to *James* he afterwards reveal'd,
Then by the whole Apostles was beheld.
And last of all was also seen by me,
As one brought into life abortively.
For I of the Apostles am the least,
Nor worthy in the number to be plac'd,
Because I brandish'd persecution's sword,
Against the servants of the living LORD.

But

But what I am the grace of GOD has wrought,
Nor was his grace beſtow'd on me for nought;
But more abundantly than all I ſtrove,
And yet not I, but GOD's aſſiſting love.
But therefore whether it were I or they,
So did we preach, and you obedience pay.
If we teach CHRIST aroſe, how then do ſome
Among you ſay, None from the grave can come?
But if there can no reſurrection be,
Then is not CHRIST from death's dominion free:
And if to life CHRIST be not rais'd again,
Vain is our preaching, and your faith too vain.
Yea, we falſe witneſſes of GOD appear,
Becauſe we teſtimony of him bear,
That he rais'd CHRIST, whom yet he did not
    call,
If truth confirms the dead riſe not at all.
For if the dead no reſurrection have,
Then is CHRIST ſtill impriſon'd in the grave.
And if CHRIST is not yet recall'd from death,
Your ſins remain, and uſeleſs is your faith.
Then they who dy'd, and hope in CHRIST re-
    pos'd,
Their eyes in never-ending gloom have clos'd.
If here alone in CHRIST we build our truſt,
We the moſt wretched are of breathing duſt.
But CHRIST, now liberated from the tomb,
Is the firſt-fruits of them that ſlept become.

For fince by man death on the world was brought,
By man was mankind's refurrection wrought.
For as in *Adam* all are doom'd to die,
So fhall in CHRIST all live eternally.
But all in order: CHRIST the firft-fruits, then
His faithful fervants among mortal men.
Then comes the end, when he fhall have re-
    ftor'd
The kingdom to his Father, GOD the LORD;
When he all pow'r and rule fhall have put down,
And made authority fupreme his own.
For he muft reign with unremitting fway,
Till all his enemies fubmiffion pay.
The tyrant death fhall be the lateft foe,
That muft fuftain a total overthrow.
For he beneath his feet hath all things laid.
But when he faith all things are fubject made,
He is excepted, plainly muft appear,
Who all things brought beneath his fov'reign
    care.
And when all things his government confefs,
Then alfo fhall the fon himfelf exprefs
His rev'rence for GOD's majefty on high,
Who fhall unrivall'd, boundlefs rule enjoy.
Elfe what muft they do who baptifm receive
For the dead, if the dead fhall not revive?
Why for the dead are they baptiz'd? and why
Do we each hour remain in jeopardy?

By

By our rejoicing, which in CHRIST I find,
I am inceffantly to death confign'd.
If, arm'd with reafon's fhafts, I war fuftain'd
With beafts at *Ephefus*, what have I gain'd,
If the dead rife not? Let us eat and drink,
We die to-morrow.—Why, then, gravely think?
Be not deceiv'd: Evil connexions fteal
Our hearts aftray, and o'er good thoughts pre-
        vail.
To virtue rife, and fly fin's baneful road,
For, to their fhame I fpeak! fome know not
        GOD.
But fome will fay, How are the dead reftor'd?
What body is allow'd them by the LORD?
Thou fool, the feed thou cafteft in the ground,
Except it die, can with no fruit be crown'd.
The feed thou foweft fhall not rife again,
But yield a crop of wheat, or other grain.
But in his wifdom GOD a body gives,
And ev'ry feed its proper frame receives.
All flefh is not the fame; but men, we find,
Beafts, fifh, and birds, have each a diff'rent kind.
Celeftial and terreftrial bodies too,
The LORD has openly expos'd to view;
But the celeftial glory fhines with light,
Diftinct from that which makes the earthly bright.
There is one glory of the beaming fun,
One of the ftars, one of the waning moon;

For

For ſtars poſſeſs a difference of rays,
And with variegated glory blaze.
So will the raiſing of the dead be found;
Sown in corruption, it ſhall be rais'd found.
Sown in diſhonor, it to glory ſprings,
And ſtrength, inſtead of former weakneſs brings.
Sown weak, and natural, and doom'd to woes,
A body pure and ſpiritual it grows.
There is a body natural and frail,
And one whoſe purity ſhall never fail.
So the firſt *Adam* a live ſoul was made,
The laſt a quick'ning ſpirit, as 'tis ſaid.
The natural did firſt precedence claim,
Afterwards that which is ſpiritual came.
The firſt man earthy is, and form'd of clay,
The laſt the LORD of univerſal ſway.
The earthy are like that whence they proceed,
And as the heav'nly, are the heav'nly ſeed.
As we the likeneſs of the earthy bear,
We ſhall the image of the heav'nly wear.
Now, brethren, this I ſay, that fleſh and blood,
Cannot attain the heav'nly realms of GOD;
Nor can corruption incorruption ſee.
Behold I now diſplay a myſtery;
All ſhall not ſleep, but a change undergo
Sudden as thought, when the laſt trump ſhall
     blow;
The trump ſhall ſound, the dead riſe, and we come
Chang'd, and ſet free from vile corruption's gloom.

Corruption

Corruption muſt pure incorruption be,
And frail fleſh put on immortality,
So, when corruption ſhall be done away,
Turn'd to a ſtate that never can decay,
Shall come to paſs the words of ancient date,
Death is abſorb'd in victory compleat.
O death, where now is felt thy blunted ſting?
O grave, what haughty triumph doſt thou bring?
The ſting of death is ſin; and from the law
We healing remedies for ſin may draw.
Thanks be to GOD, thro' JESUS CHRIST his Son,
By whom we laſting victory have won.
Therefore, beloved brethren, ſtedfaſt ſtand,
Unmoveable, inclin'd to GOD's command,
Abounding in the bleſs'd work of the LORD,
Which ſhall an heav'nly recompenſe afford.

JOHN,

LET not your hearts be overcome with woes,
Ye truft in GOD, in me too truft repofe.
The houfe wherein my heav'nly Father reigns,
A multitude of manfions contains ;
Were this not fo, ere now ye fhould have heard,
And I precede to have your place prepar'd.
If I depart, your dwelling to provide,
For my return with certainty confide,
That you I may unto myfelf receive,
And make you in my habitation live.
Whither I go ye fully comprehend,
And the right way in which your courfe fhould
  bend.
James faith, O LORD, we know not where you go,
Then how can we the proper paffage know ?
JESUS faith, I'm the life, the truth, the way,
And can alone mankind to GOD convey.
Had ye known me, my Father ye had known,
Henceforth ye know him, to your eye-fight fhewn.
Philip faith unto him, LORD, fhew the fire,
And we no greater knowledge will defire.
JESUS faith, Have I been fo long with thee,
And art thou, *Philip*, ignorant of me ?
He who hath feen me hath my Father feen,
What doth thy words, then, fhew the Father,
  mean ?

         Believe

Believe ye not that I in GOD abound,
And that in me the Father too is found?
The words I fpeak do not from me proceed,
But GOD who dwelleth in me works the deed.
Believe the LORD's in me, I in the LORD,
Or truft me for the proofs the works afford.
Verily, verily, I fay to you,
He who trufts me fhall do the works I do,
And alfo greater works than thofe compleat,
Becaufe I to my Father now retreat.
What ye afk in my name ye fhall attain,
That by the Son the Father praife may gain.
If ye fhall any thing afk in my name,
With ftedfaft faith, I will perform the fame.
If you for me would teftify your love,
To my commandments ftill obedient prove.
And I will pray the Father, who fhall give
Another comforter with you to live;
Even the fpirit of veracity,
Who will not by the world accepted be,
Becaufe that him it neither hears nor knows,
Nor rev'rence to his infpiration fhews;
But ye acknowledge him, and honor pay,
For he dwells in you, and with you fhall ftay.
I will not leave you grieving to complain,
Devoid of comfort, but return again.
Yet for a little while, and I fhall ceafe
To fhew to the furrounding world my face;

But

But ye perceive me, and becaufe I live,
Ye alfo in like manner fhall furvive.
At that day I'll be in my Father found,
And I in you, and you in me be crown'd.
He that fubmiffion to my precepts pays,
Love and attachment thus to me difplays;
And he that loveth me, fhall likewife find
My Father loving towards him, and kind;
And he fhall alfo my affection fhare,
And I will clearly unto him appear.
Then *Judas,* not *Ifcariot,* replies,
LORD, how wilt thou to our obferving eyes,
Thyfelf confpicuoufly fhew alone,
Yet be to all the world befides unknown?
Then JESUS faid, For me a man fhall prove,
By ftrict attention to my words, his love;
My Father's love he likewife fhall obtain,
And we will come, and both with him remain,
The man who will not to my words attend,
Doth not behave towards me as a friend;
Nor are the words I utter mine, indeed,
But from the LORD, who fent me here, proceed.
Behold thefe doctrines I have notify'd,
While I in your fociety refide.
But when the HOLY GHOST, the Comforter,
Who in my name fhall come, GOD's meffenger,
Arrives, he fhall teach all things, and reftore
To your remembrance what I told before.

My

My peace I give you, peace with you I leave,
Not as the world gives, you from me receive.
Let not your hearts with trouble be opprefs'd,
Nor with alarming terrors be diftrefs'd.
Ye heard what formerly I faid, I go,
Away, but will return again to you.
If ye regarded me, ye would rejoice,
That I refpect my fov'reign Father's voice.
I timely warning ere it comes afford,
That when it comes, ye may believe my word.
I will not many things hereafter fay,
For this world's prince comes, and I go away.
But that the world may evidently find,
I love the Father with a filial mind,
And to his precepts yield with willing heart.
Arife, and let us ftraightway hence depart.

S f   15th

15th Chapter.

MY Father is the hufbandman, and I
The true vine which doth wholefome grapes fup-
   ply.
Each branch in me that doth not clufters bear,
He loppeth off, with clofe-infpecting care;
And purgeth in me each prolific fhoot,
That it may bring forth greater ftore of fruit.
Now ye are render'd altogether free,
By my inftructions, from impurity.
Abide in me, and I in you. For lo!
As boughs detach'd from vines no grapes be-
   ftow;
So neither can you any found fruits yield,
Unlefs ye are with my pure fpirit fill'd.
I am the vine; ye are the boughs; and they
Who reft in me fhall loaded boughs difplay.
For without me ye nothing can produce,
Caft forth as wither'd branches, of no ufe;
But, gather'd up by men, in flames expire,
Beneath the fury of confuming fire.
If ye in me and my commands confide,
Afk what ye will, it fhall not be deny'd.
Herein my Father's glory lies, that ye
Bear fruit, fo fhall ye my difciples be.

I

As the Father lov'd me, fo did I prove
My love to you : Continue in my love.
If my commands in honour ye retain,
My uniform affection ye fhall gain;
Even as I have been obedient found
To my fire's laws, and with his love am crown'd.
Thus have I fpoken, that my joy might reft
In you compleat, and ye with joy be blefs'd.
Thus I command, that mutual love be fhewn
By you, fuch as my love to you is known.
No greater love than this we can fuppofe,
That for his friends a man his life fhould lofe.
Ye are my friends, if with fubmiffive will
Ye ftudy my commandments to fulfil.
Henceforth I fervants call you not of mine,
As fervants know not what their lords defign :
But I have call'd you friends; for all I heard
My father fpeak, has been to you declar'd.
Ye have not chofen me, but I chofe you,
And have appointed what ye are to do;
That ye fhould bring forth pious fruit, and be
Blefs'd in your increafe everlaftingly;
That whate'er in my name ye may require,
My father may accomplifh your defire.
This precept I command you to obferve,
Affection for each other ftill preferve.
If the world hate you, this retain in mind,
It hated me ere 'twas to you unkind.

If

If we were of the world, we might depend
On having, of the world, a loving friend;
But as ye are not of the world, but made
A choice by me, its hatred is difplay'd.
Remember ftill my oft-repeated word,
The fervant is not greater than the lord.
If they rejected me, they'll you reject,
If they heard me, they will not you neglect.
But for my name's fake they will you difown,
Becaufe they have not him who fent me known.
Had I not come, and preach'd, they had been
      clean;
But no cloaks for their vices now remain.
He that doth for me bitter hatred bear,
Will in my Father's hatred likewife fhare.
Had I not greater works among them wrought,
Than man before, they had been free from fault
But now have they beheld me with their eyes,
And yet me and my Father they defpife.
But this doth what their law declares, fulfill,
They hated me, though I had done no ill.
But when the comforter is come, whom I
Shall fend, the fpirit of veracity,
Proceeding from the Father, he fhall fpeak,
And honorable mention of me make.
And ye fhall alfo witneffes abide,
Becaufe your faithfulnefs has long been try'd.

16th

16th CHAPTER.

THESE things have I declar'd, that ye fhould
 ceafe
To think your junction with me a difgrace.
They from the fynagogues fhall you remove,
Becaufe to me ye fhew refpect and love:
Yea, the time cometh, when they fhall contend,
That he who killeth you makes GOD his friend.
This they will execute, becaufe they knew
Not what was to me or my Father due.
But thefe things have I mention'd, that ye may,
When the time comes, remember what I fay.
At firft no hint of thefe things ye receiv'd,
Becaufe in fellowfhip with you I liv'd.
To him that fent me I depart, and lo
None of you afketh, Whither doft thou go?
But as thefe things I have to you reveal'd,
Afflictive grief hath o'er your hearts prevail'd.
Howe'er, the truth from you I muft not hide,
I fhould not longer with you now abide;
Nor will the Comforter, if I ftay here,
Approach; but when I go he'll ftraight appear.
Of fin, of right'oufnefs, and judgment he
Will, when he comes, prove men in fault to be.
       Of

Of fin, becaufe they kept from me their heart;
Of right'oufnefs, becaufe I hence depart,
Unto my Father, and ye fhall no more
Behold my countenance as heretofore;
Of judgment, becaufe this world's prince is thought
A malefactor, and to trial brought.
Howe'er, when the fpirit of truth is come,
In falfehood's paths he fhall not let you roam;
For of himfelf he fhall not fpeak, but tell
What he fhall hear, and future things reveal.
Me fhall he glorify; for he of mine
Will be poffefs'd, and them to you define.
Mine are all the Father hath; I faid hence,
He fhall take mine, and them to you difpenfe.
Yet for a little while, and ye fhall try
In vain to view me with a ftedfaft eye:
Again, a little while, and I will fhew
Myfelf, becaufe I to the Father go.
Among themfelves then the difciples faid,
What means the declaration he hath made,
Yet for a little while, and ye muft ceafe
To fix your longing looks upon my face;
Again, a little while, as I remove
To join the Father, vifible I'll prove?
Therefore they faid, What doth this faying mean,
A little while? We cannot this explain.
Now JESUS knew the drift of their defire,
And faid, Do ye among yourfelves enquire

What

What means a little while, and ye shall find
Your eyes to see me actually blind;
Again, a little while, and I shall be
Exhibited before you visibly?
Verily, verily, I thus declare,
Ye shall lament with agonizing care,
But the world shall rejoice; and ye shall mourn,
But all your sorrow into joy shall turn.
A woman when in travail is sore griev'd
As her time of deliv'rance is arriv'd;
But when the child is born, the welcome boy
Converts her anguish into boundless joy.
Ye now feel woe; but I'll see you again;
Make glad your hearts, none shall your bliss re-
    strain.
Then ye shall ask me nought: And what ye claim,
The Father will bestow you, in my name.
Ye yet did nothing in my name require,
Request, receive, and have your full desire.
These things in parables I have express'd,
Ye shall not be hereafter thus address'd,
But I will plainly of the Father tell,
And make the paths of duty visible.
When ye petition in my name that day,
I say not for you to the LORD I'll pray;
Because the Father ye have loving made,
By your affection towards me display'd;
And with unshaken confidence believ'd,
That I authority from GOD receiv'd.

I from

I from the Father to mankind came down,
And will return to an immortal crown.
Then his difciples faid, Lo, now we hear,
Plain words, and from a doubtful meaning clear.
Now are we certain that you all things know,
Nor need that men fhould ought unto you fhew;
That you came forth from GOD we hence per-
    ceive.
Then JESUS anfwer'd, Do ye now believe?
Behold the hour approacheth, yea, is come,
When ye fhall fly me, each one to his home,
And leave me lonely, void of company,
Yet not alone—the Father is with me.
Thefe things I faid, to bid your forrows ceafe,
And that through me ye might have lafting peace.
In this world troubles fhall on you obtrude,
But comfort take, the world I have fubdu'd.

WHEN JESUS had these cheering words ex-
    prefs'd,
To heav'n he turn'd his eyes, and GOD addrefs'd,
Father, the hour is come ; glory beftow
Upon thy Son, which back to thee may flow.
As he did from thee boundlefs pow'r receive,
That thofe you gave him might for ever live.
And this is life eternal, to know thee
The only GOD, from all eternity,
And JESUS CHRIST whom thou haft fent to bring
Thy faithful fervants to their fov'reign king.
I have on earth thy praife and glory fhewn,
And have the work committed to me done.
And now, O Father, condefcend to fhed
A portion of that glory on my head,
Which I enjoy'd with thee in realms of light,
Before creation burft from gloomy night.
I have to thofe made manifeft thy name,
Whom you permit me as my own to claim ;
From thee, their LORD, they were to me confign'd,
And to thy word they have their hearts inclin'd.
Now have they known that what thou gaveft me,
Their being have deriv'd alone from thee.
For I to them the words from thee receiv'd
Have taught, which they accepted and believ'd,

And have known furely that from thee I came,
And own'd me fent thy kingdom to proclaim.
Not for the world I offer up my pray'r,
But thofe thou gaveft me, for thine they are.
All mine are thine, and thine are mine, and I
Acquir'd through them glory fupreme and joy.
Now I go from the world, but thefe remain,
And I return to thee, in pow'r to reign.
Preferve thofe, holy Father, to thy Son,
You gave, that they, as we are, may be one.
While I continu'd in the world, they were
Kept in thy name, through my inceffant care;
Of all the number which you bade me guide,
And hold fecure, not one has turn'd afide,
Except perdition's fon, who fell from me,
That thus the fcriptures might accomplifh'd be.
I come to thee, and thefe things loudly tell,
That in themfelves my joy might fully dwell.
I have deliver'd them thy word, and lo!
The world doth enmity againft them fhew,
Becaufe that from the world's fociety,
By my example led, they dar'd to fly.
That thou fhouldft take them hence I do not pray,
But to protect them from each wicked way.
The world, as well as I, they have deny'd.
Through thy true word let them be fanctify'd.
As thou haft fent me to the world to preach,
So have I order'd them mankind to teach.

2   Myfelf

Myfelf I fanctified for their fake,
That they through truth might holinefs partake,
Nor pray I for thefe only, but likewife
Thofe who through them become my votaries:
That, Father, they in concord may abound,
As thou in me, and I in thee am found;
That they may fhare of our community,
And the world own that I was fent by thee.
The glory you gave me to them was lent,
That their lives might in harmony be fpent.
That I in them, and you in me may ftay,
That perfect unity they may difplay;
And that you plainly to the world may prove,
As you lov'd me, to them you fhewed love.
Father, from thee this grant I alfo claim,
That thofe you gave me may be where I am;
And may the glory which you dealt me view;
For I was lov'd ere the world being knew.
O right'ous Father, men, perverfe and blind,
Could not the healing knowledge of thee find;
But I confefs'd thee, and thefe, too, have known
That to the world thou haft difpatch'd me down,
To them already I declar'd thy name,
And will repeatedly announce the fame;
That the affection I enjoy'd from thee,
May be in them, and they be fill'd with me,

IT came to pafs, when *Jefus* thefe words fpoke,
He went with his difciples o'er the brook
Of *Cedron*, where a neighb'ring garden lay,
Into which they together took their way.
The place, too, *Judas*, who betray'd him, knew,
For thither with the reft CHRIST oft withdrew.
Then *Judas*, having under his command,
Of officers and men, a chofen band,
Which the chief priefts and pharifees had fent,
Thither with lanterns, ftaves, and torches went.
Then JESUS knowing what things he fhould bear,
Went forth, and afked them, What feek ye here?
JESUS of *Nazareth*, they faid. Then he
Reply'd, The man ye feek behold in me.
And *Judas* alfo who betray'd him, ftood
Connected with the military crowd.
When JESUS to them, I am he, had faid,
They fell down proftrate on the ground, difmay'd.
JESUS again, Whom do ye look for? cry'd.
JESUS of *Nazareth*, they all reply'd.
He faid, You heard I'm he, your fearch now ceafe,
If ye feek me, let thofe depart in peace.
That what he fpake might be fulfill'd, Of thofe
I have loft none, whom for my fold you chofe.

With

With anger *Simon Peter* then inflam'd,
Againſt the high-prieſt's ſervant, *Malchus* nam'd,
With a drawn ſword a fur'ous onſet made,
And cut away his right ear from his head.
CHRIST ſaid to *Peter*, Sheath thy ſword, nor think
The cup my Father gave, I ſhall not drink.
The captain, officers, and *Jews* ſtraightway
On JESUS ſeiz'd, and led him bound away,
And made him before *Annas* firſt appear,
Father-in-law to *Caiaphas*, that year
High-prieſt. Now *Caiaphas* advis'd that one
By death, ſhould for the people's ſins atone.
And after JESUS, *Peter*, in the throng,
With one of the diſciples, walk'd along;
The other was unto the high-prieſt known,
And was, with CHRIST, into his palace ſhewn.
But *Peter* at the door without remain'd.
Then went forth he whom the high-prieſt retain'd
In memory, and did for him procure
Admittance, from the maid who kept the door.
Then ſaid the damſel, Art thou not, I pray,
This man's diſciple? And he anſwer'd, Nay.
The officers and ſervants gather'd round,
And as the day intenſely cold was found,
They made a fire, to warm their freezing blood,
And *Peter* at the fire among them ſtood.
The high-prieſt then from JESUS cloſely ſought
Of his diſciples, and the rules he taught.

JESUS

JESUS reply'd, I openly reveal'd
My doctrine to the world, nor aught conceal'd;
And in the fynagogue and temple, where
The *Jews* refort, my precepts did declare.
Why doft thou afk me? Afk them who heard me,
Behold they know what I faid openly.
One of the officers attending, who
Heard CHRIST's defence, towards him nearer drew,
And gave him, with his open hand, a blow,
And faid, Doft thou the high-prieft anfwer fo?
Then JESUS anfwer'd, If it fhould appear
I fpake amifs, againft me witnefs bear;
But if with ftrict propriety I fpoke,
Why do I from thee thus receive a ftroke?
Now he to *Caiaphas* the high-prieft went,
To whom in chains by *Annas* he was fent.
And *Simon Peter* ftood before the fire,
Then did the people of him thus enquire,
Art thou not this man's difciple likewife?
But he, I know not what ye mean, replies.
One of the high-prieft's fervants, kinfman near
To him from whom *Peter* cut off an ear,
Thus queftion'd, In the garden did not I
Lately obferve you in his company?
Peter again the charge with oaths deny'd,
And the cock crew, as JESUS prophefy'd.
Then led they CHRIST from *Caiaphas* away,
Unto the judgment-hall, at dawn of day,

But

But went not in themfelves; unftain'd, to make
Themfelves prepar'd the paffover to take.
Then went out *Pilate* unto them, and faid,
What charge of guilt againft this man is laid?
They faid, Had he not been a criminal,
We had not brought him to thy judgment-hall.
Then *Pilate* anfwer'd, Take him hence from me,
And by your law let him convicted be.
Therefore reply'd the *Jews*, Our law commands,
None fhould with death be punifh'd by our
   hands:
That thus might be fulfill'd the prophecy
Which Jesus utter'd, how he was to die.
Then *Pilate* went into the hall again,
And faid, Art thou King of the *Jews?* fpeak plain.
Doth this thing from thyfelf, CHRIST anfwer'd,
   flow,
Or others unto thee this knowledge fhew?
Pilate reply'd, Am I a *Jew?* You come,
By my decifion to receive thy doom;
Charg'd by the chief-priefts and thy countrymen;
Of what offence haft thou been guilty, then?
Then *Jefus* faid, My kingdom is not here,
My fervants would defend me, if it were,
And free me from this *Jewifh* infolence;
But lo! my kingdom is not now from hence.
Therefore, faid *Pilate*, Art thou, then, a king?
Then anfwer'd JESUS, You declare this thing.

       For

For this caufe did I come, and for this end
The world with my nativity befriend,
And to the truth a teftimony bear,
All that are of the truth my voice will hcar.
Pilate faid, What is truth ? And then declar'd
Unto the *Jews*, no fault in him appear'd.
Ye have a cuftom I fhould fave, he faith,
A culprit, at the paffover, from death ;
Then are ye willing pardon to proclaim
To him who does himfelf your fov'reign name?
And all reply'd, Not him, but *Barabbas*.
And he a murderer and robber was.

19th

19th CHAPTER.

THEN *Pilate* scourged JESUS, till the gore
His unoffending body cover'd o'er.
A crown of thorns the soldiers also made,
With which, and purple robes, he was array'd;
Then with their hands they smote him wan-
     tonly,
And cry'd, Hail, *Jewish* King! in mockery.
Therefore again unto them *Pilate* came,
And said, Behold I find in him no blame.
Then JESUS with his crown and robes appear'd,
And *Pilate* said, View here the prince rever'd!
When him the officers and chief-priests spy'd,
They all exclaim'd, Let him be crucify'd.
This execute yourselves, then *Pilate* saith,
I find in him no crime deserving death.
The *Jews* then answer'd him, We have a law,
Which final punishment should on him draw,
Because that he, with blasphemous pretence,
Call'd himself the Son of OMNIPOTENCE.
This saying *Pilate* heard, and, fill'd with dread,
Did to the judgment-hall again proceed,
And said to CHRIST, Who or whence art thou?
     speak:
But JESUS no reply vouchsaf'd to make.

Then *Pilate*, with aftonifhment infpir'd,
Doft thou not fpeak to me? of CHRIST enquir'd:
Or art thou ignorant, that pow'r in me
Refides, to crucify, or fet thee free?
JESUS reply'd, You could no pow'r poffefs,
But from above, to make me feel diftrefs;
Therefore the greater muft the guilt appear
Of him, who brought me unto trial here.
Thence *Pilate* fought his freedom to obtain;
But the *Jews* clamoroufly cry'd again,
If he's releas'd, you are not *Cæfar's* friend;
Who makes himfelf king, *Cæfar* muft offend.
When *Pilate*, therefore, heard them thus debate,
He brought forth JESUS to the judgment-feat,
And in a place the pavement call'd, fat down,
By the name *Gabbatha* in *Hebrew* known.
And now about the fixth hour, when the *Jews*
For the paffover preparation ufe,
Pilate faith, See your king. But they reply'd,
Bear him away, let him be crucify'd.
Then *Pilate* anfwer'd, Muft your king thus die?
They faid, All kings but *Cæfar* we deny.
Then he refign'd him up without delay;
And they took JESUS, and led him away.
And he his crofs fupporting, onwards went,
Beneath the agonizing preffure bent,
Until to a place call'd a fkull he came,
But in the *Hebrew*, *Golgotha* by name.

2

Here

Here he and other two were crucify'd,
CHRIST in the midft, and one on either fide,
And *Pilate* on the crofs fix'd this writing,
JESUS OF NAZARETH THE JEWISH KING.
This title, then, did many of the *Jews*,
For JESUS near the city dy'd, perufe ;
In *Hebrew*, *Greek*, and *Latin*, 'twas exprefs'd.
And then the chief-priefts *Pilate* thus addrefs'd,
The King of the *Jews*, write not, but that he
Affirm'd himfelf King of the *Jews* to be.
Then *Pilate* to this application faid,
What I have written, is a writing made.
The foldiers, then, when CHRIST was crucify'd,
His garments take (which they in four divide,
To each a quarter), and likewife his coat,
Without feam woven from the top throughout.
They therefore faid, The coat we will not tear,
But the proprietor let lots declare :
That thus might happen what the fcriptures fpake,
My parted raiment among them they take,
And lots pronounce who fhall my coat receive.
The foldiers, therefore, in this way behave.
Now to the crofs of JESUS there ftood nigh
His mother, and her fifter ; and *Mary*,
The wife of *Cleophas*, was likewife there,
And *Mary Magdelene* drew alfo near.
And when his mother, CHRIST, on looking round,
With the difciple whom he loved, found,

He

He to his mother cry'd, Thy Son perceive;
Then faid to him, Thy mother now receive.
And from that hour he brought her to his home,
Thenceforth her Son adopted to become.
Then Jesus, knowing all compleated firſt,
The fcriptures to accomplifh, faid, I thirſt.
A veffel there with vinegar was fet,
Wherein a fponge was, by the foldiers wet,
On hyffop put, and to his mouth apply'd.
When Jesus, therefore, had the mixture try'd,
He faid, 'Tis finifhed; then bow'd his head,
And join'd the great affembly of the dead.
As, then, it was the preparation-day,
That on the crofs the bodies might not ſtay
Upon the fabbath-day, it came to pafs
(Becaufe that fabbath-day an high day was)
The *Jews* pray'd *Pilate* their legs they might
　　　break,
And from thence, afterwards, their bodies take.
The foldiers came, and brake in pieces, then,
The legs of both the executed men.
But when they found life's pulfe in Christ had
　　　ceas'd,
Againſt his legs no hoſtile hands they rais'd.
But with a fpear a foldier pierc'd his fide,
From whence of blood and water flow'd a tide.
And he that faw it teſtimony bare,
While truth atteſteth what he doth declare;

　　　　　　　　　　　　　　　　　　And

And he knows truth confirmeth what he faith,
That in his evidence ye might have faith.
The fcriptures to fulfill, thefe things were done,
Ye fhall not find in him a broken bone.
Another fcripture thus doth teftify,
On him they pierc'd they fhall look ftedfaftly.
And then *Jofeph* of *Arimathea*
(CHRIST's fecret convert, of the *Jews* in awe)
Pilate befought CHRIST's body he might have,
Which he remov'd, when *Pilate* granted leave.
And with him too came *Nicodemus* there
(Who firft at night to JESUS did repair)
And brought, commix'd, the laft rites to compleat,
Of myrrh and aloes an hundred weight.
In linen cloaths, then, CHRIST's corpfe they in-
     clofe,
With fpices, as the *Jews* their dead difpofe.
A garden ftood near where he death obey'd,
And a new tomb wherein man ne'er was laid.
Becaufe of the *Jews'* preparation here
In earth CHRIST refted, for the tomb was near.

F I N I S.

www.ingramcontent.com/pod-product-compliance
Lightning Source LLC
Chambersburg PA
CBHW030819110726
47900CB00006B/1663